A TO

TARGET LOCKED

NEW YORK TIMES #1 BESTSELLER **TONY LEE** WRITING AS

JACK GATLAND

Hooded Man MEDIA

PREPARATION • PRODUCTION • PUBLICATION

Published by Hooded Man Media.

Cover design by L1graphics

First Edition: January 2023
Second Edition: August 2023

PRAISE FOR JACK GATLAND

'This is one of those books that will keep you up past your bedtime, as each chapter lures you into reading just one more.'

'This book was excellent! A great plot which kept you guessing until the end.'

'Couldn't put it down, fast paced with twists and turns.'

'The story was captivating, good plot, twists you never saw and really likeable characters. Can't wait for the next one!'

'I got sucked into this book from the very first page, thoroughly enjoyed it, can't wait for the next one.'

'Totally addictive. Thoroughly recommend.'

'Moves at a fast pace and carries you along with it.'

'Just couldn't put this book down, from the first page to the last one it kept you wondering what would happen next.'

There's a new Detective Inspector in town...

Before Tom Marlowe, there was DI Declan Walsh!

An EXCLUSIVE PREQUEL, completely free to anyone who joins the Jack Gatland Reader's Club!

Join at www.subscribepage.com/jackgatland

Also by Jack Gatland

DI DECLAN WALSH BOOKS
LETTER FROM THE DEAD
MURDER OF ANGELS
HUNTER HUNTED
WHISPER FOR THE REAPER
TO HUNT A MAGPIE
A RITUAL FOR THE DYING
KILLING THE MUSIC
A DINNER TO DIE FOR
BEHIND THE WIRE
HEAVY IS THE CROWN
STALKING THE RIPPER
A QUIVER OF SORROWS
MURDER BY MISTLETOE
BENEATH THE BODIES
KILL YOUR DARLINGS
KISSING A KILLER

ELLIE RECKLESS BOOKS
PAINT THE DEAD
STEAL THE GOLD
HUNT THE PREY
FIND THE LADY

TOM MARLOWE BOOKS
SLEEPING SOLDIERS
TARGET LOCKED
COVERT ACTION
COUNTER ATTACK

For Mum, who inspired me to write.

For Tracy, who inspires me to write.

CONTENTS

PROLOGUE

THE MOMENT THE CAR FOLLOWED HIM OFF THE MOTORWAY, Marlowe knew he was screwed.

He'd been watching it for a while now: a nondescript, grey Audi, registration number showing it to be new, but not *that* new, while expensive, but not *that* expensive. It had followed him for the last hour along the M4 towards London. It was what Marlowe would call a corporate car, a fleet car, something bought in bulk, and given out to the staff. A definite salesperson's car.

An assassin's car.

He wasn't completely sure of this, but the fact of the matter was that Marlowe had been driving for at least an hour down the motorway, and that bloody vehicle had been three cars behind him at all times. And that was the problem with amateurs; if you were trying not to be seen, the one thing you shouldn't do was attempt this in such a uniform manner. Cars overtook and were overtaken on a motorway. For a car to slot in exactly three cars behind you, and adjust their driving to keep to this every time one of the intermediate cars changed ... was a *red flag*. To do this in such an obviously unobtrusive car? It wasn't good. And it made you more noticeable than you might expect, especially to someone trained in this, even when the night was miserable, dark, and in the early hours of the morning.

Marlowe had been checking his phone, looking for a turnoff he could use to prove his hypothesis. If he pulled off the motorway and the car carried on, it was simply a mistake on his part, a little paranoia mixed with late-night adrenaline, he'd see the car was probably driven by someone with the cruise control on, and Marlowe would simply go round the turnoff's roundabout and come back onto the motorway behind them, carrying on with his journey.

But, if he turned off, and the pursuer did the same, he had to do more to prove things, as there was still every chance this was *also* the Audi's turn off.

There was a service station coming up after junction three, and Marlowe had waited until the last moment, veering left into the Heston Services with a screech of resisting tyres, knowing this would likely cause enough damage to the tread to force him to fork out for brand new tyres down the line. Which, for a Jaguar, was a pain in the arse, but worth it, if this saved his life.

His car was a burgundy 2015 Jaguar XJ, Marlowe's pride and joy, and a vehicle he'd won in a poker game a few years earlier. He hadn't been cheating either, which made it all the sweeter when his opponent, an East-European arms dealer, convinced Marlowe was sleeping with his wife, had demanded he be checked for hidden cards, arguing he'd been cheated, only to be proven wrong.

He was also wrong on the wife front, too, as Marlowe hadn't ever met her, let alone screwed her.

MI5 agents weren't all bloody James Bond wannabes, after all.

Three cars behind, the headlights of the Audi shifted as it pulled into the services behind him, and Marlowe swore softly to himself. It had to be a hit, but he didn't know who it could be from. After all, following the antics of a couple of months or more back, it could be any nation with a grudge against Thomas Marlowe, ex-MI5 agent – as he'd been *burnt*, his air supply cut off, and now had no backup given when needed.

Basically, it was hunting season for Marlowe right now.

First, there'd been the Bulgarian, just before Christmas. Marlowe hadn't even known what he'd done to piss the Bulgarians off, but in a toilet downstairs at *Claridge's Hotel* of all places, the stocky, balding agent had attempted to garrotte Marlowe with a razor wire hidden in a tie. There'd been a scuffle, and Marlowe had eventually stopped this sudden attack by flipping the attacker over, slamming him head-first into the tiles in front of one urinal. Which didn't sound that painful, until you learned more about *Claridges*, and the men's toilets in particular – because in the toilets, each urinal had a sheet of four inches high by fifteen inches wide glass at the base, angled out at forty-five degrees towards the person currently peeing, so any splash back missed their shoes or socks, instead hitting the glass and continuing down the slope and into the drain. Which was a nice touch, and even more painful when a Bulgarian assassin's skull was slammed into the edge at speed.

The second attack had been a group effort; while visiting an old friend in Brighton a small unit of Russians had cornered him under the Pier during an early morning run. They had pulled out small-arm weapons and sharp, vicious-looking blades. Marlowe had, however, taken the better part of valour here and instead of fighting a group of trained killers and terrible odds, he opted to use his knowledge of the area to parkour up the side of the seawall and head into the narrow lanes of Old Brighton, only emerging when he felt he was safe.

He didn't hang around long to find out what happened next. And, as far as he knew, they were still out to get him, and could even be *today's* special guests in the mysterious Audi now less than three cars behind him.

And then there was the third attack – well, more of an *attempt*, if he was being pedantic, where someone had tried to wire up the Jaguar to explode when he started the car, but in the process had electrocuted themselves on Marlowe's own, homemade security devices as they tried to pick his lock, and were still shuddering uncontrollably as he walked up to his car, climbed in – after giving them a good kicking – and driving off.

He'd not needed to interrogate the assassin, as he recognised him and knew exactly where he came from, a receipt Marlowe would be repaying soon. He'd taken the explosive device, though. For a start, you never knew when you needed a car bomb. And, watching the groaning assassin, he was a little worried he'd twitch a little too hard and set the whole bloody thing off.

People were getting sloppy, and Marlowe was getting worried. Once the sloppy people failed, they always brought in the experts.

And that was when the trouble started.

As he entered the services, he slowed down, allowing the Audi to catch up. He could see through the window, as the lights shone down on the windscreen, that it was a singular driver, alone in the car, a pair of aviator sunglasses and a baseball cap on – possibly red, but bathed in the glow of streetlights, giving it an almost golden sheen as it covered most of his face. He looked Caucasian, but that meant nothing in the world of contract-for-hire killers. Marlowe needed to know who sent him before he stopped him, and that was always the bigger problem. However, he was convinced more than ever this was a hit, as *nobody* wore sunglasses at one in the morning.

Reaching into his holdall, currently resting on the passenger seat, Marlowe did his best to not look like he was doing anything, as he slowly turned into the car-parking lanes, very aware that as much as he could see the man behind him, the man could see *him*. And, carefully and keeping it under the dashboard, and therefore under the view through the rear window, he pulled out his SIG Sauer P226, placing it into his lap. He vastly preferred the double action/single action trigger of the Sig to the clunkier constant of the striker fired weapon, and the weight felt secure as he watched through the rear window, waiting for the right moment.

The Audi turned into the car-park lane to follow him, and Marlowe knew he had to do something quickly, as soon the Audi would guess he was being set up and prepare for it. Ahead he noticed a large white van, parked a short distance away from the main Food Hall entrance, a couple of open spaces beside it and away from the main thoroughfare to the right. At this time in the morning the services weren't busy, but they weren't empty either, and Marlowe realised that using the van as some kind of visible shield from the main entrance might offer some privacy for what he had planned next.

Marlowe winced. He really didn't want to do this, especially to his car, and he hoped he could minimise the damage, at least. And, slowing down even more to enter one of the empty car-parking spots a couple of spaces down from the van, he suddenly slammed the gear into reverse, and rocketed back into the unsuspecting Audi with an expensive-sounding *crunch* of metal and glass, as the back-left part of his car slammed into the front grille of the Audi, who hadn't stopped in time.

Now he had to move quickly, the Sig gripped and held behind his right thigh, while his left hand waved an apology as he walked around the Jaguar, towards the aviator-glassed man in the red baseball cap.

'My fault!' he cried out. 'Wrong gear! Sorry! Do you have your insurance—'

He ducked back down as the driver opened the door, rising, his own gun in hand, firing wildly with a suppressed pistol, the cough of the subsonic rounds echoing in the car park.

But Marlowe had been prepared and, pulling his gun out, he used the back of the Jaguar as a shield as he fired in return. The assassin had been thrown by the accident, his nose bloody from where he'd smacked his face into his steering wheel, adrenaline flooding his system and hadn't been quick enough to react, but Marlowe was ready and had prepared mentally for this before he even left the car, and fired a double tap to the centre of Mass and a third round to the head, dropping the would be assassin instantly.

Marlowe noted people emerging from the Food Hall, nervous and looking around, listening in fear as the gunshots echoed around the forecourt. But Marlowe was aware this was West London and just after midnight, so most of the drivers wouldn't be looking at a middle-class looking white man in a posh sports car as the culprit, instead looking the other direction from where he'd stopped. And, as planned, the white van now blocked most of what had happened - to them, his gunshots would have sounded like firecrackers, perhaps some kind of prank even, so he had a couple of moments to fix this.

He quickly walked back to his car, parking it beside the van before returning to the Audi. Marlowe checked about for witnesses, and then hefted the body back into the vehicle, clambering in after it, now parking the Audi up next to the Jaguar.

The security cameras at these sites were always set up near the Food Hall, but aimed away from where he'd parked, and placed there mainly to collect number plates rather than activities. And even though the people who'd walked out of the services, seeing nothing and likely tired after a long day were returning inside, Marlowe knew the police were likely to have been called - and even at this time of night, speed was of the essence.

First off, he pulled on a pair of leather gloves he'd brought with him; he didn't want to leave fingerprints on this, even if he intended to make damn sure nobody *was* seeing this. With one eye watching the car park, he leant over the body, going through the pockets quickly and methodically, looking for anything that could give him an idea as to who this was and why they wanted him dead.

A phone fell into his hand. Using the dead man's facial recognition, he opened it up to see a photo of his own face on the screen. For a split second, Marlowe actually wondered if he'd accidentally set the phone to video call, but it was an old MI5 ID image, and one sent to the man in the aviators; a photo to show him who to kill.

Pulling a small USB-C wire from his pocket, Marlowe connected his own smartphone to the assassin's phone, using spyware placed on it by a good friend to clone everything off onto a partitioned drive. He could look into it later, and while his phone merrily scrolled along a percentage bar, Marlowe carried on searching.

A photo of a woman in what looked to be America paused him. He'd assumed this was a Russian, or East European, but the woman in the image was definitely somewhere on the east coast, maybe New York, or Boston, perhaps.

An American assassin working for the highest bidder, perhaps?

Marlowe hoped so. The last thing he wanted was the bloody CIA now going for him, too. He slipped the photo into his pocket, moving on.

The wallet was, as expected, empty apart from two fifty-pound notes in there for expenses. Marlowe tossed the wallet, pocketing the money. With nothing else on the body, Marlowe now started searching through the glove compartment, pulling out the rental papers for the car, squirrelling them away, and then searching the back seat. With nothing else, and with his phone now completed with cloning, he tossed the assassin's phone to the floor, took a photo of the dead assassin with his own camera, wiped down the steering wheel, gear stick and door, anywhere he may have left fingerprints before he'd pulled on the gloves, and then walked around to the back of the Audi, opening the boot.

Also, and unsurprisingly, there was a black duffle, likely the assassin's "go bag" in there, so Marlowe quickly removed it, tossing the assassin's gun into it as he did so, walking back to his Jaguar and opening his own boot, wincing at the cosmetic damage he'd caused in the accident as he tossed the bag into it, closing the door.

That was going to be expensive, he thought. *But rather the bumper than his life.*

Like the phone, he could check the contents of the bag at leisure later, but he knew the police wouldn't be far away – and some of the people, the ones who hadn't gone in already were now looking in his direction.

In his boot was also a small rucksack – this had housed the explosive meant for him, taken when he electrocuted the poor bastard tasked with killing him. It had been jury-rigged to work on a timer, and so he set it for two minutes, tossed it into the back of the Audi and, quickly returned to his Jaguar, pulling out a plastic, green, five-litre can of petrol from within. He proceeded to pour this liberally over the seats of the assassin's rental car and the body, tossing it onto the back seat when he shut the door, making sure to wind the back window down. Now, checking his watch and seeing a minute had already passed, Marlowe climbed into his Jaguar and started the engine.

It didn't start.

'Come on, you bastard,' he growled, trying again. 'Don't do this now.'

Again, it failed to turn over.

And, as he glanced at his watch, Marlowe knew he had only thirty seconds to get away.

However, on the third try it spluttered into life and, the car now purring, Marlowe reversed out of the parking bay, pausing long enough to take a flare from his own glove-box and light it, tossing it in through the back window of the Audi, and driving off. The flare, hitting the petrol inside the car immediately ignited it, and as Marlowe pulled out into the lane that led to the motorway, the flames were already visible, licking up the side of the car as, with a loud explosion, the timer finally connecting, it erupted into a small fireball, the petrol tank having also now ignited.

Of course, the people still outside, now seeing this explosion, started running towards it, completely ignoring the battered Jaguar that drove along the side road, its lights turned off. And then, as he passed any visual location from people at the service station, Marlowe flicked them on and, with a flaming fireball of a car left in the car park behind him, continued to head into London.

He could wait until tomorrow to work out who'd tried to kill him *this* time.

1

EN-CRYPT-ED

MARLOWE HAD SOLD HIS MOTHER'S HOUSE – WELL, HE supposed it was *his* house, and had been for a while, although it was difficult to see it as anything else but his mother's, even though she'd died over a decade earlier – after MI5 had attacked him while he was there, convinced he was some kind of rogue agent. It had been a few months back, and they'd mainly focused on the self-built bunker she'd created over the years, a bunker he'd been in when the armed agents had arrived, but even though he'd detonated that safe space, using it to escape from them, once the whole operation had ended, and he was cleared of wrongdoings – at a price – he'd felt exposed while staying there.

After all, if they knew where you were, they knew how to find you.

He'd never been that fond of Upper Epping, where the house was, to be honest. It was quiet, and there were times after a mission or an undercover op he needed that, but at the same time, he was twitchier these days; nervous, still filled with adrenaline and stress after clearing his name, and constantly needing to be on the move, rather than sitting tight and waiting for the next killer. He needed to be elsewhere, especially as he tried to rebuild his life.

After all, MI5 had effectively *ended* it.

Marlowe had started as a soldier, a Royal Marine Commando but, when his mother was killed during the 7/7 bombings in London her replacement, Emilia Wintergreen had brought him across to "Box", the nickname for the Thames-side building MI5 used, not the green-tipped monstrosity famously revealed in various James Bond movies across the river. There he'd joined Wintergreen's "Section D", a department of MI5 that was aimed at more domestic issues, and was named because it was the fourth one given permission to exist, but it didn't take long, thanks to Wintergreen's eccentric recruitment process, for the "D" to be classed as short for "Disavowed". The *Botany Bay* of the security service, the misfit toys of the spy game.

Marlowe hadn't cared, as this allowed him to operate with no expectations, and his missions over the years had all been successful, all the while moving from Box into Whitehall when the current Prime Minister took an interest in the outfit. However, almost a year earlier, while escorting a prisoner named Karl Schnitter from a secure location, he'd been betrayed by someone connected to the Government, a mercenary outfit with a score to settle with someone else entirely, and Marlowe became collateral damage, ambushed and left for dead on the side of a road, two bullets in his chest his only souvenir.

He'd spent months in therapy, both physical and mental, and it was right before he returned to duty that he found himself embroiled in an attempt to silence old spies by rogue agents – and, when the smoke cleared, Marlowe was seen as the scapegoat, losing his access, and becoming "burned".

That's what you get for saving Presidents these days.

But, at least he wasn't rotting in a black site somewhere, and that was something Marlowe could be thankful for. And he wasn't the first spy to have his air supply cut off, and the others had all had long and productive post-MI5 careers.

Well, the ones that weren't instantly executed, anyway.

With the money from the house sale, luckily arranged through a broker while he kept his head down, he'd set up a couple of shell accounts, using identities he'd created during his time in the service, effectively laundering it into a clean and untraceable fund to use on new purchases. And, once he'd funnelled it through a dozen different banks and servers, something that sounded complicated but took him less than a day, he then paid cash for a small and dilapidated "fixer-upper" church in West London. It'd been empty for a good ten years now, unable to be sold because it was a nightmare to heat, and he'd bought it for an absolute steal, on the condition he renovated it completely, including placing in new wiring and plumbing. And, more importantly, there was a garage, owned at one time by the church, now Marlowe, and a few yards down the street, that was large enough to hide his car within.

And, as he walked through the main door into what was once the Nave, he faced wooden-wall framing, the layout of the new apartment taking shape, the mezzanine area at the far end, a raised bedroom where the high-ceilinged altar once was, now built out and usable, a new staircase already set in on the right, leading up to the new, upper level that looked out onto the church.

It was here that Marlowe now walked, duffle bag over his

shoulder, passing through the plastic sheeting that worked currently as dust traps and doorways, walking down the newly plastered corridors, the high ceiling still visible above him. The whole place looked like a builder's nightmare, and in a way it was, as Marlowe had deliberately brought competing companies in to work on different areas, purely to ensure nobody had a working schematic of the location. Even the plumbers, putting in the toilets had been completely turned around while working there. And this was exactly what Marlowe wanted, as it also meant that no enemy agency, or even just someone who wanted him dead, could walk in, get hold of the blueprints, and use them against him.

There was, of course, another reason. And this was under the staircase to the right. There was a cupboard being built under the stairs, with a selection of hastily wired, shoddily placed electrical cables which were currently jutting out, enough to keep anyone away, in case the badly wired buggers started sparking. In fact, the wires weren't even connected, were purely there for show, and were there more to keep any nosey builder away than anything else.

Because the wall they jutted out of wasn't really a wall, and could be shunted aside, revealing a second set of stairs.

These stairs, heading down to the church's crypt, were the *real* reason Marlowe had bought the place.

The crypt was unconsecrated and emptied of any old coffins and general dead-people-ness, but still ran most of the length of the church. There was a small, hidden exit to the rear of the churchyard, the external entrance half covered with foliage and forgotten, and apart from that, the only other entrance or exit were the stairs Marlowe had walked down.

In effect, it was as secure as the bunker his mother had

built in the old house in Essex had been, and was now easier to escape from if there was a problem, thanks to the CCTV network he'd created, one that alerted him if anyone even came near the church. And apart from a confused plumber who didn't understand why his eccentric client needed a bathroom in the crypt, a question answered with a long explanation about home theatres and building permission for extending basements, Marlowe had been framing and designing the new location himself.

He knew he was unlikely to be here for long, as to be honest, he didn't even know if he'd be *alive* for long, especially if people kept trying to kill him; but as long as he had a London base, it meant he was near travel hubs around the world. He had enough identities squirrelled away from his time in MI5, and even if these were found and burned, Trix Preston had also created some newer, off-the-books ones he could move on to.

For the moment, he was secure in here, which was more than could be said for how he was outside.

Downstairs, the crypt was as half-finished as the ground floor Nave was, but this was less by design, and more because of Marlowe building this alone. He'd not wanted people down here, so once the toilet, shower and sink had been placed into a small bathroom in the corner, he'd started framing his "secret" apartment down here himself. It wasn't going to be pretty, just functional. He needed a place to hide his weapons, currently comprising a couple of automatic pistols, in particular his favourite SIG Sauer P226, a couple of assault rifles he'd picked up on the way, some knives, ammunition boxes and explosives, including grenades, slabs of C4 and a couple of claymore mines, named after the massive Scots battle sword, due to to their massive killing power, thrown in for good measure. These were mainly things he'd picked up over the last few months, after he'd effectively started from scratch following the destruction of the bunker – and the various assassination attempts, while failing, had provided him with a small arsenal to play with.

Of course he could always do with more, but for the moment, these items were now in the "armoury", or, to be more honest, a corner of the crypt where the plasterboard was actually up and mudded, and although still slightly damp because of the lack of flowing warm air down there, was finished enough to place some wire-meshed backing against it, allowing the effective pin board to hold the arsenal in place, a selection of metal trellis and shelving tables containing the other items, now held in metal boxes which had been stolen from an MI5 store room at some point in the past, and were now filled with his own stores, including cases filled with cash in foreign denominations and what were known as "bullion coins", basically gold one-ounce "Britannia" coins from the Royal Mint, each worth about a grand and a half, and easily transportable across borders.

He was very aware this was a similar trope to the coins used in that Keanu Reeves *assassin movie series* his Uncle Alex liked, but he felt it wasn't such a known commodity that customs agents actively looked for them. And he'd started doing this after seeing the villains smuggling gold krugerrand in *Lethal Weapon 2*, so technically he'd been considering it longer than Keanu Reeves ever had. Either way, even if he found himself in a situation where he had nothing, a couple of these coins, sold at a loss, would still give him a small and workable war chest.

It was best not to ask where he'd got a small box of them from, though.

The armoury was down the left-hand side of the crypt, just over halfway along and near the rear of the space. He'd originally planned to have this closer to the door, as if someone came in, or if he was chased into this den, he had a thought to have the weapons he needed close by – until it was pointed out to him by someone far cleverer than he was, that doing this meant that if someone actually made it into the crypt behind him, the weapons were there for *them* to use, too.

Marlowe hadn't liked this idea.

Turning on a couple of the standing construction lamps, lighting up the corridor as he walked down it, the actual lights for the basement apartment not finished yet, he placed the assassin's "go bag" duffle onto the top of the workbench and, before examining it, pulled out the photo of the woman in what looked to be America, from his pocket, placing it onto the countertop. This done, he now pulled out his own phone, connecting it to a flash drive, downloading the information taken from the assassin's own device. As his phone happily did this, Marlowe glanced at the image of the woman.

It was a holiday snap, or at least was posed to be one – Marlowe had taken his own share of similar over the years – and from the looks of things it was shot in New York, in the summer or late autumn, with an expanse of water behind the woman in the image, the familiar sight of skyscrapers on the horizon. Marlowe thought he recognised the location as Battery Park in Manhattan, but he wasn't absolutely sure. He'd need to put it through an image analyser to be certain. There was every chance this was a real image though, and somewhere out there was a woman, a wife, fiancée or girl-friend, maybe even a sister that didn't know the man carrying this was never coming back to her.

Marlowe had a brief twinge of regret, but it quickly went when he remembered the man had wanted to kill him first.

Turning the picture over, he examined the back – there was nothing written on it, nothing visible, that was, but there was a very light sheen when he angled it to the light, enough to make him pick a UV pen up from the side and give the back of the photo a quick scan with it, the UV light showing a secret message.

Tick Tock 481 8th Ave – 10am 2/4

Marlowe paused as he read the message. This photo definitely wasn't a loving memento, it seemed. And he knew where the message meant, as well. The address was that of the New Yorker Hotel, and at its base was the famous Tick Tock Diner. The question was whether the date was British or American? If it was the former, the date meant the second of April. If it was the latter, it was the fourth of February, less than a week away.

It had to be the latter, purely because the assassin had gone for him today. But why a meetup? Usually money was passed digitally, usually in crypto these days, so was this a debrief? If so, was the assassin freelance, or agency? Marlowe knew there were some corporates out there who had teams on their payroll; maybe he was one of them?

Either way, Marlowe was going to New York in the immediate future.

His phone beeped – the upload was complete. And, taking the flash drive, Marlowe looked up at the weapons on the wall, held to the mesh by pins, placing his own gun up there with them before opening the duffle and examining inside. On the top were the rental pages and the assassin's gun, a Walther PPK.

Marlowe grinned at this. *Someone had a James Bond fetish.*

Placing the gun on the wall as well, Marlowe paused as he realised there was a rifle missing from the macabre display. Picking up the duffle and the flash drive, he turned slowly, working out quickly who could have taken it, while walking through the framed doorway and into the main living area.

It was dark, there were no lights on yet, and the furniture was sparse, mainly items that could be brought down the crypt steps flat-packed, and put together down there. Because of this, IKEA heavily influenced most of the style, and in the far corner was a chair, one with a strange, almost "fake word" sounding name.

Currently, a figure sat in it, the missing rifle in their hands, and aimed at Marlowe.

'Your security is shit,' they spoke, a woman's voice as Marlowe turned on a side lamp, the woman raising the rifle as he did so.

'Bang. You're dead.'

2

HOUSE VISITOR

Marlowe ignored the woman as he walked over to a small fridge the other side of the "living room", connected to a car battery.

He sighed, opening it up and pulling out a cold can of Coke.

'Put it back when you've finished playing with it,' he said, before walking over to a second chair, sitting in it, taking a deep mouthful of the drink as he let the duffle fall to the side.

Trix Preston lowered the rifle, amused at his non-responsiveness.

'You knew,' she said. 'How long?'

'I have a motion detector above the altar,' Marlowe replied, watching across. 'You bypassed the others, but you didn't pick it up. I didn't know who it was that tripped it, but I suspected.'

'Bollocks,' Trix growled. 'I shouldn't have been caught by a bloody trip camera. Even a teenager can get past those.'

Marlowe smiled at this. In her early twenties, Trix Preston was only a year or two divested from the teenagers she criticised here, but she'd done so much more in that time. In the last year or two she'd gone from working for a dodgy corporation with connections to the Government, to becoming the main hacker for Emilia Wintergreen's MI5 "Section D", working with Marlowe on a variety of operations, most recently in the field herself a couple of months back, when she entered Westminster Hall during a terrorist attack to defuse a nuclear device.

The fact she had no bomb training and was instead forced to "hack" the terrorists themselves had impressed Marlowe immensely.

Unfortunately, it hadn't impressed MI5, smarting from the embarrassment caused by their own inaction, and although Marlowe had taken the worst of it, becoming burnt in the process, Trix had found her own security clearance affected, and was amid a dozen performance reviews the last time they'd spoken.

'Why are you here, Trix?' he asked, not confrontational, but more as a passing question, like you would a friend who'd popped by for coffee.

'Heard there was an explosion in Heston,' Trix smiled. 'Witnesses said they saw a classic sports car drive off. Guessed it was you, came over.'

Marlowe looked at his watch.

'It was literally half an hour ago,' he said. 'You live a good twenty minutes away. There's no way you could have known I'd—'

He stopped.

'Where's the tracker?' he growled.

At this, Trix grinned, almost in triumph.

'I had to place it on something you always travel with,' she replied. 'And you have such a love for that sodding car.'

Marlowe groaned, remembering a moment a couple of weeks earlier, when, after the failed explosion, Trix had examined the car to reset the security.

'You can remove it,' he said coldly. 'I don't need to be babysat.'

'No?' Trix's tone matched the iciness of his own, and Marlowe realised she was one step away from full-on anger. 'So, you were completely fine tonight?'

Marlowe went to argue about this, but stopped.

'It was close,' he admitted. 'But it's also over.'

'I'll decide when it's over,' Trix snapped, clicking with her fingers for the flash drive. 'Come on, toss it over. I saw you uploading while you were mooning at the pretty girl in the photo.'

Marlowe tossed the flash drive across and Trix caught it deftly, already pulling a laptop out of her bag, clicking the USB-C port into the side.

'I don't have Wi-Fi yet,' Marlowe apologised. 'The walls of the crypt make it impossible to get a—'

He stopped again when Trix held up a hand.

'I'm good,' she said. 'I'm connected to three spy satellites and Starlink, so I'm getting five bars on the little Wi-Fi symbol.'

Marlowe wanted to ask if she could sort out the same for him, but thought better of it as she looked down at her screen. Instead, he placed the Coke can down and pulled the duffle back up, placing it onto his lap as he rummaged inside it. As expected, there were a couple of changes of clothing, an extensive first-aid kit, some spare ammunition, a couple of Kabar combat knives, and finally a couple of clear, zip locked bags; the first contained what looked to be several thousand in UK pounds and US dollars, as well as a USB stick with the

"Ledger" corporate symbol on it – this was familiar to Marlowe as he had similar from the same company, and was a "cold wallet", a way to store crypto coins offline, while the second bag held three different passports. One was French, one was British, and one was American, each with different names; Jean-Paul Toussaint, Jordan Frazier and Edward Warner.

In each, though, was the same passport image. No hair change, no moustache. All made at the same time, and from the same photo.

Marlowe frowned. These were less quality than Government issue, which once more gave him the feeling this wasn't a country attacking him.

'I don't think this was a country,' he said, speaking his thought aloud.

Trix, still typing, looked up at this.

'There's a two hundred grand hit out on you at the moment,' she replied. 'He could be freelance, but the source is still Government.'

'Wait, there's a hit out on me? Who's put a hit out on me?' Marlowe frowned at the news. 'Government?'

'Not sure,' Trix leant back from the laptop, considering the man in front of her. 'Came through more corporate dark-net channels; if there are such things. Probably someone covering their backs, so yeah, maybe.'

'Or, as you just said, it's corporate,' Marlowe said, without naming the corporation they were both thinking of.

Phoenix Industries.

'Where were you today?' Trix asked, looking back at the laptop, almost as if trying not to catch his eye.

'You know where,' Marlowe sniffed. 'You had a bloody tracker in my car.'

'In the car, not on you,' Trix shook her head. 'I know you drove to Berkshire, stopped in Hurley-Upon-Thames, parked up and then drove away about two hours later, but what you did during that time is a mystery.'

She now looked up at him.

'And, as we both know, Detective Inspector Declan Walsh lives in Hurley,' she said, 'but you went at a time you knew he'd be at work. So, there's every chance you went to check his house.'

She frowned as a new idea came to mind.

'Or you went to some other house? Or perhaps a place of work?'

Marlowe nodded at this.

'I went to Karl Schnitter's house,' he admitted, 'and then his garage.'

Karl Schnitter had been a long-time resident of Hurley, a sleepy Berkshire village, working as the local car mechanic. But he had a secret past, that of an East Berlin border guard, and more importantly, a righteous serial killer known as the *Red Reaper*. As this, Karl had murdered Detective Inspector Declan Walsh's parents – well, in a roundabout way – and Tom had helped Declan and his team in capturing him a year earlier, mainly because his boss, Emilia Wintergreen, had told him to. And, when Karl was in custody, Tom had taken him to a black site before the CIA, having worked with Karl in the past, could take him themselves, in the process providing him with a new identity in return for sensitive information.

And there Karl had rotted, until Francine Pearce, previously CEO of *Rattlestone Security,* a mercenary force with Government approval and now in custody for a variety of crimes, had freed Karl in an attempt to gain revenge on

Walsh and his police unit for something completely unrelated.

The "freeing" had been in the form of a hijack, while Karl was being transported to a new prison after his location had been compromised, an attack that left several good men dead, and Marlowe as good as, with two bullet wounds, and Karl free once more.

Interestingly, because of his own twisted morality, Karl had felt anger at this for the death toll was not of his doing and, once more a fugitive, had found and killed Francine, blowing up a holiday cottage she was hiding in, before giving himself up to the Americans and gaining a new identity.

And, of course, the final twist was that Francine Pearce wasn't even in the house, and was still at large, having now taken this "death" and used it to her advantage.

'Why did you go there?' Trix had also had her run-ins with this and knew the entire story.

'I wondered if anything had been left, or missed,' Marlowe shrugged. 'It's empty, forgotten. Nobody lives there.'

'Nobody's hurrying to buy the house of an ex-serial killer,' Trix shook her head. 'Strange that.'

'It's because technically he's still missing,' Marlowe cricked his neck as he spoke. 'They can't sell it until he agrees, or he's classed as dead.'

'And that's why we can't have nice things,' Trix shook her head. 'So, what did you find?'

'A note,' Marlowe reached into his pocket and pulled out his phone. Tapping the *photos* app, he scrolled to an image, passing photos of dead assassins as he did so, showing the photo he was looking for across the coffee table between them.

'It says "sorry for everything," and on the back is a letter

M,' he explained. 'I like to think he went back before he travelled to St Davids and left me it.'

'Or, he left it for Walsh,' Trix was looking back at the screen now. 'You know, with an M being a W when upside down.'

She looked up with a roguish grin.

'But, you know, whatever makes you sleep at night and all that.'

'So, why are you here again?' Marlowe sighed, knowing that deep in his heart, he agreed with Trix. 'And don't just say you were checking on me.'

'I had a call from our resident Yank,' Trix half-chuckled, and Marlowe knew why. Brad Haynes was a slightly more than middle-aged poster boy for the CIA, old enough to be Marlowe's dad, and with the attitude to match. He'd helped Marlowe and Trix a few months earlier, but had kept his cards incredibly close to his chest throughout, disappearing the moment the operation was over, and, apart from a couple of cryptic messages here and there over the last couple of months, had been pretty much non-responsive, most likely locked away in an office cubicle in Langley.

'Social or business?' Marlowe asked, expecting it to be the latter. CIA spooks never really called for a chit-chat.

'A bit of both, actually,' Trix leant back, folding her arms as she considered this. 'Said he has a job, an off-the-books one. Needs a bodyguard, someone with skills and tactfulness. And, as nobody else with those skills can do it, he's looking to see if you're available.'

'I'm not a babysitter, and I'm not really looking to risk flying to America right now,' Marlowe chuckled, but the smile faded slightly as he watched Trix. 'Or am I now? What do you know that you're not telling me?'

Trix turned the screen around to show an image of the assassin. It wasn't one from the passports, nor was it the one from Marlowe's personal photo collection, but a new image, a police mugshot. It was a couple of years old, but it was definitely the same man.

'Meet Grayson Long,' she said by introduction. 'They took this lovely shot in 2019, when he was pulled in after a bar fight in Newark.'

'Let me guess, he's a New Yorker?'

Trix nodded.

'Explains the photo you haven't shown me yet,' she said, nodding at the picture resting on the duffle. 'I can see enough to work out it's Manhattan from the skyline behind. That building there?'

She leant across, tapping one skyscraper in the background.

'That's Goldman Sachs, just south of Jersey City,' she explained, taking the photo now and examining it closer. 'I recognise the slightly darker top. There's a spot to get a superb view of the New York skyline, and there's a tribute to the New Jersey people who died in 9/11 right beside it. I visited it about seven years back, while on a school trip.'

Marlowe winced at this.

'I was fifteen,' Trix grinned, enjoying the moment. 'You were what, thirty?'

'I was in my twenties,' Marlowe replied, refusing to bite. 'And I was MI5 by then.'

'Do you creak when you move?' Trix impishly continued. 'Asking for a friend who's young and fresh-faced.'

Marlowe took the path of stoic silence here, and leant back in his chair, waiting for Trix to continue. Then, after a moment of waiting, just in case Marlowe wanted to verbally spar, but deciding wisely to carry on, Trix nodded to herself.

'Anyway, he's a New Yorker, yes, but he travels the world a lot. Tons of air miles, gold-level hotel memberships. Which is odd for a man who left the US Marines with nothing about five years ago.'

'Contract killing obviously pays well,' Marlowe looked back at the photo of Grayson. 'Go on, why are you pushing this?'

'I spoke to some police contacts of ours before Christmas,' Trix returned to the keyboard, typing as she spoke. 'They found Francine Pearce and Tricia Hawkins, the two bitches that almost killed you, in a building in Wardour Street in London, back in October. I took the details of this new company they'd founded and learned they'd both travelled to Manhattan in November.'

'Pearce and Hawkins are in New York, and a month or two later someone from Newark comes after me?' Marlowe nodded. 'Convenient.'

'I won't know if it's correct until I go through his phone data,' Trix was frowning at the back of the photo now. 'I saw you buggering around with a torch. Is there—'

'Yeah, UV ink,' Marlowe passed across the torch, allowing Trix to look at the message. 'The meeting's in a couple of days.'

Trix grinned, placing the photo back on the table.

'So, you have an assassin sent from New York, who has a meeting back in New York in a couple of days, who may have been hired by Pearce and Hawkins, and while you're in town, a CIA asset you know needs your help.'

'I'm going to New York, aren't I?' Marlowe sighed, looking up at the ceiling of the crypt.

'Look on the bright side,' Trix smiled, reaching into her bag, pulling out a new passport and an air ticket for later that day, just before eleven in the morning. 'It gets you out of the way while all this shit in Heston Services goes down, and a CIA slush fund has paid your ticket there.'

Marlowe took the ticket, reading it with a growing sense of irritation.

'This was why you were watching me,' he growled. 'To give me this bloody thing and pack me off like a happy camper.'

'I'm not packing you off anywhere,' Trix pulled out a second ticket, waving it at Marlowe. 'I'm coming with you. Super excited. Never flown business before.'

'Is Wintergreen going to be happy with that?' Marlowe was surprised at this.

In response, Trix shrugged.

'I'm still suspended,' she replied. 'If they have a problem with me freelancing, they can bloody reinstate me.'

'And what exactly are we doing there?' Resigned to the situation now, Marlowe rose from the chair, walking over to his armoury through the door. He wouldn't be able to take any of this with him, but he knew that for all his faults, Brad Haynes could provide him with most of what he needed.

'No idea,' Trix grinned. 'But I can't wait to find out. Grab your go bag, get some sleep, and I'll see you in the Heathrow business lounge tomorrow morning. Or, rather, later today, as it's gone midnight—'

She stopped as the laptop beeped.

'Hold that thought,' she said, looking up. 'You won't be going to sleep just yet. I just found Grayson's hit broker, and she works in London.'

Marlowe leant across the workshop table, picking his SIG Sauer off the pegs.

'Why would a US assassin have a UK broker?' he asked as he took it apart, placing the pieces onto the table before cleaning.

'Why would an assassin have a broker, full stop,' Trix was typing again. 'As I said earlier, usually they gain their targets through the dark web, or Craig's List.'

'Brokers are still out there for the more official jobs,' Marlowe was cleaning the gun barrel as he considered this. 'This way there's a level between booker and contractor.'

'Well, the broker's Pauline Faulkner,' Trix looked back up. 'Recognise the name?'

'No, but that doesn't mean we haven't crossed paths before. Especially if she's set *Grayson kill-person,* or whatever his name is, after me.'

'She has a registered address in North London,' Trix closed the laptop with a smile. 'She's also sending emails from the IP at the address right now, so I'm guessing she's working the night shift, or she's staying really late.'

'Then maybe I should have a chat before I leave,' Marlowe said, reconnecting the gun back together, and checking the chamber. 'You know, see where the dust is settling.'

'You need a gun for that?' Trix watched him finish up with a morbid fascination.

Marlowe smiled.

'I *always* need a gun for that,' he said.

3

BROKERING A DEAL

IT WAS ALMOST FOUR IN THE MORNING WHEN MARLOWE arrived at a North London courier company, pulling up around the corner of the building and watching it for a long moment through a sniper scope, before deciding to climb out, moving from his Jaguar, and heading towards the wire fence at the side.

The company was in a small warehouse district near Lea Valley Park, north of Stratford and Hackney, with what looked to be wire fences the only boundaries. A simple looking one-storey warehouse, from the half-an-hour reconnaissance by Marlowe, he'd gathered it was mainly entered and exited by vans through a large roller-shuttered entrance, the vans all emblazoned with *"Impetus Couriers"* on the side.

Makes sense, Marlowe thought to himself as he hurried to the building and fence to the side of it. *A courier company can travel anywhere in the world, and anyone working for them can do the same.*

Trix had found more on Impetus Couriers during his drive up to the street he was now parked on, sending it as a series of WhatsApp messages, probably from her bed as, unlike Marlowe, she tried to actually sleep that night. Or was it early morning by now? Marlowe hated semantics.

The company had been created almost ten years earlier, and if Marlowe was honest, it looked as legitimate as it could be. In the decade since creation however, they'd only had a couple of speeding tickets and, after a quick browse, he saw their Trustpilot score was astronomical.

Which probably meant they were fake.

Nobody ran a courier company and didn't break the speed limit regularly. They probably took the occasional job to keep up appearances, but there were a ton of different, off-the-books jobs a company like that could do. Although "brokering contracts for assassins" weren't quite the jobs Marlowe had expected.

The building next to Impetus Couriers was a garage of some kind, closed up for the night. The main gate, however, wasn't closed, probably because the garage had nothing worth stealing, and more likely knew next door would be in and out all night – and would see anything happening next door. But one man, sneaking through the pallets and car parts, including entire door pieces and engine blocks, keeping low to not cast a shadow from the lights above the main entrance next door, could slip through the courtyard and down the side of the building, sliding into the darker shadows with a minimum of fuss.

Now hidden from all prying eyes, Marlowe examined the warehouse through the wire mesh. There was a side door, at the back, which was probably mainly used as an exit to a smoking area, one that didn't require walking through the entire building. It might even be the reception entrance, although that was unlikely, as the ground leading to it from the front was barren and untended.

You didn't send your potential clients down such a path.

No, this was more an emergency exit than professional entrance, and that suited Marlowe fine; the last thing he wanted was something used regularly. And, moving closer, he crouched beside the fence, pulling out his knife.

It wasn't his usual knife, but was an Oplita bayonet tanto blade in black. He'd been given it a while back, and found it to be a little more unwieldy than his favourite Fairburn Sykes blade, but what it had going for it was a hole in the blade itself which, when placed into a corresponding slot on the solid sheath it came in, turned the back of the tip of the blade into a very effective wire cutter. And now, holding the blade's handle in one hand and the metal sheath in the other, he used this as a poor-man's bolt cutter, taking out the mesh fence in a matter of moments, the subtle *clip* noises as he took each wire apart drowned out by the vehicle noises at the front of the building. And, when he had enough cut wires to pull it aside like a curtain, just about able to move through in a crouch, he disconnected the blade, sheathing it and putting it back into his jacket before slicing through.

He was only a couple of metres from the door now, back against the wall, letting the shadows of the night shield him, but as he reached the door itself he flung himself back against the wall as the barren ground in front of it was bathed in light. The door had opened, and a man, in his mid-thirties and wearing the clothes of a delivery driver walked out, lighting a cigarette as he continued to the fence where, moments earlier, Marlowe had moved through.

He didn't see Marlowe, and more importantly, he didn't see the gap in the fence as he pulled down his zipper, adjusted himself, facing the fence and pissed through the mesh into the garage next door's property, cigarette in his mouth.

Realising this was his chance, the door still ajar to provide light to the driver relieving himself, Marlowe quickly slipped through it, entering the warehouse proper. As he'd thought from the brief glimpse he'd had earlier through the large entranceway, the building was mostly open space, filled with vans as workers moved boxes from trolleys into the vehicles, preparing for a long day of deliveries, or, rather, whatever the items being delivered really were. At the back, however, was a raised platform, not unlike Marlowe's own bedroom designs in his church, that looked down over the area, but was large enough to hold an office, the stairs to which could be seen directly beside him, running up the wall.

Taking them two at a time as quietly as he could, Marlowe started up the stairs, very aware that the moment the driver outside finished his ablutions, he'd be walking back into the warehouse, and finding Marlowe there could complicate things a little.

At the top of the stairs was a discarded vest; fluorescent yellow with stripes, it was a pull-on sleeveless jacket of sorts, the kind that marshals at events wore, and the same type of top everyone in the warehouse was wearing. Marlowe slipped it on, finding it was a little too large for him, but not really caring about the sartorial side of things. With this on, he now looked like one of the others – or enough to pass without a second glance. And, with a clipboard resting beside it, Marlowe could use this to look like someone on a mission, there to check inventory numbers or something, whatever courier people did, rather than a very pissed off ex-spy with a grudge.

With the disguise now on, Marlowe walked more casually, looking way less furtive than he did a moment earlier. As he did so, his phone buzzed silently in his pocket. Pulling it out, he looked down at the message.

She's still emailing.

So, the target was in the office next to him, and hadn't left for the night. That was good. And, straightening, Marlowe reached for the door, opening it.

The door led into a smaller front office, with a door to the side leading into what was probably the rest of the upper-floor space. There was a window to the right that looked out onto the warehouse below, the walls were a rather horrid pale yellow, and a map of Britain, with pins placed in various spots was stuck up behind a desk, a portly, miserable-looking man in a similar garish work-top looking up at him.

'What?' he asked, frowning. 'Hold on a mo, I don't know you.'

'First night tonight,' Marlowe lied. Well, it wasn't really a lie, as he had started tonight, just not the job the man expected of him. He waved the clipboard now. 'I was told to get this signed by Miss—'

He looked at the blank clipboard, the man at the desk unable to see the lack of paperwork, with the stare of a man unsure of the names in his new place of work.

'Faulkner?'

'It's Mrs,' the man at the desk said, showing the other door with a thumb. 'You're lucky she's in. I can sign it, though, if you want?'

'I dunno,' Marlowe looked worried now, playing to the audience. 'It's my first day, and I was told—'

'Yeah, yeah, whatever,' the man said, already returning to his computer monitor as Marlowe moved quickly to the door, knocking on it before entering.

The office he now entered was slightly larger, with a set of filing cabinets to the side and box arch files nestled horizontally above. In the corner, facing another full-length window was a middle-aged woman with black hair cut into a short, bobbed haircut, a younger style that actually worked at belying her true age, wearing a blue fleece and chewing on the end of a biro, sitting at her desk and staring at her monitor screen as Marlowe entered.

'What?' she asked without looking, her accent showing tinges of South London, and Marlowe wondered for a second if he'd even arrived at the right location, because Pauline Faulkner currently looked as far from "assassin broker" as you could possibly get.

'Mrs Faulkner?' he asked, closing the door behind him.

'Yeah, what?' Pauline was still reading the screen.

Marlowe smiled, placing the clipboard down and pulling out his SIG Sauer, aiming it at her face.

'I'm Tom Marlowe,' he whispered. 'I've come to tell you Grayson Long won't be coming into work today.'

Finally looking up from her work, Pauline swallowed. If the sight of a man with a gun was new to her, Pauline Faulkner hid it well, as she placed the pen down, slowly leaning back in her chair and watching Marlowe for a moment.

'I heard,' she said. 'You blew him up. Was he dead when you did that?'

Marlowe nodded.

'I'm not that much of a monster. I shot him. After he shot at me, I add. But he died quickly. No pain.'

Pauline nodded, not replying.

'I didn't put the hit on you,' she said. 'I just moved it along. Your fight isn't with me.'

'Currently it is.'

There was a chair by the wall so Marlowe pulled it across the room, sitting in it, facing Pauline, the gun half hidden now, but still aimed at her.

'So how about you tell me who paid you to find someone to off me?'

'You know I can't do that,' Pauline straightened in the chair. 'I get seen as someone who can't keep clients' identities secret, then I lose work. And probably my life, too.'

'I get that,' Marlowe smiled. 'But I'll be honest, you losing work isn't that high on my list of things I care too much about.'

He waggled the gun.

'And currently, I wouldn't worry about the future, because your life is in danger right now.'

Pauline stared at the gun for a long moment.

'I can tell you some things,' she said. 'Who it's not, for example.'

'A Government or corporation?' Marlowe asked.

Surprisingly, Pauline shook her head.

'Wait,' Marlowe half rose. 'It's *not* a corporation?'

'You're more surprised about that?' Pauline chuckled. 'I read your file, Mister Marlowe. That is, the one they sent me, anyway. You've pissed a lot of people off over the years. I would have thought you'd be expecting countries, or diplomats calling me on *behalf* of countries.'

'Oh, I know I've pissed those off enough to come after me,' Marlowe shrugged, settling into the chair. 'Already had a couple have a go, too. I'm curious, however, why you hired a New York-based assassin, though.'

Before Pauline could continue, the door opened and the man from outside popped his head into the room.

'Everything okay?' he asked, suspiciously.

'Oh, it's all wonderful,' Pauline beamed back. 'Mister Marlowe here is a spy. That is, he was one.'

Marlowe felt a sliver of ice slide down his spine at the comment, and his finger tightened on the trigger, but Pauline carried on speaking.

'I sent him into the workforce to check on morale, thievery, all the usual things. He's now giving me his report.'

'Oh. Okay.'

The man seemed a little thrown by this, but held it in well.

'I thought you would have told me.'

'If I did, it wouldn't have been secret,' Pauline waved the man off. 'You're fine. Go keep an eye on everyone. I won't be long here.'

The man nodded and closed the door, and Pauline now returned her attention towards Marlowe.

'These are real couriers?' Marlowe was surprised.

'Of course,' Pauline looked mortified he'd think anything else. 'The tax man checks everything. We did it to cover the money at the start, but now and then we actually make more money in a month legitimately.'

'But not enough to go legit full time?'

'Hell no.'

There was a long, uncomfortable silence.

'I didn't pick Grayson,' she explained. 'I was told he was the one they wanted. Picked specifically.'

'They being the client?'

'Exactly.'

'A New York client?'

'And why would you think that?' Pauline was smiling now, and Marlowe had the strongest belief that to her, this conversation was a game she was very much enjoying.

'Because of the photo.'

Pauline frowned, and for the first time, the guard was lowered.

She doesn't know about the photo.

Marlowe leant forward now, the gun lowering as he spoke.

'A woman in Battery Park, with a message on the back to meet in Manhattan in a couple of days,' he said. 'I'd think it was a lover's message if it wasn't in UV ink.'

'Bastard!' Pauline hissed. 'He was double crossing me!'

'Grayson?'

'No! I—'

Pauline stopped, gathering herself together.

'Brokers work simply,' she said. 'We make ten percent of the fee on culmination of contract. But to do that, *we* need to see the client once the job is completed, not the assassin. If he was meeting with the client, then he was taking us out of the equation.'

She thought for a moment.

'Tick Tock Diner, right?'

Marlowe nodded.

'That's where he met us, too, when he originally planned it,' Pauline growled now. 'Ever been there?'

'As a kid.'

'It hasn't changed. Bastard.'

Marlowe guessed the last word was more aimed at the

client, rather than the interior design of a New York hotel diner.

'On a side note, how much was I?' he asked, shifting in the seat.

Pauline looked uncomfortable, as if worried Marlowe might think the amount too little, and then spoke.

'A hundred grand.'

Marlowe nodded at this, reaching into his pocket and pulling out a wad of notes, in a Ziplock bag.

'Ten percent would be ten grand,' he said. 'Here's more than that, to call off the hit. Or, at least, not to add any more people on to it, now Grayson's dead. At least until I have a word with the client?'

In truth, he didn't know how much was in the pile of money he now placed on the table; it was Grayson's own money from his duffle. But it felt to be around fifteen grand, and he was playing a hunch.

Pauline didn't even pause, taking the bag, already opening it and counting the notes as she spoke.

'Taylor Coleman,' she said without looking at him. 'That's who put the hit out on you.'

Marlowe paused as he heard the name.

'Taylor Coleman?' he breathed in a mixture of shock and anger.

'You know him?' Pauline now looked up, curious at this change of events.

'Yeah, I bloody know him,' Marlowe growled.

Marlowe rose from the chair, but Pauline held a hand up to halt him.

'Look, I know this probably isn't the time, especially with you recently aiming a gun at me, but I wasn't lying when I said I read your file,' she said. 'Or, at least the stuff we're allowed to know about. You're good, Tom. You've got top level scores in a lot of areas. And, thanks to your connections and accounts being frozen by MI5, you're friendless and out in the cold.'

Marlowe didn't completely agree with this, but he was curious where the conversation was going, and so stood still, waiting.

'We could use someone like you.' The offer was simple, and unexplained. Marlowe could work for Pauline Faulkner, likely as a contract killer, as he didn't think she was talking about his couriering skills. 'The money's good.'

'I don't need money,' Marlowe smiled. 'But you're right, I need friends. However, you sent someone to kill me. I think we're not there yet.'

Pauline gave a brief nod at this, the slightest hint of a smile on her lips.

'Give me time,' she said.

'Time is one thing you do have, after all,' Marlowe replied as he walked to the door. 'It's been a pleasure.'

Now out in the external office, Marlowe nodded to the man back behind the desk, and continued through onto the deck.

He didn't have to hide anymore.

But, he'd never felt more exposed.

Because Taylor Coleman, the man who'd placed the hit on him, was his bloody *father*.

4

BUSINESS CLASSED

Unsurprisingly, Marlowe hadn't slept after the revelation his own father was trying to kill him. That said, he hadn't spoken to Taylor Coleman in a long time, possibly even since his mum died, so there was every opportunity something else had happened, and Marlowe simply didn't know about it.

Marlowe's mum, Olivia, had met Taylor while on a mission in Kosovo. Taylor was Irish, but had lived in London most of his life, and was a black market salesman, preying on the wounded and the lost.

Marlowe had never worked out what his mum had seen in him, only that she once told him she had a soft spot for "lost causes", and Taylor sodding Coleman was definitely one of those. In fact, when she told him she was pregnant, Taylor actively disappeared out of her life for two years, and when she found him after that, his first question was whether or not she'd had an abortion.

She'd taken out two of his teeth when she punched him.

The last time Marlowe had even seen his father was over

fifteen years ago, on the night of his eighteenth birthday – the night before Marlowe signed up for the military – when Coleman had appeared out of nowhere on his doorstep with a four pack of Tennent's Special Brew hanging from his hand. He'd dragged Marlowe to a local park to chug two of them down with him, sitting on a park bench like a couple of homeless alcoholics, while Marlowe tried to drink them down as quickly as possible simply to get away from the man.

At the end of this, Coleman had solemnly explained that this was his task in life, to "make Marlowe into a man".

Marlowe had followed his mother's lead from years earlier and punched Coleman hard in the face at this, and, as the older man lay sprawled on the grass, Marlowe had crouched over him, holding a butterfly blade to his throat – not intending to slice it, but just enough to draw a bead of blood from it – pointing out that as they'd now had their father-son bonding session, if Taylor Coleman ever came near Marlowe or his mother again, he'd kill him – incredibly slowly.

Marlowe had never seen his biological father again, and if Pauline Faulkner was correct, it looked like he'd tired of waiting to confront his son once more, deciding instead to cut to the chase and just remove him from the board, as violently as possible.

He'd heard a couple of years back that Coleman had moved into arms dealing in Kosovo, and apparently had been doing quite well in it, but that was as far as he'd checked.

If asked, he claimed it wasn't worth his time to check, but the truth of the matter was that Marlowe didn't want to look into his deadbeat father's financials, and find he'd become a success without a wife and child to weigh him down.

Marlowe wanted Taylor Coleman to be a *failure*, and, in

his own mind, bereft of facts to the contrary, this is how Taylor Coleman existed. Now, to know not only did his father have a hundred grand to his name, but he also had a hundred grand to throw on a hit against him ... it was a tough pill to swallow.

By the time Marlowe arrived back at the church, around five in the morning, he only had enough time to shower, pack, and then lock the place back up; the flight was just under six hours away, and check-in started around half past seven. And, by the time he'd ferreted away enough "air travel-ready" items, as well as spare credit cards, dollars, bullion coins and fake IDs into his cabin luggage, it was already half-past six.

Driving his still-damaged Jaguar to the Heathrow Long-Stay car park, Marlowe took one last long, resigned look at the battered rear bumper, and promised to get it fixed when he returned.

If he returned, that was.

Trix was in the British Airways business class lounge when Marlowe entered, working on a small tablet-style computer that, although looking like a basic iPad, was likely souped up by a factor of a hundred.

Looking up as he approached, she placed the computer back into her leather backpack, clearing the table in front of her.

'Passport worked, then?' she asked. At this, Marlowe shrugged, sitting down in the chair facing her.

'Not had a true workout yet,' he replied. 'All they do here is check your ID is the same as the name on the ticket. That'll come on the other side.'

'It'll work,' Trix brushed away the concern. 'If Brad

wanted us that bad, he'd have got some buddies in the CIA to sort it.'

'They're CIA level forgeries?' Marlowe pulled his out again, checking the main page where a photo of him faced out into the world, the name GARTH FLEMING written under it. 'Well now I'm *double* worried they won't work.'

He looked back at Trix.

'And Fleming?' he muttered. 'Is he taking the piss or what? He might as well have written *Bond* as the surname.'

'It's still better than mine,' Trix smiled. 'I'm Winifred Hutchinson. Apparently, the name means "a friend of peace" or something.'

'Winifred?' Marlowe actually chuckled at this. 'Now I know the CIA are on drugs.'

'If they are, they're the good ones,' Trix folded her arms as she watched Marlowe. 'So, what happened with the broker? You went dead on me as soon as you entered.'

Marlowe considered lying, but Trix had done enough for him, and he felt it wasn't fair to keep her in the dark about this.

'She gave me the name of the client,' he said, leaning back in the chair. 'The one who placed the hit.'

'And?' Trix leant closer. 'Was it who we thought?'

'Hold that thought,' Marlowe grinned, rising. 'I'm grabbing a coffee.'

It was phrased as a "dick move", to make her wait while he walked off, and there was a slight element of satisfaction in doing it, but Marlowe hadn't played the card to be a prick. He'd done it to gain a moment of thought; *did he want Trix to know the truth about his father?* He wasn't mentioned in any of Marlowe's files, and apart from his mother, long dead, there weren't many actual people who knew this.

Grabbing a black coffee from the machine, he walked back to the table, Trix frowning as she watched him return.

'Okay, I'm guessing you needed time to configure your answer,' she said, 'which means it's a shit one for you. Who placed the hit?'

Damn you, Trix. For once, miss the clues.

'An arms dealer named Taylor Coleman did it for a hundred grand,' Marlowe replied diplomatically. 'It's nothing to do with Rattlestone or Pearce or any of that crowd.'

'You're sure?'

Marlowe went to reply but stopped himself.

'Actually, no,' he admitted. 'I last saw Coleman around fifteen years ago. I don't know why he'd place a hit on me if I'm being brutally honest.'

Trix had picked up on the *fifteen years* line, and Marlowe could see her doing the maths in her head.

'Who is he, Tom?' she asked, her voice softer and lower now.

'He's my biological father,' Marlowe admitted. 'And you're one of about three people in the world that knows this. I don't think even Wintergreen knows. He's literally just a sperm donor with an attitude.'

'An attitude that wants you dead.'

'Sure,' Marlowe shrugged. 'But the broker said the whole New York meet was nothing to do with her, so it's obviously something else, and daddy dearest was somehow screwing the middle man. Or woman, in this case.'

'So, you're going to the meeting?'

Marlowe pulled out the photo of the woman in Battery Park.

'Can you find her?' he asked gently. 'You know, with some spy shit facial recognition?'

'Already on it,' Trix winked. 'I scanned the image last night while you were cleaning your gun. Nothing yet, but it's an excellent shot, full face, and if she's in any database, she'll turn up.'

'And if she's not?'

'Then that makes it a far more tiresome game, as we move to Facebook and Instagram profiles,' Trix sipped at her own drink, a small glass of champagne. 'But if she's on social media anywhere, we'll find her.'

'Should you be on that, this early in the morning?' he asked, pointing at the glass.

'Unlike you, I don't get many chances to fly in business class,' Trix sniffed. 'I'll be taking every free thing I can during this flight.'

Marlowe finished his coffee, considering this.

He should be more like Trix, he thought.

After all, he had no idea if this was the last plane he'd ever get on.

THE PLANE LANDED AT JFK AIRPORT SHORTLY BEFORE TWO IN the afternoon. It'd been a fairly uneventful flight, and Marlowe had been in a window seat, with Trix across the aisle. She'd spent the eight hours of the flight sampling everything she could, while Marlowe had taken advantage of the folding-out bed, grabbing around five hours of mostly uninterrupted sleep.

He'd had the dream again during it. The one where he was ambushed while taking Karl Schnitter to a new location, a dream where masked attackers took out his team, shooting him point blank in the chest five times.

It wasn't a dream as such, it was an "almost" memory – in the real world he'd worn a Kevlar vest, one that had saved him from three of the five bullets shot at him – but here, he was naked, and because of that each bullet found their mark, slamming into him as he realised *this was it,* and he was going to die.

He'd woken with a yelp as the plane dipped with turbulence, realising his skin was clammy to the touch. People called it "flop sweat", the act of sweating because of nervousness, especially the fear of failure.

Failure to save his friends.

Failure to stop Karl from escaping.

No. You can't think about that.

Marlowe had risen, making his way to an empty lavatory, where he faced himself through the mirror, splashing cold water on his face to wake himself up. It had been a full-on twenty-four hours, from the journey to Hurley, the investigation of Karl's house, the journey back and self-defence killing of Grayson Long, the conversation with Trix and then the journey to Pauline Faulkner, resulting in the news about his father ...

No wonder he was having nightmares.

Trix was watching for him as he returned to his seat.

'Okay?' she asked, nodding to herself when he replied with a single thumbs up gesture. He didn't want to go into it with her. He didn't want to go into it with anyone.

And, after a breakfast provided an hour before landing, Marlowe prepared his lies for the US Immigration.

As Garth Fleming, he was travelling for business, staying at the Mayfair Hotel off Times Square, and was flying back in a day or two.

It didn't matter if this was true, as all he needed to do was get past them. Then Garth Sodding Fleming was returning into his box.

Once off the plane, the line for immigration was longer than expected, a Chinese flight having arrived directly before them, and so Marlowe and Trix waited patiently as the line snaked back and forth towards the exit. Usually, if he flew as himself, Marlowe was part of the *Global Entry* travel scheme, which slipped him through immigration and customs in double time; but now, as Fleming, he had the same wait as everyone else, taking it step by step, "called forward" case by "called forward" case.

Eventually, Marlowe arrived at the counter. He saw Trix, at the counter beside him, have her passport scanned, her fingerprints taken and then get waved on; he hoped his journey was as quick.

It wasn't.

'Reason for travelling, Mister Fleming?' the customs official, a terrifyingly muscled black man, asked, holding up the passport, matching the image to the man in front of him.

'Business,' Marlowe replied.

'What kind of business?'

'Exports.'

The customs officer grunted and placed the passport under the scanner.

However, after a moment, he looked back at Marlowe, narrowing his eyes.

'Problem?' Marlowe asked, already feeling a trickle of ice down his spine.

Something was wrong.

'It's just taking its time,' the officer said, tapping a button under the counter.

That's not good.

'Casey, can you grab the sarge?' the customs officer said to a second arrival, most likely attending because of the button pressing. The new arrival, another obviously ex-military officer nodded, staring at Marlowe before walking off.

Marlowe wondered what the best exit strategy was here – did he bluff it, or fight it out? If they took him in, there was every opportunity this was because of some other issue, rather than a dodgy passport forgery. What else could it have been?

Now two additional guards walked up, hands on their sidearms.

'Mister Fleming, could you come with us, please?' the one that had first arrived said, nodding towards a side door. Marlowe wanted to complain, or at least argue with this, but the customs officer in the booth passed him his passport back, and nodded.

'I'd go with them, sir,' he said.

And now Marlowe was confused. If there'd been some kind of irregularity with the passport, it would have been kept from him. *This was something else.* Quietly, and noting Trix, standing by the door to baggage claim, watching him, he followed the guards into the room.

'Is there some kind of problem, officers?' he asked, instantly regretting it. Of *course,* there was a problem. He was being placed in a quiet, out-of-the-way room, rather than being allowed entry into the United States.

The guards said nothing, simply motioning for Marlowe to stand before a metal table. On the other side of it was a burly woman in her fifties. And, before Marlowe could protest anything, she placed a small backpack onto the table.

'Welcome to America, Mister Fleming,' she said simply,

her voice giving no hint of emotion. And, this message given, she pointed at another door at the end of the room. 'You can go through there when you're done.'

This said, the woman and the two guards left the room through the door they had brought Marlowe through, leaving him alone in the room.

This was unexpected.

Quickly and quietly, Marlowe turned his attention to the backpack in front of him. It was a grey, thin material pack, and inside it, when opened, Marlowe found a loaded Glock 17 pistol and two 17 rounds spare magazines.

Picking up the weapon, he ran a fingertip along the right side of the slide. Just behind the ejection port he felt a raised bump, the pistols loaded chamber indicator confirming a round in the chamber. Next to this was a wallet with the driving licence and ID of a "Dexter Garner", his face mysteriously resembling Marlowe's own.

In the wallet were also credit cards in Dexter's name, as well as three hundred dollars in cash. With that was a smartphone, turned off, a small, yet sharp, knife that clipped to his waistband, a US Marshals ID for Dexter Garner, and a shoulder holster for the gun.

Turning on the smartphone, Marlowe was amused to find it already primed for his fingerprint.

Nice, he thought to himself as it came to life. *Way to make an impression, guys.*

There was one number on the phone, and one message. An address, nothing more.

Placing the address to memory, Marlowe emptied the backpack, moving everything into his own bag while taking off his jacket and shouldering the holster.

This done, he replaced his jacket, concealed the gun and, now with a completely new persona, left through the other door and into the baggage claim, to find Trix, and whatever was going to happen next.

Personally, he was just happy he wasn't getting a cavity search.

5

FRIENDS REUNITED

THE ADDRESS WAS THAT OF A HOTEL ON EIGHTH AVENUE IN Manhattan; a midtown address that held the building between 44th and 45th Street, facing bars and liquor stores, while only a block from Times Square and Broadway.

The text message Brad had left on the burner phone stated the hotel and room number, but hadn't provided a key to enter the elevator with, so as Marlowe watched the other guests in the lobby, wondering which one to lift a card from, Trix tapped quickly on her tablet, hacking into the system.

Eventually, deciding he couldn't be bothered with more spy shit, Marlowe walked over to the counter.

'I'd like to place a call to room—' he stopped, checking his phone. 'Room six-oh-thirteen.'

'Do you have a name?' The receptionist asked.

Marlowe frowned.

'Haynes?' he suggested.

This wasn't the correct answer, as the receptionist now looked up at him suspiciously. Before she could say anything, Marlowe pulled out the US Marshal badge, showing it to her.

'I was told to go to that room,' he said. 'Nothing more.'

The receptionist stared at the badge for a moment, and Marlowe wondered if she could see it was a fake, but then she looked at the screen and smiled.

'I think there was a confusion at your end, Mister Garner,' she said, tapping on the keyboard. 'Room six-zero-one-three is in your name.'

'Oh,' Marlowe hadn't expected this, and placed the wallet away. 'Of course. That makes sense. Can I get two keys then, please?'

'Already sorted,' the receptionist passed over two plastic credit-card-sized room keys. 'And if you download our app, you can turn your phone into a digital card.'

'I'll remember that,' Marlowe smiled back, nodding as he held the cards up. Walking back to Trix, he saw her now playing with her phone.

'I can't hack a room key without the right equipment,' she moaned.

'They do it in the movies,' Marlowe chided, almost backing away as Trix looked up, her gaze burning through him. As a defence action, he held up the cards.

'Old school?' he suggested.

Trix, seeing the cards, visibly relaxed.

'How?'

'It's what I'm trained to do,' Marlowe replied, deciding it was better not to explain the truth here.

'After you,' Trix said, impressed, as they walked to the elevators, Marlowe nodding to the security guard as he tapped his card against the scanner. The guard had been watching them since they arrived, and was probably one step away from kicking them out, so it was a good idea to play nice.

As the elevator doors opened, Trix looked at Marlowe.

'I could have done this, you know,' she protested. 'If I had the right tools.'

'I know,' Marlowe smiled as he entered. And, to be honest, he believed her. 'So, shake it off and get ready. We don't know what we're walking into, but let's go speak to the Yank.'

THE YANK WAS INSIDE THE HOTEL ROOM – OR, RATHER, THE hotel *suite*. A two-bedroom apartment of sorts with a middle "lounge" area, Brad was setting up what looked to be an ornate computer system, a bank of three large screens connected on the hotel suite's desk, all removed from form-fitting, black, plastic, cargo boxes. These were military-level screens, or at least ones that were expected to suffer bumpy travel conditions.

As they entered, Trix gave the most cursory of nods to Brad, before pushing him away from the system, already leaning over the desktop box, checking the cable arrangement. Grinning, his hands in the air in mock surrender, Brad Haynes turned to face Marlowe.

As ever, Brad gave the appearance of a middle-aged man in good condition, a bomber jacket open over a New York Yankees T-shirt, blue jeans completing the casual ensemble. His hair was still thick and dark, his body stocky but not fat, the jacket hiding the fact he was as solid as a prize fighter, his jawline strong, and, the only difference from the last time Marlowe had seen him, heavily stubbled, the beard peppered with white hairs.

He looked like Captain America, if he'd had a decade of working as a rock band's roadie.

'Brit,' he said, pulling Marlowe into a manly embrace. 'You're not dead. That's a start.'

'He's doing his best to fix that,' Trix said from the monitors, not looking up as she spoke.

'I've had a few moments,' Marlowe admitted. 'But why get killed in the UK when I can come here and do it for you?'

Brad smiled, walking to the fridge and pulling out a couple of beers. Passing one to Marlowe, he took a long drink from it.

'Sorry for the cloak and dagger shit and all that, but I know you get off on it, so I thought it'd be a big adventure for you.'

'I didn't "get off" on thinking I was about to be cavity searched,' Marlowe growled, showing the gun. 'And a Glock?'

'What about it?' Brad asked, frowning. 'It's your favourite.'

'The SIG Sauer's my favourite,' Marlowe replied, and realised he was whining about a gun of all things. 'My concern is why I needed one the moment I stepped off the plane.'

'You're a wanted man,' Brad shrugged his wide shoulders at this. 'People want you. Want to *kill* you. I thought you'd want your own equaliser.'

'And the Marshal's badge?'

'You wanted to be a cowboy as a kid, right?' Brad flashed a grin as there was a spark, a crack, and a yelp of pain from beside the window.

'I'm alright,' Trix quickly commented. 'Forgot your US plug sockets are bloody death-traps.'

She pointed at a grey box connected to the wall socket.

'What's that?'

'It's an electromagnet,' Brad replied, nodding at it. 'Not that strong, but enough to wipe any drives placed directly onto it. CIA self-destruct plan.'

'Nice,' Trix smiled patronisingly as she carried on working through the network cables. 'Probably doesn't work, though. Or it'd be screwing with the entire network by now.'

Marlowe walked to the sofa, placing his duffle bag down on the ground as he sat on it, watching Brad.

'What's the plan?' he asked carefully. 'This isn't a CIA op, but you're flashing CIA money.'

'How do you know it's not a CIA op?' Brad sat in a chair opposite, holding his beer bottle in both hands. 'Maybe when I came back to the States, I was treated like a hero.'

'Saving the US President would do that,' Trix commentated, half-listening as she started working on the operating system. 'Unless you're Marlowe. And then you get fired. Although he wasn't Marlowe's President, so maybe that's why he got the shit end of the stick.'

'I heard your mom was still on the list when it was shared around,' Brad's face darkened as he looked back at Marlowe. 'That was the deal, wasn't it? To keep the girl out of the spotlight while you took the brunt of the anger?'

Marlowe now shrugged, leaning back onto the sofa. *Or was it a couch over here?* He couldn't remember.

'I had less to lose,' he admitted. 'They already wanted me out. They just found a way to cause doubt on whether or not I was a threat.'

'The CIA doesn't see you as a threat,' Brad raised his bottle in a salute.

'The CIA doesn't even know I'm here, do they?' Marlowe raised his own in a mocking response. 'They don't call in burned spies or hackers on suspension. You've dipped into the slush fund to finance this, haven't you? This means it's not a CIA case, it's personal. And the amount you've spent shows how important it is.'

'How so?' Brad folded his arms as he waited.

Marlowe waved his bottle around the room.

'A suite rather than a flophouse room. Business Class tickets.'

'I wanted you to be comfortable.'

'You wanted us to be *ready*,' Marlowe snapped back. 'You fly us economy, we arrive tired, cramped, sore and aching, not at our best. But give us space to relax, to stretch our muscles and a bed on the flight? We're more relaxed. Ready to hit the ground running. And then I get the ID and the gun in the airport? You couldn't even wait for us to get here? You were concerned you'd need to call on us before we even arrived, maybe even as soon as we left the airport.'

He pulled out the US Marshal ID.

'This is CIA grade, just like the passports. The systems over there are the same. There's a lot of CIA-level hardware, but you're going with known assets the CIA probably isn't happy to see, so you're keeping them out of the loop. I'd like to know why, and what you need from us.'

'I'd like to know if I'll get time to see *Phantom Of The Opera*,' Trix gave a winning smile across the room. 'It's only next door.'

Brad pursed his lips, and then curtly nodded.

'I was going to wait until the teenager had finished,' he said, nodding over at Trix who, having returned to her operating system, didn't seem to either hear or react to the jibe. 'I've got a problem, and I wanted your help.'

'Something you went to the CIA for, but got turned down.'

'Yeah.'

'Something personal.'

'Yeah. Unsurprisingly, saving the President didn't make me hero of the week.'

Brad picked up his phone, scrolling through some images on it, before stopping at one and passing it over. It was of a woman, in her late twenties or early thirties. She was slim, with short, brown hair in an asymmetrical haircut, blue eyes contrasting against her olive skin. She wore a grey suit and salmon blouse, and the photo was very much a posed shot, one of those you'd see on a website when telling the viewer "about the team".

'She's the target?' Marlowe passed it back.

'In more ways than one,' Brad replied, leaning back in his chair. 'Her name's Roxanne Vasquez. She's an environmental lawyer for *Rehbein and Pope*, one of the smaller Manhattan law firms.'

'Environmental lawyer,' Marlowe repeated slowly. 'Who's she decided to go for?'

'There's a company downtown, well, more of a financial hedge fund case,' Brad explained. 'Donziger. They're massive, but mainly work through shell companies and cover names. Have a few outlets, mainly in the oil, gas and finance areas.'

'So, they're big enough to make governments sit up and take notice. I get that.'

'Roxanne was passed a case, a small town in the Midwest, Jericho Falls, that had been almost decimated after one of Donziger's funded purification plants had set up shop nearby. She took on the whole town as clients, aiming a class-action case against Donziger. Billions of dollars.'

'And it was swept away quickly? They usually are,' Marlowe replied dismissively.

At this, however, Brad shook his head.

'No,' he smiled, and Marlowe, for a brief moment, thought he saw an expression of pride on the older man's face. 'They had some smoking guns, some definitive proof of corruption at higher levels. Governors and Senators being given sweeties to look the other way. The case, even if it gets into the courtroom, doesn't just embarrass the corporation, but also Capitol Hill.'

'This is still going to court?'

'Monday, ten am,' Brad nodded. 'Four days from now.'

Marlowe considered the date. The meeting at the Tick Tock Diner was on the Saturday morning, and it was now mid-afternoon on Thursday.

'So, this is a babysitting mission?' he asked. 'Keep her alive until the case? Surely the feds can do that?'

'They did that,' Brad rose, now angrily pacing. 'Until last Monday. Two of the Jericho Falls witnesses were killed when the safe house they were staying in exploded. "Gas leak," people claimed. But that's bull.'

He glowered out of the window as he spoke.

'Three FBI agents died in there. But dozens knew about it. Any of those people –and we're talking about trust representatives in high up places – could have sold the information to Donziger.'

'And Vasquez?'

'Once she heard about this, she decided if she was going to die, she'd do it on her own terms. Told the FBI to go screw themselves. Said she was going to carry on the week like nothing was going on. And for the last two days, she's done just that, with the tiniest of NYPD support teams.'

'And you.'

Brad wrinkled his nose as he tried to reply, without giving too much away.

'And me. And a SEAL buddy, who's watching her right now.'

'This is why I'm a Marshal, isn't it?' Marlowe was understanding now. 'If I was an FBI agent, then it might go back to the mole that I'm a ringer. But if I'm a Marshal, they have more of a national remit. I could have come from anywhere.'

'Partly,' Brad gave a weak smile. 'But mainly I wanted to see you play *cowboys*.'

There was a *ping* from beside the window, and a triumphant hiss from Trix, finishing up the set up.

'Who's she to you?' Marlowe asked. 'Roxanne?'

'I'm helping because—'

'I didn't ask why you're helping,' Marlowe interrupted. 'I asked who Roxanne Vasquez is to you.'

Brad didn't want to answer; that much was obvious. But, eventually, he gave a brief nod.

'I had a buddy in the Agency,' he explained. 'Danny Vasquez. Great guy. Saved my life twice.'

He stopped, looking at the ground.

'I lasted longer than he did.'

Marlowe understood what Brad was saying here – Daniel Vasquez had died while in service to the CIA, and was most likely now immortalised in an anonymous star on a Langley wall.

'And Roxanne is his daughter?'

Brad shook his head.

'Niece,' he replied, but added nothing else to the statement.

'I'm guessing you went to the CIA with this, but they didn't bite.'

'The CIA is political,' Brad slumped a little as he spoke. 'They understood it was the right thing, but they have a lot of Senators and governors in their orbits.'

'Including the ones she's gunning for,' Trix walked over now, a Diet Coke in her hand. 'What? I was listening to everything.'

'You're majorly off-books,' Marlowe realised. 'You could get kicked out, or worse, for what you're doing!'

'Danny saved my life,' Brad looked up at Marlowe now, and the intent was clear in his gaze. 'I never returned the favour. Until now.'

Marlowe understood that. He'd been guilty of the same thing a few times.

'Okay, so we keep her alive until Monday,' he finished the bottle, placing it on the table. 'What's the first task?'

'She won't be happy she's being tailed,' Brad admitted, looking from Marlowe to Trix. 'She's like her uncle for that. But she'll understand when the bullets fly.'

'You're expecting bullets?'

'Hell yes, I'm expecting them,' Brad reached into his jacket, pulling out an invitation. 'There's a swanky party tonight at the New York Public Library, beside Bryant Park. Black tie, the whole shebang. She's going, mainly to confront a couple of people, I reckon. If there's gonna be an extraction made, it'll be there. This is for you, "Marshal Dexter." Go in, make contact, keep her the hell alive.'

'I'll need a tuxedo,' Marlowe said, looking at the invite. 'And I won't be able to take a gun in.'

'You're a US Marshal,' Brad smiled. 'You'll be able to bring what you want in. And as for a tux, it's in your room. Sized by eye, but should be fine, unless you've been stuffing your face and letting your body go to hell since we last met.'

Marlowe smiled.

'That's the dream,' he said. 'Okay then, let's go save a lawyer.'

He stopped.

'I have one problem, though,' he added. 'There's a hit out on me—'

'A hundred grand? Yeah, I've been monitoring it,' Brad nodded. 'I don't know what you did in London, but someone killed it in Europe.'

Marlowe smiled. *Pauline Faulkner had been true to her word, it seemed.*

'But over here?'

'Open season,' Brad admitted. 'People will be gunning for you. There's even talk it came from the East Coast, either here or in Boston. It's why I dumped your Garth Fleming passport the moment you arrived. Someone will work out Fleming was you, and then they'll know you're stateside. But, with luck, by the time this occurs, you'll already be flying back to Limey-land under a different name.'

'Courtesy of the CIA?'

'Not this time,' Brad shook his head. 'I'll use a local guy. Safer. But until then, Dexter Garner, the floor is yours.'

Marlowe nodded.

'I have a list of things I'll need,' he started.

6

PARTY FLAVOURS

The New York Public Library was actually two libraries, the Astor and Lennox Libraries, combined into a new building in the late nineteenth and early twentieth century, to the east of Bryant Park. Known as the "Main Building" for over a century, it was after billionaire investor Stephen A. Schwarzman donated over a hundred million to rebuilding in 2008, that they renamed the building the *Stephen A. Schwarzman Building.*

In fact, it was in Astor Hall, in the Stephen A. Schwarzman Building, where the evening's event was planned.

Marlowe had checked the website before changing into his party clothes. The event in question was a fundraiser for climate change awareness, honouring writers, activists and philanthropists who, over the last year had brought positive attention to the issues relating to ways to change the planet's reliance on coal, oil and gas, among many other believed culprits. Many of the guests were members of the social media community, as well as actor activists, some even hopping on their private jets and flying over from Hollywood to attend, and in the process ignoring the whole *point* of the situation.

This year, they had invited both Roxanne Vasquez and the partners of Rehbein and Pope as special guests, with Vasquez giving a keynote speech. That within days they would go up against Donziger wasn't missed by either side, and the event organisers knew this would gain them publicity, while Rehbein and Pope knew this would gain public support for their point of view in the upcoming case.

It was large, glitzy and extortionate, with Astor Hall, being the entrance to the building itself, giving an imposing and opulent beginning to the experience. An immensely high, stone-vaulted ceiling, above a white marble interior, the bay windows were ceiling-high and arched, with equally arched porticos on the other side leading into the library itself, while a staircase to the left, also in white marble and stone, took you to an upper balcony where you could look out at the party below.

As Marlowe entered, passing his invite to the suited security, he stepped before the metal detector, pulling out his US Marshal ID and quickly flashing it.

'I'm carrying,' he breathed, and the guard nodded, looking back at the guard standing on the other side of the scanner.

'He's coming through hot, but it's allowed,' he said as Marlowe walked through the metal detector's frame, the light flashing red, but the guard waving him on, past security and into the party itself. Nodding thanks, Marlowe continued into the Hall itself, lit with a warm-white, almost golden lighting scheme, a couple of projectors shining white, revolving shapes onto the marble walls above him.

To the left and right were drinks bars, both with white-jacketed barmen serving cocktails, and in the middle was a small, raised dais with a string quartet playing what sounded like show tunes, arranged spectacularly, or ironically, depending on the mindset of the arranger.

It was busy, with maybe two hundred people already milling around, and it looked like the speeches were later in the evening. Marlowe took a deep breath, manipulated his neck from side to side to take out any kinks, and turned away from the party, examining a plaque on the wall.

'Testing comms,' he whispered.

'Comms check,' the voice of Trix replied.

'Comms check two,' the voice of Brad Haynes added. 'Can we get on with this? It's bloody cold out here. There's talk of snow and this car's heating is crap.'

'Should have got a better car,' Marlowe smiled as he looked back.

'Spent the money on bringing you two over, you smug limey prick,' Brad replied in a sarcastic but good-natured way. At least Marlowe hoped it was good-natured.

'Stay for twenty and then move to a warmer spot,' Marlowe instructed as he walked towards the bar. 'Try to stay within a block, though, in case I need extraction.'

'Roger.'

Marlowe took a glass of champagne from a tray as it passed, but he had no intention of drinking tonight, no matter how vintage the drinks were. He needed to be clear-headed, and he could feel the slightest twinges of jet lag hitting him, pushing at the sides of his skull.

Looking around, he spied Roxanne almost immediately, standing across the Hall at the other bar, talking to an older man with a pair of half-glasses. From the body language, Marlowe could tell they knew each other. They weren't close enough for him to accurately read lips, but he could see from the expressions this was a social conversation and one both parties were happy to have. It was probably her boss, and they were discussing her speech, as Marlowe made out the word "keynote" mentioned.

Pretending to sip at his champagne, Marlowe continued across the Hall, but stopped as a second woman caught his eye. Her hair was also short and brown, but cropped in a more traditional cut, the hair lighter than Roxanne's. She wore a simple black dress, which hugged her figure, but didn't stand out from the others. In fact, if she hadn't worn an expensive-looking diamond necklace, Trisha Hawkins wouldn't have even caught Marlowe's attention. Which, being honest, was probably the plan here. The last thing she wanted to do was gain the attention of anyone taking photos.

Marlowe knew she was in New York, and had expected to see her at some point, but he hadn't expected to walk into her path within hours of arrival. This did, however, cause a slight problem.

Trisha Hawkins knew Tom Marlowe. She'd been involved, in some way, in the breakout of Karl Schnitter, and she'd researched Section D in detail during the planning of the operation. She would know instantly the nervous man in the tuxedo wasn't Dexter Garner, US Marshal, but was instead an unemployed, disavowed MI5 agent. And, if he did anything about this, she could easily blow his cover there and then.

'Hawkins is here.'

'What? Where?' Trix's voice now, concerned. 'I've not connected to the CCTV yet. Have you—'

'On it now,' remembering what he had planned to do before seeing the woman, Marlowe quickly turned from Hawkins, walking over to the white-marbled wall and a low-down power socket. Pulling out a small device, no larger than a plug, he slotted it into the two pin outlet and rose. 'Found you a spot.'

The adaptor would use the power socket to enter the library's system, apparently, and Trix was convinced this would give her a back door into the network. The library wasn't expecting any kind of major cyber-attack in the immediate future either, so it was likely she'd be in and out with no one noticing. And the fake USB outlet on the back meant that if found, it'd be discarded as a phone charger, forgotten in the event's franticness, and tossed into a bin before anyone was the wiser.

'I'm going to talk to her.'

'Is that code for kill her?'

'Going comms silent.'

Marlowe hadn't answered the question with an actual answer because he didn't have one. Hawkins and her people had destroyed his life, leaving him for dead, bleeding his lifeblood out on a side road in the middle of nowhere, and he wanted more than anything to return the favour.

But he wasn't here for her.

Still, that didn't mean he couldn't have a little fun. And, with the glass in his hand, he walked over to her, currently standing beside the left-hand-side bar, watching the other partygoers, seemingly as alone as he was this night.

'Drink, Miss Hawkins?' he said, the sound of her name

pulling her attention from the crowd, her eyes widening in horror as she realised who was beside her.

'My guards are near,' she whispered, and Marlowe almost believed she made the sign of the cross against him. 'If you're here to kill me ...'

'Don't worry, I'm not here for you,' Marlowe smiled now, pulling out his fake ID. 'Dexter Garner, US Marshals.'

Trisha Hawkins' eyes narrowed at this.

'I'm supposed to believe this is a coincidence?' she muttered, just loud enough for Marlowe to hear. 'I didn't place the hit on you. I know all about it, but I wouldn't use US killers.'

'I know,' Marlowe smiled wider, knowing this was more unnerving than reassuring for her right now. 'I already spoke to the broker. The client's known to me. And I'll get with them, eventually.'

'So why are you here?' Trisha frowned, relaxing a minuscule amount, and Marlowe knew this was a pivotal moment. He couldn't say anything about Roxanne in case Trisha exploited it. He also couldn't use anything connected to her, as she'd invariably class this as a threat and, once more, all bets would be off.

'Karl Schnitter,' he said, looking around the room. 'I have a CIA source who said his new identity is based in Manhattan. Working for an environmental agency.'

Trisha's eyes widened at this, and Marlowe could almost see the cogs whirling around inside her head. There was no way she could know who or where Karl was now, unless he'd reached out, and knowing he'd been the one to try to kill Francine Pearce, Trisha wouldn't be looking to make friends with him soon. That said, he *had* tried to kill Francine Pearce, and, looking at Marlowe, Trisha could now realise an option to find and remove Karl for this.

The enemy of my enemy is still my enemy, but for a brief moment, they could be usable and all that.

'He killed Francine,' she said, continuing the line that Pearce had died the previous summer. 'If there's anything I can do to help ...'

'If you see him here tonight, I'd appreciate a heads up,' Marlowe nodded, passing her a white card – no name, just a phone number, typed in bold letters. He didn't know whose number it was, to be honest, as he'd picked it up as he entered, bumping up against a security guard while in the queue. It was a force of habit and probably a high-end escort service. Marlowe killed the idea of Trisha trying to work out the "cypher", as some high-end call girl gave her the prices in code.

Trisha, to her credit, didn't bat an eyelid and, pocketing the card, simply nodded, walking off into the hall without another word, effectively ignoring Marlowe once more. That was fine by him, and Marlowe hoped that, this small piece of misdirection started, Trisha Hawkins would now see Karl Schnitter behind every pillar.

He looked around, wondering whether Francine Pearce, in whatever new identity she'd cooked up since her "death" was also there, but his attention was distracted by the other bar, across the hall, where Roxanne was now talking to a newer, younger man, and it was, from the postures, a far more confrontational situation.

'What does Vasquez drink?' he asked, turning his earbud back on by tapping it.

'Is Hawkins dead?'

'No, I decided she was more useful alive, so I gave her

someone else to worry about,' Marlowe replied, his eyes still on the two people across the hall. 'She's now jumping at shadows. Cocktail. Now!'

'She used to be partial to Porn Star Martinis,' Brad's voice cut in. 'I remember Danny complaining about this once when she was in law school.'

Marlowe turned to the barman, pulling out a twenty-dollar bill and holding it up.

'Porn Star Martini, and this is for you if I get served first.'

The old couple being served glared daggers at him as the barman, sensing a quick tip, placed their wine glasses down and quickly made the cocktail. Marlowe shrugged apologetically at them. In the grand scheme of things, having to wait a minute or two more for your swanky party drink wasn't that high on his concern factor.

'Are you about to make contact?' Brad sounded concerned.

'I'm about to remove an irritation,' Marlowe smiled darkly. 'Quick question. Her file said she was single. That still right?'

'You're not about to—'

'Brad, she's having a heated conversation with a strange man,' Marlowe accepted the Martini, passing the twenty-dollar bill as payment, and started across the floor. 'If I'm about to walk into a relationship issue, I need to know.'

'Social media says single, no photos with any male or female I'd call "relationship close", if that helps,' Trix replied. Taking this as a tacit agreement, Marlowe walked up to the two people.

The man was young, in his thirties, and bore all the semblances of money. He was in expensive clothing, his watch was five figures, his hair was messy but expensively so, and his stubble, almost a beard, was expertly curated. Roxanne, however, didn't seem to be bothered by any of this, instead choosing to glower at him, her body language showing a woman one step away from murder.

'Ah, there you are, darling,' Marlowe slurred, sliding into the space between the man and Roxanne, his back now to the corner as he offered the drink. 'Porn Star Martini, just as you like it.'

Before Roxanne could say anything, though, Marlowe turned to the man, as if surprised he was still there.

'Oh, hello,' he said. 'I'm Dexter. And you are?'

'Leaving,' the man grumbled, walking off, back into the party. After this finished, Marlowe looked back at Roxanne.

'I had that,' she growled irritably. 'I don't need a white knight to save me. And how did you even know what I drank ...'

She tailed off, looking down at the glass.

'Ah, goddamn, you're one of them,' she muttered. 'Babysitters. Did he send you?'

'By "he," you mean—'

'Your CIA buddy!' Roxanne almost exploded. 'Treating me like a goddamned porcelain doll!'

'All I know is someone asked me to keep an eye out for you,' Marlowe, realising this wasn't going the way he expected, tried to return the subject to her ongoing safety. 'Keep you alive until Monday. I'm Dexter Garner, a US Marshal—'

He stopped as she held up a hand while he was halfway to revealing his ID.

'Please, that'll be as fake as the one the other guy showed me,' Roxanne muttered. 'Turned out he was a SEAL friend of

Pop's, before he died, although I'd never heard of him. Just as paranoid as the others.'

'When did you speak to him?'

'About half an hour back,' Roxanne sighed. 'I'd seen him following me a few times. Realised he was either a well-connected stalker, or security. Which one are you?'

'Was that the last time you saw him?' There was a gnawing, nagging feeling that tugged at Marlowe as he spoke. 'Half an hour ago?'

'I saw him heading to the washrooms maybe five minutes later,' Roxanne wasn't stupid – she could tell something about this bothered Marlowe. 'Why?'

'Hold that thought,' Marlowe said, looking away as he tapped his earpiece. 'Brad, can you get through to your guy?'

'Already been trying, he's not answering,' Brad's voice replied in his ear.

Marlowe looked around the party, checking the faces.

'Who was the man I interrupted?' he asked, still scanning the room.

'One of the Donziger flunkies, sent by his son to sort a settlement,' Roxanne tried to follow his gaze. 'What are you looking for?'

'Things that shouldn't be there,' Marlowe looked back at her. 'Look, I'm aware we just met and you have no reason to trust me. I'm not Dexter whatever his name is, I'm Tom Marlowe. I'm British, and ex-MI5. And trust me when I say something's wrong here.'

Roxanne didn't reply to this, as the seriousness of the situation now caught up with her.

'Stay here, in public, and don't move,' Marlowe ordered. 'I need to find your other babysitter.'

With this he strode quickly across the hall, ignoring

Trisha Hawkins as she watched from the balcony, heading through the doors at the back, and walking down the corridor to the left, heading to the men's washroom.

'Brad, what's your SEAL's name?'

'Trevor Sinclair, why?'

'Call him.'

'Already done that—'

'I need to hear a phone ring, Brad, in case it's been dropped.'

'Gotcha.'

Marlowe walked into the washroom, noting the four cubicles at the end. Walking up to them, he saw three were open, the last one, beside the wall, closed. And, as he lightly rested his hand against the door and pushed, it was locked as well.

'Trevor?' he asked softly, but received no answer.

Instead, a faint buzzing, like the vibration of a phone, came through the door.

Marlowe didn't have time for niceties; the washroom was currently empty and so, with a hefty kick, he slammed the heel of his shoe against the cubicle door, smashing the lock apart as the door swung inwards at speed – to reveal a muscular, middle-aged and rather dead black man.

'Stop calling,' Marlowe muttered.

A second later, the vibration stopped.

There were no signs of a fight on Trevor Sinclair's hands or face, but a blossom of blood on the shirt around the chest area showed what had happened. Without even checking the body, Marlowe started back towards the door and the party.

'Trevor's dead,' he breathed. 'Silencer on a pistol, I'd say. Someone's taking out the security. They're making a pass at Roxanne.'

'When?' Trix's voice was nervous, the sound of keyboard keys being tapped at speed in the background.

Exiting the washrooms, Marlowe spied the three burly men now walking with purpose across the floor of Astor Hall, heading towards the now alone and unsuspecting Roxanne Vasquez.

'Right now,' he said as he broke into a sprint.

7

BALLROOM BLITZ

ROXANNE VASQUEZ DIDN'T NOTICE THE THREE MEN approaching through the crowded party. What she did notice, however, was Tom Marlowe as he slammed into the side of the lead man, sending him stumbling to the floor.

'Sorry, my fault,' Marlowe said, turning to face the other two. 'I'm all over the place right now. Hey, is that The Rock? I'm a massive fan—'

As the left of the two men followed his finger, Marlowe brought his foot up quickly, catching the one on the right hard between the legs, sending him crumpling, clutching at his personal and now painful parts. The final attacker standing, realising he'd been played, turned to find Marlowe jabbing, his hand straight, fingers pointed, straight into his throat with enough force to send him also staggering back, gasping, as Marlowe spun to face Roxanne.

'We run, now,' he said sharply, grabbing her by the arm and pulling her away from the three men, now gaining a rather unhealthy amount of attention from the surrounding guests.

'What the hell were you thinking?' Roxanne replied, half following, but half pulling from him as they headed up the stairs, away from the dance floor. 'I can't leave now! I'm giving the keynote speech in half an hour!'

'If you don't leave now, you won't be alive in half an hour.'

'So you say.'

'Trevor Sinclair, the SEAL guy you had a go at earlier? They killed him,' Marlowe replied matter-of-factly, pulling Roxanne through the white-marble archway and into the library itself. 'He's in the bathroom if you want to see. They probably thought he was the only one, and with him dead, you were open season.'

'Or you pissed them off when you interrupted them,' Roxanne argued.

Marlowe turned right into a side corridor, dragging her behind him.

'That flunky was probably giving you a last chance to make things right,' he said. 'Once you said no, he realised the only available offer was to remove you.'

'Kill me?'

'Well, probably not here,' Marlowe admitted. 'They'd probably drug you, take you out back and dump you in a van.'

'And then what?'

Marlowe paused, partly to check behind them, but also to face Roxanne.

'You really don't want to know,' he said. 'Come on, we can leave through the Forty-Second Street entrance.'

There was another staircase in front of them, heading both upwards and down.

'If we're going back down, why go up?' Roxanne snapped.

'Because the party wall blocks the entrance to *these* stairs,'

Marlowe explained as they turned to face the steps, pausing for a second as he wondered whether anyone had come this way to cut them off. 'And also, if they don't see us doubling back, they'll think we've gone upwards.'

There was a *spang,* however, as a bullet fired from down the corridor hit the marble behind them, and Marlowe saw the lead assassin, the man he'd called *Stumbled*, raising his suppressed pistol, likely the one that killed Trevor Sinclair, for another shot.

'Run!' he snapped at Roxanne, drawing his Glock out and firing back, sending Stumbler back into cover, but another unsuppressed gunshot from down the stairs forced him to pull Roxanne back.

'Run upstairs!' he suggested instead, firing down the stairs at who he thought was *Neck Chop*, and wondering if they could even make the gunshots out in the party's noise.

Now on the third floor, Marlowe pulled Roxanne down the corridor until it turned right, the ceilings once more high and white-arched, pausing her as he did so, now standing beside a wooden double-door with signage hanging above it, claiming it was the "Berg Collection."

'Keep going,' he waved down the hall. 'Turn right when you hit the rotunda and head into the reading room. Find a place to hide, and I'll be back when I've sorted these three out.'

'You're insane—' Roxanne started, but yelped and ran as another gunshot echoed around the corridor. Marlowe fired again and followed her into the McGraw Rotunda, an ornate rectangular space beneath arched bays, above seventeen-feet-high paired Corinthian walnut pilasters. It felt more like a church than a library, with a ceiling vault painting of Prometheus bringing mankind fire and knowledge stolen from the Gods shining down on him, while the wooden and painted-plaster walls had various paintings of people ranging from Moses holding the Ten Commandments, to scribes writing illuminated manuscripts, all the way to the creation of the Gutenberg Bible and the Linotype machine. In the middle was a glass display case, beside the door he'd sent Roxanne through, leading into the Bill Glass Public Catalogue Room was a desk and chair, and finally, white pillar lamps were either side of the doors on the left and right of the Rotunda.

Marlowe knew he needed to get close to whomever was following, and so he slid against the wall to his right, waiting for the first attacker to emerge. If he carried on around the wall, he would have hit stairs heading down to the lower level and the narrow gallery above the party, and he wondered for a moment whether he'd have attackers arriving from *both* levels.

However, before he could consider moving places, he heard running feet and the first of the attackers, the man he called *Stumbled,* came running into view, turning to face Marlowe, his eyes widening as Marlowe, Glock aimed close range at Stumbled's chest, fired and dropped his attacker, sending him, well, stumbling to the ground. However, although the gun was placed against the chest – the muffled shot was loud enough to confirm a gunshot had been fired – the man groaned and clambered back to his feet, as Marlowe saw, through the now shredded shirt, that he was wearing a thin Kevlar weave vest; not enough to properly remove the kinetic energy, but enough protection to halt a bullet.

Basically, he knew *Stumbled* would have broken ribs, but he wasn't down for the count.

As *Stumbled* rose, he reached for his fallen gun, but

Marlowe moved forward quickly, stepping in and grabbing *Stumbled* by his torn shirt and physically slamming him, head first, into the glass top of the exhibit case with a sickening *crunch*. The shattering sound echoed around the rotunda, and this, added to the chest wound, was enough to send the injured assassin to the floor.

Marlowe knew the sound would have alerted anyone else approaching, and so he pulled the body closer, checking for a pulse – there wasn't one anymore, probably because of the narrow length of shattered glass now jutting out of his bleeding right eyeball – before quickly checking through the pockets.

Stumbled was ID-less, but made up for it in weapons. In addition to his suppressed pistol, he carried two full spare magazines, a vicious-looking blade and a capped syringe of something, most likely to use on Roxanne.

'How did these guys get in with these?' he spoke aloud into his earpiece, as he carefully pocketed the items.

'Same as you?' it was Brad that replied. 'Used an ID?'

'Nothing on him,' Marlowe complained. 'I had to go through security, they would have had to do the same. So somewhere they were given these, like I was in the airport.'

'You got those because the agents thought you were CIA,' Brad muttered.

'Maybe these guys were believed to be something, too?' Marlowe went to continue, but stopped as he heard movement at the end of the corridor. Taking a photo of the dead man, he now slid into the doorway of the Public Catalogue Room.

'Nothing more than high-end Kevlar. He'd have ID of some kind if he was a normal person. No phone, either.'

'Maybe they're point and clicks?' Trix spoke now through

the bud. 'Told where to go, do it, come back?'

Marlowe cursed – he hadn't checked the ears for any kind of earbud device. However, someone was coming up the stairs, and in the background, he could hear the sounds of shouting.

'Have they heard the gunshots yet?' he asked. 'There's been enough of the bloody things.'

'No, believe it or not,' Trix was almost laughing. 'They thought they were fireworks outside. People even went to look. They've just found the body in the bathroom though, so the gala's about to go south real soon. You need to get out now.'

Marlowe peered around the door again, but whereas he was sure someone had been coming up the stairs, now there was nobody.

Apparently, they decided to get out before they were found, he thought to himself before looking through the door into the reading room.

'Roxanne! We're getting out of here!'

Roxanne must have been waiting, as she came out of the room quickly, stopping, holding her hand to her mouth as she saw the body, frowning as Marlowe ran back past her, heading into the Public Catalogue Room, and the Rose Reading Room the other side.

'Where the hell are you going now?' she muttered. 'This is a dead end! I looked for a door!'

'They'll be watching the entrance,' he said, pulling her through into the room and turning right, heading towards a wooded partition that reminded him of old-style bank-teller windows, with a door on the right-hand side. 'We're taking the side exit out by Forty-Second Street.'

'There isn't an entrance there,' Roxanne shook her head

in exasperation. 'It's the floor below us that goes out onto the street.'

'We're not aiming for the street,' Marlowe replied, carrying on past the enclosure where the librarians would have worked during the day, passing through the door and stopping beside a narrow door elevator. 'We're heading for the stacks.'

By now, the lights were red, and there was a siren blaring.

So much for keeping things quiet.

The door to the elevator opened, and Marlowe pushed Roxanne in, hammering the bottom button as he did so.

'What the hell is a stack?' Roxanne asked. 'And why are we heading to the basement?'

'When you fill out a form for a book here, and it's not on the shelf, it's transferred to the stacks,' Marlowe said as he waited for the elevator to hit the bottom, still ready for anything. 'They find it, stick it in a little red trolley and it comes upstairs again.'

'You know a lot about this,' Roxanne shook her head as the doors opened to reveal a battered-looking basement area, metal poles supporting the ceiling.

'I like to read,' Marlowe smiled as he pulled her to the left, following a white-walled and low-ceilinged corridor filled with pipes, vents and, along the top of the walls, a line of trolleys on tracks. 'I also like to know all the exits if a kill team tries to end me. See? Little red trolleys.'

Marlowe smiled, pointing at them as he pulled Roxanne through a series of doorways, eventually finding themselves in a corridor of white book-stacks.

'And here are the stacks,' he said, looking around as he tried to gain his bearings. 'That's the north wall, behind those.'

Little black controllers controlled the stacks on each one, with green arrows for left and right on either side of a red "stop" button. He ran along these, counting as he did so.

'Stacks can be really close together when they're not being used, and therefore save space, better than normal shelving,' he explained as he stopped at the sixth one, nodding. Then, pressing the button, he watched as the door slid open, peering down at the end.

'Shit, it *was* seven,' he said, doing the same with the one to the left, revealing a new narrow corridor.

Looking down it, Roxanne could see that unlike the other stack corridor, which ended at a white wall, this one had a grey fire-door at the end. Marlowe waved for her to follow as he walked along the line of books on either side before stopping at the end, tapping the door as it made a metallic *clang*.

'It's a fire exit that goes nowhere,' he said, crouching as he examined the lock built into the handle. 'But once it opens, it leads to a service tunnel that takes you to the subway station next door. It's still accessible as long as the right stacks are open, but it's not been used in years.'

Roxanne nodded, understanding now.

'You're talking about the Forty-Second Street, Bryant Park and Fifth Avenue Station,' she replied. 'Runs underneath the library.'

'Exactly,' Marlowe stood back up, opening the door. 'And right now? We're underneath the library, too. When they built the Flushing Line in 1926, they had to deepen the library's foundations. And, while they did this, they created a connecting tunnel from here to the main platform, one that wasn't used until they started talking about using the station as a bomb shelter during the Cold War. After that, they closed it up.'

'How do you know all this?' Roxanne shook her head, incredulous.

'I have an interest in secret passageways,' Marlowe grinned as he turned back to the doorway now they were through. 'Remind me to tell you about the time I escaped an execution by a knowledge of tunnels in Westminster.'

The door behind them closed, Marlowe turned his phone's torch on as they continued down the passage.

'We can get a train out of here and work out the next steps,' he said, gingerly moving over a small pile of something that could be dead, or more likely discarded. About fifteen feet further on was another door, and he started working on the lock once more.

'My shoes are ruined,' Roxanne muttered. 'Still, better them than my life, I suppose.'

Marlowe swung the door open and ushered Roxanne out into the subway corridor.

'We turn right, go down the stairs—' he started, but stopped, yanking Roxanne hard to the side as rounds slammed in to the wall beside them, the gunshots echoing back to the main entrance as commuters and tourists alike ran in all directions, screaming.

'There's no way they knew about this!' Marlowe cried out in annoyance as, ducking back into the doorway, Roxanne behind him, leant out and snapped off a triple tap, two rounds to centre of mass, one to the head, dropping the first of the attackers instantly. As a flurry of new gunshots echoed and bullets ricocheted around the corridor, Marlowe dropped the clip out of the gun, slipping a new one in and locking it into place. Then, with three well-placed shots, he fired up the walkway, before pulling a spare magazine from a pocket with his off hand and punching the magazine release on the Glock, dropping the spent mag and quickly loading a fresh one—

Only to have the gun knocked out of his hand by someone to the right of the door, someone he hadn't seen. Glancing right, he saw *Neck Chop* swing what looked to be a viciously sharp machete at him. He stepped back, avoiding the swing and grabbed the arm, spinning *Neck Chop* around so that he was now on Marlowe's left as he pulled off his tuxedo, twirling it around, turning it into a thick rope. Now, he hoped the gunman up the walkway, possibly the third of the attackers in the library and now called *Crotch Kick*, would think twice before shooting, in case he hit his fellow killer. Or, he wouldn't care and the body count would go even higher, but Marlowe didn't really want to think about that as, with the jacket now coiled tight and held between his arms, he used it to wrap around *Neck Chop's* arm as he slashed at him, taking the trapped arm and wrenching it hard against the door frame, hearing the audible crack as the forearm connected hard against the metal, the blade falling from *Neck Chop's* hand as, with his other arm he reached for something else, possibly his gun.

But he didn't have time to use whatever it was, as Marlowe reached down and grabbed the machete, letting go of the jacket with one hand to do this, rising as he stabbed upwards, slicing into *Neck Chop's* gut and pulling upwards, the jacket now used as a shield as the blood spurted out. Before anyone could see, Marlowe pulled *Neck Chop* into the corridor, pulling off the now dead attacker's jacket as he did so, pulling it onto Roxanne's shoulders as he used his own jacket to wipe the handle of the blade, tossing it to the floor as he folded the bloodied jacket up, inside out, to hide the stains.

'What the hell are you doing?' Roxanne asked, as this time Marlowe checked the ear, finding a similar earbud to the one he also wore.

'My jacket is covered in blood, and my prints are on the blade,' Marlowe fired his gun once more up the walkway, taking a second, quick photo, this time of *Neck Chop's* face as he pushed the bloodied jacket under his arm and dragged Roxanne after him, running down the passage towards the platform. 'They'll have CCTV footage, but that's of US Marshal Dexter Garner. If my real prints turn up on, say, a major murder site? I'll get interest I really don't want.'

'And the other jacket?'

'It's the start of February and it's bloody freezing,' Marlowe replied. 'Or if you want, I could wear it and you could freeze?'

'I thought you knew secret tunnels?' Deciding not to argue about the warm gift, Roxanne was glancing behind them as they ran onto the platform; a train was there, the doors about to close. Quickly, Marlowe pulled her into it. 'They didn't seem to be *that* secret.'

'There's no way they knew we were down there,' Marlowe mused, watching the platform entrance. Either the gunman had found the body and was delayed, or had given up the chase. 'The only way—'

He stopped, paling, tapping his ear as he walked to the still open carriage doors.

'You there?' he asked.

'Just about, the signal's shit,' Trix replied.

'We've got eavesdroppers,' Marlowe whispered, watching the entrance still. 'They've known where we're going every step of the way. I'm going dark.'

'Roger,' Trix replied, not even bothering to ask for more

information. This was a place they'd both been in before. 'How do we get to you?'

'Budapest protocol,' Marlowe said, pulling the earpiece out and tossing it into the gap between the train and the platform – only a couple of seconds before the train doors closed – and walking back to Roxanne, standing beside one of the orange plastic seats of the carriage.

'Where now?' she asked.

'They'll know we're on this train so we'll get off at the next station, do a little back and forth to truly lose our tails,' Marlowe replied, already pulling items out of his bundled tuxedo and placing them into his trouser pockets. 'We'll find a place to lie low for tonight and then we'll work a plan out in the morning.'

'Budapest.'

Marlowe nodded.

'I'm sorry,' he said. 'I was only supposed to babysit you, not overturn your life.'

'The alternative was death,' Roxanne forced a smile. 'I can live with overturning.'

Marlowe nodded, forcing his own smile back. But inside, he was far from smiling. That'd been too close for comfort, at an event Trisha Hawkins had been at. The three attackers had got weapons through security and were connected to the same feed he was, hearing everything he'd said.

This wasn't a corporation trying to remove a thorn. This was a *war*.

And Thomas Marlowe had just been *conscripted*.

8

HONEYMOON SWEET

MARLOWE HAD TAKEN ROXANNE ON A TOUR OF NEW YORK over the following hour, skipping trains, doubling back on themselves and even leaving one station to walk a block to a separate line. During this time, he'd also sent the photos of the two assassins to Trix before breaking up and discarding the phone, and then walked into a tourist shop and bought two hoodies and a velour bomber jacket, all emblazoned with "NYC" on them, getting Roxanne to wear one under her tuxedo jacket while he threw the other on under the bomber jacket. It wasn't great for warmth, but it was better than just a shirt, and the blood on the front, minimal as it was, had still been enough to raise some eyebrows.

Only after he'd doubled back enough, making sure nobody could follow him, did he hail a yellow cab, paying in cash to be taken to the New Yorker Hotel.

He was glad that New York wasn't as bad as London was yet for security cameras, but at the same time he knew there were enough around, and he needed to make sure they didn't pick him up in too many spots. So, a block from the hotel, he leant forwards, paid the driver and stepped out outside Penn Plaza.

'What are we doing here?' Roxanne, already hurting thanks to the shoes she was wearing – evening shoes that were not created for pavement running – grumbled.

'We'll lie low here tonight,' Marlowe said as he crossed the road, heading towards the entrance, Roxanne behind him. 'Just keep your arm linked in mine, and laugh at anything I say. We're tourists returning from a party, okay?'

'I don't see how you're going to steal a room key from here,' Roxanne muttered. 'I could have used my points card if it helped. But that's still in a cloakroom at the New York Public Library.'

'And we'll pick it up later.'

'My phone's with it,' Roxanne grumbled some more as, beside Marlowe, she walked up to the elevators, surprised as Marlowe pulled out a plastic room card and tapped it against the elevator button. As the doors opened, Marlowe ushered her into the carriage quickly before anyone paid too much attention to them.

Roxanne went to speak, but Marlowe shook his head, nodding imperceptibly at the camera in the car's corner. When the seventh floor opened up, Marlowe led Roxanne into the hallway, down a corridor and into a room on the right, which opened the moment he tapped the card against the lock.

It was a suite; a large room with a sofa and TV led into a double bedroom to the left of it, a selection of gold and burgundy furniture scattered around. In front of the window was a writing desk, and a door led through to a modest bathroom.

'Whose is this?' Roxanne breathed, as Marlowe threw the

card to the floor, walking over to the wardrobe and pulling out a towelling robe, throwing it to her.

'Here, you must be freezing,' he said. 'We'll sort out new clothing in a bit.'

'Dammit, could you just answer *one goddamned question?*'

Marlowe stopped and nodded.

'I thought I might need a safe house,' he said. 'Better safe than sorry. And I never rely on what's been given to me on an op, especially when the CIA's involved. So, while we prepared for tonight, I also came here. Using a fake ID and card, ones that the CIA doesn't know about, I hasten to add, I booked a suite.'

'Why a suite?'

'Because you get the bed, and I get the sofa,' Marlowe replied, as if it was the most logical answer possible. 'They'll look for places the average spy goes to ground. Pay by the hour sleaze bag hotels and flophouses. They won't consider looking a few blocks down the street, in an expensive, five-star room.'

As he spoke, he'd removed the tuxedo jacket, hanging it onto the back of a chair.

'I didn't expect to need new clothes though, so that's on me.'

'My coat would have been nice, but I'll settle for being alive.'

'You've had a tough night, and you need a break,' Marlowe said, appreciating the pragmatism. 'I need to get some supplies and arm up, so I need to check the business suite downstairs for a message. While I'm gone, feel free to drink the minibar dry, and eat whatever you want from room service. The CIA's going to be paying for it anyway, whether or not they know yet.'

'Why the business suite?' Roxanne asked, before answering her own question. 'Budapest Protocol.'

'I'll explain in a bit,' Marlowe was already at the door, the key back in his hand. 'Don't call anyone, okay? We're off the grid, just doing it in style.'

'And how long am I supposed to be in here?' Roxanne snapped back – but Marlowe had already left the room.

THE BUSINESS SUITE OF THE NEW YORKER HOTEL WAS A SMALL, understated room, with three mahogany desks in a basic, modern style placed against three of the four white walls of the room, with one also holding a printer. On each desk was a monitor, keyboard and mouse, the desktop PC likely under the desk and near the power socket. Marlowe took a moment to sit down, open a browser, and search for an old Reddit group. It was created for fans of a UK-based, science-fiction comedy called *Red Dwarf*, and hadn't really been used for several years, apart from the occasional thread or spam message, removed when the moderators of the group saw them.

This was why Marlowe needed to move fast, as he needed to see a message before it was removed. And there, on the screen, was a new post.

L1sterRawx: 20:53pm

Marlowe didn't need to read the message below. Instead, he simply sent the whole page to the printer, closing the browser once it had finished printing, standing up, taking the printout and heading back to the room without another

word. Everything he needed was on the printout – he just
hoped it was good news.

Roxanne was drinking a minibar vodka as he returned.

'Anything happen?' he asked as he locked the door
behind him.

Roxanne shook her head.

'No, it was quite uneventful,' she said as Marlowe walked
to the writing desk, sitting down and pulling the pad and pen
closer, using the edge of the menu as a straight rule, as he
drew horizontal lines on it. 'Although I called my sister. She'll
be worried, and I always call her. It's okay though, I didn't say
what name we were under, just the room number in case she
needs to call—'

She stopped as Marlowe turned to face her, his face ashen
in horror.

'You did what?' he asked incredulously, but the look
turned more into irritation as he watched Roxanne laugh.

'Of course, I didn't call anyone,' she said. 'I've seen the
movies.'

She walked over, looking at what Marlowe was drawing.

'I didn't realise it was art class,' she said, picking up the
printout. 'What the hell is this? Some kind of soliloquy about
a cat in space? And Christ, the grammar is terrible, half the
words are misspelled, and I'm not talking about the English-
American discrepancies.'

'It's my message,' Marlowe finished drawing rough lines,
finishing with a sixteen by sixteen grid. 'I just need to work
out what it says.'

As Roxanne went to answer this with another sarcastic
comment, Marlowe wrote the message, letter by letter, into
each of the two hundred and fifty-six spaces. The message
only reached a hundred and ninety-seven of these, and so he

continued from the beginning again until all the spaces were filled. Then, underneath, he wrote out the alphabet, writing the corresponding number under each.

'A cypher,' Roxanne smiled. 'This is the Budapest Protocol, right?'

'It's not a protocol,' Marlowe leant back in the chair, looking at the scramble of random letters in front of him. 'I said that to throw them off the scent. All I needed was to say "Budapest", as that's the cypher.'

He tapped the letters.

'So "B" is the second letter. "U" is the twenty-first. "D" is four, and so on. I take each corresponding letter, write them out, that's the message. When I hit the end, I start again until I have what I need.'

'How the hell did she do this so fast?' Roxanne was already counting letters, writing the answers as she spoke.

'She has an app,' Marlowe explained. 'You type in the message, then add the cypher, and it creates the message for you. I'd usually just place it into an app on my phone, but—'

'But you dumped it into a bin near Times Square,' Roxanne nodded. 'Clever. Looks like one of those spam messages bots send. Which, in a way, it is.'

Roxanne was moving quickly, and Marlowe read what she had found so far.

'They've sorted me a bag,' he said. 'I need to go get it.'

Roxanne carried on pulling up letters, writing them into a recognisable phrase.

'What the hell is LuggageBuddy?' she asked. 'Should there be a space? Did I miss a letter?'

'Since the Twin Towers fell, luggage lockers in stations became the stuff of movies,' Marlowe explained, tapping the message. 'But there are left luggage shops near all stations.

That's the name, address and locker number for one a colleague of mine has organised.'

'But there's no code number,' Roxanne was examining the message. 'The message stops.'

'I don't need it,' Marlowe grinned. 'She always leaves me the same three-digit code. Double-oh-seven.'

'James Bond. Figures,' Roxanne threw off the robe. 'So, when do we go?'

'*We* don't go anywhere,' Marlowe shook his head as he moved away from the table. 'You're a target. I'm a US Marshal and unknown element.'

'Can you at least get my phone and my handbag from the library?' Roxanne pouted. 'My laptop is in it. And people trying to kill me or not, I still have a ton of work to sort before court on Monday ...'

She trailed off, her eyes widening.

'You're not going to allow me to go into work tomorrow, are you?' she breathed. 'Oh, no, we're not having that. I need to be in meetings.'

'We'll discuss that when I get back,' Marlowe was already walking to the door, checking his gun was loaded before sliding it into the back of his trousers. 'I'll be an hour, tops. Get me some chips from room service.'

'I'm gonna spend a shit-ton on room service!' Roxanne cried out angrily as he closed the door behind him. 'A shit-ton!'

IT WAS JUST PAST TEN AT NIGHT WHEN MARLOWE ARRIVED AT the LuggageBuddy office to the south of Penn Street Station. He could have been there quicker, but he wanted to make sure he wasn't followed, and even though he didn't think he was, it was better to be safe than sorry. Walking into the store, he turned and walked over to a bank of luggage lockers at the side, finding the relevant locker, a small sticker with a drawing, in red pen, of one of Disney's Seven Dwarves stuck on it, a literal "Red Dwarf" as a clue, and typing the three-digit code into it. The door opened with a soft chunk and swung open, revealing Marlowe's own holdall, the one he'd brought from London.

I hope you kept everything in it, he thought to himself as he walked out of the store saying nothing.

The city was changing as he walked back to the hotel; the evening commuters and the theatre visitors were gone, the shows were yet to finish, and the partying nightclubbers were yet to appear. It was a transitional time, and it felt uncomfortable, as if this was the moment people would let their guard down, and the dark side of Manhattan would rear its head.

There was an Irish bar on the right, the neon sign stating it was called *Dun Dealgan*. Marlowe checked his watch, working out if he had time to break here, or whether he continued on. He'd promised he'd be an hour, and so far it'd been just under forty minutes, so he slipped through the door, walking over to the bar.

'Guinness,' he said, dropping a ten-dollar bill on it. 'Where's the toilets?'

The barman, a young lad with short blond hair, nodded towards a door marked "FIR", which was Gaelic for "Men". The bar was a tourist haunt, and Marlowe knew the washrooms would be clean and safe. If it was a real Irish bar, like the ones in Boston, or Staten Island, he might have thought twice, or at least held onto his gun as he entered, but he needn't have worried.

Entering a cubicle and closing it behind him, he placed the lid of the toilet bowl down and sat on it, holdall on his lap. Unzipping it, he was relieved to see his spare clothing was there, as well as a medium-sized first aid kit, and the Ziplock bag of dollars he'd brought across from the UK, taken from the now dearly departed Grayson Long. In the bag was also a new phone, a single number within the contacts app. Marlowe almost called it, but at the same time, he didn't know where the leak came from right now. He didn't want to consider it, but there was every chance Brad had brought him over purely to be the fall guy as they took Roxanne Vasquez out.

There was another, smaller medical kit in the bag; something he hadn't seen before. Marlowe had furrowed his brow at this, confused why Trix would throw such a thing into the bag when there was one already in the bag, but a note inside explained everything.

This should reveal what's in the syringe

In the kit was a selection of liquids and litmus paper strips; Marlowe had assumed the syringe he'd taken from the assassin was poison, but this way he could check for sure. Zipping it back up, he searched the bottom of his bag, pulling away at a home-made Velcro base, revealing two passport blanks, some bullion coins and a selection of credit cards.

If things go south, get out as quickly as you can.

Taking a coin and sliding it into his pocket, Marlowe rose from the toilet, flushing it and walking back out into the washroom. Exiting the room and walking to the bar, he found the barman placing his pint of Guinness on the counter.

'Where's a good place to find clothing this time of night?' he asked. 'Airport lost our bags. Need to find some nightwear for my wife.'

'Shop on the corner closes at twelve,' the barman nodded with his head towards the wall, his barman X-ray vision seeing through it. 'They'll do what you need. Londoner?'

Marlowe considered his answer; the barman had the slightest of Irish twangs, but it sounded a little too Disneyfied – as if he was told being Irish helped with the tips. But under it there was the slightest hint of a Birmingham accent. Marlowe played a hunch.

'Londoner? Piss off. I'm Brummie, if anything,' he smiled. 'Accent comes from the army.'

The barman grinned in response.

'I was born and bred in King's Heath, South Birmingham,' he said. 'You need anything, you let me know. I'm Dermot.'

'Garth,' Marlowe shook Dermot's hand, deciding to keep to the Garth Fleming legend, rather than the US Marshal Dexter Garner one, because of the more Irish-sounding first name.

However, he paused as he saw a small tattoo on Dermot's wrist: a slightly faded tribal style image of a bird, above what looked like wavy lines. It was filled with straight edges and angles, and Marlowe recognised it immediately as the *Standing Rock tattoo*, made famous on Instagram a few years earlier. It had been designed by Stephanie Big Eagle, a descendent of the Great Sioux Nation, in solidarity of the ongoing issues with the US Government over the Dakota Access Pipeline, which at the time threatened the water supply for the Standing Rock Sioux. The protest had finished shortly after the National

Guard evicted the last protestors, and the pipeline had been built.

Marlowe hadn't been there, but he'd made one of the FBI agents there into an MI5 asset a couple of years later, and he remembered being told this story by the now-apologetic double agent.

'Were you there?' he asked, nodding at the tattoo.

'No, but my girlfriend was,' Dermot replied. 'She still tries to fight it. But big corporations always win.'

Marlowe quickly reassessed the barman in front of him – suddenly, this was an asset he could use in case of backup plans being needed. He'd had an idea when he left the hotel – there was every chance Donziger wouldn't wait until Monday now, especially after the attempt at the library, so Marlowe had to take the mission as blown. It was still a baby-sitting mission, but at any moment, it could turn bigger and wilder.

'Actually, I do have a couple of things I need to find,' Marlowe leant in now, lowering his voice. 'And I'm not that familiar with the country. I think you might actually be able to assist me with something.'

'I'm not connected to crime—'

'No, no,' Marlowe held up his hands in mock surrender. 'I'm not a criminal, I'm an activist, like you. I just don't have the tattoo. I'm here because of the Donziger case on Monday.'

'Oh aye, that,' Dermot shook his head sadly. 'Poor buggers in Jericho. They won't see a penny.'

'You don't think?'

'They'll settle before Monday, and it'll be pennies on the dollar,' Dermot cleaned a glass as he spoke, pouring himself a whisky. 'Money begets money and all that. Just ask ...'

He held up his hand, showing the wrist tattoo again.

'You disapprove?' Marlowe raised an eyebrow at the response.

'What, seeing the little guy get screwed over by the one percenters?' Dermot downed the shot. 'Of course, I do. But what can we do about it? You might as well get on the first flight back to Birmingham.'

'What if I *could* do something about it?' Marlowe smiled.

'Illegal?'

'Not at all,' Marlowe shook his head. 'I'm looking to protest. Bigger than Standing Rock though, and here in the city. Something more than just Donziger. Something where the people can really raise their voices.'

'Aye, that'd be grand,' Dermot grinned. 'Our voices have been woefully quiet of late.'

'I'd need a couple of things, though, and a willing crowd. If the case doesn't happen, that is.'

'Could cost you.'

Marlowe placed one of the bullion coins on the bar.

'You know anyone who buys gold?' he asked. 'That's about fifteen hundred bucks there. Take it. Whatever I don't use, you can keep.'

Dermot stared at the coin for a long, agonised moment, before palming it away better than any sleight-of-hand magician could.

'You turn out to be illegal, I call the cops,' he muttered carefully.

Marlowe smiled at this.

'Completely understand,' he said. 'But seriously, how would you like to stick it to the man, Dermot? Because I think I have just the thing.'

9

ABDUCTEES

'You said an hour,' Roxanne said as Marlowe walked back into the suite. 'I got you a burger on room service, but it's probably cold now.'

'That's fine,' Marlowe placed his duffle onto the sofa as he sat down facing the lawyer. It was almost eleven now, and the long day, the jet lag and the fading of the earlier adrenaline were all hitting him now.

'You look like shit,' Roxanne said, reaching over to the writing desk, where remnants of the food lay, and passed across a plate of crisps. 'Here, this'll help.'

'What are these?' Marlowe stared at the crisps suspiciously.

'You said you wanted chips,' Roxanne said.

Marlowe groaned.

'I forgot the language barrier,' he said. 'We call these crisps, not chips. And we call chips what you call—'

'Fries,' Roxanne slapped her hand against her head. 'Goddammit. I should have guessed. I wondered why you'd want that for dinner. It's why I got you a burger just in case.'

Her face brightened.

'That came with fries,' she said, now pulling across another plate of food. Taking the bun, Marlowe bit into it. The food wasn't cold, but it was obvious it'd been on the table a little while. But, considering the last thing he ate were canapes, and before that it was airplane food, his stomach growled at the opportunity for anything edible, no matter how lukewarm it was.

'I got you some things,' he said, nodding at a carrier bag with NYC on it. 'Some sneakers, jeans and some T-shirts. Oh, and a jacket.'

'Why?' Roxanne was already rummaging through the bag. 'I only need to stay until tomorrow. I can get a change of clothes from my apartment—'

'Yeah, we're not doing that,' Marlowe replied, his mouth half full as he spoke. 'They'll be watching for you. And if they were ready to shoot up the library during a public event ...'

He stopped as he spoke, remembering and, as he placed the food down, he rose from the sofa and walked over to his discarded tuxedo jacket, carefully removing the syringe.

'Now wait,' Roxanne instinctively backed away, but Marlowe shook his head.

'I'm not going to use it on you,' he said as he walked back to the duffle, pulling out the first aid kit filled with testing strips, placing one on the table. 'I want to find out what it was. If it's fast acting, then they wanted you dead quickly and quietly. If it's slow, like Novichok, then they wanted you to suffer.'

He lightly pressed the end of the syringe, making sure not to splash any of the liquid, allowing only a couple of tiny drops to hit the paper before carefully wrapping the end in a napkin, placing it to the side, watching the paper as it slowly turned blue.

'That's interesting,' he said, pulling up a colour chart and comparing it to the colour he'd just made.

'Interesting how?'

'It's not poison,' Marlowe looked up at her. 'It's *Gamma-Hydroxybutyric Acid*, better known as Liquid Ecstasy, or GHB. A naturally occurring neurotransmitter and depressant drug, synthesised to give the user a feeling of euphoria. But there's a dark side to it.'

'It's a date-rape drug,' Roxanne's expression was emotionless as she replied coldly. 'I've heard of it. We all know about drink spiking around here.'

'This is a little more than drink spiking,' Marlowe looked at the syringe again. 'This amount would definitely have you incapacitated because of the sedative effects, within seconds of it hitting your bloodstream, and in the moments before it hit, you'd be disorientated, unfocused, or worse.'

'So, you said that fast poison was quick death, slow poison was what they wanted me to suffer ...' Roxanne was also looking at the syringe as she spoke. 'What does this mean?'

'It means I was wrong, and they weren't there to kill you,' Marlowe returned his attention to Roxanne. 'They were there to get in and inject you: maybe a jab in the hand, or your bare arm, whatever, maybe even squirt it into your glass. You'd ingest it, be affected by it, and they'd have no trouble taking you out of the event, and to wherever they wanted you to go.'

'So, they didn't want to kill me?'

Marlowe pursed his lips as he tried to decide which answer to give.

'Honestly, I don't know,' he eventually explained. 'But to

me, and the knowledge I have, I'd have to say this looked like them taking you somewhere else to kill you. Possibly even gaining information first. What do you have on Donziger?'

Roxanne looked away for a moment, and Marlowe thought she was avoiding the question, but her expression when she turned back to him was one of fear. She'd been gathering her strength of will, probably just to not scream.

'I have witness statements on the crimes they've performed in the purification plant at Jericho Falls, and I have footage of some of the cleaning operations in places they've had spills,' she said. 'I—'

'Cut the shit, Roxanne,' Marlowe snapped, finally tiring of the dance. 'I've had a long day and I've barely slept since yesterday, I've killed several people tonight, not by choice, and I know when people are telling me what they think I want to know. So, what do you have on Donziger, because it's enough to have them send in a bloody extraction team?'

Roxanne hissed in air between her teeth.

'My father worked for them,' she eventually admitted.

Marlowe didn't know what to say to this, and Roxanne wasn't continuing, so the silence stretched out for a long moment before she spoke again.

'Nathan Donziger and my father, Brett, went to Harvard together,' she carried on. 'They were roomies. Or whatever you are, in a place like that. Nathan Donziger came from money, his family were oil magnates in the south. But Nathan hated oil. He hated getting dirty, was a germaphobe. And so, his plan was to gain a finance degree, move into banking. He'd take the family money and clean it for them, in more ways than one.'

'This was the hedge-fund financiers?'

'Eventually, yes,' Roxanne nodded. 'But before that, they

worked in the City, before the Towers fell. The day the planes hit, my father and Nathan weren't in the offices, they were buying out a small private helipad in the Hamptons. If they'd been there, they would have most certainly died with the others in the firm.'

'Jesus,' Marlowe picked at the fries, eating them as he listened.

'Jesus wasn't anywhere near them,' Roxanne growled. 'After the Twin Towers fell, Nathan Donziger saw an opportunity and hit the ground running. While other financial firms mourned their dead, he made alliances and bought out all the smaller fish, ones who'd lost their entire board in the space of a morning and didn't know what to do. He was a goddamned vulture, and the financial district was an all-you-can-eat buffet.'

'And your dad helped him?'

Roxanne nodded, her face tight.

'In the beginning,' she said. 'He had this misguided loyalty and a survivor's guilt. But after a year, it really got to him. He'd fight with Mom, bad ones, and eventually she packed our bags and we left. They divorced two years later, and I took her surname, rather than his, Hendricks.'

'Like the dead rock star?'

'No, C-K rather than X,' Roxanne smiled. 'Although Pops really believed he was a rockstar back then. Even started living the life when he was single again.'

'So how does this affect the case?'

'My father and Nathan fell out, about ten years back,' Roxanne leant back in the chair, almost hiding in it as she remembered. 'Nathan Donziger destroyed him overnight. Took away all his expense accounts, made him pay back corporate loans, the lot. Even took away his company apartment in the city, which he found out when he tried to use his keys, finding they had already changed the locks. They sent his personal items to Goodwill. It was like Mom leaving him all over again, and I think it got to him.'

'So, what happened next?'

'He came to me,' Roxanne leant over, stealing one of the fries. 'I was in my final year doing law in Stanford, as far from here as I could be, and he flew out to California to visit.'

'Why?'

'Guilt, I expect,' Roxanne munched on another of the fries. 'I think it hurt him I took Mom's name instead of his. But he also needed a confessor, someone to listen to his stories.'

'Or he wanted an ally, someone to help him gain revenge.'

Roxanne laughed at this.

'Oh, he wanted that, all right. He was brimming with pent-up rage and anger at what happened to him. I think he even thought I'd pass the Bar and take them to court for him.'

'But you didn't?'

'No.'

It was something in how Roxanne spoke the word, but Marlowe knew there was something more to this.

'What happened?' he asked, no longer eating.

'I told you, he ...'

'Come on,' Marlowe insisted. 'I've already said one thing I'm fantastic at is knowing when I'm being lied to.'

'I listened to his stories, and I nodded at all his comments, playing the dutiful daughter, and then he left again,' Roxanne began reluctantly. 'I think he realised I wasn't going to be the solution he needed. I didn't hear from him for a while after that. And then, about five years back, I was practising at a firm in Los Angeles, and I heard the news. He'd died in a house fire.'

Marlowe wanted to say something supportive, or offer some condolences, but once more, his years of spy craft stopped him. *There was something more going on here.*

'You don't think it was an accident, do you?'

'No.'

Roxanne rose from the chair now, walking over to the window, staring out across night-time Manhattan.

'It was dodgy as hell. It wasn't even a part of the city he'd hung around in. I had a friend, someone from college, who now worked for the New York Attorney's office. I hit her up, asked if she could look into it for me. She agreed, but then sent me a message a week later, saying she wasn't going to look into it anymore, and I'd do well to walk away, remember him as he was.'

She looked back at Marlowe.

'I heard a few weeks later that she'd also died, killed in a hit and run on Broadway.'

'You think Donziger did it?'

'I think Donziger did both,' Roxanne said icily. 'They killed my friend and made it look like an accident, and they killed my father, making it look like he died in a fire.'

'So, you went after them,' Marlowe watched Roxanne carefully. 'No, you don't rush to anger, do you? You took your time, made a plan. I'm guessing you looked at ways to come at them from different angles. This case, maybe?'

'I moved to a firm in New York that specialised in environ-mental issues,' Roxanne shrugged as she looked out of the window again. 'I planned to find someone with an axe to grind against Nathan Donziger and then use them as my crowbar to get into his company. But it was harder than I expected. Nobody had the balls to go up against him, so I knew I'd have to bide my time for a couple of years until I found someone. And even then, I knew I'd have to build my reputation in the firm, so that when I called for this, they'd give it to me.'

She smiled.

'And I was damned good at it,' she said. 'I *am* damned good at it.'

'So, you moved to New York, and Rehbein and Pope, and waited until the right case came up,' Marlowe wiped his mouth with a napkin. 'And then comes Jericho Falls, a small town that's been screwed over by a company Donziger helped finance. You go for a big settlement, knowing it'll force everything out into the open, and you know you'll win, because you have something on them. You have your father's war stories.'

'And more,' Roxanne admitted. 'He had a lockup in Greenwich Village. Held all the paperwork he'd squirrelled away after his exile. He sent me a key, and a note on how to get in before he died.'

'Sending you that muddies the waters on how and why he died, though,' Marlowe scratched his chin as he rose from the sofa. 'You know, a suicidal person will make sure everything's sorted before they go off and do something bloody stupid ...'

He trailed off.

'Oh, wait, it *wasn't* suicide that made him send it to you, was it? He was going to war, and didn't think he'd make it.'

'They didn't have the right address, so it took two months to get to me,' Roxanne nodded. 'By then I'd been told of his death, and I'd been told to walk away. The note said he'd paid six months' rent in advance, so the day after I learned of Stacey's death – that's my friend – I bought a ticket to New

York, and took the key with me. Once I saw what he had, I quit my job immediately. I had an interview prepped with Rehbein and Pope before I even caught the plane back.'

'And then you went to Jericho and, with this information in your pocket, had a kind of legal *Rosetta's Stone*, a way to see into Donziger's hand every time he tried to play a card,' Marlowe was impressed. 'No wonder he wanted you dead. Does he know who you are? That Hendricks was your father?'

'No, I don't think so,' Roxanne shook her head, walking back to the minibar and pulling out another tiny bottle of vodka. 'Vasquez is my mother's maiden name. But when I win my case, I'll make sure to tell Donziger the truth. That Brett Hendricks did this from beyond the grave.'

'You need to survive until the case starts to do that,' Marlowe mused.

'That's for you and your team to sort out,' Roxanne said as she poured the tiny bottle down her throat. 'How many of you are there, anyway?'

'Three,' Marlowe admitted. 'A friend from London, Trix, she was the voice in my ear you could hear last night. And then there's Brad. He brought me onto the mission.'

'I heard you say his name into your earbud thing,' Roxanne nodded. 'He also sent the SEAL?'

Marlowe nodded.

'Okay, so what's this to do with him?' Roxanne continued.

'It's personal,' Marlowe moved to his bag now, pulling out the phone. He was half tempted to call in, see if anything else was happening, as by now Trix would have worked out who gave the enemy their comms signal. 'He was in the CIA with your Uncle Danny. Owed him his life. He sees this as a way of returning the favour.'

Roxanne turned slowly to face Marlowe.

'Bullshit,' she said.

'Look, I know, it's a shock when you realise someone you love is a spook—'

'No, I mean that entire story is utter bullshit,' Roxanne snapped. 'I don't know what the hell garbage you've been fed, but I don't *have* an Uncle Danny. And according to my father's notes, the ones I found in that lockup, the CIA has been taking funding from Donziger for years.'

Marlowe tried to keep the surprise off his face, while internally he wanted to scream.

Brad bloody Haynes had screwed him again.

But, had it been deliberate, or by accident? Had Brad given Marlowe a story to get him to help, using dead relatives and life debts as dressing for the pitch, or had he brought Marlowe in, knowing he'd bring Roxanne Vasquez to him?

Marlowe worked through the plan for earlier that night. Brad was supposed to be in the car, waiting if there was a problem. Marlowe was to bring Roxanne to the car, and they'd take her back to the hotel.

Brad could have taken him out at any time. Hell, Trix could be dead by now.

But there was something in the background, a belief that Brad wouldn't do that to him, naïve or not.

'Porn Star Martinis,' he blurted.

'It's nearly midnight and I'm exhausted, I really don't want—'

'No,' Marlowe shook his head as he worked through the question. 'Who else knows about you drinking these at Law School?'

'Probably the lawyers I drank them with, why?'

'Because Brad, the CIA guy you've just told me is full of

shit, told me to use it to get close to you,' Marlowe was pacing now. 'He knew this was a drink you'd recognise, because he said, "I remember Danny complaining about this once when she was in law school." That's word for word what he told me.'

'My father complained about it,' Roxanne was frowning now, her brow furrowing as she thought back. 'When he came to see me. I don't think he realised it was the only way I could get through the meetings I had with him at the time.'

'Something's not right here.'

'Yeah. Your buddy's talking about an uncle who doesn't exist.'

'There's something else. Just in the corner, out of reach. I'll keep working on it,' Marlowe checked his watch. 'It's almost midnight, and therefore it's almost Friday. What did you need to be doing tomorrow?'

'I needed to be working on the case,' Roxanne snapped. 'Which I'm not going to be able to do, am I, because you're going to tie me up and keep me here all weekend, aren't you?'

'You're thinking of the movies again,' Marlowe smiled. 'I want you to win this case. And I'm guessing your offices have security. Once we get you in there, hunker down until I come and get you.'

'Wait, you're not hanging around?'

'I have questions to ask,' Marlowe hadn't realised how angry he was as he spoke the words, but the venom was audible in them. 'I think we should call this a night, and start tomorrow bright and early.'

Roxanne nodded, looking down at the mess of food on the table.

'We should clean this up,' she said.

'I'll sort it, you go sleep,' Marlowe indicated the bedroom.

'I'll leave them outside the door. And we'll be gone first thing in the morning.'

Roxanne took one of the oversized T-shirts, walking off into the bedroom, closing the door behind her. Now alone, Marlowe reached for the new phone in his bag, but stopped.

If Brad was playing with him, did he know about the phone?

'Actually, I'll be back in a minute,' he said, reaching for the plates. 'Just stretching my legs.'

———

THE BUSINESS SUITE WAS QUIET FOR THIS TIME OF NIGHT, which was to be expected, as Marlowe slipped into the chair in front of the closest computer screen. He pulled a USB flash drive, one he'd brought with him from the UK and taken from the holdall before leaving the room, out of his pocket, slotting it into the USB drive port at the side of the screen.

There was a flicker on the monitor as the software on the USB drive activated, and after a second a screen opened up on it, the program on the drive bypassing the operating system and doing its own thing. Marlowe had a series of options appearing on the screen, and he scrolled the mouse to the third one down.

STARBUG

This was the spacecraft used in *Red Dwarf*, and was named by Trix in one of her bouts of nerd-dom. Clicking the mouse button, he then had a text box to write a brief message in.

Danny doesn't exist. Brad playing us. Meet
me Wash Squ Fount 10am

It was short because of the maximum number of words he could use, but then, with a click of the mouse again, the words disappeared to be replaced with a random series of sentences that looked like a spam post. Copying it, Marlowe now opened a browser, searching for the same Reddit forum he'd visited earlier, logging in as his own account, *RImm3rBoy*, and pasting the text into the message, pressing send.

This done, he removed the USB stick and pocketed it once more; with luck, Trix would look for messages, and would see a cypher message on the board. She would check the message in her own app, and with luck, get out of there as quickly as possible.

Or, she was already dead, Brad knew the code, and he'd be waiting.

Marlowe leant back on the chair, placing his hands behind his head as he stretched.

That was a risk he'd have to take, and a risk he'd look at tomorrow.

He looked at his watch.

'Nope, I'll look at it later today,' he muttered as he closed the terminal up and left the business suite.

———

Roxanne had Marlowe's gun in her hands as he entered the suite.

'You scared the shit out of me, running off like that!' she snarled, as Marlowe walked over to her, taking the gun, and trying not to stare at her, currently wearing nothing more than an oversized t-shirt that only just reached her rather tanned and nice-looking thighs.

'You should go to sleep,' he said, averting his eyes. Realising he was being a gentleman, Roxanne choked a laugh back, patting him on the arm and walking back to the bedroom.

'You Brits really are wound up tight,' she purred mockingly as she looked back at him, while Marlowe forced himself to look directly at her face, her eyes, anything that wasn't large swathes of bare skin.

'Goodnight, Marlowe,' she continued, her voice now serious. 'Thanks for saving my life tonight.'

'All part of the job,' Marlowe forced a smile. 'I'll see you in the morning.'

As Roxanne closed the door to the bedroom, now out of sight, Marlowe breathed out a long sigh. There was no doubting she was attractive, and he wasn't a monk.

But as he kept saying, this wasn't the movies.

He couldn't be bothered to pull out the sofa bed, and so, pulling the spare duvet and pillow from the suite's wardrobe, he made a makeshift bed upon it and, facing the door, gun under the pillow, tried to get some sleep in the second uncomfortable seat-bed he'd slept on in two days.

10

CLOAKED ROOM

MARLOWE WAS ALREADY UP, THE SOFA BACK TO ITS ORIGINAL intent, the pillow and duvet squirreled away by the time Roxanne emerged from the bedroom around seven in the morning. She'd already showered and dressed in jeans, sweater and t-shirt, and slumped into the chair, accepting a cup of coffee.

'I went down to the diner,' Marlowe explained as he walked to the desk, sipping at his own cup. 'Thought you might need some caffeine after last night. There's sugar sachets on the table.'

This wasn't quite true, however – Marlowe had gone down to gain coffee, but there was a perfectly fine coffee machine in the suite, one that used pods to create passable blends. But Marlowe had wanted to check out the Tick Tock Diner, on the ground floor of the hotel, so he could gain an idea of the best exits and entrances, and the breakfast time situation.

In around twenty-four hours the mysterious meeting, the

details found on the back of a photo, would happen and Marlowe wanted to be there.

'Will your company let you in like that?' Marlowe smiled, nodding at the sweater. 'I mean, I've heard of "dress down Friday," but that looks to be taking the piss a little.'

'It's my travelling clothes,' Roxanne made a face at Marlowe as she sipped at her own drink. 'I can change when I get to the office. I changed there last night before the ball, so apart from a blouse and underwear, I can pretty much re-use what I have. And I can wear a t-shirt for a blouse and go commando until I can buy some nice new lacy panties.'

She spoke the last part of this in a purr, and Marlowe knew she was once more trying to get a reaction from him. But he had other thoughts on his mind now, dangerous ones, and the slight flirtation slipped past without a response.

'We need to get my bag first,' she said, finishing her drink. 'It has my phone and my ID in it. Without that, I can't get into the office.'

'I'll pick those up,' Marlowe nodded, pulling on a sweater-hoodie with NEW YORK METS emblazoned on it. 'I'd rather mine was the face seen than yours. The problem is, though, it won't open until ten this morning, and I'm guessing you need it before then.'

'Preferably, I'd like to gain it within the next hour,' Roxanne passed a chit with a number on over to him. 'This is what they gave me when I checked it in. My coat's with it, too.'

Marlowe took the chit, placing it away.

'I'm good to go whenever you're ready,' he said.

'You don't want a shower?'

Marlowe nodded at a door to the side.

'Suite has two bathrooms, one with a shower, one with a bath,' he smiled. 'I'm clean and scrubbed.'

He reached into his holdall, pulling out a jacket; a thin, brown leather one. Pulling it on and placing the hood of his Mets hoodie over the collar, he took the Glock 17 from the table, placing it into his holster, clipped to the inside of his belt. Taking the hint, Roxanne walked into the bedroom, checking for anything she'd missed.

'I have to wear the velour jacket again?' she said as she examined the remaining clothes.

'You'll be getting the coat you checked into the cloakroom in a bit,' he shrugged. 'Thought you'd prefer that to something mis-matched.'

'You mean you forgot to find me something nice,' Roxanne chided. 'So, what's the plan?'

'We go to the lobby, get a cab to the library. I gain entrance, get your things, we then go to your office on ...' Marlowe faltered for a moment.

'Broadway and Worth Street, way down south,' Roxanne smiled. 'Like, waaaay down.'

'We'll go there then, I'll make sure you're set up, then I'll disappear for an hour or two,' Marlowe continued as he checked his pockets, rummaging in the holdall as he realised he was short an item or two.

'Wait, you're leaving me alone?'

'Not for long, and I'll pick you up before lunch and bring you here,' Marlowe replied. 'So, gather what you need for the weekend, because once we're out, we're hunkering down.'

Roxanne went to argue this, but then nodded.

'Fine,' she said, walking to the door. 'It'd better not be snowing out there if all I'm wearing is this.'

Roxanne waited for Marlowe to prepare the suite – first,

he placed the DO NOT DISTURB sign on the door, and then pulled a hair from his head, licking his finger and running the hair along it, placing it low and on the door, across the gap between door and frame.

'You know that doesn't work in the real world,' Roxanne commented as she watched.

'You'd be surprised,' Marlowe rose from his crouch. 'Come on, let's get out of here.'

THEY CAUGHT A CAB FROM THE MAIN ENTRANCE, MARLOWE offering cash if the driver promised to wait while he gathered the items from the library. And when the car pulled up outside, he told Roxanne to wait inside as he walked up to the main doors.

They were open, as expected – the police were still examining the scene of last night's crime, and a uniformed officer watched him approach.

'Library's shut, pal,' he drawled, his Brooklyn accent clear to hear. 'Come back this afternoon.'

Marlowe flashed his US Marshal ID.

'I need to speak to someone inside,' he said officiously, a slight twang to his voice, just to sell it. 'In and out, two minutes, won't touch a thing in the two crime scenes.'

'How d'you know there's two scenes?'

'Two bodies in different situations,' Marlowe shrugged. 'I guessed two scenes.'

With Marlowe knowing enough of the case to show he wasn't off the street, the police officer grudgingly moved out of the way, and Marlowe passed through the main double door, back into Astor Hall.

It didn't look the same as last night, even though nothing had been moved. The lights were on, but it was a colder, utilitarian white than the muted colours of the previous night, and the bars, once thriving and full of life were now empty and bare, the glasses discarded when the partygoers ran once the bodies were found.

A couple of CSI officers were still checking the ground, and an overweight, already sweating detective looked up at him.

'You a Fed?' he asked.

'Marshal,' Marlowe replied, showing the ID again. 'Working on something connected. Need to pick up something from the cloakroom.'

'Is it another dead body?'

Marlowe chuckled.

'Nah, it's a bag and a coat. We picked up a drug mule last night, she reckons she was set up and her purse is here. Until we have proof, we can't move on.'

He pulled out the chit.

'Mind if I go look?'

'Go wild,' the detective said, turning back. 'Any problems from the uniforms, tell them Detective Forte said it was fine.'

'Appreciated,' Marlowe tapped the brim of his baseball cap – he'd placed it on as he entered the taxi, and it was grey with NYM on it, the three letters and logo of the New York Mets, matching the hoodie.

'Just don't talk to Harris,' Detective Forte added. 'He's a Padres fan, and he's sore about the recent game.'

Marlowe smiled, nodding again. He didn't know what the scores of the last few games had been, he'd only picked the Mets because they were often the underdog, and the Yankees' hats were so commercialised, they almost made you stand out more if you wore one – a sure sign of "tourist" if added to a British accent.

And Brad had been wearing a Yankees top when they met, he smiled. *You did it to bug him, too.*

The cloakroom was empty when Marlowe arrived, and after hopping the counter, being careful not to leave any fingerprints on the surface, he went through to the back of the rows of coats and bags, searching for Roxanne's clothes. As he did so, he also kept an eye out on the other items there, coats and bags forgotten when the crowds ran out, items not being picked up for a few hours.

Items a spy could use.

It was all insured, and Marlowe didn't feel too bad about taking a couple of items as he walked along – a thick, winter pea coat in navy was grabbed, as was a small can of pepper spray and a length of metal chain that had been wrapped around a briefcase handle. It looked inoffensive, but Marlowe had recognised it as a steel self-defence bracelet chain, something that not only deflected knives but also, when held loose, became a metre-long whip of vicious steel. They were illegal in the UK, but obviously not here, and that was enough for Marlowe.

This now wrapped around his left wrist and secured by the dragon-head clasp, Marlowe grabbed Roxanne's bag and coat. The former was a Louis Vuitton bag in brown and gold, while the coat was a DKNY quilted fur jacket with fur-trimmed hood, all in black.

Marlowe smiled. *Being an environmental lawyer paid well.*

With these in hand, and also a small backpack picked up for good measure, its contents poured onto the floor, Marlowe made his way to one of the other exits, nodding to the police officer guarding it as he passed through. The officer, expecting to stop people entering rather than leaving, simply stepped aside as the man in the hoodie and cap walked past with two coats and a couple of bags.

Climbing into the cab, Marlowe passed the jacket and bag to Roxanne, who eagerly pulled the quilted jacket on, sighing as she finally felt the warmth within.

'See you got yourself something new,' she said as she noted the new pea coat. Marlowe was pulling off his thin leather jacket, emptying it and placing it into the backpack as he now pulled the coat on, transferring the items into it, while the taxi pulled back out into the street.

'That's a solid fashion choice,' she said as she saw the wrapped chain bracelet. Marlowe smiled, saying nothing as it now disappeared into a sleeve, the hoodie's hood now placed over the coat's collar instead.

'You have any defence in that?' he asked, pointing at the bag.

'I have a rape alarm whistle,' Roxanne shrugged. 'Never really worried that much before. I never went anywhere I'd be attacked.'

'Take this,' Marlowe passed over the pepper spray. 'In case I'm not around to shoot.'

'You say the nicest things,' Roxanne smiled, leaning back in the seat.

———

THE OFFICES OF REHBEIN AND POPE WERE ONLY A TEN-MINUTE drive away, the day still early enough to drive without too many breaks. And, once outside the building, Marlowe paid the cabbie his fare, as well as a couple of extra twenties.

'You never saw us,' he said as they both exited the car,

allowing it to drive off into Manhattan once more as they looked around.

'Move fast,' Marlowe said, leading Roxanne to the glass doors that led into the building. 'Anyone could be watching.'

The doors led into an ornate, marbled lobby, silent and echoing as they walked across it. To the right was a long reception desk with security standing behind it – a man and a woman – who watched the two new arrivals as they walked to a series of glass-walled, waist-high entrance gates.

'We're on the seventh floor,' Roxanne explained as she nodded to the guard on the other side of the gates. 'Hey Hank. He's with me.'

'Gonna need to see some ID,' Hank the guard said as Roxanne used her own ID to buzz herself through, and Marlowe complied by once more showing the US Marshal ID.

Seeing this, Hank's eyes widened, and Marlowe leant in close.

'I'll be back in a minute, and I'll need to speak to you and your team,' he said. 'Let me get Miss Vasquez to her office first.'

Hank nodded, pressing the call button for the elevator, and Marlowe and Roxanne entered it, the "7" already lit.

'This feels different to the last elevator we were in,' Roxanne joked as it lurched slightly and rose.

'We're not being shot at,' Marlowe replied.

'Day's still early,' Roxanne winked as the doors opened and they entered the reception of Rehbein and Pope. Roxanne nodded to the receptionist, a young man who looked no older than twenty. That didn't mean he wasn't capable, though, as Marlowe had learned over the months he'd spent working with Trix.

'This is US Marshal Dexter ...' she stopped, realising she didn't know Marlowe's fake surname.

'Garner, Ma'am,' Marlowe drawled as he tipped his cap.

'When he comes back, he's to be brought straight to me,' Roxanne ordered, before looking back at Marlowe. 'Stay safe, yeah?'

Marlowe nodded and walked back to the elevators, ignoring the conversation Roxanne was now having with the receptionist, the latter likely asking why the hell she needed a US Marshal escort to work, and why she was dressed like a tourist. Marlowe entered the carriage, pressing for the ground floor, and was convinced he heard her asking the receptionist to get someone to "nip to Victoria's Secret" when it opened, and he couldn't hide his smile as he carried on down.

Hank, the guard, was waiting for him as the door opened.

'Should I know something?' he asked with no form of introduction, and Marlowe saw from his posture that not only was Hank armed and ready for a fight, but that he was trained.

'What were you?' he asked softly. 'Marines?'

'Oorah,' Hank replied.

'Good,' Marlowe actually felt a little relief at this. 'Miss Vasquez was the subject of an attempted murder last night. You hear about the New York Public Library attack?'

'Two deaths,' Hank nodded, giving nothing away on whether the news surprised him. 'I knew she was up against bastards, but didn't know they'd go that far.'

'They did, and they will again,' Marlowe replied, looking around the lobby, checking for entrances and exits as he spoke. 'One death was an ex-Navy SEAL who was watching over her. The other was one of the killers.'

'Killed by the SEAL?'

'Killed by me,' Marlowe said quietly. 'I'm off to sort out a safe house in East Sixty-Eighth Street, down by Lenox Hill. I'll be back in a couple of hours. Keep an eye out, be wary of everyone.'

'Sir, yes sir,' Hank replied, and Marlowe could see he would do just that. The address he gave was fictitious, but if Hank mentioned anything to anyone, it'd at least give them a nice wild goose chase.

'Good man,' Marlowe patted Hank on the shoulder and moved back out through the gates. 'I'll be in touch.'

And, this done, Marlowe walked back out of the lobby of Rehbein and Pope and onto the Lower Manhattan street. It was a mile or so walk to Washington Square Park, where he was to meet Trix, and he could be there by nine, easily. That'd give him enough time to scope the place out, make sure this wasn't a trap.

He hoped to hell it wouldn't be, but right now, he simply wasn't sure who he could trust.

11

PARKING METERED

MARLOWE HAD BEEN WATCHING THE FOUNTAIN FOR HALF AN hour by the time Trix Preston arrived. He'd taken the journey north from Rehbein and Pope in a leisurely fashion, allowing the cold, February wind to wake him up, grabbing a bagel from a delicatessen down the street. With a Coke in his other hand, he'd eaten it as he sat beside the Robin Kovary Dog Run for small dogs – a little playground for four-legged visitors – half watching the morning dog walkers as they brought their charges to the area, allowing them off lead to play before connecting the leashes back on and walking off into the city.

There were a lot of transitional walkers here, unleashing dogs, sitting down and then rising to leave, and they left Marlowe to his own devices as he ate his breakfast quietly, watching the fountain through the trees.

He hadn't seen anyone following Trix, and he gave it a good five minutes before getting up and walking over to her. She'd come into the park from the north, which fitted where she'd have been travelling from; if she'd come from the south, he would have wondered what she'd been doing near Roxanne's place of work. And "being a tourist" wouldn't cut it.

'You okay?' she asked as he approached, not bothering with the niceties of greeting. Marlowe shrugged as he sat down on the edge of the fountain beside her. The park was almost empty, the cold weather keeping most casual visitors away, and they had the space to themselves.

'I've had better gigs,' he said. 'And I've had fewer trust issues with them.'

'Yeah, I get that,' Trix nodded. 'You're off grid, right?'

Marlowe didn't reply, and Trix smiled.

'Where does he think you are?' he asked instead.

'I showed him your Budapest message, but I changed it before he could see it,' she explained. 'He saw it come up, so I couldn't deny it. But instead of showing it, I told him you'd asked for more supplies, that you needed more ammo and a first aid kit, as well as a couple of small things I had in my bag. Currently, he thinks I'm back at Penn Station, sticking another bag into a locker.'

She looked around, sniffing.

'Or, he's watching us through a sniper scope and realising I've been less than truthful,' she added fatalistically.

'Why do you think he lied to us?' Marlowe was scanning the edges of the park now.

'How do you know he did?'

Marlowe looked back at Trix, and she sighed.

'Yeah, he lied,' she continued. 'There's no Daniel Vasquez. Not in the SEALs with Brad, nor to my knowledge in the CIA. I'm still checking though.'

Marlowe leant back a little, his hands on the edge of the fountain to stop him from overbalancing.

'Why lie?' he muttered. 'It doesn't make sense. If he wants Roxanne to die, then he leaves us back in London. We don't turn up to help, she's taken last night after Trevor dies.'

'Trevor Sinclair,' Trix pulled out a phone, opening up a notes app. 'I found some stuff on him. He did work with Brad. They both served in Afghanistan together. From the looks of everything I read, they were close, too.'

'This is what I mean,' Marlowe forced himself to keep his voice low. 'Brad might be a Yank prick at the best of times, but he's CIA and a patriot through and through. He wouldn't have left an old Navy buddy to die without saying anything.'

'He was pissed at that,' Trix replied. 'He came back to the hotel after you ran, absolutely steaming with rage. Spent the next hour looking at a photo. I saw it, and it was what you'd expect – young Brad with other SEALs. One of them was likely young Trevor.'

She pursed her lips as she contemplated her next words.

'But even if he's on the level, he's definitely keeping things from us,' she said. 'And it's not like he doesn't have priors on this. He left you out to hang when we last worked with him.'

Marlowe nodded.

'And a leopard doesn't change their spots,' he added. 'Look, all we have to do is keep her alive a couple of days more. I'm off the grid, and if I don't have Brad next to me, I don't need to worry about what he's *doing* next to me. Can you survive the weekend?'

Trix grinned now, and Marlowe actually smiled, it was so infectious.

'I've lasted longer and with worse threats against me,' she said. 'I had your uncle sold on my innocence for a month, remember?'

There was a long pause in the conversation. Trix's smile became more impish.

'So, how is she?'

'The lawyer?'

'Who else?'

Marlowe thought for a moment.

'She's tough, no nonsense, listens to orders, doesn't freak out,' he said.

'She's pretty,' Trix said, watching Marlowe. 'Just your type, too. Where did you sleep last night?'

'Not in the same bed, if that's what you're asking,' Marlowe's tone was a little too short, and he mentally pulled himself back, so as not to give Trix any more ammunition. 'It was a pay-by-the-hour hotel in Harlem.'

At this, Trix's expression became considerably colder.

'You might not trust Brad, but that hurts when you don't trust me,' she said. And, before Marlowe could reply, she held up a hand. 'I sorted out your fake IDs, remember? You think I don't get an alert when you use a card? Like, when you book a suite at the New Yorker?'

Marlowe sighed.

'I do trust you,' he said, turning to fully face her. 'And to be honest, I probably trust you more than anyone at the moment. But Brad might not trust you. And if he asks if you know where I'm staying, I wanted you to have plausible deniability.'

'You don't think I could sell it?'

'That's not it at all, Trix. I didn't want you to be in a position where you *had* to sell it.'

'Yeah, okay, I see that,' Trix's expression softened at this. 'What's your plan, then?'

'I think I'm going to have to chat with Brad, sooner than

later,' Marlowe was clenching and unclenching his hands as he spoke. 'I need to know what the hell is going on.'

'And apart from that?' Trix looked around. 'I don't see any lawyer.'

'She's in her office,' Marlowe replied. 'It's safe, I checked it. I'll go back when I'm finished.'

'Talking to me?'

Marlowe didn't reply.

Trix frowned at him.

'Marlowe, what the hell are you planning?'

'I thought I'd go have a word with Nathan Donziger,' Marlowe said, as if it was the most casual thing in the world. 'See if we can stop this before it gets out of hand.'

Trix swiped through her phone once more.

'You need to be careful if you're doing that,' she said. 'I had details come back about the two men you killed.'

'Did they work for Donziger?' Marlowe was interested again, leaning closer to see the phone. However, what he saw was enough to make him feel sick.

'Shit,' was all he could whisper.

'Yeah,' Trix looked up, but the smile was gone now. 'Meet Shaun Lord and Trey Attwood. Both, until last night, active agents in the US Secret Service.'

Marlowe rose, almost as if by backing away from the phone and the information displayed on it, he wouldn't have to look at it.

'Donziger had Senators connected to him, according to Brad,' he said, looking around the park again. This time, however, he wasn't looking for Brad, he was instead looking for Presidential security, and the various technological assets they had at their disposal. 'You think he could have convinced them to pass him some agents?'

'To kill a lawyer?'

'No, to retrieve her,' Marlowe shook his head. 'The syringe I obtained had GHB in it. They weren't looking to poison her, they were there to remove her from the location and take her somewhere else.'

'What about Trevor?'

'They weren't told he was a SEAL, maybe they were given details that compromised him,' Marlowe was thinking on the fly now, and he knew it. 'I don't know. Maybe they were corrupt. Look into their records. I'm guessing they were military before they became agents.'

He stopped, looking back at Trix.

'Check if they were CIA,' he added quietly. 'Maybe perhaps even working with Brad.'

Trix nodded, tapping on her phone as she rose, placing it away and passing Marlowe another holdall bag.

'Here,' she said. 'Put this with the other one. It's the ammo and first aid kit I told Brad I was giving you. There's also a USB in there with the CIA file he had on Vasquez. There might be something in there you can use.'

'Tell him I want to meet him today,' Marlowe opened the holdall, throwing the backpack with his leather jacket inside, into the larger space. 'Don't make it sound like we have a problem, though.'

'Do we have a problem?' Trix backed away slowly, not because she feared the conversation, but because she was eager to get going. Marlowe understood this, as there was every chance they were being watched, even targeted right now.

'I'll tell you after we speak,' he said. 'Stay safe, Trix.'

'Keep an eye on your girl,' Trix turned to walk away. 'Brad will be, too.'

Now alone in the park, Marlowe shifted the duffle onto his shoulder.

'I should have let that bloody hitman shoot me,' he growled as he returned south.

THE DONZIGER OFFICES WERE NEAR WALL STREET, A CHROME and glass monstrosity of a building on Nassau Street, and smack-bang in the middle of New York's financial district. Which made complete sense, even if it was a nightmare to get to.

Marlowe didn't intend to make the two-mile journey on foot, so he caught a cab there, once more paying in cash. The driver had been quite negative about the area, and Marlowe got the impression yellow cabs weren't being used as much down there, so he gave a healthy tip before leaving.

The building wasn't just Donziger's, although they seemed to own the top half. The main reception was covering at least four different companies, so Marlowe entered swiftly, keeping his cap low to hide his face from the CCTV, and showed his US Marshal ID to one of the receptionist / security guards, saying he needed to speak to someone in the company that occupied the floor below, which, from the list at the door was called *Troopers Industrial*. He didn't know who they were or what they needed, but the duty security guard, on seeing the ID, went to call up.

Marlowe stopped him.

'This isn't what you'd call a scheduled meeting,' he said, noting the wedding ring on the guard's finger. 'My target has missed three court sessions for aggravated assault on a minor, and I don't want him to leave when I arrive, kapeesh?'

'Aggravated assault on a minor?' the security guard frowned.

'Hit his kid,' Marlowe continued, playing a hunch. 'His wife, too, when she tried to stop him. Ended up holding a kitchen knife at her throat before the police turned up. But he had good lawyers, you know?'

The security guard's face darkened, and Marlowe knew he'd thought correctly.

'You got kids?' he pressed.

'Two, a boy and a girl.'

'Then let me do my job and get that piece of shit,' Marlowe smiled. 'If he doesn't know I'm coming, he won't be able to run.'

Marlowe winked.

'And if you were to have a malfunction in the elevator's CCTV, I could even ... you know ... on the way down.'

'Second elevator on the right as you pass through the gates,' the security guard, already waving at the guard at the security gates, smiled. 'The camera's a bit iffy. I think it might be down for the next twenty minutes.'

'That's all I need,' Marlowe smiled. 'Appreciate that.'

Walking through the gates and now at the elevator, Marlowe took a breath. He didn't enjoy lying to guards, but it was part of the job. And besides, the guard would now be even more vigilant with everyone working at Troopers-what-ever-the-hell-it-was, purely as he didn't know which of the employees was the piece of shit the nice Marshal had spoken about.

Once in the elevator, Marlowe noted the camera in the corner – the light winked off. And, before it could turn on again, or if the security guard changed his mind about this, Marlowe quickly pulled out a roll of electrical tape, placing a small piece over the tiny lens. This way, even if they turned it back on, there would be no footage.

This done, he waited until the elevator reached the floor below Donziger, and then pressed the "hold" button. There was a ringing as the elevator alarm went off, usual for when an elevator was stuck, but Marlowe wasn't listening, bracing himself against the corner as he pushed himself up, back to the wall, like a climber, punching out the panel at the top of the car.

Then, dropping down, he slung his holdall over his shoulder and jumped up, grabbing the edge of the hole and pulling himself through, closing it behind him.

Now on top of the elevator car, Marlowe pulled on a pair of light leather gloves and moved across to the wall. There was a service ladder, and with a determined effort, Marlowe started climbing it. Although the next floor was Donziger, he didn't want to enter through that door, as that would be where the reception was. On the journey there, he'd googled the layout of the building, and he knew that two floors up was a closed and empty floor while they repositioned departments.

That was the entrance he needed.

He'd barely started up the ladder when the elevator beneath him dropped.

They'd realised something was wrong, he thought to himself, *but they'd be looking at the wrong floor.*

Now moving faster, climbing harder, Marlowe reached the elevator door to the empty floor and, pulling a small metal plate from the wall, the wires connected to it allowing it to hang loosely, pressed a switch within. The doors, on override now opened, and Marlowe used his momentum to swing through them, landing in the empty corridor.

The space was a mixture of open-plan office and building site, with framed wall dividers still not covered in plaster-board or paint, the whole place looking like an office floor should look, but not quite enough.

Pushing through some tarpaulin, used as a doorway and most likely to stop dust contaminating the entire floor, Marlowe spotted a table next to a circular saw. This was likely the workmen's dining area, although a little too close to the wood chips and sawdust for his liking, and it was covered in junk food wrappers and bags; it was almost as if the workers had gone home the previous day and not turned up this morning.

Marlowe checked his watch; it wasn't yet eleven, so there was every chance they worked later hours, or even into the night – if they were loud, as he could imagine the other offices complaining – so they may have done most of their work during the hours of darkness, working the evening and night shift instead.

The fast food bags gave Marlowe an idea, however. And, pulling one closer, he checked inside to see the remains of a meal, in its wrapping, tossed away. Looking around, he took a few more pieces of discarded wrapping and threw them in as well, re-folding the top of the paper fast-food bag down as he hefted it. Even though it was filled with trash, it now looked like a full bag of takeaway food.

This would be his way in.

Quickly, Marlowe removed his pea coat, rolling it up and stuffing it into his duffle bag, slinging that once more over his shoulder by the long strap in a cross-body manner.

He couldn't wear the pea coat in his plan; it was likely worth hundreds of dollars, and the character he was about to play didn't have that kind of money.

Readjusting his hoodie and baseball cap, Marlowe grabbed the bag and continued towards the far staircase. He'd bypassed the reception, but now he had to get to the finish line.

He just hoped Nathan Donziger was hungry.

12

DELIVERY MAN

For a Friday morning, the offices of Donziger were strangely quiet.

That said, Marlowe didn't know how many were working from home, connected wirelessly to the network, or, rather, how many were making sure they were nowhere to be seen days before a rather nasty court case was about to start.

Marlowe made his way along the corridors, a man in a hoodie and cap, a delivery bag over his shoulder, and a food order in his hand. He looked like he knew where he was going, and reception had obviously passed him through, and so the employees he walked past barely paid him a glance, enwrapped in their own daily problems.

He'd worked out from the website he'd checked that Nathan Donziger's office looked out towards the north; he saw this in a photo piece, had reverse engineered the view using Google Maps and the three-dimensional view it offered to work out the angle, and from that he knew the office had to be at the end of the northern corridor and on the right. What he didn't know, though, was whether Nathan would actually be in it.

However, he didn't reach the room, as the moment he turned into the corner to walk towards it, he faced a man in his mid-thirties, pink tie over expensive white shirt, staring at him in confusion. His hair was filled with product, he wore horn-rimmed glasses, and if he'd worn braces, Marlowe would have been convinced he'd walked onto the set of *American Psycho.*

Before the man could speak though, perhaps even question this intruder to his level, Marlowe held up the bag.

'Breakfast order,' he said, now looking at the receipt, pretending to read the name. 'Are you Nathan ... Dansacker?'

The man snorted, hiding a laugh, and Marlowe knew he'd thought correctly. Nathan might have been feared, but he wasn't liked.

'He's down the end, on the right,' he pointed. 'I don't think he's in there, though.'

He frowned as a thought came to him.

'Don't you guys leave it at reception usually?'

'Yeah,' Marlowe replied, returning to the receipt, pretending to read from it. 'But he left a note on the order. "Bring it to my office, don't leave it with those pricks on the front desk because they never tell me before it goes cold. Fifty buck tip if you do this." Tip sounds kinda good.'

'That sounds like Donziger,' the man smiled. 'If I give you a hundred, would you lose it for me?'

'Sorry man, no can do,' Marlowe shrugged apologetically. 'Tip sounds nice, but I'd lose my job.'

The man nodded at this, stepping to the side to allow Marlowe to pass.

'Don't call him Nathan,' he said, holding back a laugh.

'Call him Mister Dansacker. He loves that.'

Marlowe made a "thanks" gesture and carried on towards the room, making a silent promise to find out who that smug, horned-rimmed prick was. Deliberately sending a poor bloody delivery driver into the office of a man who could literally destroy his life on a whim, and letting him mispronounce the name was not cool.

'Mister Donziger?' Marlowe said, tapping on the door. He knew it was the right one because it had the name on the door. In gold.

N. D. DONZIGER – CEO

Marlowe idly wondered what the "D" stood for, deciding it was probably "dickhead" and, after a few seconds, he decided nobody was in and entered through the door, closing it behind him. Gone were the days of secretaries or PAs outside the door, waiting to be called, as now with messaging and emails and everything else, they might not even be on the same floor, or the same building even. The lack of people around was probably deliberate though, as with nobody nearby, you could speak freely, and Marlowe felt that Mister "Dansacker" was likely to be someone who had conversations he didn't want others to hear.

The office was spacious, although Marlowe expected this from the article he'd read, and the photos taken here. One and a half of the walls were full length glass, showing an incredible vista of the Manhattan financial district, currently preparing for work, the painted-white brick and plasterwork part of the second wall behind a metal and glass desk, and covered with a filled black bookcase. On the shelves were self-help books, awards and ornaments; Marlowe recognised the red felt of a Chinese book, the souvenir you received when you walked along the Great Wall of China, the certificate likely held inside. Beside that was a Russian doll, attached to a wooden base and a brass plaque in Russian, placed in front.

Marlowe guessed Donziger didn't read Russian, because if he did, he wouldn't have placed it so visibly. He'd probably been told it was a great award, but the plaque read *"Most likely to kill his family to be an Oligarch"*. Which, to be honest, was probably true, as well.

Marlowe walked behind the desk, sitting in the chair. The desk itself was quite sparse, with a laptop, a lamp, a mouse mat to the side with a wireless mouse on it, and an orange casino chip in a clear acrylic display. Marlowe knew it was a thousand-buck chip, as the orange chips, more currently known as "pumpkins" were uniform around the world. It seemed a strange flex for a billionaire magnate to have. To someone like Donziger, chips like this were nothing more than tip coins.

Marlowe was going to look around for some kind of desk drawer when the door to the office opened and Nathan Donziger walked into the room. He was tall, slim and had dirty-blond hair, wavy and turning white at the sides. He was in his early sixties, his face leathery and tanned, but more because of expensive holidays than sunbeds, and his suit was well-tailored and visibly expensive. His tie probably cost more than everything Marlowe wore, but that wasn't difficult at the moment.

Donziger stopped in the doorway and stared at the delivery driver lounging in his chair.

'You're in my seat,' he eventually said, closing the door and walking to the table. 'I'd like you to get out.'

Marlowe didn't move. In fact, he doubled-down, leaning back in the chair and placing his feet on the edge of the glass-topped desk.

'Take a seat, Nate,' he said, waving at the single chair on the other side of the desk. 'We need to have a chat.'

Without thinking, Donziger heard the authoritative tone in Marlowe's voice and instantly sat.

'You're the Marshal,' he eventually said, watching Marlowe. 'The one who took Vasquez out of the party.'

Marlowe nodded.

'And you're the one who hired Secret Service officers to come to the same party and abduct her,' he replied. 'And blew up three FBI agents to kill some Jericho Falls witnesses.'

If Donziger was surprised at the accusations, he made a good job of hiding it as he looked at his fingernails, considering this.

'You know, in the US, I think killing a Secret Service agent is not only murder, but treason,' he said, looking up at Marlowe. 'And if it isn't, it really should be. And you killed two last night. I wonder what they'll do to you when they find you, Mister Garner?'

Marlowe shrugged, noting Donziger hadn't denied either of the accusations he'd made.

'All depends on the context, I suppose,' he replied casually. 'I mean, self-defence is an appropriate term, especially when they were off books, and not working for the government.'

'How do you know they weren't?'

Marlowe grinned at this.

'Touché.'

Donziger looked around the office, as if expecting to see someone else.

'I don't see her here, so I guess you've placed her somewhere safe,' he smiled, and it was a bitter, humourless one, nothing more than a crooked gash against his face. 'I hope it's safe enough. I'd hate to see you fail her.'

'She's safe enough.'

Donziger listened to Marlowe, and cocked his head slightly, like a dog trying to understand something.

'Your accent's dropped.'

'I never really had one, if we're being honest,' Marlowe answered in his usual voice now. 'I felt I owed it to you to be transparent. I don't want you complaining at the end that I'd misled you.'

'What are you, MI5?' Donziger asked. 'MI6? Ex-service, perhaps? What does the British Government want by getting involved in this?'

Marlowe didn't answer. Instead, he pointed at the chip.

'Why the souvenir?' he asked. 'Seems a little odd.'

'My father gave it to me,' Donziger looked over to it, allowing the change in conversation. 'When I first started in finance, I asked for a loan, something to get me started. My father was a big name in the oil and gas industry, and I'd hoped for something substantial to help me begin, but all he did was give me this chip, a thousand lousy bucks, and tell me to bet it all on black.'

He half rose, leaning over the desk as he picked up the acrylic case now, turning it around in his hands, lost in the memory.

'I never cashed it in,' he breathed. 'I found other financiers, and I built up the firm without my father's help. And in time, I created all this.'

He looked up, making sure Marlowe understood what he was saying. And, seeing Marlowe still paying attention, he placed the chip back down on the table, sitting back in the chair as he continued, pulling a small squeeze bottle of antibacterial gel out, and squirting a little into his hands, wiping them with it as he spoke.

'It's a reminder,' he mused. 'To remind myself never to rely on others, to take their insults with grace, and wait until the right moment to strike. The casino that chip came from, all those years back, doesn't even exist anymore. The plastic is useless. But to me, it's worth everything.'

'And your father?'

'Never spoke to me after I became a success,' Donziger's eyes sparkled as he remembered. 'Mainly because I bought his company out from under him and asset stripped it in front of his eyes. I left him with a modicum of money, enough to say he'd done well, but I took his reason for getting up in the morning and threw it as far as I could from him.'

He chuckled.

'I even invested it in renewable energy. Built a wind farm and a solar field where his now dry oil rigs once stood. I seriously thought that'd be the thing that killed him. Still, he was never the same again. Had a heart attack a couple of years later. So sad.'

Marlowe didn't reply to this; he already hated this man with a vengeance, no matter how much he resonated with the story told.

'So, I'm a busy man, Brit spook, and I'm sure you have a message for me,' Donziger's expression cooled as he looked back at Marlowe. 'So, give it and let me get back to work.'

'You have a very important court case on Monday,' Marlowe rocked back on the chair, his feet now leaving the desk. 'I suggest you concentrate on winning it. Let the chips fall where they land. Don't try to take out the lawyer fighting you. If you do, you'll be facing me, and you've already seen how that goes.'

'That's the speech?' Donziger looked unimpressed. 'I expected more. Vasquez has jack shit on us. It's all smoke and mirrors, especially after the terrible accident with the witnesses.'

'Accident?'

'Gas explosion, wasn't it?' Donziger sneered, proving as far as Marlowe was concerned he had everything to do with it, and it had been no accident. 'Anyway, if she had something, she'd have asked for a pay-out before now.'

'Not if it's personal,' Marlowe suggested.

'Ah. You know why she's doing this,' Donziger leant forward now, interested. 'I'll give you ten grand, in cash, right now, if you tell me what her problem with me is.'

'Not my secret to give,' Marlowe shook his head. 'No deal.'

'Worth a try,' Donziger relaxed again. 'So, this was what, a warning? You come all this way to be the alpha male? Or is it more the white knight?'

Marlowe frowned at this, his brow furrowing as he tried to work out the angles. There was something wrong here. Donziger was too relaxed, too calm. There wasn't a panic button here, but Marlowe felt ...

'You're delaying me,' Marlowe rose from the chair. 'You're waiting for what, your security to come? They'd better be better than yesterday.'

Donziger waved around the room.

'Now how would I be able to call for help?' he asked innocently. 'You've been with me since I arrived.'

'Then you're delaying me because ...' Marlowe trailed off as a sick realisation took hold.

Seeing his expression, Donziger leant closer, smiling.

'Now you get it,' he said. 'How shall we begin this? Oh, I know. "*Hello, Mister Bond. I've been expecting you.*" But you're not James Bond, are you? You've got the look, the accent, but so far you're more like that – what's the name of the film with the guy from *Mister Bean*? When he's a shit secret agent? Oh yes. You're less James Bond, and more *Johnny English*.'

Marlowe looked out of the window, realising the truth, that right now, someone was heading to Rehbein and Pope, and Roxanne Vasquez *wasn't* being guarded.

'You think I didn't know you were here?' Donziger rose to match Marlowe now, venom spitting from his lips. 'I knew the moment "Marshal Garner" appeared downstairs. And when we found the piece of tape on the camera, we knew you were in. We just didn't know where. The man you met with the pink tie. He's my son, Cody. He was there to guide you here, to sit you down and make you wait for me, distract you with meaningless crap conversation while I sent my hounds out to hunt.'

Marlowe could feel his world spinning. He had to force his mind to relax, to quieten while he worked out what to do next.

'If you touch Roxanne; if you try to take her—'

'You'll what, kill me?' Donziger held his hands out. 'Go on. Do it. I'm sure you're armed. I won't be taking her this time, though, I'll be removing her.'

He mimed a knife across the throat as he said this, emphasising it with a *crrrrkkkttt* noise, before leaning his hands upon the glass desk, watching Marlowe with a vicious glee as he continued.

'We wanted her last night, because I wanted to know how much she knew, how much her father had told her. Yes, I know it was Brett Hendricks. And the fact he'd taken files from me was well known. I'd hoped they burned up in the fire, but apparently not. I needed to know what she was using against me, so the plan was to get it out of her. And then you turned up and did it for me.'

'I did nothing of the sort—'

'*Of course, you did!*' Donziger bellowed, interrupting Marlowe. 'You took her off the grid! You sent her to Rehbein and Pope to gain all the information she'd need on Monday, right? All that vital information, all on something portable, all on one external drive. And now, all my woman has to do is take it when she kills your pretty little lawyer.'

'How do you know she's there?' Marlowe flailed now, knowing the answer. Donziger probably owned half of Rehbein and Pope by now.

The receptionist.

The people in her office.

Anyone could have been the mole.

He started for the door.

'Security has been alerted to your presence, but don't worry, they'll be letting you pass,' Donziger laughed now. 'I told them you'll probably be leaving at a run. It's a good ten minutes from here in traffic, and I sent my hound out to hunt about … oh, yeah. Ten minutes ago.'

Marlowe had a final line, a last insult to shout at Donziger, but he didn't say it as he ran from the room. He didn't have the time to stop, to say the line and leave. He was already behind.

Getting into the elevator, he pulled off his hoodie, tossing it to the side as he pulled the pea coat out of his bag, throwing it on. He couldn't breathe, his heart was hammering—

You got played. Suck it up. Fix the mess.

Marlowe pulled the phone Trix had given him out of the jacket pocket as the elevator reached the lobby. As he ran out, noting the security guards standing to the side, idly watching him with no curiosity on their faces, he made a choice, dialling the one number in it. The phone had been sent before Marlowe had told Trix about Brad lying to him, and therefore, the number in it could only be that of Brad Haynes.

'Hi, this is Brad,' the voicemail message spoke. 'Leave a message.'

'It's me,' Marlowe said as he ran onto the outside pavement, looking for a cab. The one-way street was heading south, though, and he needed to go north. 'I don't know which team you're playing for at the moment, but if you're currently watching Roxanne and you *are* genuine, you need to get to her right now. A killer is on her way and I'm ten minutes from you.'

He disconnected, looking around.

'*Dammit!*' he shouted angrily, before heading north at a run. It was just over a mile from the office, and Donziger had been right about the traffic. But he could run a mile in six minutes easily, so he made the calculated guess it'd be quicker to run.

Marlowe dialled another number as he started – the main number for Rehbein and Pope.

It was engaged.

Marlowe quickened his pace, hoping to God that Brad Haynes was not only on his side still, but close enough to help.

Because, if he wasn't, then everything was over.

13

HOSTILE TAKEOVER

MARLOWE REACHED THE OFFICES OF REHBEIN AND POPE AT A sprint in just over five minutes.

It wasn't a personal best, but at the same time he hadn't run through the streets of Manhattan with a half-filled duffle bag over his shoulder before. Surprisingly, it wasn't anywhere near the same kind of run as a comfortable Saturday morning Parkrun, or a treadmill session at the gym. Not that he did those much, but it still made the point, and Marlowe decided on a mental note that, if he survived this, he'd start training with weights and distractions. After all, when he did deep water training, he had to pick up items from the bottom of a swimming pool with his hands and feet tied.

Of course, that didn't help him right now.

As he ran through the doors, he saw the guards at reception, the same ones he'd seen the last time, but over at the elevators, Hank the guard was strangely missing from his post.

'Where's Hank?' Marlowe asked, looking around. The

female security guard closest to him, still behind the reception desk, followed his gaze.

'He was here a moment back,' she said. 'He was speaking to a woman, and then a man came by—'

Marlowe held up a hand, stopping her, noting the word *woman*, and remembering his conversation with Nathan Donziger.

'And now, all my woman has to do is take it when she kills your pretty little lawyer.'

'Call Rehbein and Pope!' Marlowe cried. He didn't wait for any more information, instead running for the gates, vaulting over them as he saw, against the far elevator and out of sight to the lobby, the downed figure of Hank, his neck flowing crimson with a vicious wound to the throat.

'Call an ambulance!' Marlowe shouted back into the lobby. 'Man down!'

Using a military term galvanised the other guards into action, and the female guard who'd spoken to him ran over, to see if she could help, paling when she saw Hank.

'Is he dead?' she whispered.

'No, they nicked the throat, but not the artery,' Marlowe was checking as he spoke. 'He's alive, but he's lost a lot of blood. Here, place your hand on it, put pressure on the wound.'

The guard did this, watching Marlowe draw his Glock, already pressing the elevator button.

'What are you doing?' she asked.

'I'm going to find and kill the woman who did this, before she kills Roxanne Vasquez,' Marlowe hissed, already entering the elevator before the doors fully opened. 'Keep him alive.'

ROXANNE HAD BEEN WORKING IN HER OFFICE WHEN THE gunfire rang out.

She'd managed to pretty much upload everything she needed onto a small and rugged external drive, one of those "travel ready" ones with the orange neoprene outer skin, in case she accidentally dropped it off a roof or something – she didn't know why she'd do that, but the adverts for the drives seemed convinced that was what happened to these – and was closing up the laptop when the screams echoed down the corridor.

Marlowe wasn't here to help, was the first thought, followed by the rather more morbid *they're here for you.*

Quickly disconnecting her laptop, and throwing it into her bag alongside the external USB drive, she frantically rummaged through the other things inside it until she found the can of pepper spray Marlowe had passed her earlier that morning. It wasn't much, but at least she had something if they came for her.

Which they were literally doing right now.

Another gunshot, another scream, and this time, the sounds were getting closer. Roxanne looked around the office, wondering if there was anywhere she could hide, maybe under the table—

The door to the office smashed open, and a middle-aged man stood there smiling, a small revolver in his hand. He was stocky, and his peppered hair was in a buzz cut, giving him the air of someone military.

'Miss Vasquez,' he said.

Roxanne raised the pepper spray, waving it at him.

'Back off, mister, or I'll give you a dose of this,' she called out, sounding way more confident than she actually was.

The man simply chuckled, raising his gun.

'Your spray has an effective range of about three feet,' he said, waving his gun at the nine feet of space between them, before aiming it at her face. 'While this can kill you easily from here. Do you have the external drive?'

'You work for Donziger?' Roxanne was suspicious as, in the background, she heard another scream.

'I ask the questions,' the man continued, boring of the conversation. 'You can die, or I can take you with me. Which would you prefer?'

Reluctantly, Roxanne lowered the can of pepper spray and started towards him. She knew this was the cowards way out, and that Marlowe would have fought rather than give up, but there was a part of her mind, a survival instinct that whispered *if she went with the man, she'd stay alive longer for Marlowe to find and rescue her.*

'And your bag, with the information in it,' the buzz-cut man waggled his revolver, stopping her. 'Time is of the essence, after all.'

THE FIRST THING MARLOWE SAW AS HE ENTERED THE LOBBY OF Rehbein and Pope was the blood on the reception desk.

The second thing he saw was a woman, in her twenties, her black pant-suit bulky, likely hiding a a ballistic vest and a weapon or two – nothing major though, as she would have had to get through the lobby without suspicion, but enough to take down Hank. She stood down the corridor, facing an office, a pistol in hand - a scream from within cut short as she fired twice.

The woman looked back at him, ducking his first shot and raising her gun to shoot back at him, but Marlowe had the element of surprise and speed in his favour, and before she could pull the trigger, he'd made the distance between them, and slammed into her as they spun across the floor, locked in combat.

She broke free and sprang to her feet, a vicious little serrated blade push dirk in hand. She stabbed at Marlowe, who stopped the blow with a forearm block, then spun away from a followup wide backslash.

He tried to sweep the leg, but she was ready for this, allowing her momentum to send her into a roll over it, coming back up closer to him as she moved once more – but the sweep had been a feint, and Marlowe now grabbed her arm, the blade extended, twisting as he held onto it, pulling it over his shoulder and then, using the momentum of the move, bending forward, throwing her bodily over his shoulder and onto the floor. But she still moved in, stabbing and swinging and finally caught Marlowe hard on his arm, drawing a line of blood before he grabbed her, throwing her heavily against an office door, sending her off her feet as it crashed open behind her, the lock breaking as she fell through it.

The room was empty, and Marlowe was glad for this. He looked for his gun, fallen in the fight but couldn't see it as the woman, now back on her feet kicked out, catching him hard in the gut, sending him staggering backwards before she tossed aside the blade and, grabbing at her ankle, pulled another small gun from it.

Marlowe dived behind the desk, pulling it with him, the computer monitor falling to the floor as the bullets hammered into it, thanking whoever was watching over him they hadn't scrimped on the furniture, and had desks with solid tops rather than simple chipboard, which likely wouldn't have stopped anything.

The woman had emptied the clip in quick succession, though, but as she went to check on the assumed dead body behind, she found nothing there. This was because Marlowe had moved in the other direction and, grabbing the T-hilted blade from the carpet as he did so, he ran across the room before she could click a new clip into the gun, using the over-turned lip of the desk to gain speed and height as he rose, and then slammed down into the woman, the blade stabbing into her throat with the force of a gravity-enabled punch.

As she staggered back, blood gushing from the open wound, her eyes open, Marlowe took a moment to gather his breath.

'Are you alone?' he asked.

The woman, wide-eyed and dying, didn't answer as she fell to the floor.

'This is your last chance to do the right thing,' he said to her, staring into her eyes. 'You're dying. You'll bleed out before anyone gets to you, and your secrets don't save anyone. Did Donziger send more than one of you?'

The woman didn't speak, just gurgling weakly as she nodded.

'... man ...' she whispered, and then her eyes unfocused, no longer staring at Marlowe as the life left her body.

Marlowe stared out of the doorway of the office.

There was another out there.

'Shit,' he said, running back into the corridor and grabbing his gun.

THE MAN WITH THE BUZZ CUT AND THE GUN STOOD BEHIND Roxanne as they walked hurriedly along the corridor.

'Did Donziger send you?' she asked, trying to get something out of him. 'Did he tell you to bring me or kill me?'

The man said nothing, a hand on her shoulder halting her as he listened.

'He's here,' he whispered. 'Wait. You say a word, you die.'

Roxanne felt a tremor of fear run down her spine as she stared up the corridor. She could see through the window of one office, and there was a body, a woman's, on the floor. She couldn't see a face, and she didn't know if she knew the victim or not, but there was a good chance she did, and now they were dead because of her.

I should have listened to Marlowe, she thought to herself. *I should have taken a gun rather than a can of pepper spray.*

There was a right-hand turn off, halfway down the corridor, and Roxanne could hear hurried footsteps down it, heavy steps that were probably from someone large, maybe male.

She went to back away, but the hand on her shoulder gripped tight, and she felt, rather than saw the barrel of the revolver to her right-hand side as the man, using her as a shield was moving to the right for a better aim.

There was a shadow on the floor before the walker appeared, and a second later, Marlowe, covered in blood, emerged into the corridor, gun in his hand.

He turned to face Roxanne and the man, his face paling as he saw the man's face for the first time.

And as he did so, Roxanne realised he knew the man who currently held her.

'You—' he started, raising his gun, but that was as far as he got, before the man raised his own gun in response, and fired three shots down the corridor in quick succession.

MARLOWE WAS TIRED, SORE AND ANGRY AT HIMSELF FOR throwing Roxanne into this situation. He'd killed the woman Donziger had sent after her, but now there was another out there, and he didn't know who this man was, or where this man could be.

However, as he walked into a T-junction corridor, he heard a sound to his left, preceded by a slight gasp. Turning to face Roxanne, he saw Brad Haynes behind her, as if using her as a human shield, Smith and Wesson Model 19 Carry revolver in his hand.

He didn't know if Brad was here because of him, or whether Brad was the other man, the one the dying assassin had named, but he sure as hell wasn't going to waste time asking, and brought his gun up.

'You—' he started, but stopped as Brad's gun rose quicker and more determined, with Brad firing three times.

Marlowe threw himself to the side, landing hard against the wall facing him. He almost went to fire back, but realised as he rose back up that Brad hadn't caught him with a single bullet.

There was no way he'd missed that many times.

Marlowe heard a thud behind him and turned to see a man, slim with short white hair, a suppressed pistol in his hand, and three bullet wounds to his chest now lying dead on the floor.

'He came out behind you,' Brad explained, lowering the gun. 'Didn't have time to warn you.'

'Thanks,' Marlowe rubbed at his shoulder. 'I took out the woman, so I think that's all of them. Body count?'

'Receptionist made it out, but there was an old man with those half-glasses who'd been shot when they entered,' Brad said. 'The receptionist tried to give CPR, but he bled all over the desk. I didn't see anyone else.'

'There's a woman in an office who's dead,' Marlowe was already hearing the faint sounds of police sirens in the distance. 'They took out the elevator guard, too.'

'Get a photo?'

Marlowe shook his head.

'Wanted to check on Roxanne,' he said, nodding to her now. 'You okay?'

'This man's with you?' Roxanne pulled away from Brad now, glaring at him. 'I thought he was here to kill me! He pulled a gun on me! Told me he wanted to kill me!'

'In fairness, you had a can of mace aimed at me,' Brad replied. 'It was the easiest way to get you out. And I didn't say I wanted to kill you, I gave you a choice. I said you could die, or I could take you with me.'

He pointed at the dead, white-haired man.

'If you'd stayed, *he* would have got you. Or the other killer. Marlowe could have screwed up and been killed by her.'

'Thanks.'

'Just saying. You're a Brit. You don't enjoy fighting women.'

'I was happy to fight that one. She was vicious,' Marlowe looked around, working out his next steps. 'Anyway, they're both dead, but Donziger will watch the building. He'll be looking for us leaving. And, after the mess in the lobby and the gunshots here, the police will be all over the place.'

'You got an idea?'

Marlowe nodded, looking back at Roxanne.

'Take off the jacket,' he said.

'But it's a DKNY,' Roxanne protested. 'And I only just got it back!'

'And you'll get it back again later,' Marlowe looked at Brad. 'I didn't see the receptionist?'

'Hiding in the stationery cupboard, where I told him to go,' Brad pointed down the corridor. 'I think he was still trying to give the poor dead bastard CPR in there. You need a diversion?'

'Yes. Go get the receptionist, and I'll be right back.'

Marlowe ran back down the corridor, entering the room with the dead female assassin. Turning the body over, he pulled out the phone, taking a shot of her face, before rummaging through her pockets. As expected, she had nothing to say who she was, where she worked, not even a set of apartment keys, just ammunition and a second blade, luckily one she'd not thought to pull out, relying on the gun in her ankle holster.

This done, he rose, picking up an olive-coloured winter coat that was hanging on the door, holding it as he ran back to the reception area.

An unhappy receptionist was staring at him as he arrived, currently wearing Roxanne's coat.

'I'm not happy about this,' he said as Marlowe passed Roxanne the olive-coloured one.

'I know, but it's for the greater good,' Marlowe replied, pulling the hood up over the receptionist's head as he looked back at Brad. 'Take Roxanne out of the back entrance with the other office workers. I'm going out the front with—'

He looked at the receptionist. He didn't know his name.

'Ezra,' the receptionist muttered.

'I'll go out front with Ezra, get in a cab and drive around for half an hour,' Marlowe continued. 'Anyone following will see me and a face-hidden companion and assume it's Roxanne. After we lose any tails, Ezra can return, no longer pretending, and you guys can go back to the Madison and the suite in my name.'

Roxanne glanced at Marlowe, but he gave a subtle shake of the head. She was clever enough to understand what was going on, and nodded.

'Okay, let's go,' she said, glancing out of the window. 'There's a hell of a crowd out there.'

'One moment,' Marlowe pulled Brad away from the others.

'I don't know what your problem is with me—' the CIA operative started moodily, but Marlowe held a finger to stop him, leaning in as he whispered.

'I know there's no "Uncle Danny" out there,' he said. 'I don't know what your gameplay is, but I know you've lied to me from the start. So, when we get out of this, if we're still alive, you and me are having a chat.'

This now said, he looked back at Ezra.

'We'll take the stairs,' he said.

THE GROUND FLOOR WAS CHAOS AS MARLOWE, HIS PEA COAT pulled in close to hide the bloodstains, walked out of the service entrance. He held his US Marshal ID up to get past the police at the barriers, noting with a little relief that Hank, his neck bandaged, was being placed in an ambulance outside.

Exiting the building with the crowds, Marlowe pulled Ezra in closer, keeping the hood up, making sure to anyone watching that he was leading someone away – someone who didn't want their face seen. Calling a cab, he bundled Ezra in, giving an address uptown as the car pulled off.

Now alone in the back seat, Marlowe looked at Ezra.

'Good job,' he said. 'I think we're being followed, too, so that's good for Roxanne.'

'Not good for us, though,' Ezra muttered.

'Nah, it's fine for you,' Marlowe smiled. 'Donziger doesn't kill his loyal workers, after all.'

Ezra tensed, and Marlowe leant in.

'There's no way you survived without knowing the killers,' he said. 'Or they knew not to kill you. Donziger told me he'd bought people's loyalty in Rehbein and Pope, and these spies kept him informed. You were in the perfect position to not only let him know when Roxanne arrived but also to let the assassins in at the moment they turned up. But there was a complication, wasn't there? Someone was with you when they came through the doors, and they had to kill him to keep your secret.'

'You're mad,' Ezra pulled back, staring in horror. 'I want to get out.'

'And you will, in ten minutes,' Marlowe smiled. 'And when you get out, I suggest you run. Because if I find out you were the one who informed – and believe me, when I tell you I know people who can and *will* find this out – on Roxanne's arrival, that caused those deaths, I will come find you and *kill* you. And while I'm hunting you, I'll also let Donziger know the only reason he failed was because you were working with us. How do you think that'll play out for you?'

'He'll kill me,' Ezra said, his voice flat, his eyes wide and terrified, no longer pretending his innocence.

'So here are the rules,' Marlowe glanced out of the back window, making sure they were still being followed. 'You run. You tell Donziger, or whoever your contact there is, that I'm gunning for him, and I will not wait until the court case now. He's made it personal, so I'm going to kill *him* this weekend. And his dipshit son who thinks he's an extra in *Wall Street*. Leave them both as dead as Shaun Lord and Trey Atwood.'

'Who are they?'

'Don't you worry. Just tell him the names. And then, once you've done that, you pack your bags and get the hell out of New York. Because once Donziger's finished? *I'm coming for you.*'

Marlowe tapped the window, dividing the driver and passengers.

'Can you pull over quickly?' he asked. 'My companion is feeling sick.'

As the cab pulled to the sidewalk, Marlowe leant over Ezra, opening the door for him.

'And take off the damned coat,' he said. 'You don't deserve it.'

Now feeling the cold and dressed in only his shirt and tie, Ezra stared at Marlowe as he closed the door, telling the cab driver to carry on. And, as Marlowe watched out of the back window, he saw the car following pull over, likely hoping to find out what the hell was going on.

Marlowe leant back on the seat. The most Ezra could give them was that Marlowe had mentioned the Madison, a hotel the other end of Manhattan. With luck, that'd give them some time.

But staying alive for the weekend wouldn't be easy. He needed a new plan.

Luckily, he had the start of one brewing.

'Actually, can you make a stop near Madison Square Garden?' he asked through the small grille. 'I have something I need to sort out in an Irish bar near there.'

14

HOME TRUTHS

Marlowe had spent another ten minutes in the cab after stopping at the Irish bar, asking the driver to wait. Dermot hadn't been in, and the bar had just opened, but Marlowe had dropped a message, and the woman manning the bar had said Dermot would be in for the evening shift, so there was still time, if needed. After that, he'd had the cab take him to the hotel he'd originally arrived at with Trix, what felt like days ago, but was actually less than twenty-four hours before.

Paying in cash, Marlowe stepped onto the pavement, hugging his pea coat around him. Not to hide the blood, although that was a definite advantage, but because there was a biting wind now blowing through Manhattan.

Marlowe looked at his watch; it'd been about an hour since they'd left the offices of Rehbein and Pope, and in that time, although Marlowe had taken Ezra and the Donziger watchers on a tour of Manhattan, he'd hoped Brad had understood the message and brought Roxanne back here, to the suite Brad had originally placed in Marlowe's fake name.

He still had the room key in his wallet, so he entered quickly, keeping his head down.

However, as he walked across the lobby, the concierge, seeing him, waved his hand.

'Mister Garner?' he called, using the name Marlowe had been booked under. 'Sorry, but I have a message left for you. I was told it was very urgent.'

Marlowe walked over, expecting it to be from Trix or Brad, saying they'd moved locations, but instead, it was from a very surprising source. Taking the note and dropping the concierge a twenty-dollar bill for his trouble, Marlowe read it.

Nice little game with the number – I didn't indulge in her expertise though.

Marlowe chuckled to himself, imagining the awkwardness of the call as he continued to read.

You're about to need my help. I'm happy to do so for a price. A cease of all activities against us. Call the number when you realise you've been screwed. I can get you ears of power. T.H

T.H. Trisha Hawkins.

Marlowe looked around the hotel lobby, but he knew Trisha wasn't stupid enough to wait around. She'd probably learnt the name he gave at the party and called every hotel – or, rather, got someone else to call every hotel – until she found him.

What did she know, though? This was a message given with serious advance knowledge.

'When was this dropped?' Marlowe asked.

The concierge checked his watch, and Marlowe could see from it that it was almost twelve-thirty in the afternoon.

'About fifteen minutes ago,' he said. 'A lady in her thirties. I offered to call your room, but she said you weren't there, but were likely to return soon. So, I held on, in case I saw you. Oh, and she gave me this.'

He passed over a business card. On it was a telephone number. There was nothing else written. No name, no company, just the number. Trisha was returning the favour, it seemed. Marlowe just hoped it went somewhere useful, and she wasn't just offering him an escort as well.

'It's appreciated,' Marlowe held up the folded note and card, and then with a last nod to the concierge, walked over to the elevators. Trisha Hawkins not only knew he wasn't in the room but also when he was likely to return. He didn't know whether to be flattered at the attention, or concerned at the creepiness. He decided it was a question for later, though, as the elevators opened and he walked in.

First, he had to sort out another issue.

ROXANNE WAS IN THE MAIN ROOM OF THE SUITE WHEN Marlowe entered, Brad talking to Trix at her bank of computers.

'I thought you were dead,' she said, rising with relief. 'I thought they'd got you. How's Ezra?'

Last I saw, he was getting into a Donziger car and probably telling them to stake out the Madison,' Marlowe replied, walking over to the minibar and pulling out a small can of Sprite. 'Sorry, but he worked for the bad guys.'

'That's why he said Madison instead of here,' Brad explained to Roxanne. 'He knew we'd know to come here, especially as he never said to us where he hid you last night—'

'Do you blame me?' Marlowe didn't mean to, it was an unconscious movement, but his hand rested on the grip of his revolver as he replied. 'I think you and I may need to have a talk.'

'I don't know what your problem is with me, Marlowe, but I don't appreciate it,' Brad snapped back, noticing the movement, and adjusting his position in the room, likely to move back and use Roxanne as a shield if things went south.

'Porn Star Martinis,' Marlowe spoke quietly now.

At this, Brad frowned.

'What?'

'Porn Star Martinis,' Marlowe continued. 'It's what you told me to take to Roxanne, in the party. Something she knew well that'd instantly get me close. A drink, however, which isn't in her records, and isn't known by anybody apart from her uncle, who told you, according to ... oh yes, *you*.'

Brad shifted on his feet. Marlowe pressed on.

'An uncle that doesn't exist. But you knew that already.'

'I dunno, maybe I must've read it in the file,' Brad suggested.

'I've read the file too,' Marlowe snapped. 'Trix passed it to me. There's no mention at all about porn star martinis, in fact, there's nothing at all about her entire time at university. The only way you would know her favourite drink is if you'd spoken to somebody who knew that she drank them. And that sure as hell wasn't her "Uncle Danny" because he didn't exist. Which either means you believed there was, and someone played you, or you decided to lie about it, and play both of us.'

Marlowe waved at Trix as he spoke, and she turned to watch the conversation.

'How can we trust anything you say?' Marlowe finished. 'How do we know you're not playing us and working for Donziger?'

Brad stared opened mouthed at Marlowe for the briefest of moments, and then looked away, nodding.

'I knew about the drink because I spoke to her dad,' he said.

'What do you mean, you spoke to my father?' Roxanne, hearing this, spun to face Brad now. 'My father died years ago.'

'I know,' Brad sighed, walking over to a chair and slumping into it. 'I was dealing with him before he died. '

'He was an asset,' Marlowe was understanding now.

At this, Brad simply nodded, leaning forward on the sofa as he explained.

'It was after he was fired. Brett was angry, and he had information that could be used,' he began. 'I was working on something similar for the CIA, in relation to some senators that were working with Donziger.'

'Working with or owned by?' Roxanne's tone was icy.

'What's the difference?' Brad made a weak attempt at a smile, but then thought better of it. 'They'd been compromised, and we knew this was an issue for Washington and Capitol Hill, going forward with them. We had concerns about security leaks, and then Brett turned up with a ton of information for us.'

'He was working for the CIA?'

Brad nodded.

'He had one stipulation to the deal, and that was you and your mom were looked after and kept safe, no matter what happened to him. He wasn't a fool, he knew he was playing with live ammo here. And as we saw what he had, we knew Donziger would kill anyone who saw this. He wanted to go into witness protection, start a new life—'

'Why didn't he tell me this?' Roxanne interrupted, her voice tight and coiled, holding back the urge to shout, to scream.

At this, however, Brad rose to face her, and his face was bitter as he spoke.

'He tried to,' he said. 'He told me he'd come to see you in Stanford, and that you wouldn't speak to him.'

Marlowe looked at Roxanne, remembering her story from the previous night. Brad, not noticing this, continued.

'He wasn't happy with the way things had ended, that he hadn't seen you grow up. And your mom, well, he knew he treated her bad. He knew the divorce hadn't helped, but when he came to you, he realised you were angry at him for the wrong reasons.'

'I thought he needed an ally to fight Donziger,' Roxanne, slowly realising the truth here, whispered.

'No, it was because he needed you to understand what he was about to do,' Brad replied. 'That all this was done for you, and for his estranged family.'

'All he had to do was tell me—'

'He wanted to,' Brad held up a hand to pause her. 'But he couldn't because he was working with us and I was his handler. I told him before he even got on the flight to see you he couldn't tell you the truth. He told me afterwards he'd spent a night with you drinking Porn Star Martinis, as he tried to explain his plans, without actually telling you them. But you saw these plans purely as revenge rather than a chance to redeem himself.'

Brad looked at the hotel carpet.

'We worked for years on this, they gave Brett a new ID and he effectively joined the CIA, working in Langley with me as we took out a few of the corrupt governors and Senators who Donziger owned. It was slow work though, as we knew the moment Capitol Hill heard what we'd been doing, we'd be stopped. I was going through a messy divorce at the time, and he kept me sober.'

He looked up at Marlowe, his eyes haunted.

'He was like that, you see, always thinking of others first, I think it was his way of making up for what he'd done in the past. And then, a few years into our working relationship, he jumped into a flaming apartment block to save people, and died in the fire.'

'Donziger started that fire,' Roxanne was shaking her head now. 'He did this.'

'I don't know that, and I wish I could give you an answer,' Brad shrugged. 'I know it was an apartment that was connected to an asset of his, an old lady on the top floor, as I dropped him off there after we had a catchup. As I called for help, he ran in to save his asset, knowing that with her age and her mobility she couldn't get out in time, but the floor collapsed, and neither of them escaped. I disappeared before anyone turned up, as there no way a CIA operative standing outside a flaming building could be seen as anything but suspicious, especially with Brett under a fake name. *Daniel*.'

'Maybe—'

'No,' Brad knew what Roxanne was about to say, and

immediately shut her down. 'There was no faking of his death. No witness relocation. This wasn't some kind of clever CIA plan to keep him off the radar like we had for four years by then – he didn't live. There was nothing I could do about it, and for years I regretted the fact that I'd let him go into the fire ... that I hadn't helped him.'

'You'd have died too,' Trix, watching from the side, spoke.

'Maybe, maybe not. All I knew was I'd let him die, and then years later, a chance for me to redeem myself turned up, because I get the message his daughter is going to battle against the very man who wanted him dead.'

'Why didn't you use his information before this?' Marlowe asked.

'We never had it,' Brad turned to him now. 'Brett had hidden it. I didn't even know Roxanne had found it until she started the case for Jericho, and things were appearing in court requests, things only Brett had known. Of course, they stopped me from getting involved – the same Senators who worked for Donziger back then are still in power, so I knew if I did something, I had to do it on my own without backup. I just hoped people like you and Trix, Marlowe, people who had your own reasons for not trusting the CIA would come and help, and so I called you.'

Brad let out a long sigh, pursing his lips as he nodded to himself.

'And yes, I should've told you the truth, but I didn't because I was ashamed to tell you I'd known her father and let him die. What kind of person does that make me?'

'The same sort of person we all are,' Marlowe snapped back. 'You could've told me, Brad. You could have trusted me. What you *did* is make me think you were working for Donziger.'

He looked at Roxanne.

'If I'd had known this, we wouldn't have gone off grid, we wouldn't have had all these problems—'

'Guys,' Trix spoke now, watching the screen.

'I know! And I'm sorry! Can you trust me now to—'

'*Guys!*' Trix shouted, ending the conversation as both men turned to face her. 'Turn on the news, Channel Nine right now. You need to see this.'

Marlowe looked around, spying the television remote on a side cabinet. Walking over, he picked it up, turning on the television. As he clicked onto the channel Trix had requested, he saw a suited news anchor talking to the camera.

'—return to today's main story,' he said to the camera, caught in mid-flow. 'Donziger Industries have settled out of court for an undisclosed sum against the inhabitants of Jericho Falls.'

'No ...' Roxanne's face paled as, on the screen, obviously recorded footage of Nathan Donziger, his pink-tied son beside him, spoke at a hastily set up press conference.

'I'm very grateful to the people of Jericho Falls for allowing me to fix this inadequacy in proceedings,' Nathan said. 'The court case next week would've caused pain and stress, especially with Rehbein and Pope now grieving their own, who unfortunately were the victims of a domestic terror attack earlier on today.'

'Domestic terror?' Marlowe was fuming. 'It was his own people who killed them!'

On the screen, however, Nathan Donziger was continuing, having not heard Marlowe's outburst.

'Because of the violence that happened at Rehbein and Pope, we felt, with the tragic deaths and the personal losses that company has had, that it was only fair that we did not force them to go to trial for Jericho Falls at such a time, especially considering the conflict of interest they now have, and so we've offered a settlement that the people of Jericho Falls have accepted.'

'You traitorous *bastard!*' Roxanne went to throw a mug at the screen, but Marlowe quickly took it from her as Donziger continued.

'In the meantime, we apologise to anybody who has suffered in Jericho Falls. We weren't the people responsible, but we have a cause for guilt, having funded their actions. We promise to utilise our resources to make a better situation for the town, and we apologise and offer our sincere condolences to anybody who was affected by the terrible domestic terror attack earlier on today—'

'Why does he keep calling it a domestic terror attack?' Roxanne was shaking now. 'How can he be so sure? And what does he mean by "conflict of interest" there?'

Trix looked up from her screen, where she'd been reading a news board thread.

'They're saying that somebody from Jericho Falls came into the Rehbein and Pope offices today and shot it up,' she explained. 'They're saying Rehbein and Pope had been accused of trying to settle for way less, and someone didn't like it, that they didn't give due care to the Jericho Falls citizens who were killed a few days back, with the three FBI agents. The conflict was relating to your company being attacked by the very people they were defending.'

She looked at Marlowe now.

'They're on a manhunt now for two people, one of which is pretending to be a US Marshal, name unknown.'

'No, this can't be right, they wouldn't do this ...' Roxanne was shaking her head, backing away as she stared in horror at the now muted screen, now showing b-roll footage of the police outside the offices of Rehbein and Pope. 'There's no way they agreed a deal that quickly unless they'd already started talking. It's been what, an hour? No goddamned way!'

'Roxanne, they lost their own,' Marlowe said as Roxanne walked to her bag, now rummaging inside it. 'At least two people died I know of. I don't even know who they were. There was a guy with half glasses who was killed beside Ezra, and there was—'

'Oh my God,' phone in hand, Roxanne shook her head. 'Half glasses? That's Sebastian Pope, one of the founders.'

She had been tapping on the phone as she spoke, and now she held it to her ear as she waited for it to connect.

'Joanne, it's Roxanne. I need to—'

She paused.

'Yeah, sure I'll hold.'

'What's going on?' It was Brad who asked the question on everyone's lips.

'I'm on hold for one of the junior partners,' Roxanne looked sick. 'They said they needed to speak to me. I ... hello, yes, yes, this is Roxanne ...'

Roxanne listened to whoever was on the other end of the line for a long moment.

'But I don't understand ... okay, no, of course I didn't want this to happen,' she carried on. 'Please send my condolences—'

Her face angered, however, as something else was said.

'Goddammit, Peter, you can't do this!' she exclaimed down the phone. 'We could've taken them for *billions!* You saw what *Info Wars* lost! We had everything on Donziger and we had the information to take them down, we could've—'

She stopped, tears filling her eyes.

'You goddamned coward, Peter,' she snapped. 'You all took the deal before this happened. You know they came for me. You're covering your own asses—'

She stopped, staring at the phone, the call now disconnected.

'I take it the phone call wasn't a good one,' Marlowe commented.

'Donziger made a settlement for fifty million, and those cowards accepted it,' she sighed. 'That's nothing – that's the *coffee money* Donziger spends a year.'

She looked around the suite, realising the gravity of the situation.

'I've got nothing,' she said. 'They've won. Donziger said they had proof from Washington I'd been looking into them way before I spoke to Jericho Falls. They said it was deliberate and personal, connected to the firing and death of my late father, and that I had a harassment case about to be placed against me, unless I was removed from the company and the information I'd stolen illegally was returned.'

'Stolen illegally? You mean the paperwork your dad left you?'

'Yeah. But they couldn't do that, because I moved it all to the drive in my bag, and when I pulled the drive out during the attack, I'd corrupted the source file there,' Roxanne looked like she was about to laugh or cry, but couldn't yet decide which. 'So ... they just fired me.'

'You don't have nothing,' Marlowe walked over to her now. 'You've got an external drive filled with information. That's information on Donziger, smoking bullets that can be used. Go to the press, get it out there and people will pick up on it.'

'Give me the drive and I'll make damn sure it gets out

there,' Trix winked. 'I have enough favours owed with people who can get shit like this done.'

'He's not going to win,' Marlowe snarled. 'He attacked me, and I take that personally.'

He looked at Brad.

'There must be somebody who has power over him. What about the Senators?'

'Senator Kyle,' Brad thought for a moment. 'She's been with Donziger the longest, and not by choice, if you get my drift. If anybody's got information, she would.'

'And I have several pieces on her in my drive,' Roxanne, seeing a lifeline here, nodded eagerly. 'Maybe we can use that? She'll want to keep her own skin rather than risk anything for Donziger.'

'There's a few Senators funded by Donziger, and their loyalties can't be bought,' Brad added. 'Trust me, we know. However, if we make things tough enough for them to stay impartial, eventually they'll have to do something about this.'

'I've got something on Senator Kyle,' Trix was working on the computer, and from the logo at the top of the screen, looked to be deep in the White House network. Marlowe decided it was better not asking. 'You know I said the two guys Marlowe killed at the library were Secret Service? Well, it looks like they were part of Senator Kyle's security detail.'

'They came from Arizona?' Brad was surprised, but Trix shook her head.

'No, she's an Arizona Senator, but she's in New York at the moment for the weekend. In fact, there are several Senators in town for no reason. There's nothing political worthwhile going on, but their calendars are all booked for some kind of Saturday night gala event near the Donziger building.'

'He's bringing in the troops,' Marlowe nodded at this. 'He

wants to make sure everything's sorted. Probably booked them before he knew he could pay off this case, but now he's just making sure they're on the same line.'

'Either way, Kyle has skin in the game and blood on her hands,' Brad growled. 'Her men are the ones that killed Trevor. I'm in.'

He looked at Marlowe; the gaze steeled and serious.

'I used a lie to get you in,' he explained, 'And for that I apologise. But my friend Danny I spoke about, the CIA agent who has a star in Langley ... Brett Hendricks was given the name Daniel Sutton when he joined the agency. I didn't lie about that. And he saved my life, every time he stopped me from falling into a bottle and ending things.'

Marlowe nodded. He understood how debts worked.

'We're good,' he said. 'Just trust us more next time.'

'So, what do we do now?' Roxanne asked, looking a little more hopeful now.

'Well, you're going to check your external drive's data with Trix and see if there's anything that we can use,' Marlowe nodded over at Trix, who nodded back. 'She speaks fluent *hacker*, so if anybody can find a way of using it, it'll be her.'

'But don't put it anywhere near that,' Trix pointed at the small grey box connected to the wall socket. 'It's an electro-magnet. It'd corrupt the drive.'

'Why do you have that here?' Roxanne was horrified.

Trix shrugged.

'If we're compromised, I'll be wiping this computer with it,' she replied. 'But to be honest, it's CIA tech. It probably doesn't work half the time, or at best it's dialled down so low it doesn't interfere with anything else in the room. Second-rate, shitty toys.'

Marlowe looked over at Brad now.

'What do you have for me, kid?'

'I need you to check your contacts, see if we can find out anything about this event tomorrow night,' Marlowe instructed. 'And I need to know if we're compromised.'

Brad went to reply again, but Marlowe shook his head.

'I'm not accusing you again, but someone hacked our comms last night, and I want to know how they did that,' he said. 'These were CIA-given earbuds. Someone had to give the frequency.'

'I'll get on it. And you?' Brad asked.

Marlowe remembered the note in his pocket.

'I'm going to speak to an old enemy, and see if I can make them my ally,' he said.

———

15

ENEMY OF MY FRENEMY

MARLOWE HAD DECIDED TO CALL TRISHA HAWKINS FROM somewhere public, and far from the hotel. He didn't know if she could backtrack anything, but it was enough of a risk as it was to bring her in, so he felt a little more secure doing it outside.

She answered on the third ring.

'I only gave this number to one person, so this had better be Tom Marlowe,' she said, her voice amused. 'I saw the news. I'm guessing you did as well?'

Marlowe bit back his first reply.

'You knew,' he said. 'You knew they'd settle. How long had that been arranged?'

'Longer than you've been hanging around with that pretty filly,' Trisha's voice was amused as she replied. 'Nathan had offered the amount before, but your firebrand kept stopping it. Now she's out, and one of the founders of the company was brutally shot down in a—'

'Don't say it,' Marlowe interrupted. 'I don't want to hear the words "domestic terror attack" again for a long time.'

'I was going to say, "badly botched assassination," but I'll agree to your terms,' Trisha purred. 'Either way, your woman could never win. When you're as rich as Nathan Donziger, you play for chips way larger than someone like you can ever imagine.'

Marlowe also bit back a reply to this, forcing his face to smile as he replied.

'You said to call when I was out of options, and I think you know I'm very close to that.'

'Oh, you think you still have options?' Trisha mocked. 'That's sweet.'

'I have a plan in mind,' Marlowe snapped. 'I didn't think Donziger was going to play fair, so I've been sorting out backups.'

'Killing him isn't a backup,' Trisha's voice wavered as wind hit the microphone; Marlowe could tell she'd walked into the open while talking to him. He couldn't help but wonder where she was going. 'Maybe you could use Karl Schnitter? You were looking for him the last time we spoke, after all.'

'And you know by now that was a ruse,' Marlowe didn't need to lie anymore – the chances were Trisha already knew where Karl was. 'I didn't know how you played into this. In fact, I still don't.'

There was a long pause on the line, and for a moment Marlowe wondered if the call had disconnected.

However, a moment later, she replied.

'I hate him.'

'Okay, I'm happy to hear more,' Marlowe smiled.

'His son, Cody, is a ... known commodity,' Trisha replied. 'He's a full-blown psycho. Runs security, has fingers in a dozen pies and doesn't play well with others.'

Marlowe considered this; Trisha Hawkins had worked with Francine Pearce when they created the mercenary heavy security force known as *Rattlestone*, and although this had been dismantled because of Government intervention, the new company, *Phoenix Industries,* was still connected into the same circles. If any of the Donziger brats felt Trisha was an interloper to their personal playground, Marlowe could understand why she'd feel this way.

'He's cost you work,' he spoke as a statement more than a question.

'You speak more like it's past tense,' Trisha replied. 'He's a constant bloody irritation, and that's why I want him stopped.'

'And that's why you want to help me take down Donziger?' Marlowe was suspicious of this.

'Oh, no, I don't give a shit about your argument with Nathan Donziger,' Trisha said coldly. 'I can work with him if I have to. I want Cody removed.'

'Trisha, I don't have time to—' Marlowe started, already regretting making the call.

'I can get you Senator Kyle,' Trisha interrupted, and this single statement froze Marlowe where he stood.

'What do you mean?'

'Exactly what I said. I know people close to the Senator, and I know where she is tomorrow evening. I can get you a one-on-one with her if that's what you want.'

Marlowe very much wanted that. If he could speak to the Senator, alone, with no one from Donziger there, he could work out what hold Donziger had on her. And it had to be something large, as she'd so far lost two of her secret agents to his cause.

'You mean the gala,' he said. 'Are you going?'

'I have an invitation, yes,' Trisha purred. 'Embossed card in my name, everything. Very secretive, very swish. So, do you want to speak to her or not?'

'I want, but I need to know what I'm selling to get it,' Marlowe replied cautiously.

'I told you, I want a truce,' Trisha said. 'I've already got rogue policemen and serial killers looking for me, the last I want is some MI5 assassin taking pot shots. And if you do what I ask you to, we all win.'

'How do you see that?'

'You help me, I kill Cody's chances of replacing Daddy,' Trisha explained. 'And I then get you in with Senator Kyle, and she ends Donziger for you.'

'And you sweep in and gain a bucket load of security contracts in the process,' Marlowe mocked. 'You must think I'm stupid.'

'No, I think you're desperate, and I'm offering you a life-line,' Trisha, obviously tiring of the conversation, retaliated. 'Cody has secrets hidden deep in one of the Donziger shell companies upstate. I need someone to break in and get them for me. You do that tonight, then I can provide you with a golden ticket tomorrow. You can have Donziger wrapped up like a Christmas turkey by Sunday. Sound good?'

Marlowe didn't really have an option here to say no, but there was a small part of his pride that wanted to argue this.

'If it's so simple, why haven't you done it yet?' he asked.

'I was planning to,' Trisha replied. 'But it's more fun when not only do you get the thing you want, but you're able to resolve another problem at the same time.'

Marlowe sighed. *She had a point.*

'Send me the information and we'll get—'

'Uh-uh,' Trisha interjected, and Marlowe could almost imagine her waggling her finger as she spoke. 'No "we" is happening here. I don't want anyone else involved. This is *our* deal. No burned out Americans, and definitely not Miss Preston, considering it was her revelations that gave up Francine in the first place.'

Marlowe winced. He'd forgotten the first time Pearce Associates had appeared on anyone's radar was when Trix, pretending to be an intern in a City of London police unit while secretly working for them had been caught altering the direction of a case, and forced to reveal everything she knew rather than go to prison. In the end she'd started working for Section D, another of Emilia Wintergreen's misfit toys, but probably just the sound of her name was enough to cause tantrums in Phoenix Industries, especially if Francine Pearce was alive and working there.

'Besides,' Trisha added. 'Trix Preston's fantastic with tech stuff, but Donziger's old school. He's completely analogue.'

'Notes and paper?'

'Files and paperwork, yeah,' Trisha agreed. 'So not as easy as hacking into a server farm, it's more making your way through a warehouse the size of an IKEA, with shelving either side, filled with boxes.'

'Do you have an idea where or even what the secrets are?'

'If I told you that, where would the fun be?' Marlowe was convinced Trisha was smiling as she replied, and it irritated him immensely. 'I'll send you what I have, to your New Yorker room, okay?'

Marlowe froze once more as she spoke. *She knew about the New Yorker Hotel.* This was a serious power play, a "see what I know about you" flex, and to be honest, it worked.

'Leave it in reception,' he said in return. 'If you try to be clever and break in, your asset might get a shock. I booby trapped a lot of things in there.'

'Good to know,' Trisha had gotten into a car, the wind in the background now muted. 'Go steal me something, Mister Marlowe. And in return, I'll be your Fairy Godmother and make all your dreams come true.'

'You can't make them all come true.'

'Oh? And why's that?'

'Because you'd still be alive.'

Marlowe disconnected before Trisha could reply and forced himself not to toss his phone across the floor. There wasn't much he could do here – she knew he was in a bind, and she knew he'd need her help. What was frustrating, however, was that she knew the problems before even Brad did.

They'd been playing on the back foot here, and Marlowe hated that.

Looking around the square of grass he'd used for the phone call, Marlowe considered his next steps. It was early afternoon now, and the sky was already darkening. Roxanne and Trix would be sifting through data from the drive by now, and Brad would hunt through his little black book. The only option was to return to the New Yorker, take stock of what he needed to do, and wait for Trisha's gift.

There was an unpleasant taste in his mouth, and he spat to the floor, apologising with a wave at an elderly lady around ten feet away, who muttered "disgusting" and walked off. She was right, but it had been a knee-jerk reaction. And Marlowe knew the foul taste was psychosomatic – he hated the fact he was now in league, or even possibly in debt, with Trisha Hawkins, the woman who'd almost caused his death.

He knew she'd try to screw him over at some point – scorpions always stung; it was in their nature. He also knew if he did this, if he found information to help her, he'd likely be held to account for the theft, most likely leaked by the woman herself, so now his task was twofold; he needed to break into some upstate archive, find some secret files that Donziger had hidden there and get them out, passing them to Trisha to use, while covering his tracks to the point there was no way he could be hit with this.

And if wishes were horses and all that, he thought to himself as he started south.

HE TOOK HIS TIME RETURNING TO THE HOTEL, AS HE WAS NOW very paranoid about who exactly was around him. He wasn't sure how Trisha had worked out his hotel room, but if he was brutally honest, he hadn't done the best job of keeping things secret. His Garth Fleming ID would have been shot to hell by now, with him having flown in that day, and the US Marshal Dexter Garner ID would have been flagged the moment he ran from the library event. If it hadn't been so early in the day when he returned, he might even have been taken in by FBI agents there and then.

Of course, that would have involved them being able to catch him.

He stopped at the Tick Tock Diner at the base of the hotel, once more grabbing a coffee inside as he watched the surrounding people. By the end of the breakfast rush the following day, there was supposed to be a meeting here between a now-dead assassin in West London and ... well, Marlowe wasn't sure. The one thing he knew for certain, however, was he intended to be there for it, no matter what happened.

Unless he was dead, or arrested by then.

Shaking the thought from his head, he walked into the hotel, checking with reception whether anything had arrived yet – it hadn't. And so, taking his room key out and using it on the elevator, he quickly and quietly travelled up to his suite, walking down the corridor and past the room before doubling back, a last chance at catching any final tails—

The hair wasn't there anymore.

Marlowe looked to the carpet; there was every opportunity it had simply dried and fallen off, or a gust of wind as someone passing knocked it aside, but it wasn't that common. In fact, in maybe the last fifty times he'd done this on a room door, he'd had the hair accidentally come off maybe four times.

Glancing both ways up and down the corridor to make sure he was alone, Marlowe crouched down, pretending to do up a lace as he examined the base of the door. He could see the hair, and it had fallen off the door – but it was also caught *under* the door now.

There was no way this could have happened without the door moving, the hair falling as the door opened in, and then sticking to it as it closed outwards once more. What it did mean was someone had been inside.

Rising, pulling his Glock 17 out as he did so, Marlowe took a long breath, allowing it to leave his body slowly as he counted to five, calming himself, preparing himself for whatever happened, as he placed the key card against the reader, seeing it turn green, the door unlocking as he grabbed the handle—

Marlowe moved in fast, his gun up and ready. He moved in low, hoping anyone trying to get a quick shot off would aim head height, shooting over him in the process.

Nobody did because nobody was aiming a gun at him.

The room was exactly as he'd left it, and by that he meant dishevelled and rough, but the coffee table had been cleared of items, except for one small glass, filled with a measure of what looked like scotch, or at least some kind of whisky. Beside it was a small bottle, from the minibar, and Marlowe spun, expecting someone to be waiting by the bedroom, but again, there was nobody there.

Slowly, Marlowe walked over to the glass, to see it had been placed onto a circular, white coaster, one of those paper ones that cafes and bars used; completely disposable, and mainly there to soak up spilt drink. Also, one that *wasn't* from the hotel room.

Removing the glass, Marlowe stared down at the coaster. It had the logo of a beer stein on it, confirming it wasn't from the hotel itself. However, as he picked it up carefully and examined it, he saw a simple message written on the other side.

Moriarty's Final House 7pm

Marlowe took a step back as he saw this.

'If you're still here, you'd better show yourself,' Marlowe spoke aloud now, spinning around in a circle, looking for anywhere someone could have hidden. But nobody revealed themselves. Nobody even answered him.

Marlowe stared at the note. It was obviously in code; they wanted the message to be for Marlowe's own eyes.

Marlowe pulled out his phone, opening a search engine. He wanted to google "Moriarty", but that was too obvious. He tried several other words and phrases, but apart from events and talks, none of which were soon, nothing appeared.

Eventually, Marlowe focused on the coaster, narrowing his range of vision, trying to think of words he missed.

Moriarty's Final House.

Moriarty's Final ... Problem.

In "The Final Problem", Moriarty died on the Reichenbach Falls.

So, with a quick look around the room in case he was being judged on his speed of solving, he typed in "Reichenbach NYC" to see what happened. And the first search result stood out above all others.

Reichenbach Hall – hearty German eats & fine beers

Marlowe almost laughed. Moriarty's final house would be *Reichenbach Hall.* He could almost envision it. And someone requested his presence there that night, in a restaurant only a few blocks from here.

He spun as the door to his room banged, but it was a knocking, rather than a violent crash. Walking over, keeping the gun out of sight, he opened the door to find a bellboy, an A4 manilla envelope in his hand.

'Arrived at the front desk, sir,' he said. 'Was told to pass it to you alone.'

Marlowe hid his gun, passing the bellboy a tip as he took the envelope, closing the door behind him and turning back to the room.

He didn't know what had happened while he was gone; if

someone had been in here, they could have left all manner of devices, all kinds of poisons and toxins.

Nodding to himself and grabbing his duffle, the only thing in this room he actually needed, Marlowe turned and left the suite, leaving his room ID card inside.

He wouldn't be coming back.

———

16

COMIC CHARACTERS

Marlowe kept to himself for the next couple of hours. He left a message with the others, telling them he'd found a solution, but it needed to be done alone and was likely keeping him out of the suite until early morning the following day, then went to find a coffee shop to read through the notes.

He hadn't told them he was working with Trisha Hawkins, or that some unknown prankster had been in his room; the first was so he didn't have to argue with anyone, but the latter was because he still didn't trust Brad completely, and there was every chance it'd been Brad himself in there having a root around, or someone alerted by him, who wanted to meet.

The paperwork Trisha had given him was simple, but detailed enough for what he needed. There was blackmail information on Cody Donziger in the file-filled warehouse, information kept by the father to ensure the son stayed on track, and this information was kept in New Rochelle, in Westchester. It was a county to the north of Manhattan, and about half an hour by car, especially at the time of night he intended to travel.

Of course, this meant he had to steal a car, but he felt that once he got out into the suburbs, this would be easy to do. Far easier than attempting to do it in Midtown, that was for sure.

The paperwork was light on what the blackmail information on Cody Donziger actually was, but having met Cody earlier that day, and knowing he'd been an integral part of his father's plan to screw Marlowe over, he held no concerns that he wasn't "doing the right thing" by finding and passing it on. From what he was reading here, Cody sounded like a piece of work, a coke-ravaged narcissist, living a life beyond his means, and relying on Daddy to bail him out whenever he got into some kind of shit too deep to crawl out of.

Marlowe hated him already, and now actively looked forward to not only finding this information but also screwing him over.

Of course, doing this meant helping Trisha, and he wasn't a fan of that, but he'd been in espionage long enough to know you picked your battles.

Sure, right now he was playing nice with both her and the people behind her, likely Francine Pearce in whatever new identity she was using, but there'd be a point, sooner rather than later, where the gloves would come off.

After all, she was likely working out how to screw him over the moment he gave her the information, so it was only fair he worked out his own details.

In fact, he was so engrossed in his plan, he almost missed his seven pm meeting, noting it was six-forty on the wall of the coffee shop when the waitress wandered over to let him know they were closing in twenty minutes. Thanking her and placing everything back into his backpack, Marlowe left quietly, pulling his pea coat's collar up against the wind outside, rushing to the Reichenbach Hall.

He'd originally intended to check the place out, and gain a rough idea of what to do, but it wasn't that large, and only had two exits, the front entrance and a back door that led out of the kitchen. It was pretty straightforward as meeting places went, and Marlowe had decided early on he wasn't going to spend too much time on planning.

Whoever this was, they could have killed him in the suite a dozen different ways rather than leaving him a message. This, to him, sounded more like an asset-gathering situation, with Marlowe as the asset.

Of course, although he knew this was likely to be that, he still didn't know who the contact was going to be.

As it was, the contact turned out to be a woman in her late thirties, red hair in a bob that had grown out of its style, a charcoal business-suit over a pale-blue blouse. She looked relaxed and confident as Marlowe entered the restaurant, a glass of red wine already in front of her. Seeing him enter, she gave a little wave at him, as if a woman seeing her date, and calling him over.

Forcing a smile, wondering how many others in the restaurant were there with her, and deciding the answer was *all of them*, Marlowe complied, opening his jacket as he did so. She looked Irish with the red hair; she had minimal makeup on and although she was attractive, she overdid nothing, revealing a woman who felt she didn't need to seduce to move ahead.

Or, she simply believed she was attractive enough without it.

'Tom, please, take a seat,' she said, nodding at the chair facing her. 'I haven't ordered yet, I wasn't sure if you'd be staying past the starter.'

Marlowe nodded, smiling again, taking his jacket off and placing it on the back of the chair. He didn't want to eat anything, even though his stomach was growling at the idea.

Whoever this woman was, if she controlled the restaurant dining area, she probably controlled the kitchen too, and that meant anything coming from it could be tainted.

'I don't think we've met,' he replied cordially as he sat, observing her. 'I'm guessing you're some kind of security service. You don't look corporate to me.'

'Oh?' the woman seemed surprised at the comment. 'Go on.'

Marlowe shrugged slightly, pointing at her jacket.

'Cut of the suit is a bit cheap,' he smiled. 'I've seen Midtown money, and corporate go for better. Government offices go for practical.'

'Fair point,' the woman conceded. 'My name is Sasha Bordeaux, and I'm—'

'Already lying to me,' Marlowe sighed. 'Sasha Bordeaux was a spy in DC Comics. She might still be. I'm not sure, as I don't read them anymore.'

'Grown up?'

'No time.'

'From what I hear, you have all the time in the world.'

Marlowe cocked his head slightly at the jibe.

'So why do the CIA want to meet with me here, of all places?'

'Why CIA?' Sasha gave an inquisitive look in response. 'I could be NSA.'

'True, but I'm hearing hints of an East Coast accent, I can see that you're university educated, and I'd say you're a Langley resident currently.'

'And how do you get there?' Sasha was almost amused by the deduction.

In return, Marlowe nodded at the suit she was wearing.

'Your suit,' he said. 'It's quite distinctive. I'd say you bought it in Tyson's Corner, the mall? It's not too far from McLean, where the CIA is based, and I know a few who shop there for ease.'

It was a guess, maybe a calculated one at that, but it was also a lie. Marlowe had only ever been to the George Bush Center for Intelligence in McLean, Virginia, once. Even though the building was better known in the trade as "Langley", one of the closest shopping areas had been Tyson's Corner. In fact, he'd met his contact in a Starbucks inside the shopping centre.

This was because his contact had been a Mossad agent who was currently infiltrating the building, but Marlowe wasn't about to admit this.

Sasha, or whatever her true name was, seemed impressed.

'Very nice,' she smiled. 'And you're right. We're quite the fan of yours in Langley.'

'Aw, shucks, you're making me blush,' Marlowe deadpanned. 'So, come on then, why are we here? Why all the cloak and dagger?'

Sasha shifted in her seat, leaning closer slightly.

'We picked Reichenbach Hall because of you,' she replied. 'We know you're a fan of Sherlock Holmes, and we thought this would be a nice little code for you to break. Also, if I'm honest? I wanted to see how quickly you'd do it.'

'What if I didn't arrive back at the hotel until tomorrow?'

'Then I would have been here tomorrow at seven instead.'

Marlowe nodded as he took in the new information. This

wasn't a simple code breaking game, in the way she suggested; this was a message. Although a fan of them as a child, he hadn't been a reader of Sherlock Holmes books for years. In fact, he barely considered the fictional detective.

For Sasha, and therefore the CIA, to say they knew he *was* a fan wasn't a mistake, it was a message, where they were saying "we know what you've been doing since your childhood. We have an extensive file on you."

'I don't know whether to be worried or flattered,' he eventually said.

'You should be flattered,' Sasha sipped at her wine. 'We don't spend time like this on anybody.'

She swirled the wine in the glass as she looked into it.

'You've been working with a friend of ours,' she said. 'Brad Haynes.'

'Friend? Don't you mean "employee", or am I missing something?' Marlowe replied, not answering the implied question.

'You've been using several of our legends recently,' Sasha continued, ignoring the question, still staring into the glass. 'A certain US Marshal, and a Mr Fleming, have both been popping up around New York.'

Marlowe hid his internal grimace. It seemed Brad hadn't been as cautious as he'd made out.

'What can I say? I felt coming here as me would cause ... problems,' he leant back on the wooden chair. 'Do I get a drink?'

Sasha looked up from the glass now, staring at Marlowe, and he knew she was trying to work out how much of this was stalling, and how much was simple stupidity, or some kind of professional arrogance on his part.

'As soon as these sightings started appearing, we knew

something was going on, and we looked into it,' she continued. 'Imagine our surprise, when we realise Thomas Marlowe, ex-MI5, turns out to be on our doorstep, running around and killing people regularly – all while using an established CIA legend.'

'There's a difference between killing people, and doing it in self-defence,' Marlowe raised a hand in protest. 'I think you know that just as well as I do.'

'True, but at the same time, we need to look into this,' Sasha replied, almost apologetically. 'You're burnt, after all.'

There was a long, uncomfortable pause after this comment. *Of course, she knows you're burnt,* Marlowe thought to himself. *They probably knew before you did.*

'You might think I spoke that as a threat,' Sasha continued. 'I didn't. We saw what happened, we read the notes, and I know you deliberately left your mother's name on a sleeper NOC list in order to give an innocent civilian a chance at a quiet and uneventful life. I actually applaud you for it. I also applaud you for not trying to make any political hay out of your selfless act of saving President McKay last year.'

Marlowe frowned. Sasha was being too nice. This was too comfortable.

'So, what is this, some kind of job interview?'

At this, Sasha grinned for the first time, but Marlowe still felt it was a smile more for "oh, well done, you worked it out" than of humour.

'You could say so,' she said. 'You do, after all, have no team to play for.'

'Just because I've not been picked by my team doesn't mean I'm looking for a new one,' Marlowe snapped, perhaps a little too sharply. The sting of being effectively fired by MI5 still burnt deep. 'Perhaps I enjoy being on my own.'

'On your own, on the run and marked for termination,' Sasha's smile had gone now. 'Watching constantly over your shoulder, so you don't get taken out by a foreign agency, while your own family put hits out on you.'

'I wouldn't really class Taylor as my family,' Marlowe tried to calm himself, feeling the anger brewing. 'He was more a sperm donor, and a reluctant one at that.'

Sasha made a little cock of her head, accepting the comment.

'You could come in from the cold.'

'You'd want a burnt, British spy?'

'Please don't play hard to get,' Sasha sighed. 'Self-deprecation doesn't become you, even though it's second nature to you Brits.'

Marlowe folded his arms, considering the words, and the unspoken implications of what the agent named after a DC Comics spy was insinuating.

'I wouldn't betray my country,' he said.

'Even though they betrayed you?' Sasha said, before holding her hand up, warding off a response. 'Don't worry, we're still all friends there. Special relationship and all that. But if you were looking to change your team colours, we'd need to talk about something.'

Here we go, Marlowe smiled to himself. *We had the carrot, now we get the stick.*

'If you're going to tell me to stop looking into Donziger, we're going to have a problem,' he replied coldly. 'That man deserves to be taken down. And, being brutally honest, he's attacked me frequently now. I think I'm within my rights to demand that he's removed.'

'Unfortunately for you, Mister Donziger is an ally to the CIA,' Tasha gave her most apologetic face as she spoke, but

Marlowe knew it was for show. 'And because of that, we can't let you continue this chaotic mission that you have with Agent Haynes.'

'At last, we get to the point,' Marlowe leant closer, elbows now on the table. He'd given up waiting for someone to come and take his drinks order, and so instead leant over and took a sip of Sasha's wine. 'Do you mind? Throat's a little dry, and I guessed of all the drinks in here, yours is likely to be the most un-doctored. If you have a problem with Brad Haynes, why let him get involved in this in the first place? He's one of your own. You should have stood him down.'

Sasha shifted uncomfortably, and Marlowe knew without a doubt it wasn't because he'd sipped her drink. She was irritated at Brad's actions. He'd gone off the grid, and they hadn't expected it.

'We thought Brad Haynes was professional enough not to let his personal side get into his business,' she replied slowly and carefully. 'We were wrong.'

'Damn right you were,' Marlowe saw a chink in the armour and started picking at it. 'But what he's done isn't immoral. He's helped people. And regardless of what you think of Donziger—'

'Let me get one thing perfectly clear here,' Sasha snapped, and her violent reaction almost toppled the wine glass before she caught it. 'I think Nathan Donziger is scum. I think even less of his Nazi shitwit child. I said he was an ally, not that we liked it. We know he was behind the deaths of three FBI agents. And when we're done with him, he'll swing for it.'

Marlowe mulled over the comment for a moment. *Here she was. Here was the real woman, regardless of whatever fake name she used.* There was a way here to get what he needed, but he had to be careful.

'Is his son an asset?'

'Cody? Christ, no. Stupid little cokehead's nothing but a liability—'

Sasha stopped, smiling.

'Ah, this is the favour you're doing for Hawkins, isn't it?' she shook her head. 'You'd get in bed with the woman who happily ordered your death, but not with us.'

'I know where I stand with her,' Marlowe shrugged. 'I know she'll try to betray me. I'm planning for it. You? Well, you might actually be on the level.'

Sasha stared at Marlowe and then pulled her phone out of a pocket. She tapped on it for a moment, composing and then sending a message, before looking back up at him.

'I get you're a white knight, and I get you hate leaving something unfinished, so I'll make you a deal,' she said. 'Anything that removes Cody Donziger, or causes him to be less than the shining light of his father's eye, is profitable to us. So, we'll help you find the information. Do you have an equipment list?'

Marlowe pulled his own phone out, opening a notepad app. He showed it to her.

She raised an eyebrow.

'I expected more.'

'I'm low maintenance.'

'We could have this with you within a day—'

'I go in two hours,' Marlowe stated. 'Class this as a test to see how much you want me.'

'We can do that,' Sasha reluctantly muttered as she stared once more at the list. 'But if we play for your team, you play for us ...'

'Brad.'

'Brad,' Sasha agreed. 'We can't have someone go off the reservation like that. We understand his history, but that doesn't excuse what he's done. He's an old dog, Mister Marlowe. He's had a good run guarding the farm, but now he's too far gone, and sometimes you just have to take him out back and—'

'If you say, "shoot him," I'm out of here,' Marlowe snapped.

'God no,' Sasha looked horrified. 'I was going to say, "take him somewhere quieter". Maybe a desk job, in a small, sleepy town, where nobody needs to worry about spies, and guns, and any of that. You know, where corporate temptation doesn't cause him a loyalty issue.'

Her face darkened.

'Basically, Thomas – can I call you Thomas? Basically, it's up to you. We can give you a future, one that keeps you safe from enemy agents, one that gives you purpose, even has you teaming up with old friends, although doing it from our side of the room. "Poacher turned gamekeeper", I believe you call it over there. But the payment for this is Brad Haynes. You do what you need to do, but by the end of this weekend, I want him in our custody.'

She sipped at her wine, letting the moment linger.

'And if it helps your peace of mind, consider this. How easy have you been to find since you allowed him to control your identities? How easy has it been to hack your comms?'

Marlowe clicked the roof of his mouth with his teeth. He knew this was likely a line given out purely to make him doubt Brad, but it was a good one, poking at thoughts he'd already considered.

'Do you know where the files are in the warehouse?' he asked in response.

'We do,' Sasha, sensing an agreement to her terms, smiled. 'But as it's analogue, we've never been able to find someone with enough plausible deniability to send in. Until now.'

'You'll want copies of whatever I find, I guess?'

'Of course. Oh, and there are a couple of additional files we'd like you to pick up. Things on Senators working with Donziger, just so we can check they've not been compromised. I'm sure you understand.'

'Then if that's it, we have a deal,' Marlowe nodded. 'One more thing though … do you know if there's anything in there that's detrimental to Trisha Hawkins?'

'Yes, we know there is,' Sasha frowned. 'I'm guessing you'd like that location too?'

'Oh, absolutely,' Marlowe smiled, rising from the table. 'Thanks for dinner. Really helped with my intermittent fasting. I'll be in contact.'

'I think you'll find we'll be the ones contacting you,' Sasha smiled back, her grin as faked as Marlowe's was. 'We have your number, don't you worry.'

Marlowe looked down at Sasha, now sipping at her wine again.

'My file,' he said. 'The one with my childhood love of Sherlock Holmes in it.'

'What about it?'

'It told you about DC Comics, didn't it?'

'We almost used Diana Prince,' Sasha replied. 'But we thought it was a little too on the nose.'

'No, Sasha suits you,' Marlowe turned from the table and

started towards the door. 'I wouldn't check her Wikipedia page, though.'

'No? Why?'

Marlowe stopped at the door and smiled.

'It didn't end well for her,' he said simply as he opened the door and left.

17

LIGHTLY SALTED

SASHA BORDEAUX MAY HAVE BEEN A FAKE NAME, BUT THE AGENT behind it was top-notch, Marlowe thought to himself as he sat in the Ford Mustang, staring across at a small New Rochelle warehouse through a newly gained sniper scope.

He'd received a message an hour after the meeting; there was a car park to the west of Central Park, and they had placed a vehicle for him to use. The key was on the driver's wheel, hidden by the wheel arch, the parking garage fee covered. And, when Marlowe had arrived, he found a case on the back seat filled with everything he'd asked for, as well as a couple of extra little things he hadn't even considered.

The CIA really wanted to recruit him, it seemed.

There was also a folder that held a few sheets of paper; on them were lists of aisle and box numbers, the first for Cody Donziger, the second for Trisha Hawkins, the others locations of other people the CIA had interests in, with a tacit suggestion to try for these "if the opportunity arose", while demanding Marlowe *made* the opportunity arise.

Marlowe noted the first two were only a couple of aisles from each other, too, which made things easier.

Brad had tried to call him while he was driving to the warehouse; he'd diverted the call to voicemail, but knew he had to do something before Brad decided he was in trouble, and came to help. He'd done that before. Brad had also done nothing a couple of times Marlowe was in trouble, however, so his help was a bit of a coin toss.

In the end, Marlowe sent a text, explaining he was hunting a lead to gain access to Senator Kyle the following day, and would be back early in the morning.

A glance at the time on the phone said it was almost eleven at night, and the warehouse seemed quiet. Unlike the courier company he'd visited a couple of days earlier, one that worked a twenty-four-hour shift, this one seemed to have more sensible business hours.

The problem was, however, that it didn't seem big enough. The building was in the middle of an industrial area outside the town, but Marlowe reckoned there was only enough space inside for maybe a few trucks. No way was there space for aisles upon aisles of shelving.

But this was the right location, the logo "HAVENFORD ENGINEERING" emblazoned on the front. Trisha's notes had explained Havenford had been picked up around twenty years earlier by Nathan Donziger's father during some kind of hostile takeover, and when Nathan had taken the family reins, or, rather, removed his father via his *own* hostile takeover, this was one of the few locations he'd kept, even though the records showed it hadn't really been used in over thirty years.

Instead, Nathan had taken the land that the company

owned and turned it into this industrial park. He'd made a healthy profit too from the looks of things, as many of the building names were ones Marlowe recognised.

But Havenford Engineering was small. Uneventful. Not worth keeping.

Marlowe had spent the time waiting for the car checking through old records of the area, and requesting images from various educational establishments, on the off chance he could gain more information on the security used here. It was optimism rather than planning, but Marlowe had the time, and didn't want to leave any stone unturned.

However, as he was about to leave the car, his phone *pinged* with an email from one of the antiquated map sites he'd contacted. Attached to it was a map of New Rochelle in the nineteen forties.

Opening the map, Marlowe scrolled to where he currently was and zoomed in.

And then he groaned as he saw the name.

Havenford Salt Mine

'Shit,' he muttered as everything fell into place. Trisha Hawkins had to know this; she'd deliberately not told him just to keep him on his toes. The reason the building was small was because it didn't need to be large. The whole damn thing was a hundred feet underground, maybe even under where he'd parked.

Salt mines had been used as archive locations across the world for a while now; Marlowe had even been in the Winford Salt Mine, deep under the Cheshire countryside, now run by a company named *DeepStore*, where during the war, Whitehall paperwork had been placed, and now, companies and council departments all over the country used the specially built archive spaces, over a hundred metres underground, to house their most precious papers.

Still a working salt mine, the conditions offered ideal temperatures and very low humidity, the salt pillars creating a naturally occurring dry atmosphere and an ambient temperature of fourteen to fifteen degrees Celsius, great for long-term storage of archival materials, important documents and even priceless artefacts, all held safely below.

And it looked like New Rochelle had one purely for Donziger's paper archives.

Which wasn't good, as it meant that Marlowe's plans now had to change. He wouldn't be able to simply sneak in and out, as he'd already decided, but would now most likely have to gain access to the elevator that would take him down to the mine's level, and that meant a choke point, a single in-and-out exit location that, if compromised, was *terminal*.

The only plus point so far seemed to be that unlike the UK one, which was still a working salt mine and ran twenty-four hours a day, this had been closed, or at least worked in only during the day. With larger, more profitable salt mines elsewhere on the Eastern seaboard, the chances were Donziger had kept the company as a front. It's what Marlowe would have done, after all.

Deciding he couldn't wait any longer, Marlowe cricked his neck and then leant over to the back seat and the CIA-provided case. Opening it up, he pulled out a tranquilliser gun, shaped like a large Luger pistol. Marlowe wasn't a fan of these; unlike in the movies, tranquilliser guns didn't really work on humans. They worked on large animals because the person using the gun would have a much larger margin of error, but with humans, it was very easy to get the dose wrong.

Too little tranquilliser and the gun did nothing. Too much and it killed the person.

Still, if anyone was going to say they'd worked the dose out accurately, it would be the CIA.

Checking the cartridge in the handle, Marlowe could see there were six darts inside, and a quick rummage in the case they'd provided him showed this was all he had. He'd have to take things a little easier if things went sour.

Either that, or he'd start shooting with a real gun, and that was unlikely to end well.

There was a small, hand-held taser device he'd used before, an extendable baton he placed away for later and a Kabar combat knife, although Marlowe was more comfortable with his own Fairbairn–Sykes one. If it was good enough for the SAS, it was good enough for him, after all.

He'd pulled a thin-layer carbon-weave Kevlar vest over his hoodie; it was chunkier than he'd expected, and now his pea coat didn't fit correctly, but as he opened the driver's door and shivered in the late February air, he decided that once he hit the ambient temperature of the mine, this wouldn't be a problem. And he'd much rather not be shot than suffer the discomfort of being a little chilly.

Once he'd added a few more items to his arsenal and closed the case, he climbed out of the car, shutting the door behind him and started across the road, aiming for the building beside his target. Like the courier company, his plan was to find a place to cut the chain-link fence and—

He stopped as he moved closer. The fence between buildings was actually made of metal vertical fencing, each tine a spiked, metal spear, with a very thin amount of wire between.

It was too narrow to slide through, and it looked a little off for standard wire mesh. It was when he got really close, he realised why.

It was electrified.

Okay, so a subtle side entrance was out of the window. That left a more public arrival through the front gate. However, he was in combat Kevlar and with a weapon in his hand – he couldn't see that going down well, or anyone waving him through in the immediate future.

Time to see if the CIA knows their stuff, he thought to himself as he tiptoed towards the main entrance. He knew what his plan had to be now; he'd seen there were two guards in the booth beside the main gate. They wouldn't let him through, even if he waved his fake Marshal ID at them, and the chances were they'd been alerted to his identity anyway, following his abysmal meeting with Nathan earlier that day. So, he needed a new, quicker plan.

Walking up to the gate, he kept to the side, tapping on the closed wall at the back of the booth as he paused. He heard the door open on the other side of the booth, and a voice say, 'hello?'

Marlowe walked around the corner, crouched over. This way, the vest wasn't instantly visible, and this gave him a couple of vital seconds.

'Please ...' he groaned. 'Mugged ...'

'You've been mugged?' the guard acted exactly as Marlowe had hoped, a momentary compassion replacing his suspicion at the new arrival. This was only a second, but it was enough time for Marlowe to stagger a couple more steps closer, rising and firing his tranquilliser gun into the guard's throat.

As the guard staggered back, grabbing at the dart now

jutting out of his neck, Marlowe spun around the next corner, firing once more into the booth itself, taking out the inside guard before he could press a button to alert anyone. This one struggled, grabbing at his neck and pulling out the dart, glaring furiously at Marlowe as the nerve agent took hold, his eyes widening and then rolling back, the guard collapsing to the floor without a sound uttered.

Quickly, Marlowe moved back to the first guard, now also unconscious, and pulled him into the booth, placing him beside the other. Now with the door shut, and with a moment's respite, Marlowe considered his options.

The second of the targets was around his height but heavier set. Marlowe quickly pulled off the guard's shirt and tie, pulling off his own vest and hoodie, placing the vest back on, the stolen shirt and tie now placed over it. He pulled the hoodie over the torso of the guard – after all; he didn't want him to freeze to death in here – and, tucking in the shirt, looked at himself in the window looking outside, the light from within turning it into an effective mirror.

His beard was growing out now, and his hair was longer than the other two, but with a hard hat on and a fluorescent vest over the shirt, his black trousers matching the guards own, he could probably pass as a guard at a distance, especially at this time of night.

Pulling on the brightly coloured vest and hat, Marlowe quickly tied and gagged the two guards with zip ties, mainly as he didn't know how long the tranquilliser would work on them. Then, this done, he left the booth, closing and locking it behind him using a ring of keys found on the desk, and walked over to the warehouse.

Nobody stopped him.

He kept his head down as he walked to the side, finding a

locked door facing him. Pulling one of the IDs he'd just stolen, he tried it against the reader, hearing the door softly click open. Without looking around Marlowe moved through – if anyone saw him open the door and then look for witnesses, this could have been taken as a suspicious activity, and so he hoped his attitude matched that of a guard who believed he should be there, and entered a small corridor.

To the left was a toilet and sink, the next door some kind of canteen area, or break room. And next to that, the last door on the left was a room filled with lockers, likely where the security placed their items before going to work.

There was a sign on the door, a "punching in" list, likely of who was on shift that evening. Of the five names on it, two matched the gate guards' names. This was good, as it meant there was a strong chance only three others were even here right now. Marlowe noted the remaining names, and then looked to the door on the opposite side of the corridor, the only one heading right, and leading into the warehouse itself.

Marlowe had been correct – the warehouse was nothing but a front for the mine. There were some racks of shelving to the side, but the fundamental structure within the building was an old, late-nineteenth-century mine shaft elevator, placed in the middle and to the rear of the space. It'd been freshened up, but the workings still looked like the original mechanics, and Marlowe hoped this meant they'd been upgraded a little over the years, or this was going to be a bumpy ride.

The door to the elevator was nothing more than a pulled-across, concertina mesh made of metal slats, with "up" and "down" buttons within being the only electronics, apart from a lamp above. Marlowe closed the slats, pressed the down button, and prepared himself for whatever was at the bottom.

When visiting the salt mine in Cheshire, the elevator had been a slow journey of over a hundred metres – this was shorter, only fifty. And, when he lowered fully into the cavern made from salt, the pillars reached half as high as he'd expected. It was as if the salt was half as deep as the UK mine, but just as long.

There had also been a tangy, salty taste on his tongue in the UK one, mainly as it was still a working salt mine. Here, the air smelt and tasted different. They had mined no salt for years, and this was clear from the lack of any in the air.

Instead, the lights along the cavern's ceiling lit up a series of racking levels; a two-storey metal and mesh creation that started three feet from the ground, and at least the same from the walls, ensuring no boxes touched the salt. The whole thing was self-contained, and Marlowe could see the metal steps that would take him onto the mesh flooring.

Moving fast now, unaware of how long it'd be until someone else appeared, Marlowe walked determinedly towards the steps – but paused as a voice called out behind him.

'Who the hell are you?'

Marlowe turned to face a Hispanic guard, walking towards him.

Ramos, Heckler and Wilde, Marlowe thought to himself. *He has to be one of them.*

'You Ramos?' he asked, deciding that confrontation was the best option here. 'I've been looking all over for you.'

Ramos paused, unsure of what to say next. The stranger knew his name, and this meant the conversation wasn't going the way he'd expected.

'Nobody told me someone was looking,' he said suspiciously. 'How'd you get down here?'

'I flew,' Marlowe snapped back sarcastically. 'How the hell do you think? Management is pissed. Seems Wilde hasn't been as law-abiding as the rest of you. And when I arrived looking for answers, Munro sent me down here.'

Munro had been the guard he'd taken the ID and shirt from, so he knew Ramos would most likely know the name. And throwing one of the other two guards under the bus would make Ramos feel like he'd dodged a bullet.

'Well, Munro needs to mind his own business,' Ramos muttered, but stopped as Marlowe walked closer.

'Should *I* be minding my own business?' he growled, well aware Ramos still didn't know who he was, or how much power and influence he wielded. 'Where are Wilde and Heckler, anyway?'

'Heckler went home,' Ramos replied without thinking. 'Wife was hit by a bike or something. Wilde took the message, not me. He's on perimeter duty. But surely you'd have seen him—'

He didn't finish – Marlowe whipped out the tranquilliser gun while he spoke and shot him in the chest. Knowing he was now alone, with the second guard upstairs and the third not even on site, he didn't even bother to watch the guard fall as he ran to the steps now, taking them two at a time, and then running down the walkway.

Every few feet there was a walkway to the left, with high shelving, filled with boxes on either side. There was another walkway above him, and this led to even more shelves on an upper level, the stairs to this located every fifty yards. Marlowe knew he didn't have that much time, and so he took the important boxes first; he didn't know how long he'd have before Wilde, on his route, visited the gate guards, only to find them down.

If this happened, all hell would break loose, and Marlowe really didn't want to be underground with only one way of escape when that occurred.

Pulling a box from the shelf to his right, letting it clatter loudly to the floor, he began searching.

18

MIDNIGHT MEETINGS

'Are you still open?' Marlowe asked as he leant through the door of the *Dun Dealgan*.

'Aye, we close at two on a Friday night, so you've got a good hour of drinking to go,' Dermot smiled from behind the bar, waving around the almost empty pub. 'As you can see, Friday night is also our busiest party night.'

Marlowe smiled, hefting his backpack on his shoulder as he entered the bar. He'd re-parked the Mustang in the car park he'd picked it up from, and had left the keys back on the driver's wheel.

'You look like you've been in a bit of a fight,' Dermot tapped at his nose. Marlowe absent-mindedly wiped at it to see a sliver of blood on the back of his hand.

'Got punched in the face by a pissed-off gate guard,' he muttered. 'Thought he was still asleep. My mistake for removing the zip ties. I'll have a Guinness, please.'

If Dermot thought Marlowe's reply was strange, he said nothing, instead turning to the tap and, with a pint glass in his hand, started pouring the drink. Marlowe pulled out a tissue and dabbed his nose. It was still sore, and he felt stupid. He'd gained all the information he needed, returning to the surface with it, and still not bumping into the mysterious Wilde. However, as he returned to the gatehouse to pick up his discarded backpack, he decided, over-charitably, to release the arms of one of the two men on the floor; after all, it was bitterly cold in the gatehouse, and with Ramos down in the archive and Wilde apparently AWOL, he worried they might both freeze to death before anyone got to them.

Unfortunately, he picked the wrong guard, who, the moment the hands were free, swung hard at him. And, even though he'd been in a lying down position, the bugger still smacked hard into Marlowe's face, sending him rocking back.

Marlowe had quickly subdued him, leaving him unconscious but untied, as he returned to his borrowed Mustang. And, with the time being almost midnight by then, Marlowe had then spent the next fifteen minutes searching for a fuel station or other twenty-four-hour business that had a photocopier he could use. In the end he found a late-night bodega that had copies for ten cents each, and he spent the next twenty minutes copying everything he'd stolen and, when he eventually returned to the carpark, he'd left a copy of each of these on the passenger seat, with a "thank you" card he'd picked up from the store.

Now, he just had to finish the rest of his business.

'I've got a friend meeting me,' he said, nodding at a booth at the far end of the bar. 'Well, more a miserable harpy I'd like to see brutally executed, but you know how it goes.'

'I'll wave anyone asking for you down,' Dermot passed Marlowe the pint, and Marlowe returned the gesture with a twenty-dollar bill.

'Get yourself something,' he said. 'Also, I have a quick question before it gets busy in here.'

Dermot didn't rise to the joke, instead raising an eyebrow. 'Aye?'

'You said you had people who were looking for things to pass to the press,' Marlowe smiled. 'You know, sticking it to the man and all that.'

'What about it?'

Marlowe placed a folder onto the bar, sliding it over.

'Have a look at that, and see if it's worthwhile,' he smiled. 'If it is, go wild. But until then, keep it under the counter, yeah?'

Taking the pint of Guinness, Marlowe walked over to the table, ignoring the audible 'Jesus!' from Dermot as he opened and started reading the file. Marlowe knew it'd be of interest because it was Cody Donziger's file. And it was explosive.

There was a *ting* as the door opened again, and Marlowe looked up to see Trisha Hawkins enter. She was in a far more relaxed look than she was the last time she met Marlowe, this time jeans and an expensive fur coat – worn over some kind of cream cable-knit jumper – replaced the party dress. Dermot, on seeing someone arrive, had hidden the folder, but didn't need to do anything else, because she didn't even acknowledge him, walking straight over to Marlowe, sitting down opposite.

'I didn't expect a late night meeting, Thomas,' she growled irritably. 'I'm losing my beauty sleep.'

'You said you wanted this ASAP,' Marlowe replied, sliding another folder across. 'Cody Donziger's grubby little file. From birth to, well, now.'

Trisha opened it, reading the first page.

'You read this?' she asked.

'Yup.'

'You copy this?' Trisha looked up at Marlowe.

'Should I have?' Marlowe looked surprised.

'Probably best not to,' Trisha smiled to herself as she flicked through the file. 'Oh, Cody, you have been a bad little boy.'

'I think you might not want to use "Cody Donziger" and "little boy" in the same sentence, after reading that,' Marlowe smiled. 'Seems he has a bit of a kink. One where he's been caught a couple of times, and there's been a few payoffs. Add the drug-filled orgies, all with minors of both sexes, and he's really not going to come off well.'

'If this ever comes out,' Trisha replied. 'I have reasons to keep this off the media's table, and it'll help me when I tell Cody I have this.'

'I know,' Marlowe leant back in the booth as he sipped at his Guinness. 'I saw you in the file. Shame on you.'

'I didn't know his appetites when we dated,' Trisha shrugged. 'I'm as much a victim as these – well, these children.'

'Of course, you are,' Marlowe replied soothingly. 'Poor you.'

Trisha closed the folder with a triumphant grin, her eyes sparkling, and Marlowe knew she was already working out how to use this information to her advantage.

'So, I gave you what you needed,' Marlowe placed the half-finished pint glass down. 'Now you give me what I need. A one-to-one with Senator Kyle.'

'Yeah, that's not happening,' Trisha was already placing the folder in a tote bag she'd pulled from her pocket. 'I decided I don't like the idea of you hanging out with my friends. Or, even, anyone.'

'What did you do?' Marlowe frowned now, glancing at the front of the bar. There was nobody in with her, but that didn't mean they weren't outside.

'I hear there was a problem at Havenford,' Trisha said, leaning back to take in more of Marlowe as she spoke. 'Terrible situation. Apparently, someone broke into the warehouse and stole valuable information from one of the richest and most vindictive men on the planet.'

'That's terrible,' Marlowe watched Trisha as he replied, his voice calm and level. 'What did you do?'

'Well, luckily for me, I had an asset, someone in the warehouse who, the moment it happened, could pass me a message. And, knowing this, I contacted Nathan Donziger himself, telling him I'd heard of the break in.'

Marlowe almost laughed.

'Your asset wouldn't be a guard named Wilde, would it?' he asked. This was why he hadn't seen the last guard; the bloody man had been told to step back and allow Marlowe to do what he needed to do first. He'd even told his fellow guard to go home, probably inventing the accident to get him out, to make it easier for Marlowe. 'If he was working for you, why send me in?'

'Because he could never go into the salt mines,' Trisha replied, like it was the most obvious answer in the world. 'The moment he did, then Nathan would know it was him, and he'd give me up. And trust me, he would. I've seen what Donziger does to people he hates.'

'So, you killed two birds with one stone,' Marlowe nodded. 'You let me do the work, knowing Donziger already hates me, and while I take the blame, you get the information you need.'

Trisha waved her hand as she gave a mocking half-bow.

'So, as you see, I can't really let you speak to Kyle, as Nathan would know we've spoken,' she said. 'I'd probably run if I were you. And maybe, in the future, don't consider yourself equal to your betters, or take on jobs you can't get out of cleanly.'

She went to rise, but Marlowe chuckled.

'Great,' he said. 'I'm being given espionage tips by an ex-ice dancer.'

Trisha looked down at him, eyes blazing.

'How did you know about that?' she snapped.

'Oh, you told Cody about it while you were screwing,' Marlowe said. 'And he put it in your file. Interestingly, he doesn't call it "dating," but he's a little more crass in his penmanship than you.'

'My ... file?'

'Oh, yes,' Marlowe raised his eyebrows in mock surprise. 'Didn't you know about it? Apparently Donziger senior was so concerned about you snagging his son, he sought all your dirty little secrets. And he must have enjoyed it, because even after Cody dumped you for a school-bus-load of teens, he carried on doing it. All the way to ... well, right now.'

Trisha continued to stare at Marlowe, and he smiled. She hadn't expected this from him. She'd badly underestimated him, and now she needed to re-evaluate the situation.

'Where is my file?'

'Oh, don't worry, I didn't take it,' Marlowe shook his head. 'I did, however, take photos of the pages within it though, and then emailed those to Whitehall. There's some very interesting details on those pages, things I'm sure the current Prime Minister – who really hates you, remember that – would like to see.'

Trisha paled.

'You've just signed your death warrant,' she stated icily. 'When Donziger finds you, he'll—'

'When he does find me, how will you know?' Marlowe interrupted. 'Will he call you? Would it be the same number you gave me?'

'That number's dead now.'

'Yeah, but he could still find out you owned the phone, right? I mean, he's Nathan Donziger.'

'What did you *do*?' now it was Trisha's turn to ask the question.

'I have a bit of an apology to give you, actually,' Marlowe theatrically sighed, as if about to give up a massive secret. 'I'm glad you closed that phone service, because, well, I ... I think I lost the card.'

'What do you mean, you *lost the card*?' In a mixture of shock and anger, Trisha sat back down again.

'It was so nicely printed. I felt honoured you'd take the time to do that. So, I kept it on me. Like a keepsake. But during the night, it ... well, it fell out. Now, I just need to retrace my steps, but I think it'll be in the gatehouse, with the guards I took out, or it's in the salt mines. Or ...'

Marlowe leant closer now. He wanted Trisha to really take this in.

'It's in the now empty folder for Cody Donziger, with "Fuck You" written on the other side. In a very passible copy of your handwriting, I have to say. Thanks for the hand-written note you sent me, by the way. It helped me a lot. And I really hope you never held the card, because then your fingerprints would be on it, too.'

'I can get around this.'

'I wouldn't even start worrying about that just yet,' Marlowe replied, looking at his watch. 'It's already six am in

London. I reckon there's a dozen people poring over every page I sent them, working out how they can use it to destroy you and Phoenix Industries. All they have to do now is find you ... before Nathan Donziger does. And when he finds you, I expect he'll be pissed.'

Trisha half-staggered back from the table, but Marlowe rose to match her.

'I'm a damn good spy,' he snapped. 'And you're nothing but an amateur, playing at being a movie villain when you're actually just the girl who turns up and gets herself killed in act two. I knew you'd try to screw me. A scorpion never changes. But you never once believed *I could screw you.*'

'Senator Kyle—'

'Will meet me before her gala,' Marlowe picked up the pint, finishing it as he stood facing her. 'I have *her* file too.'

Trisha stared in a mixture of horror and anger at Marlowe, who indicated the tote bag with the glass in his hand.

'You'd better make the most of that while you can,' he suggested. 'I feel it's a limited time offer. You know, before someone spikes the story – or spikes *yours.*'

He walked up to Trisha now, face to face.

'And when you're on the run, wondering if it'll be an MI5 or a Donziger-funded bullet that'll take you out, remember this is all because you killed my friends – and tried to kill me.'

He reached into her jacket, pulling out an embossed card.

'And I'll be taking the golden ticket you promised me too,' he smiled. 'Let's be honest. You won't be using it. Going there would be a death sentence for you now.'

He turned, walking to the bar.

'Oh, and before you *do* go pack, tell Francine she's next,' he finished. 'We're done now. You can go. Can't say it's been a pleasure. And maybe, in the future, don't consider yourself equal to your betters, or take on jobs you can't get out of cleanly?'

Speechless and outplayed, Trisha turned and stormed out of the bar.

Marlowe breathed a sigh of relief, and waved for another from Dermot, who stood at the other end of the bar, watching with interest.

'I see you're an expert at making friends and influencing people,' he grinned, walking over. 'Sorry to overhear, but I couldn't help note she called you Thomas.'

'You heard right,' Marlowe replied. 'My name's not Garth. And I'm not from Birmingham. Sorry. It's a bad habit. I'm Tom. Tom Marlowe.'

Dermot shrugged.

'I appreciate the honesty,' he replied. 'And it sounds like you pissed off a major corporation, so you can't be all bad. And you gave me a gold coin like a leprechaun, so I feel you're on the level.'

Marlowe grinned.

'Don't be too sure,' he said. 'Have you read through the file?'

'Yeah,' Dermot shook his head. 'That guy's screwed up. If this gets out, it could destroy him.'

'So, you don't want to send it?'

'Are you kidding?' Dermot laughed. 'I've already put feelers out. The money people would pay for these puts your little coin to shame. You want to split it?'

'Thanks, but I actually have another idea for that,' Marlowe relaxed a little. 'It's connected to another request. And this one could be a little more problematic, and is incredibly short notice.'

Dermot nodded at this, already on board, thanks to the provided file.

'What do you need?' he asked.

And, as Marlowe sipped at his second pint, he told the barman exactly what he needed.

'Do you know what time it is?' Trix was tired and unimpressed as she answered the phone.

'No, I'm running on UK time,' Marlowe replied cordially. 'Of course, I know the bloody time, Trix. I'm still sorting things out. Hopefully, I'll be back soon, but I need a favour.'

There was a pause, and Marlowe knew this was likely Trix wiping sleep from her eyes.

'Go on then, what is it?'

'Can you send me details of where Senator Kyle is staying tonight?' Marlowe shivered as he stood outside the *Dun Dealgan*. 'I want to pop by and say hi.'

'Tonight? It's like two in the morning.'

'Things are about to run very fast,' Marlowe replied. 'I'll explain when I return. Is everything okay?'

'Well, Roxanne is unhappy about being here still, and Brad pissed off a couple of hours back in a huff, but apart from that everything's going swimmingly. You?'

'Well, I've destroyed Trisha Hawkins, I'm about to cancel Cody Donziger, and I've managed to really piss off the CIA, so the night's going great.'

Marlowe looked up at the night sky.

'And it's not over yet.'

19

BEDTIME STORIES

TRIX HAD COME BACK TO MARLOWE WITH AN ADDRESS WITHIN ten minutes.

The Lotte New York Palace Hotel was a luxury hotel in Midtown, on the corner of Fiftieth Street and Madison Avenue, and built out of a portion of the Villard Houses: six separate residences in a U-shaped plan with three wings, surrounding a central courtyard on Madison Avenue. It was built in the 1880s, and now sat under a fifty-one storey skyscraper, built a century later.

Marlowe had never been in the hotel, but he'd heard about it. Then-President Obama had decided in 2015 that meetings of the United Nations General Assembly for that year would have a headquarters at the New York Palace Hotel rather than at the Waldorf Astoria New York, following the latter's takeover by Chinese financiers. Marlowe hadn't been in the British contingent during the visit, but he'd heard from fellow agents how opulent the suites had been, and had always wanted to visit.

Of course, he'd assumed it would be during the day, not

at two-thirty am on a Friday night. Or, rather, a Saturday morning now.

Senator Kyle was staying in what was called a "Skyview Suite" on the fiftieth floor, a suite which the website boasted had "a master bath and walk-in closet, besides a library, gym, entertainment room, living room, office, dining room, and kitchen." It also placed the room at around eight grand a night, likely funded this weekend on Arizona taxpayer's money.

The problem was, of course, getting to it.

He couldn't walk in through the front entrance, as the tower the suite was in had its own elevator system, one that was likely guarded. But the hotel would have to bring up chefs, housecleaning staff, and everyone else required for such luxury guests, and so there had to be a service elevator. So, moving quickly through the back of the hotel using the original, century-old building – complete with brickwork corridors and antiquated security systems – to his advantage, he gained access to the service area, stealing a uniform from the locker room. Now dressed in the livery of a guest services manager, he found the elevator, entering it quietly, allowing the doors to close before examining the panel.

The moment he'd walked in he'd used a small clicker device in his hand, something the CIA had left in their supplies for him. It was purely aimed at digital footage cameras, connecting via Bluetooth, or Wi-Fi, or something wireless and magical, forcing its way along the fibre optic wires in a nanosecond, freezing the screen on the last image recorded and allowing someone to enter the location without being seen. It was only workable on low security systems – he wouldn't be able to waltz into MI5 with it, although he was seriously tempted to try, but a hotel service elevator was fair game.

Now alone, and at this time in the morning not expecting anyone to be using the service elevator, Marlowe used a small, battery-powered screwdriver to quickly remove the panel's securing screws, pulling it away from the wall carefully, allowing the cables that still connected to it to stay attached as he snipped a single cable, before securing the panel back on. This done, he pressed the button for the fiftieth floor.

The elevator was quick, and it was quiet. As it opened on the fiftieth floor it didn't even *ping* to announce its presence – in case a guest complained about the noise.

The elevator opened into a half-lit service corridor, with a single door at the end. Marlowe assumed this led to the main hallway where the suites were, so he opened the door carefully, peering through.

As expected, there were several doors along the hallway, each to varying suites, but only one of them had a suited Secret Service agent sitting on a chair outside, currently reading a novel on his Kindle.

Marlowe recognised him from the party. He'd been part of the three-man team with *Stumbler* and *Neck Chop*. Although they were both dead, this one had only really been involved up to the moment Marlowe had kicked him hard between the legs.

He'd named him "*Crotch Kick*" at the time, and the only other time they may have met was in the role of "other gunman" in the subway tunnel later that night, although the jury was still out for that appearance.

Moving quickly, he walked over to the man who, seeing

someone approaching in the hotel's uniform, looked up at Marlowe suspiciously.

'We didn't order anything—' he started, before his eyes widened with recognition. 'You—'

'Hello again,' Marlowe said as he jabbed the taser into *Crotch Kick's* side, watching dispassionately as the man spasmed uncontrollably as several thousand volts of electricity shut down his nervous system. 'Now have a little nap.'

As *Crotch Kick* collapsed to the floor, unconscious, Marlowe leant over the body, pulling it back up and placing the guard into a sitting position on the chair, as if a little slumped over. He looked as if he'd simply dropped off, which was what Marlowe needed. Checking through the pockets, Marlowe found the backup suite key, in case there was a problem inside.

This gained, Marlowe carefully opened the door and snuck into the suite, closing the door behind him. He almost let out a noise of alarm as he saw the man in front of him – until he realised it was a full-length mirror, with paths leading left and right.

The walls were white, the floor hardwood, and Marlowe noted the right-hand direction was bare, with only a lamp and a table in a small hall that led to a door. Marlowe worried it might be louder to go this way, so instead moved left, turning right at the end of the corridor, passing a small bathroom and emerging into a living area. To the right was a small office, a desk and table facing him, and to the left and in front were windows overlooking Manhattan at night. A dining table for eight led into an expansive two-room seating area, with sofas and armchairs spaced around the room, half placed upon expensive looking rugs as they faced a huge wall-mounted TV.

In the second, smaller room, Marlowe saw another large TV on the wall, and the walls this time were wallpapered, and had small bookshelves scattered around them to break things up.

At the end was a closed door, and Marlowe assumed this was the main bedroom of the suite. Quietly turning the handle, he moved into the bedroom with as minimal noise as he could.

The room itself was as large as the entire suite Marlowe had picked in the New Yorker; to the left was a double bed, with a middle-aged woman asleep under the duvet. In front of this was another TV, this time on a sideboard, the windows looking out into the city behind it. To the right was an en suite bathroom and walk-in closet, and towards the other door, the one Marlowe had been worried about approaching was another settee, leading into a room with an exercise bike – the "gym" the hotel had proclaimed existed up here.

Marlowe stared down at the woman in the bed. She was in her late fifties, her curly hair a gun-metal grey as she faced to the side. Marlowe moved to the side of the bed, sitting down on it, now beside the sleeping woman.

'Wakey wakey, Senator Kyle,' he whispered.

The woman moaned softly, obviously annoyed at the interruption, opening one eye sleepily and then jerking back in horror at the strange man sitting beside her.

'What the hell … who are you?' she stammered, and Marlowe held up a finger.

'Inside voice only, please,' he said calmly. 'I don't mean you any harm. My name is Tom Marlowe. I'm an MI5 agent – well, an *ex*-MI5 agent, really.'

Senator Kyle rubbed the sleep from her bleary eyes as she stared at the stranger in her bedroom.

'And I'm supposed to believe that?'

'Fair point,' Marlowe nodded. 'I was going to tell you a different identity if I'm being honest. You know, keep my real name secret, tell you I'm a US Marshal, or something along those lines, but I want us to start our relationship with complete transparency.'

'Our relationship?' Senator Kyle frowned as she realised a horrifying possibility. 'You're MI5, and they sent you to kill me?'

'Actually, Senator, I'm here to be your fairy godmother,' Marlowe smiled.

'So you're not the domestic terrorist who shot up my security team?'

'I'm not the first part of that, anyway,' Marlowe admitted. 'And they shot first. And tried to stab me first.'

'And why would they do that?'

'Because they work for Nathan Donziger,' Marlowe smiled. 'Who has a file on you. Which, I'm guessing you already know, and all this was to give you a moment to clear your head. Well played.'

Senator Kyle folded her arms.

'So Donziger has a file on me. What about it?' she asked. 'I'm not the only one in Washington with this problem. He's got half a dozen of us in his archives, all held over because of mistakes we made back in the day, when we were hungry and we needed funding.'

She stared off out of the window, looking at night time New York.

'Now we do what he tells us to, or he threatens to release the files,' she said. 'He knows to do so would kill our chances in any election. Not only that, some of us would end up in prison.'

'You mean people like Senators Tyler and Jones, and

Governor Williams,' Marlowe said. The names weren't random, these were also files he'd seen in the salt mines.

'You know your stuff, I'll say that for you James Bond spooks,' Senator Kyle muttered. 'So, is there a point to this?'

'You're in New York because Nathan Donziger told you to come,' Marlowe continued. 'Do you always dance when he tells you to?'

'Didn't you get the bit about the files he has on us?' Senator Kyle snapped. 'We don't have a choice.'

'But what if you *did* have one?' Marlowe placed a cardboard file onto the bed, making sure Senator Kyle saw it.

'What's that?'

'This, Senator Kyle, is your file,' Marlowe leant back slightly, allowing the Senator to pick the file up and scan through it. 'Seems Donziger had a break in at his New Rochelle warehouse a few hours back.'

'The salt mine?' Senator Kyle sniffed the file. 'Yeah, I can smell the salt. This ain't no copy.'

'There is no copy,' Marlowe replied. 'And as for this one, you can keep it, hide it, set it on fire for all I care.'

Senator Kyle placed the file down, sliding across the bed and exiting on the far side, pulling a dressing gown on as she turned to face Marlowe.

'I'm not sleeping with you, if you think that's on the table,' she said. 'But a gift like this is definitely up there. What exactly do you want, Mister Marlowe?'

'A friend,' Marlowe smiled. 'Maybe a few. I gave my real name. You have clearance with the Pentagon, probably have buddies at Langley. You can check into me, see how my own country cut off my air supply for helping a CIA agent and saving your boss in London. And, while I'm persona non grata in the UK, I thought I might look at the private sector in America.'

'And having friends in the Hill could help you,' Senator Kyle nodded, understanding. 'Am I your only potential friend?'

'Depends,' Marlowe replied carefully. 'I also have files for Tyler, Jones, and Williams. If they want them.'

'Oh, you'll be the belle of the ball if you do that,' Senator Kyle frowned. 'No copies?'

'I don't need them,' Marlowe shrugged. 'I want goodwill, not more bitter, blackmailed politicians.'

Senator Kyle sighed, walking to a side cabinet and pouring a glass of water from a bottle.

'Donziger will destroy you,' she said. 'By now he'll know it was you that stole the files, and tomorrow he'll kill you, your friends, family, anyone who's ever been nice to you—'

'What if I get him first?' Marlowe smiled.

'You think you can take down Donziger?'

Marlowe nodded for a water.

'Donziger Senior is about to have a terrible day later this morning,' he said as Senator Kyle passed it over. 'I'm guessing you know the issues his son has?'

'Everyone knows,' Senator Kyle growled. 'But the sick little paedo's fine while there's no proof.'

'If there was proof, where do you think it'd be?'

Senator Kyle had been taking a sip of water – she spluttered it back into the glass.

'You have *Cody's* file?'

'No,' Marlowe shook his head. 'That is, not anymore. A trusted connection is now passing it to any media that will listen. Multiple copies all over the world. However, we both know the media won't spend time on this, unless people higher up the food chain convince them.'

Senator Kyle nodded at this, already working out the possibilities.

'If Cody gets thrown to the wolves, then Daddy takes his eye off the ball,' she said. 'There's an event later today. Big gala thing downstairs. It's why I'm staying here. It was a smokescreen for him to order us to close the court case, but now that's over—'

'It's not,' Marlowe shook his head. 'Roxanne Vasquez has information, valid and provable intel that shows decades of corruption. And she too will place it online, right after Cody gets cancelled. And I've heard rumours of a protest march, too. Maybe one that stops right outside these doors?'

'You're killing him with public opinion,' Senator Kyle placed the glass on the table. 'He won't care. He's bulletproof.'

'Not if he doesn't have your security helping him,' Marlowe shook his head. 'I'm removing his sources, one by one. Cutting his air supply in the same way MI5 cut mine, and believe me, Senator, it's not fun. I'll guarantee you by tonight, everything will be in place. And you, and the other politicians being screwed over by Donziger can finally stand up against him, with no chance of reprisal.'

'You won't get in.'

Marlowe held up the card he'd taken from Trisha an hour earlier.

'Got an invitation,' he grinned.

'Why me? Why not go to the others?'

'Because I read your file,' Marlowe said honestly. 'I saw what he had on you. Corruption, sure, but you went into politics back at the start with good intentions, and it was your family that cost you your freedom. Your sister, right? You bailed her out of a drink driving charge, and then the whole thing snowballed from there. A lot of the decisions you've made over the last ten, fifteen years have been because of that file, on the bed, being held over you.'

'That's accurate enough,' Senator Kyle nodded. 'And it shows you *have* read it, because nobody knows about my sister. She had problems. Nathan... capitalised... on them.'

'Then make a change. Now you have nothing holding you down. No secrets about to fall out. Or, at least, none that Donziger has on you,' Marlowe stepped closer. 'Now you can pick your moment and be seen by every news channel in the world, and believe me, at this point in the story, they'll be watching.'

'You make it sound like it's already made up,' Senator Kyle chuckled. 'You almost sound like a politician.'

Marlowe held out a hand.

'If you agree, I ask one thing,' he said. 'Fire your agents and bring in a new security team. As I said, they work for Donziger.'

'I guessed before you told me,' Senator Kyle looked back at the bed and the file. 'They weren't exactly subtle about it. Done.'

'Then we'll speak soon, Senator,' Marlowe smiled. 'Enjoy your night-time reading.'

THE AGENT OUTSIDE WAS STILL UNCONSCIOUS AS MARLOWE passed. Pausing, and pulling on a pair of latex gloves before grabbing *Crotch Kick's* wallet, ID and his holstered weapon, carefully placing them into his pockets, Marlowe smiled.

He had a story in mind. Because the court case wasn't happening, they had to find a higher courtroom.

And luckily, there was one outside, filled with millions of jurors.

He just had to convince Roxanne Vasquez to do something incredibly dangerous.

———

20

BREAKFAST SERVING

'I still think this is risky,' Roxanne said as she ate a slice of toast, recently sent up via room service. 'You're playing with cogs and gears that aren't aligned, and the whole damn thing is going to collapse on us all.'

Marlowe sat on the sofa and rubbed his eyes, nodding at this. He'd got back to the hotel just before three and had managed five hours shut-eye before Roxanne, stressed and furious, had woken him up. But now it was almost nine in the morning, he had a meeting to check on in just over an hour, and a pissed-off woman in front of him.

'We don't have that many options,' he explained. 'Donziger outplayed us in the courts; he knew the moment you were gone your law firm would settle. He knew he could send someone in and cause utter chaos, and even if you died, he could still use the same problems and the same excuses to get what he wanted. Going public is the only option.'

'No newspaper will go near me,' Roxanne bemoaned. 'People like Donziger own them. The Senators you mentioned, too.'

'Not anymore.'

Marlowe rose from the sofa he'd spent the night on, the third such night in a row, if you included the plane's reclining chair-cum-bed. His back was screaming because of this, another night wrenched into odd positions, and he needed a solid massage more than anything right now.

It was only when he heard the sharp intake of breath did he realise he was only wearing his shorts.

Roxanne, flustered by what she'd seen, turned away. As she did this, Marlowe grinned. Two nights ago, the shoe had been on the other foot, but it seemed he wasn't the only one thrown off guard by a half-naked companion. And Marlowe knew he looked good – there wasn't much more to do than cardio and weights while you were waiting for a recall. And when you were burnt by your agency, the regimen was good to keep your mind focused.

Currently, Roxanne was trying to focus on anything else in the room as Marlowe pulled a bathrobe on.

Picking up the remote, he turned on the television. It was the same news channel they'd watched the previous day, but now it was a weekend anchor, and behind her was a photo of Cody Donziger.

'—no statement after serious sexual abuse allegations appeared on forums across the globe last night,' she continued, in mid-flow when the television had come to life. 'The yet unknown source has provided media companies across America with printouts of what seems to be a dossier on Mister Donziger, with details travelling back as far as his High School, where he was alleged to have killed another student in a hit-and-run accident, yet was never arrested, or even contacted in relation to the death.'

'Cody's just been cancelled,' Marlowe smiled darkly. 'I read the file. He's a piece of shit.'

Roxanne stared at the screen in surprise.

'It's gossip,' she frowned. 'Usually, they wouldn't be so brazen …'

'Unless they knew he was toothless to stop them,' Marlowe smiled. 'They have pages upon pages of the stuff. And they know the moment Cody does anything about it, they can hold the information they *haven't* made public over his head. They've been held back for years, decades even. And every story they'll give has probably been finished and waiting for ages.'

'Your plan might work after all,' Roxanne was reluctantly admitting now, but stopped as the door to the suite opened, and Trix walked in, a paper takeout bag in her hand.

'Bagels for breakfast,' she said. 'Oh, for God's sake, Marlowe. Stop flashing your bits about.'

Marlowe raised his hands in surrender, moving towards the bathroom.

'What's the temperature out there?' he asked.

'It's cold and windy,' Trix replied with a smile, as she placed the bag of bagels onto the table. 'But if you mean Cody and his dad, the public are loving it. People are always happy when an entitled, rich prick gets their comeuppance.'

'You knew about this?' Roxanne raised her eyebrows in surprise at this.

'I was up last night, he sent me the files – well, some photos of the sheets, and I had a quick read,' Trix shrugged. 'It's chaos incarnate and Marlowe does that very well.'

Ignoring the conversation, and actually a little glad Roxanne was now transferring her anger onto Trix, Marlowe entered the shower and forced himself to wake up by keeping it on cold. After a minute under the freezing jets, he finally felt awake enough to continue the day. And, by the time he returned from the shower, Trix and Roxanne were on the sofa, eating bagels and watching the television. Currently, there was some kind of expert on, explaining the ramifications of such bombshell revelations to the Donziger name.

'What did you get from the drive?' he asked as he dressed quickly.

Trix looked up from the news report, but Roxanne was still glued to the television.

'It's dynamite,' she said. 'I found about seven or eight catastrophic hits in the data, things that, if they get out, will destroy Donziger. They know we have the data, though. And, after this—' she pointed at the screen '—they'll come after us.'

'I know,' Marlowe pulled a sweater on. 'You need to get ahead of that. Sort the recordings out, get everything uploaded. I can do the rest remotely.'

'You can't,' Trix shook her head. 'It can't be done remotely, as it needs a hard wire.'

'Then we need to get you in there then,' Marlowe jumped up as he pulled on his jeans, pulling both legs up at once. 'You know how that works.'

'Yeah, it's not my first dance,' Trix rose, walking over. 'But what about us? Are we expendable here?'

'You know I'll rescue you if it all goes to shit,' Marlowe grinned as he did his belt up. 'I'll even bring Brad with me. Hey, where is he, anyway?'

'In the lobby, guarding,' Trix replied, walking back to the sofa and picking up her takeaway coffee cup, sipping from it before replying. 'I think he feels you still don't trust him.'

Marlowe sighed.

'I'll speak to him when I leave,' he said, and at this, Trix's eyes sparkled.

'Oh yeah,' she said, walking over to the desk and placing the cup down on it, she now sat down in front of the computer. 'You have a date with your mysterious hit placer. You need backup?'

'Always, but I think I should be okay this time,' Marlowe pulled his coat on, running a hand through his still slightly damp hair. 'I'm just going for a chat, after all.'

'With your shit bracelet,' Trix mocked, pointing at the steel defence chain around his wrist.

'It feels comfortable there,' Marlowe waved his arm in a flouncing gesture, and moved to the door, checking his pockets to make sure he had everything he needed. 'Want me to pick up anything for when I get back?'

'Just for this whole mess to be finished,' Roxanne said, and her eyes, when she looked back at Marlowe, were haunted. 'Too many people have died over this. I want them gone. If I have to pull the trigger myself, I will.'

'It'll be over tonight,' Marlowe promised. 'Believe me.'

He looked at Trix.

'Do whatever works to get you in,' he said. 'And on the network.'

'Sure, sure, let me do all the work while you flounce about with your jewellery on,' Trix mocked, already getting down to work.

Walking out of the suite and closing the door behind him, Marlowe stopped, leaning against the wall as he took a deep breath to calm his emotions. They'd both worn the same mask as he had in there, pretending everything was fine, that this was just a mission, but deep down they all knew what was at stake here.

Cody Donziger would want blood for this. He'd come for them.

And for the plan to work, Marlowe had to let him.

Taking another deep breath to centre himself, he shifted his position, straightened up, and headed for the elevators.

TRIX HAD BEEN RIGHT – BRAD HAYNES WAS SITTING IN THE lobby, staring at the main entrance with what could only be described as a murderous scowl upon his face, when Marlowe walked over.

'You went without me,' he grumbled, ignoring Marlowe. 'It's my op and you're treating me like the office bitch.'

'I'm doing what you brought me here to do,' Marlowe replied curtly. 'I'm keeping Roxanne alive. And to be brutally honest, Brad, you're not exactly filling me full of faith.'

'I was in the suite,' Brad rose now, turning to face Marlowe. 'I saw a clicker on the side table.'

'This clicker?' Marlowe pulled it out of his jacket pocket – it was the device he'd used on the hotel service elevator. 'It wasn't on any table. Care to change your story?'

'Fine, I went through your pockets while you slept,' Brad muttered. 'But I know that damned thing. It's CIA tech. And I didn't give it to you.'

'No, you didn't,' Marlowe was tiring of this now. 'The CIA gave me it. And yeah, they helped me get into Donziger's file archive, in return for copies of some files. It was an audition.'

'You were *poached?*' Brad looked like he was about to be sick. 'What did you offer for that shiny prize?'

'Just you,' Marlowe snapped. 'They want you manning a desk in the middle of nowhere. You've pissed off a lot of people by going rogue.'

'I'm happy for you,' Brad said, his face showing anything but happiness. 'When's the team arriving to take me in—'

'*Goddammit, Brad!*' Marlowe half-shouted, the noise bringing attention to them across the lobby. 'Do you think I'd tell you about this if I intended to go through with it? I needed them, and I used them. And when the CIA realise I've played both sides, do you think I'll be allowed to play with their toys again?'

He sighed.

'The mission, Brad. It's all about the mission. You know that. And, as it's *your* bloody mission, you should be happy I'm sticking to it.'

Brad shifted his posture slightly, becoming less confrontational.

'Oh, right,' he muttered, a little more relaxed now.

'I couldn't have you with me last night in case the CIA were watching,' Marlowe continued. 'And to be honest, I was a little concerned about the comment the red-haired, nameless agent who spoke to me gave. She asked how easy I had been to find since you controlled my identities, and let's be honest, it's been pretty bloody easy.'

Brad didn't say anything here.

'She also said they wanted to place you some place "where corporate temptation doesn't cause him a loyalty issue," and it was a message. You're cosying up with companies. Is it Donziger?'

Brad looked hurt.

'I'd never ...' he started, but then he gave out a long, ragged breath.

'Sure, I've been looking into the private security sector of late,' he said. 'Someone must have noticed.'

'Why?'

'Why do you think? I saved the goddamned President last year, and I got nothing for it.'

Marlowe avoided the fact Brad had been nowhere near Westminster Hall when *Marlowe and Trix* had saved President McKay, and simply stayed quiet, allowing Brad to continue.

'I wanted something for my retirement,' Brad continued. 'I started giving information for money. Nothing bad, nothing that could cause any issues, just things to prove I could be of more worth down the line ...'

'But?'

'I mentioned one legend I'd created, Garth Fleming, in one of these conversations,' Brad admitted. 'I didn't even think about it until later. This was weeks, months ago, even. And when I gave the legend to you for the op, I'd forgotten.'

'Who did you give it to?' Marlowe fought to keep his voice steady.

'A buddy from the corps,' Brad sighed, looking away. 'Trevor, the poor dead bastard. I was showing what I could offer, how I could help with witness relocations, stuff like that. But last night, while I checked about, I learned he wasn't as independent as I thought.'

'He worked for Donziger?'

'No, but almost as bad. *Phoenix.*'

Marlowe wanted to scream. *The Garth Fleming legend was well and truly burnt now if Trisha Hawkins had it.*

'And you weren't going to tell me?'

'Trix told me you'd put the kibosh on Hawkins,' Brad argued. 'I assumed you'd realised and moved on.'

'You knew Hawkins would be at the library event, didn't you? And Trevor, who you hired to look after Roxanne, was working for her? Some kind of asset deal?'

Brad nodded.

'I didn't know, I swear,' he replied. 'Not until the end.'

'This was how they had the comms frequency? Trevor gave it away?'

'I reckon so. That, or if he didn't give it to Phoenix, and they didn't pass it to Donziger, then Donziger's men got it from him when they killed him.'

Marlowe ran a hand through his hair.

'Are you compromised?'

'No, I don't think so, at least,' Brad was almost pleading now. 'Look, Marlowe. I owe this to Danny – to Brett. I need to see this through.'

'Then you do what I say and when I say it,' Marlowe growled. 'This is my mission now. My op. You work for me, not the other way around, because I can't have you going off book today. I need you to use all your skills and get settled into somewhere you'll need to be one hundred percent ready for.'

'And the girls?'

'They know the score. Trix is probably putting the next stage into play right now.'

'And you trust her?'

'Trix?' Marlowe paused. 'Why wouldn't I?'

'She's as burnt as you, Marlowe,' Brad shrugged. 'She just doesn't know it yet. And when she realises MI5 won't be calling her back either, she'll start working out how much she can make for the other side. I know you've wondered that.'

'If Trix turns, I'll cross that bridge when I come to it,' Marlowe said.

Brad breathed in, letting it out, nodding.

'Okay then, Brit. What do you need?'

Marlowe told him.

SURPRISINGLY, BRAD HAD ACCEPTED THIS WITH GRACE, AND had headed out of the lobby immediately once Marlowe had finished. Which was fine, as Marlowe had other things on his mind now, a concern which, two blocks from the hotel with Marlowe walking into the wind, his head down and his collar up against the icy blasts, was proven by a quick view into a building's window front.

He was being followed by a familiar face.

That said, it wasn't a face he knew that well, just enough to recognise, and so he started moving westwards, cutting down streets and up avenues in a zig-zag motion to see if she was fully committed to this course of action.

And, after three turns, it looked as if she was.

The hair was different, the face harsher, the coat bulkier, but it was definitely the woman from Grayson Long's photo, the one at Battery Park. She'd found Marlowe, the man who'd killed Grayson, and now she either wanted to kill him or talk to him.

Unfortunately, until he stopped and spoke to her, he wouldn't know which was more likely.

Deciding to nip this in the bud as quickly as possible, he turned into a small side alley, a cul-de-sac with high walls on all sides, and, seeing there wasn't any way to leave, or any witnesses to what was about to happen, he turned to face the entrance.

The woman moved around the corner a moment later, pausing when she saw him standing alone, watching for her.

'I don't know what you want from me, but I—' Marlowe started, but the sentence was cut short with a yelp of surprise as the woman drew a fighting knife from a leg sheath, moving in fast and slashing down with it, forcing Marlowe to step back.

'You killed my partner,' she snarled. 'I'm gonna cut you up for that.'

'I killed Grayson in self-defence,' Marlowe replied, his hand moving up to block another slash, the blade deflecting off his steel-link bracelet. 'He shot first.'

'He was dead the moment he came for you!' Another slash, followed by a stabbing motion. Marlowe, noting the time, and needing to speed this up, clicked the dragon-head clasp on the bracelet, allowing the metre-long chain link to slide off his wrist, turning into a vicious-looking whip in his hand.

'Then he shouldn't have come!' Marlowe flicked the chain, and the tip of it whipped up, slashing at the woman, who only just managed to deflect it with the blade. She moved in again without another word, and Marlowe stepped in, using the chain as a rope, looping it around her wrist and then falling backwards, his foot kicking out and pressing against the woman's chest as he did so.

The foot braced against her, his body pulling back, the chain link around her wrist snapped tight and wrenched her arm almost out of her socket with the force of the movement. There was nothing she could do, and as she screamed in pain, the blade dropped from her fingers as Marlowe, now allowing momentum to keep him moving yanked again, sending her off balance and crashing to the ground. With a whip, he released her now wrenched wrist from the chain, and looped it over her head from behind, the chain links biting into her throat as he moved in, knee to her back, pulling hard as she scrabbled at it with her good hand.

'Stop,' he said. 'I have no urge to kill you as well.'

As a show of good faith, he lessened the pressure, allowing her to breathe.

'Your partner was outclassed when he came to me,' he said.

'You think we didn't know that?' she replied. 'He'd only done minor hits before, and suddenly he's being offered six figures to take you down. Six figures!'

'He should have turned it down.'

'He did!' the woman cried out, and Marlowe, surprised at this, let the chain go, allowing her to crawl back, turning to face him, her face a mask of fury.

'Explain.'

'He was called in personally by the client,' she carried on. 'He was told if he refused, he'd never work again. There were bigger threats made. And so, he took it on.'

Marlowe thought back to the night several days earlier. The assassin hadn't known how to work cleanly, or even how to tail correctly, and even then he'd known the killer was untrained.

But this was deliberate.

'Your fight's not with me,' he eventually said, holding up his hands as he stayed crouched on the pavement. 'They sent your partner as a message, nothing more. He wasn't expected to live. They expected him to die.'

'For what?'

'For this,' Marlowe rummaged in his jacket, holding his other hand up to calm the woman as he pulled out the Battery Park photo, tossing it to her.

'Gray always carried this,' she said, her voice softening. 'You took it?'

'Not for the reasons you think,' Marlowe tossed a torch across now. 'Use the UV light on the back of the photo.'

Fiddling with the torch, the woman turned on the purple light, looking at the words on the paper.

'I didn't write this.'

'I know. But how did *you* know I was at that hotel?' Marlowe asked.

The woman looked up, the fury visible on her face.

'A message,' she said. 'Told me you'd be walking out of that hotel this morning.'

'And you don't find it strange you were shown how to find me, moments before I took the meeting written on that photo?'

The woman, now calming, nodded.

'You're meeting the client?'

'Yes.'

'You're killing the client?'

'No.'

'Why not?'

Marlowe rose now, offering a hand to the woman, but then thought better of it as she gripped her painful wrist.

'Because you deserve that honour,' he said. 'Look. Go to the Tick Tock Diner. Sit somewhere you can hear the conversations and, when I arrive, you listen to mine. If it sounds like I'm lying, you can come and fight me again. I'll even give you the first shot. But if you realise I'm on the level here, and that Grayson Long was set up for a fall? Well, then I'll leave the decision of what you want to do up to you.'

The woman considered the offer.

'I'm Vanessa,' she eventually replied. 'If you're lying, I'll be the last voice you ever hear.'

This threat given, the woman turned and stormed out of the alley, leaving Marlowe, breathless but otherwise unhurt, to coil the defence bracelet back around his wrist.

Looking at his watch, he saw he had fifteen minutes to get to the diner. But that wasn't the thought on his mind right now.

Vanessa, the woman from the photo, had been told where he was. If his father had sent the photo and the hitman as a message, why would he do that? More games?

No. The chances were someone else had sent her. Which meant there were other, unknown players on the pitch.

Marlowe sighed.

'Let's look at that life-threatening situation after I deal with the first one,' he muttered to himself, kicking the knife to the side of the alley as he left it, looking for a cab to get him to his next, probably dangerous, maybe even similarly life-threatening meeting of the day.

21

FAMILY LIES

BEFORE HIS UNPLANNED MEETING WITH VANESSA, THE DEAD-hitman's girlfriend, Marlowe had earlier decided that, unlike his usual op planning, when he would start early and scope the location out well in advance, this time he would arrive late, and let his father arrive first.

He'd visited the location several times over the last couple of days, and he knew all the choke points or problem areas, and he knew what Taylor Coleman looked like, but more importantly there was every chance Taylor was expecting to see Grayson Long, and Marlowe didn't want his father to walk in, see him, and immediately leave the Tick Tock Diner, aware that he'd been rumbled.

And so, it was five minutes past ten when Marlowe walked into the Tick Tock Diner, looking for his estranged father, and seeing him sitting by a window in the corner.

Also, as he scanned the diner, he saw Vanessa a couple of booths away, close enough to eavesdrop, but not close enough to be a hindrance of any kind.

Good. She listened.

Bad. She should probably go to the hospital with that wrist. Waiting around probably makes it worse.

Good. If she tries to kill you again, you know her weak spot.

Taylor Coleman had changed little in the years since Marlowe had last seen him. His hair was greyer, his face was darker, likely more from overuse of sun beds than sunny holidays in the Dominican Republic. But he still had that arrogant look Marlowe remembered from a park, around fifteen years earlier.

A look on a face that had stared up at him from the floor in fear, blood pouring from the nose, when Marlowe had threatened his life.

Taylor, seeing Marlowe, didn't appear to be surprised by this unexpected arrival, once more adding to the possibility this wasn't as unexpected as Marlowe had believed, nodding at him and pointing with his hand for Marlowe to sit opposite him at the booth.

Marlowe crossed the diner, sat down, and faced his father.

'You don't look surprised to see me,' he said.

'Should I be?' Taylor spoke, and Marlowe had another flashback, the accent reminding him of the conversation in the park before the punch.

'Well, that depends. You're the one who put hundred grand hits out on me.'

'A hundred thousand dollars, not pounds,' Taylor argued.

'Is there a difference?'

'Yeah. About twenty grand,' Taylor sneered. 'I didn't think you were worth a full six figures in sterling.'

Marlowe leant back in the booth, observing Taylor. The

confrontational attitude only went to cement this was a conversation not meant to happen.

'And why did you put the hit on me?'

'I wanted your attention,' Taylor sipped at his coffee. 'Only I knew you wouldn't come to see me.'

'Let me get this straight,' Marlowe shook his head at the ludicrousness of the situation. 'You wanted to speak to me, so the one thing you did was send a hitman after me.'

Taylor smiled.

'I didn't send a hitman,' he replied coldly. 'I sent a shitty hitman that I knew wouldn't be able to beat you.'

Marlowe didn't want Taylor to see Vanessa, but he couldn't help himself, his eyes flicking over to her, seeing the expression of anger on her face. *She knew the truth now.*

Marlowe took this in.

'You asked for him in particular?'

'No, but I asked for a particular level of assassin. I checked his credentials and knew he wouldn't be able to do this,' Taylor replied. 'The funny thing was that even he didn't believe he could do it. I had to really big him up, even pressure him, to get him to take the gig.'

He sighed.

'I gave the shitty hitman—'

'His name was Grayson Long.'

'Why should I care about his name?' Taylor shook his head in amazement that Marlowe would even know the name. 'Anyway, I gave him some money, enough to cover any expenses he needed to find you. I then made him write the date and time of this meeting on the back of a photo, something he'd carry with him.'

'And you sent him out to die.'

Taylor laughed at this, a barking sound that drew nails down a chalkboard in Marlowe's head.

'I kind of saw it as a *win-win* situation, to be perfectly honest,' he admitted, waving to the waitress for a refill of his coffee. 'If he killed you, I'd get rid of a problem, a thorn I had in my side. And if you killed him, my message would have been given, and I'd save money.'

'And if I hadn't looked at the photo, if I hadn't checked the back of it with a UV pen?'

'Then you wouldn't have been half the spy I thought you were.'

'You know nothing about the spy I am, Father,' Marlowe replied coldly, fighting the urge to lean across and throttle the older man. 'In fact, that's the last time I'm going to call you that, *Taylor*.'

'I've not been called father by you for thirty-odd years. It's not going to mean much to me if you don't bother starting now,' Taylor smiled.

'You deliberately picked Grayson Long, and told the broker Pauline Faulkner to hire him, knowing he wouldn't be able to kill me, and then sent him after me half-cocked, purely there to send a message.'

'Pretty much.'

'Why not just get him to send a message instead?'

'Where would the fun be in that?' Taylor looked horrified at the suggestion.

Marlowe sighed, examining the man in front of him. Taylor Coleman's clothes were well made, but not extravagant. His watch was five figures in cost, but not six. And he'd already decided the tan was more sunbed than sandy beaches.

'I see you haven't done as well for yourself as I thought

you might have,' he said. 'I hope you know how happy that makes me.'

'We're going to talk about money, are we?' Taylor laughed. 'This from a man who has none.'

'Just because I have no job at the moment doesn't mean I'm not without means.'

'No, you have your fake credit cards and your gold coins that you took from some job ten years ago,' Taylor snapped, his face freezing as he realised he'd said too much, given away more than he intended to. And he had every right to look concerned, as Marlowe had gained some very interesting information there.

He knew about the bullion coins.

Only a handful of people knew this, and it looked like one of them had been keeping tabs on Marlowe for his dead-beat dad. *But which one was it?*

Sensing Marlowe was about to respond to this, Taylor quickly continued.

'I know everything about you, Thomas,' he said. 'I've been monitoring you, and even though you haven't seen me in the shadows, I've been there every step of the way.'

There was something about the way Taylor said this that sent a sliver of ice down Marlowe's spine.

'Why have you been watching me?' he asked carefully. 'You didn't seem to give a shit when you wanted to abort me before I was even born.'

'Just because I didn't want you, doesn't mean I don't appreciate you,' Taylor said, and for a moment Marlowe had a vision of a proud father patting his son's shoulder. He wanted to rise, to scream and shout, to take the mug of coffee in front of him and slam it into his father's face—

But he didn't. He still didn't know what was going on here.

As far as he knew, Taylor Coleman was waiting for this so he could claim his own story of self-defence, as his army of bodyguards – all waiting in the diner pretending to be customers – leapt up and executed him. So, instead, he calmed his breathing and smiled darkly.

'You have no right to say that to me,' he said. 'You've nothing in common with me. You sent a man to kill me, and I killed him in self-defence. Something that when I get back to England, I'm sure I'm going to have to deal with, but you're happy with that as well, aren't you?'

'Of course,' Taylor smiled. And this time, it was more genuine. 'I wanted you gone, but I wanted to make sure that if you survived, and if things weren't that great for you in the UK, maybe you'd consider staying in America. Maybe you consider staying with me.'

Taylor's tone had changed; now it was more melancholy.

'You're kidding me,' Marlowe shook his head. 'You want father-son time? That's not how this works.'

'I wanted to see you one last time,' Taylor replied calmly, the smile gone as the tone carried on darkening. 'I'm a realist. I'm aware there's no reason you'd want to speak to me. I've seen you three times in your entire life.'

He counted off on his fingers.

'When you were eighteen. When you were three months old. When you were ten—'

Marlowe raised a hand, stopping his father.

'You never saw me when I was ten.'

'Yes, I did,' Taylor nodded. 'Do you remember a man in a van, a guy in his thirties, long hair and a straggly beard, trying to convince you to go for a drive with him? When you were walking out of school?'

Marlowe considered this.

'I remember there was a guy with a beard who hung around the outside of school. And I remember one day he wasn't there.'

'He was there to take you hostage,' Taylor replied solemnly. 'Somebody had a problem with me and used you as a bargaining chip. Your mum at the time wasn't as high in the security services as she ended up being, so I took him out personally and brought you home.'

'Mum never told me this.'

'Of course not. As far as she was concerned, everything that happened was brought on by me.'

Taylor chuckled sadly, looking down at his mug.

'She had a point – your mum always did. I'm sorry, by the way. I know she died a while back and I should have sent flowers to the funeral, except nobody told me there was one.'

Marlowe didn't like the way this conversation was going. He'd expected a confrontation, but this was sounding more like a therapy session by the moment.

'You're being very fatalistic,' he said, checking his watch. 'Could you get to the point, because I'm having a really awful weekend at the moment, and I need to be leaving soon.'

'I'm dying, Tom. Is that blunt enough for you?'

Marlowe looked up from his watch.

'Yeah, that's pretty blunt,' was all he could think of.

'I have cancer. It's eating away at my lungs,' Taylor continued. 'The annoying thing is it wasn't actually from smoking. It was from various carcinogenic shit I've inhaled while working on weaponry. But it doesn't matter now, the doctor says I've got weeks, months, maybe years if I'm super lucky. No one seems to know. Nobody wants to give me a solid diagnosis just in case I prove them wrong and take them to court. But chances are, by the end of this year, you'll be an orphan.'

Marlowe glowered at Taylor Coleman.

How dare you throw this on me, he thought to himself. *How dare you try to make me feel sympathy after you send a hitman to kill me.*

'I brought you here today, because I wanted you to know that when I die, I'm not leaving you anything,' Taylor continued.

Hearing this, Marlowe felt relieved.

Ah, there you are again, you devious bastard.

'Wait, the whole reason for bringing me here was to tell me I'm out of your will?'

'No Tom, you *are* in my will,' Taylor stared Marlowe directly in the eyes now, as if trying to gain some sort of connection. 'And it's an important thing to know. So, there are people in my life. A family. A half-brother and half-sister who you've never met, and these will receive the bulk of my money when I pass. But even though you're illegitimate, you're the oldest. And if you wanted, you could contest the will, saying you're owed as much as they are. I don't want you to do that.'

'So why not just have me killed? It's not like you haven't tried that already.'

Taylor shook his head.

'As much as that would help me immensely, I'm also aware I let you down, and I let your mother down. So, when I'm gone, there'll be an item that I will send you. My last apology to you. And when you get it, I hope you use it.'

Taylor grinned. But it was a sad, almost mocking one.

'Class this as my last gift to you,' he continued. 'You will never get what you hope for. Instead, you will always get what you deserve.'

His message given, he leant back on the chair, waving his hand dismissively.

'Here endeth the lesson,' he said magnanimously. 'You can go now. I'm sure you have other things to do. Thank you for coming.'

Marlowe got up now, staring down at his phoney onetime father.

'Never contact me again,' he said. 'Don't give me the details of your funeral, I'd only turn up to gloat. Don't send me this item. I want nothing from you.'

'When I die, and not before, my children, your brothers and sisters, may contact you,' Taylor said. 'Don't even think about talking to them while I live.'

Marlowe couldn't help himself, he laughed. It wasn't the situation; it was the fact he'd looked at Vanessa, and saw the impotent rage on her face. It was the face of a killer, and for once, it wasn't aimed at Marlowe.

'Dad,' he said, leaning in, relaxing. He wanted these last words to count. 'You are dying. And yes, your time is short. But it won't be cancer that ends you. And it won't be me, either.'

He patted Taylor on the shoulder.

'Watch your back,' he said, turning away from the man who'd conceived him, and walking purposely from the diner. He'd expected to be attacked, he'd expected to have to fight for his life.

He hadn't expected to be made to feel like a failure.

Walking out into the street, he looked through the diner's window. But, as expected, Taylor Coleman was already gone.

Interestingly, so was Vanessa. Still, as long as she wanted to kill Taylor instead of Marlowe, he was fine with that.

According to his watch, it was almost half past ten. After one more stop, he could be back in the hotel in an hour, and the plan could start in earnest. So, shaking away the demons of his past, Marlowe walked north, away from the Tick Tock Diner, his father, and his past.

———————

22

CIVIL ON REST

TRIX HAD BEEN STANDING BY THE COMPUTER WHEN THE DOOR to the suite had been kicked in by armed men.

'Get on the floor!' the lead armed man, a chunky, quite overweight-looking black man with dreads and a tatty goatee beard cried out, aiming a gun – likely a Glock – at them. Trix frowned as Roxanne, knowing her role in this stepped forward, allowing Trix to grab the drive and briefly rub it against the electromagnet beside her. The man looked capable, but in no way looked the kind of security someone with means would hire.

Which meant Cody Donziger had gone to a more freelance type of guard.

Which also meant there was a very strong chance here that the men in front of them had short tempers and quick trigger fingers.

'Hey!' the man waved his gun at her. 'Get the drive away from that!'

Trix went to argue, but a second wave of the gun stopped

her. She nodded, stepping away, placing the drive onto the desk.

'You don't need her,' Roxanne said, hands in the air. 'You want me. And my information—'

She didn't finish the sentence as the man backhanded her across the face, falling to the ground, clutching at her cheek.

'You want the same?' he growled at Trix, now standing, her hands on her head, away from the desk. 'Get on the floor.'

'Cody won't pay you for damaged goods,' Trix replied, getting onto her knees, hands on her head. She looked at the other four men, entering behind the lead – they were young, white, and all had short, tidy haircuts. One had a Confederate flag patch sewn onto his jacket, and Trix pursed her lips.

There was every chance that instead of going to professional organisations, Cody Donziger had been forced to conscript Proud Boys, or various other alt-right organisations for muscle. And that wasn't good. Everything relied on the security being professional if they wanted to stay alive.

'Who are you?' the lead man asked.

'Steph,' Trix lied, forcing a quiver of fear into her voice. 'I'm Miss Vasquez's PA.'

'Well now, you're her fellow hostage,' one of the young men in the back smiled. 'And later, you're gonna be our evening entertainment.'

'Back down, Dean,' a new, hooded figure walked into the room, the jacket bulky and unflattering, but also deliberately worn to hide the man's identity as they walked through the hotel downstairs, an identity revealed the moment the hood was pulled off, and Cody Donziger stood in the doorway. 'I need my hostages fresh and uninjured.'

He smiled.

'And Miss Preston there is an honoured guest.'

'Too scared to do your dirty work yourself?' Roxanne muttered, rubbing her cheek where a vicious-looking welt had appeared. 'Your men seem a little less professional than your usual hired help.'

'Needs must, and all that,' Cody looked at the surrounding men. 'It's interesting how deep you need to go when the usual channels ignore your calls.'

'They're older than the males you usually order,' Roxanne smiled.

And at this, Cody's own smile dropped.

'Bring them,' he ordered. 'And the drive, too.'

'I don't know what drive you mean—' Trix started, but stopped as the lead man, who she'd decided to call *Chunk*, pulled the muzzle of his gun up to the level of her face.

'The only reason you're useful right now, Trixibelle Preston, is because you can break whatever shitty encryption you put on it,' Cody said.

'Get up,' *Chunk* growled. 'You're going on an adventure.'

As she helped the still-smarting Roxanne up, Trix knew without a doubt that she really *didn't* want to go on this adventure.

LIBERTY JONES HAD ALWAYS KNOWN SHE WOULD BE AN ACTIVIST. After all, with a name like "Liberty", you'd expect to move in that direction.

If she was honest, most people who met her assumed this was a *fake* name, an identity she thought a protest organiser should have, but even if she'd become a bank manager, Liberty Jones would still have been just Liberty Jones.

Although she could never see herself as a bank manager.

Now, Liberty was sitting in an Irish Bar during the Saturday lunch rush, facing an unknown British man, someone her boyfriend Dermot had vouched for, and unsure quite what he was looking for.

She was young, in her mid-to-late-twenties, but she'd been planning protests and acts of corporate chaos since she was a junior in High School. She knew, though she looked like butter wouldn't melt in her mouth, her long black hair, pale skin and blue eyes making her look like the "girl next door" who wouldn't even say boo to a goose, she'd been inside more police cells than half the drinkers in the bar in that short time, and was even known to half the New York police force on a first-name basis.

Of course, when it was "Liberty", it wasn't exactly a hard name to forget.

'Explain this to me again,' she said, pulling a notebook out. It was a dotted bullet journal, her only way to keep things straight in her head, and from what she'd just heard, her head was about to become incredibly confused.

'I need to know how someone would organise a protest at the last minute,' the man, named Marlowe, asked. 'I know the UK rules, but I'm not sure how the US works, and I've been told you're the best.'

'By Dermot?' Liberty tried not to blush. 'I love him, but he doesn't know shit. But in this case, he's right. I'm the person to speak to.'

She leant forward, over the table now, her voice lowering.

'The First Amendment protects our rights to assemble and express our views through protest,' she explained. 'However, police and other government types can place certain narrow restrictions on how we exercise these rights.'

'They can shut you down?'

Liberty considered this for a moment.

'If we go off the guideline areas, sure,' she replied. 'But if we can keep to the rules, there's not a lot they can do. It's why peaceful protest is so dangerous.'

'Explain it to me,' Marlowe smiled. 'Like I'm an idiot.'

Liberty thought through the best way to explain this, and then nodded.

'Okay, so our rights are strongest in what are known as "traditional public forums", yeah?' she started. 'And no, I don't mean internet forums. I mean things like streets, sidewalks, and parks.'

'So, marches?'

'Kinda. You also likely have the right to speak out on other public property, like plazas in front of Government buildings, but this is only if you don't block access to the building, or screw around with any of the purposes the property was designed for.'

'This isn't anti-Government,' Marlowe nodded. 'It's in Times Square, and outside a hotel.'

Liberty noted this down in her journal.

'Okay, so if it's a hotel, private property rules differ,' she said. 'Owners can set rules for speech on their property. According to the law, the government can't restrict your speech if it is taking place on your own property, or with the consent of the property owner.'

'I don't think we're going to get consent here.'

'Okay, good to know. Also, you should know that counterprotesters also have free speech rights.'

'You mean if we hit a rival protest that's completely opposed to us? I think we're okay there,' Marlowe looked off to the side for a moment, thinking. 'Do we need a permit?'

Now it was Liberty's turn to look away, working the logistics through in her head.

'You don't need a permit to march in the streets or on sidewalks, as long as marchers don't obstruct car or pedestrian traffic,' she explained. 'But if you *don't* have a permit, the police can make you move to the side of a street or sidewalk to let others pass.'

She was writing notes down as she spoke.

'Certain types of events might require them,' she continued. 'Marches or parades that block traffic or cause some kind of street closure, maybe a large rally requiring the use of sound speakers, and definitely large rallies at most parks or plazas.'

'That's the kind of march I was hoping for, though,' Marlowe admitted.

At this, Liberty looked up, smiling.

'Well, luckily for you, there's a loophole,' she said as she waggled the pen in the air. 'While most protests have to process applications well before the event, police can't use those procedures to prevent a protest in response to breaking news.'

Marlowe smiled.

'Something like a one-percenter being outed as a terrible person. Maybe with dodgy as hell free-time activities involving teenage boys?'

Liberty nodded.

'Exactly,' she said. 'Hypothetical situation. People are already pissed about Cody Donziger. The environmental brigade have wanted to kick off since they announced the Jericho Falls case, and the settlement yesterday, added to the attack on the law firm, was enough to push it over the edge.'

She leant back, nodding to herself, working out the moving pieces.

'There's a powder keg ready to explode, and the right buttons need to be pressed, and soon. But it'll depend on what we get out of it.'

'Financially?'

'God no!' Liberty looked offended at the offer. 'If someone's coming out at short notice to protest in the early February snow, then they need to know it's not in vain. I need to know, when I tell my lieutenants, that they're doing something good, something important, and that it won't be for nothing.'

She looked over at Dermot, watching them from the bar, before looking back at Marlowe.

'You need to tell me what I'm missing,' she said.

Marlowe now shifted his position, as if considering her words and working out what to say.

'Roxanne Vasquez is my ... well, my client,' he said. 'I work in a very specific form of troubleshooting, and I've been brought in to help take down Donziger.'

'But the case was settled, and from what I hear they fired Vasquez from the firm,' Liberty replied, curious where this was going.

'That's also true, but the information she had still exists out there,' Marlowe continued. 'Information which, once it comes out, is fatal to some of the top people in Donziger Industries. Proof of years of illegal activities by Nathan himself, for example, as well as more on Cody, the Senators they've controlled ... Senators that are now freed from following the rules.'

'And how does she have this sort of information?'

Marlowe made a self-depreciating shrug.

'I stole some of it,' he admitted. 'And the rest was given to her by Brett Hendricks, who used to be the second-in-command there. He was with Nathan from the start, and saw – and noted down – every illegal act in case he ever needed to use it against the company. That information was, after his death, left in the care of his daughter. Roxanne Vasquez.'

'Damn,' Liberty couldn't help herself. 'You're serious, aren't you?'

Marlowe nodded.

'This evening there's a gala dinner at the New York Palace Hotel,' he continued. 'Set up before the court case was closed, and mainly a way to get all his paid-for politicians into town so they could give him options out of this mess. Now, it's a way for him to check in, make sure they're all on his side still. The file that was released on Cody today has destabilised that.'

'That your work?'

'It was,' Dermot spoke now, having walked over with two drinks, a bottle of lite beer for Liberty and a Guinness for Marlowe. 'And he gave it out for free.'

'We can hack the networks,' Marlowe leant closer as Dermot joined them. 'I have an expert sorting that out. And tonight, at seven, the exact moment Nathan Donziger gives his speech, we're going to give our own. Roxanne is going live, globally, and every piece of her hard drive that relates to Donziger's corruption is being uploaded to file share sites around the world, with two more appearing for every one they take down.'

'But the media could mute a fancy speech and a file drop,' Liberty mused. 'Therefore, you want a protest rally. Therefore, you need people.'

'The media won't be able to hide this,' Marlowe sipped

from the pint. 'They'll have to show the protest, and the ones that aren't in Donziger's pocket will have a field day. He needs good publicity, he'll be bringing press into the gala. What he doesn't know is half the Senators and governors he owns have been given their files back, and, well, they don't seem to be singing from the same hymn book anymore.'

'Seven pm,' Liberty checked her phone. 'That's a lot of quick-turnaround items to be sorted. That costs. What's your activist budget here?'

Marlowe reached into his jacket pocket and pulled out a handful of gold coins, placing them onto the table.

'Each coin is worth one and a half grand,' Dermot said as Liberty picked one of the five coins, turning it in her hand. 'I have a guy who can take all of these off our hands right now. Untraceable. And seven grand should be enough to start the war chest.'

'They're called—' Marlowe started, but paused as Liberty looked at him.

'They're called freedom,' she smiled. 'I think we can do business, Mister Marlowe. Two rallies, one at Times Square, and a second one outside the Lotte New York Palace Hotel, a couple of blocks away. I'll get started on it right now.'

'How will you get people to turn up?' Marlowe rose from the chair, already buttoning up his jacket.

'I'm Liberty goddamn Jones,' Liberty laughed. 'If I post there's gonna be something massive happening tonight? Then *everyone's* turning up. And tell your expert I'll throw in ten minutes access to the Times Square screens too ... for free.'

MARLOWE FELT AS IF THINGS COULD ACTUALLY WORK AS HE returned to the midtown hotel. There was a protest brewing, the files were ready to be uploaded, and Roxanne's message would be seen around the world. He wouldn't be there for that, though, as he intended to be in ground zero for the speech at Donziger's gala.

His phone ringing, however, pulled him out of his revelry as he walked through the hotel lobby, staring down at it.

Caller ID Withheld

'Hello?' Marlowe answered the phone, wondering who it could be. There was every chance it was Brad, or Trix, but at the same time it could be Trisha, or Sasha Bordeaux – maybe it was time to change the number again.

'Hello, Marlowe,' a male voice spoke, and Marlowe stopped, standing in the middle of the lobby as he focused on the call. 'We need to have a little chat.'

Marlowe recognised the voice. He'd only had a brief conversation with him once, but the accent was unmistakable.

'Sorry Cody, but have you seen the news?' he asked with a hint of concern. 'I don't think anyone's going to want to have chats with you. And you shouldn't be using "little" in a conversation.'

'Cut the shit, you limey fuck!' Cody shouted down the phone. 'I know you did this! You and Trisha Hawkins! I'll get that bitch too, believe me!'

Marlowe fought the urge to smile; his plan had at least worked in that aspect, and Trisha Hawkins had her own price on her head now.

'Yeah, I did it,' Marlowe replied casually. 'And I'd do it

again. You deserve every piece of shit thrown at you.'

'I want what you took,' Cody snarled. 'I want the files you stole from my family.'

'Or what?' Marlowe asked. He needed Cody to reply, to answer this – only then would he know if his plan worked.

'Or I kill your girlfriend,' Cody said.

There was a pause down the line.

'Oh, did you think I wouldn't find them?' Cody sounded triumphant now. 'She put up a fight, but bitches get stitches. You have files on a few prominent Senators that I want back. Tonight.'

Marlowe looked around the lobby, working out his next move. *Were they still in the hotel?*

'You don't want to go down this road,' he shook his head as he spoke. 'Once you step off the pavement, I'll run you the hell over.'

'I have the bitch lawyer, I have her drive filled with secrets, and tonight I'll have you, the bastard who stole my family's files,' Cody snapped. 'Do you really think this shit about teenage boys will stop me? I'm rich, you prick. Like "buy countries" levels of rich. I do what I want, when I want. And you can't do a thing about it.'

'You touch either of them, I'll kill you.'

There was a long laugh down the phone.

'Then you'd better come do it because I've already smacked them around good,' Cody said. 'Tick tick tick, you Limey prick.'

The call disconnected, and it left Marlowe alone once more. Roxanne and Trix had been captured by Cody Donziger. And from the sounds of things, the drive was with them.

The only way Cody could have found them, though - and

Marlowe had expected this to be the case - was through Brad or Trix. And whether Marlowe knew what was happening or not, one thing was obvious. Tonight, Marlowe needed to end this, one way or another.

He looked at his watch again. He had eight hours. Nathan Donziger's speech was at seven. Which meant Marlowe needed to get in, find the girls, break them out and face down with Cody before then.

That was good. You could start a *revolution* in eight hours.

Before he walked to his room, however, he went to check his messages at the reception desk, a habit he'd picked up from years in the field. And he was glad he did this, as there was a new tuxedo waiting for him at reception, a gift note attached. To begin with, he thought this was Cody, flexing a little more, but then he read the note.

I don't like how Sasha Bordeaux ended in the comics. But I'm keeping the name.
British spies look great in these, I'm told.
We look forward to seeing Brad again.

Marlowe smiled as he took it upstairs. He knew he'd have to scan it for trackers and bugs, but at the end of the day, this saved him the hassle of finding a new one, the last one he owned being covered in blood, and also saved him the cost of a new tuxedo, as his recent donation to activism had brought him scarily close to being cash broke.

The corridor was empty, the door ajar. Knowing the room would now be empty, and had likely been this way for a while now, Marlowe walked into the suite and looked around. The suite was strangely untouched, but someone had trashed the computer system against the window.

Cody Donziger was a terrible loser, it seemed.

Marlowe placed the tuxedo onto the bed in the other room, taking a deep breath. If his plan failed, then Roxanne and Trix would both be dead by the end of the night.

'You need help?' a woman's voice spoke from behind him, and Marlowe spun around to see Vanessa watching him from the doorway. 'The door was open.'

'The door's broken,' Marlowe walked back into the living area. 'Are you here for round two?'

Vanessa shook her head.

'You were right,' she said. 'I looked into him. Your pop's a piece of shit, and you didn't have a chance.'

'Neither did Grayson,' Marlowe admitted. 'So, why're you here?'

'You looked like you were about to commit mayhem,' Vanessa smiled. 'I thought I might want in on it. I happen to have a lot of pent-up rage I need to get rid of right now.'

'Well then, you've come to the right place,' Marlowe smiled. 'Because I have enough mayhem brewing for everyone.'

He looked around the suite, locating the phone. Picking it up, he dialled the front desk.

'It's Mister Garner, I have – yes, thank you. I need a couple of things. First, can you send a man to fix our door? It seems to be broken.'

He looked Vanessa up and down.

'And could you send someone up from the dress shop connected to the lobby?' he added. 'I need help to buy a very expensive dress.'

23

PARTIED DRESS

I<small>F THERE WAS ONE THING</small> T<small>RIX</small> P<small>RESTON COULD SAY ABOUT</small> Cody Donziger, it was that he at least placed his prisoners in nice places.

The "cell" they were currently held in was the Imperial Suite of the Lotte New York Palace Hotel, a place that was larger than the entirety of her apartment back in London, and she had a pretty pleasant apartment. There was almost five thousand square foot of space here, all over one level, with four exits from the door to the suite, with ornately designed marble floors merging into expensive carpets, and white and gold walls looking down from above; walls which wouldn't have looked out of place in Versailles.

This wasn't a suite they could enjoy, though; they'd been brought into the room while unconscious, the guards having chloroformed them both in the truck outside, and after a few hours left alone had eventually woken up sprawled on the carpet of a room in the far right corner, a frankly over-whelming ensuite room filled with teal, gold and white furniture, a king-sized bed covered in gold silk one end, and some ornate chairs around a flat-screen television on the other.

Here Trix and Roxanne had slowly awoken from their forced sleep, only to be told by the men to wait, while *Chunk* wandered off into another room to speak to his boss, Cody, probably to let him know they'd woken.

For the next hour, they hadn't been allowed to watch the TV, but this was probably because every news channel was still talking about Cody's bombshell revelations, and he didn't want to be reminded more than anything else, and so they'd sat there in silence, mainly glaring at the two men facing them.

Interestingly, there was only one doorway to the room, but it didn't have a door; the suite was in a way more "open plan" than most others, with a large and heavy curtain pulled across the middle of the room to provide privacy for anyone in the bed.

It also helped Cody and the others see what was happening, as a guard down the other end could see into the room without moving or having to open a door.

There was a lot of noise from elsewhere in the suite, and Trix assumed that somewhere to the left of them, through the wall behind the bed, was another large living area, and this was where the remaining guards, and maybe even Cody himself were situated. This was the war room as Cody tried to salvage what he could.

Around five in the afternoon, one of the guards had brought in some cans of Coke and a vegetarian pizza from down the road, so it was heartening to see they wanted to keep their hostages alive. But, even though she'd kept her tone relaxed and jovial when talking to Roxanne, Trix was a little more concerned about a couple of things, concerns she hadn't brought to light yet.

The first was the plan. It relied on a lot of fast moving and complicated pieces, and all it would take was for one of these not to work for the whole damned thing to collapse.

It could be as simple as Brad not connecting with Marlowe, or his friend in the Irish bar not succeeding in his own task – hell, to even get the message out there, Trix needed to gain access to a dozen different things, none of which were here in the room with her right now.

The second, more worrying thing, was *everyone around them*. The guards, even Cody himself; nobody was wearing a mask of any kind. They literally didn't care if Trix or Roxanne saw their faces.

And this was bad, because it meant they didn't worry about Trix or Roxanne identifying them down the line.

This was most likely because they intended to *kill* both women before the end of the night.

Of course, they wouldn't be able to do this until they had everything they needed. And that was going to be a little difficult, a fact Cody and his team had realised, gathering from the raised voices now shouting from next door, as someone finally checked on the drive they'd taken. Blame was being passed, and nobody wanted to be the scapegoat.

The voices stopped, and a moment later an angry Cody Donziger walked into the room, *Chunk* following behind.

'What did you do, you little bitch?' Cody exploded at Roxanne, who looked over at Trix, confused.

'I think he means you because I've done nothing,' Roxanne said.

'What did you do to the external drive?' Cody snapped.

'The goddammed thing's corrupted! We've had a guy working on it for hours.'

Roxanne shrugged.

'Maybe you dropped it?'

'She put it on a grey thing,' *Chunk* offered, pointing at Trix. 'When we caught them.'

Cody slowly turned to face the dreadlocked guard.

'She did what?'

'I stuck it on a powered-up electromagnet,' Trix replied. 'I was hoping it'd wipe the whole damn thing, but obviously not.'

Cody stared back at Trix.

'Look on the bright side,' she offered with a smile. 'You wanted the information Roxanne's dad had on you gone, right? Alakazam! I did it for you.'

'You corrupted the files,' Cody muttered. 'I don't know what they were beforehand. This could be a drive filled with holiday snaps, not data taken from Rehbein and Pope.'

'If they were holiday snaps, they'd be a little different to yours, I suppose,' Roxanne snapped. 'It's the drive. You win. Let us go.'

'Too quick to admit failure,' Cody shook his head. 'No. We're gonna look at it together. You're supposed to be a shit-hot hacker, Miss Preston, you can show us your skills and uncorrupt it.'

'That's not how drives work.'

'You'd better hope it is,' *Chunk* held his gun up, aiming it at Trix now. 'Or you—'

'Or I'll what?' Trix snapped. 'You're going to kill us, anyway. Either when your dad has his gala or shortly after. We've seen your faces. You think we don't realise what that means?'

'There are ways to die,' Cody said now, walking towards them. 'You can go peacefully, painlessly, or you can scream as I skin every last piece of your flesh off you. And believe me, I can keep going longer than you can keep screaming.'

He grabbed Trix's arm, dragging her into the corridor.

'You're going to show us what's on that drive, if it's the last thing you do,' he growled.

'Don't you have a party to go to?' Roxanne shouted out after him.

'I'll go later!' Cody shouted back. 'Sit that bitch down while I deal with this one first!'

Trix, being dragged along behind Cody, looked to the floor, hiding a small, secret smile.

So far, everything was going swimmingly.

'You don't have to pull so hard,' she muttered sullenly. 'After all, I'm the one who called you, remember?'

Cody ignored her as he continued into the next room.

'You screwed the drive up.'

'I had to! Your guard was about to give me away!'

'Just fix this,' Cody said angrily. 'You do that, and the deal we made this morning stays.'

THE GATE GUARDS AT THE ENTRANCE TO THE LOTTE NEW YORK Palace Hotel were thorough, that was for sure.

As Marlowe walked up the steps towards the main entrance, Vanessa beside him in an extravagant black dress and matching fur, he wondered if he'd bitten off a little more than he could chew.

There was a full-on security checkpoint for anyone entering, and Marlowe knew without a doubt that every identity he'd had created was probably burnt or known by Donziger.

The couple ahead of them passed through, and a woman with an iPad in her hands looked up, disinterested, at Vanessa and Marlowe as they stopped in front of her.

'Invitation,' she said, bored and likely cold, and Vanessa pulled the invitation Marlowe had given her ten minutes earlier out of her jacket, passing it across.

'Trisha Hawkins,' she said, in possibly the worst fake British accent Marlowe had ever heard, maybe even worse than Keanu Reeves in *Dracula*, or Dick Van Dyke in *Mary Poppins,* and that was saying a lot. 'This is my plus one.'

The woman took the invite, scanning a QR code on the corner of the card. On her pad, the name "TRISHA HAWKINS" appeared.

'ID?' she asked.

At this, Vanessa seemed to rise a foot in height.

'And who are you to demand to see identification from *me?*' she boomed, her voice commanding, if a little ridiculous, with the accent. 'Where's your manager? Hell, where's Nathan? Get him now!'

Marlowe hid a smile – he'd told her to do exactly this. And to be honest, this wouldn't have been the first guest to throw the "don't you know who I am" card at them that evening.

Sighing, the woman pressed a checkbox, confirming "Trisha" as having arrived, and looked across at Marlowe.

'Name?'

Marlowe passed over the Secret Service ID wallet of *Crotch Kick*, who had turned out to be named Neil Haskell. The woman read it and looked back at him.

Marlowe hadn't had time to change the image professionally, so it was still Neil that stared out of the photo, but with dark hair and eyes, the clean shaven man in the photo could easily be the bearded man in front of her, given time.

'The beard—' she started, but Marlowe chuckled, interrupting her.

'Undercover for four months,' he said, rubbing the beard. 'And it ain't coming off until this wind stops.'

'Senator Kyle has loaned Agent Haskell to me,' Vanessa interjected. 'Or do you want to call in and check *her* passport too?'

Seeing the queue building up behind, and *really* not wanting this argument, the poor woman decided to simply go with it, and waved Marlowe and Vanessa through.

He wasn't carrying any weapons, but his arm beeped as he walked through.

'Prayer chain,' he said, showing the edge of the steel around his wrist, under the dress shirt. The guard with the scanner waved over it, decided it was too much hassle to argue, and stepped to the side, allowing them to enter the party.

'You did well there,' Marlowe said as they entered the hotel reception.

At this, Vanessa scoffed.

'Grayson and I did way more than this, back in the day,' she said. 'I thought you were giving me a challenge.'

'You still not telling me who told you where I was staying?'

Vanessa kept silent. Marlowe decided not to press this and carried on into the main ballroom, guiding Vanessa towards a bar along the side.

'You know, I'm gonna kill your dad, right?' she asked casually.

'When you do, take a photo, yeah?' Marlowe replied with a tight smile. 'I need something new to stick on the fridge.'

As they reached the bar, a middle-aged barman with a buzz-cut walked over, wiping a glass.

'Who the hell's this?' Brad snapped. 'You brought a hooker?'

'Call me that again and I'll end you,' Vanessa growled, already holding the end of a stirrer in her hand.

Brad smiled.

'I like her more than you already,' he said.

'Brad, meet Vanessa,' Marlowe said. 'CIA, meet hit woman. There. All secrets out, let's carry on with the mission.'

'Kitchen's through the left door, go to the freezer and look at the back of the bottom right shelf,' Brad spoke calmly and softly. 'I didn't know you'd have a friend, though, so you might have to share your toys.'

'You?'

Brad tapped his hip.

'Ready to go. Just let me know when the call is.'

Marlowe looked back at the entrance.

'I didn't see any protesters,' he mused. 'They should have been here by now.'

'Oh, don't worry, they'll be here,' Brad grinned evilly. 'I've been getting the gossip from some of the late arrivals. They've snarled up Times Square already with their anti-Donziger rally, and the police are doing what they can to stop them continuing here.'

He nodded at the main doors.

'They won't manage it. The numbers are too many,' he finished. 'They'll arrive just as Nathan starts his speech, up there on the stage, in front of that lovely, massive screen.'

'Trix and Roxanne?'

'In one of the suites, but I can't work out which one,' Brad growled. 'It's the Imperial one, or they're around that area of the building, though. There's been a lot of furtive movement that way.'

Marlowe nodded, already heading for the kitchen.

'Vanessa, mill around, see if you can work out who's plain-clothed security,' he said as he walked away. 'Brad, feel free to quit your job and upgrade your situation any time soon.'

Brad watched Marlowe leave and turned back to Vanessa.

'So,' he said with a winning smile. 'How do you know Marlowe?'

'He killed my partner.'

'Good talk,' Brad groaned inwardly, the smile plastered on. 'Good talk.'

MARLOWE HAD GOT INTO THE FREEZER WITHOUT ANYONE seeing him, and once in, pulled a small case from the lower shelf.

This was one of Brad's jobs that day; to get his New York assets to help him smuggle arms into the party. The other job was to stay around and gather what information he could about where Trix and Roxanne would be held.

Checking his watch, he saw it was still fifteen minutes until Nathan Donziger started his speech, which meant that he couldn't go to the suite the women were likely held in yet, as there were other things that still needed to be done in order.

Opening the case, he growled as he stared down at a Walther PPK pistol and spare cartridge.

'Oh, you're so bloody funny, you Yank prick,' he muttered as he pulled James Bond's favourite gun from the box, slipping it into his shoulder holster. This done, he took an earbud, placing it in his ear.

'Trix?'

No answer.

And that was expected – when Trix needed him, a message would come through.

Grabbing the other pieces left for him, including a knife, some kind of acidic spray in a small can and a small chunk of C4 explosive, complete with detonator, he placed them into his pockets as he rose, walking out of the freezer and pulling out his phone.

Typing quickly, he sent a text.

> Zero minus fifteen. Where are you?

After a moment, three dots flashed on the screen. And then

> Getting push back on 47th. Will be there.
> Video?

> It'll come.

> It better.

Marlowe placed the phone away, deciding to end the little back and forth with Liberty Jones.

He could understand her nervousness, but he couldn't

really fill her with hope when he still didn't know if the whole thing was going to work.

Checking his watch one more time, he walked back into the ballroom.

It was time to start the performance.

———

24

TEMPTATION

They'd sat Trix down at a desk, a laptop connected to an ethernet cable in front of her. Beside it was the drive, connected on the other side of the laptop by a USB-C adaptor.

'This wasn't part of the deal,' she muttered, typing as she did so. 'I just told you where she would be. I wasn't supposed to be taken with her.'

'Plans change,' Cody snapped, walking out of the room as he spoke. 'You're the one who did this when you corrupted the drive.'

'I already explained that! Your goons came in trying to kill me!' Trix snapped back, raising her voice as he stopped in the doorway. 'I panicked! You were supposed to wait until I found an excuse to leave!'

'You were taking too long!'

'Bullshit! We've been here for hours! You couldn't pick a later time?'

Cody pinched the bridge of his nose, avoiding the impending headache.

'Just fix it,' he pleaded. 'I'll double your fee, yeah? I need to change.'

Trix stared at the laptop in an almost disgusted expression.

'This?' she asked. 'You expect me to decrypt the corrupted drive with effectively a Speak-And-Spell?'

'It's top of the line!' Cody screamed from the room next door. 'It's enough to do what you need! For Christ's sake, *it's what you asked for!*'

'I asked for the GX version,' Trix muttered as she looked at the others in the room; two of the mercenaries who'd captured her were still there, including *Chunk*, who stood nervously by the door, watching her.

He's the weak link, she thought to herself as she started tapping on the keyboard, opening up the drive's file structure.

'Yeah, this is buggered,' she said. 'You can see—'

'Then un-bugger it,' Cody, now in black trousers and an expensive white dress-shirt, walked back into view, tying a black bow tie. 'Or the deal's off, and you can go explain to your pal next door how you betrayed her.'

'Okay, okay, keep your hair on,' Trix flashed a smile. 'You gonna go see Daddy? Really sure he wants you near him when he does his speech. You're a little ... you know ...'

She ended by mouthing the word "toxic" at him.

'My father's speech is about the media following the woke left's mandate of smearing those they hate,' Cody was pulling on a tuxedo jacket now. 'To remove from power those that go against their new world order.'

'Yeah, but in your case, it was more because you were a creepy perv, though, weren't you?' Trix looked up from the screen.

Cody, his face reddening, stormed across the suite and

backhanded her across the face, sending her tumbling from the chair.

'You work for me, so act like it,' he growled.

Trix rubbed at her cheek, now reddening from the impact.

'Sorry.'

'Sorry what?'

'Sorry, *sir*.'

Cody looked content with the answer and returned to his bow tie.

'I want this un-encrypted by the time I get back,' he said. 'I want proof this is the drive you claim it is before any money changes hands.'

He looked at the others.

'Come with me,' he said, already moving towards the door. However, he paused, looking over at *Chunk*.

'Monitor them,' he said. 'If they try anything stupid, kill them. Let me know when she fixes it.'

With this order given, Cody and his men left the room.

Trix sighed. The "kill them" order had been expected – as she'd already worked out, the lack of masks pretty much confirmed Cody wanted them both dead.

She stared at *Chunk*. And, in return, *Chunk* stared back at her.

'How you gonna monitor us both?' she asked with a smile, and *Chunk* frowned. After a moment, he leaned back into the corridor.

'Hey, lawyer woman!' he shouted. 'Get your ass in here.'

A moment later Roxanne walked past him, sitting moodily onto a chair as Trix looked back at the screen.

'You ever killed before?' she asked.

'Sure,' *Chunk* said, but the concern on his face spoke a different story.

'Really?' Trix turned to face him. 'You've killed?'

'Yeah.'

'Unarmed women?' Roxanne added.

At this, however, *Chunk* didn't answer.

'You'd better swot up on it, considering that's what you're about to be asked to do,' Trix said, looking back at the laptop, working on it once more. 'That's why he left you here. To do the job, to take the blame.'

'What d'ya mean?' *Chunk* frowned at this. 'You're doing what he asks—'

'And he'll still kill us,' Trix interrupted. 'We saw your faces, remember? You heard him. It wasn't about if we die, it's how slow we die. And you'll be told to do just that by Cody. When he's far away from us, so there won't be any kind of collateral damage landing on him when they execute you.'

'What, the courts?' *Chunk* looked over at Roxanne, probably because he knew she was a lawyer.

'No, you bloody fool. The SAS, when they hear what you did.'

Chunk didn't reply to this, his eyes narrowing, and Trix turned to face him, almost in shock.

'He didn't tell you who we were, did he?' she said.

'She's a lawyer, and you're an uppity Brit who betrayed her for money,' *Chunk* snapped. 'That's all I need to know.'

'Not quite,' Trix shook her head. 'I offered to help, as the Donzigers have files on my family I need back.'

'Your family?'

'I'm Lady Trixibelle Preston-Windsor, of the Farnham Windsors, and I'm thirteenth in line to the throne of Great

Britain,' Trix snapped angrily. 'And going back to your earlier comment, the Royal Family is not "uppity", okay?'

'Bullshit,' *Chunk* shook his head. 'No. I would have known.'

'Oh, you would, would you? You're NBC's Royal correspondent or something? It's on my bloody driver's licence, you cretin,' Trix pointed at her jacket, in the room's corner, dumped with Roxanne's, taken when they arrived. 'Look in my purse.'

Chunk looked conflicted now. Trix pressed on.

'My uncle is the Duke of Hastings,' she said. 'Open my bloody purse and look. He'll give you double, triple what the Donzigers are offering.'

Reluctant to agree with this, but curious enough to check, *Chunk* walked over to the jacket, and pulled out a small Burberry purse.

'This one?'

'That's the one,' Trix replied, standing up as *Chunk* opened the clasp at the top, about to look into it – before staggering back as the purse released a vicious jet of pepper spray into his face. As he dropped the purse, clutching at his eyes, Trix moved fast, taking the lamp from beside her on the table, yanking the cable from the socket, and slamming the base into the side of *Chunk*'s head with considerable force, sending him to the floor.

'Get something to tie him up, grab the gun and guard the door,' she said, already returning to the laptop.

'Why am I the one to do that?' Roxanne asked, already grabbing a curtain tie.

'Because I'm a hacker and you're a lawyer,' Trix smiled. 'I know which one would scare me more if I faced them.'

'Duke of Hastings?' Roxanne asked as she tore a rope from the side of the curtain. 'Isn't that from *Bridgerton?*'

'I didn't think he was the sort of man to watch a show like that, so it was a calculated choice,' Trix shrugged. Now back into the file structure of the drive, she typed in a line of code, watching as the folders changed from being corrupted into clean, uncorrupted file chains.

This had been the plan – to get into the building somehow and connect into the ethernet land lines, otherwise the videos wouldn't be able to hack into the audio-visual system in the ballroom. From the moment she'd placed the drive on the crappy CIA box of shitness, she'd held the cards. The drive was made to look corrupted, and the only person who could fix it was her. Even when she'd phoned Cody, offering to betray everyone for six figures and a private jet home, she'd been playing a long game.

Cody had been guilty of underestimating before, but now he was about to pay for it.

'Mic check,' she said, turning on the laptop's microphone and speaker.

'Check,' the voice of Marlowe came through.

'Check two,' the voice of Brad now spoke.

'Package is on its way,' she said, pulling a selection of files off the drive and placing them in an open window of an app she'd just installed. 'Have fun, guys.'

MARLOWE WAS IN THE BACK CORRIDOR WHEN THE MESSAGE from Trix came through. He knew where she was; he knew how Cody would come down to the ballroom, and so he'd waited near the service elevator, knowing he'd be a matter of seconds now.

The door opened, and Cody emerged from the elevator, three guards with him. They weren't dressed like the agents had been, however, and they looked younger, off the streets, perhaps.

Cody's air supply was being cut, and he wasn't getting the level he usually expected, Marlowe thought with a smile. *Shame.*

Pulling out his phone, he turned away, gaining some distance as he dialled a number, placing it to his ear as he waited.

'You finally grew a pair,' Cody's voice was almost amused. 'I thought you'd be running home to your shitty little country.'

'Have you hurt them?'

'Who? Oh, you mean the bitches? I'm treating them nice, just for you. And after you give me the files, I'll let them watch as I gut you.'

'You'll do it? Not one of your lackeys?'

'Come to the hotel and I'll show you,' Cody sneered down the line. 'It's okay, your name's on the door. They'll let you in. You know, after they kick the shit out of you for me.'

'No need,' Marlowe started walking back around the corner. 'I'm already here.'

Cody was facing away, frowning into his phone as Marlowe disconnected.

'What do you mean you—hello? Don't you dare hang up on ...'

He looked up with horror as Marlowe moved into view, the three guards slow to react as he gathered up the open ground between them at speed, hurtling into the first guard, sending him sprawling as, with the small can of acid he grabbed the second, spraying his face at close range, the man staggering back, clutching his skin.

Unleashing his wrist chain, Marlowe smashed the second with a chain covered fist, then slashed the thirds gun arm, sending his weapon clattering across the floor. The first guard, recovered, grabbed Marlowe, pinning his arms.

Marlowe threw his head full weight backward, the back of his skull crashing into and shattering the guards nose. The man slid down the wall, bleeding heavily, as the second, burnt-faced guard now came at him with a knife, but Marlowe side-stepped the move and, while watching Cody, his eyes never deviating from him, he grabbed the wrist, twisting it and slamming the blade into the second guard's gut, holding it there as the second guard slumped against him, before tossing him to the side.

However, now the third guard had returned, pulling his gun out. But before he could do anything Marlowe side-kicked him through the doors, back into the elevator and, as they closed, he tossed the small lump of C4 in after him, arming the detonator as he did so.

A moment later there was a faint crump as the bomb exploded in the confined space.

'So, tell me again what you wanted to do to me?' Marlowe enquired, turning back to face Cody.

He'd actually expected Cody to run, but the man was surprisingly made of sterner stuff, and instead threw a wicked haymaker of a punch at Marlowe, catching him on the side of the head as Marlowe quickly flinched back. The bulk of the power had missed the target, but it was still enough of a blow to send him staggering backwards, already re-evaluating the man in front of him.

Cody grabbed Marlowe around the throat, his anger too

much, and Marlowe leaned into this, head butting Cody hard, the pair staggering from each other as Marlowe kneed upwards viciously between Cody's legs. However, he either missed the target, or Cody was so amped on adrenaline he didn't feel it, because the impact didn't seem to do anything, and Cody spun, throwing Marlowe against a rack of shelving, Marlowe wiping his head to see if he was bleeding as he rose back into a fighting position.

Cody now went on the offensive, kicking out at Marlowe, but his ankle was caught and twisted hard to the right, flipping the now off-balance Cody to the floor. However, Cody found himself beside the fallen knife, and grabbed at it, slashing with it at Marlowe, who, sick of this, kicked hard at the hand, the knife sent flying with the impact.

Before Cody could do anything else, Marlowe pulled the gun out of his holster, aiming it at the billionaire.

'I don't want to kill you,' he said. 'I want you to face every crime you've done. Death gives you escape. But don't think for one moment I'll not kill you if I get pissed off.'

'I'll kill your friends ...' Cody wheezed, and at this, Marlowe laughed.

'You think?' he asked. 'Hey, Trix, how are we doing?'

'Ready to go,' Trix's voice replied through his earbud. He looked back at Cody.

'Seems they're not under your control anymore,' he smiled.

'She works for me!' Cody stared in horror. 'She called me, gave you up!'

'That was the plan,' Marlowe replied apologetically. 'Sorry.'

'I left a guard!' Cody was almost apoplectic at this, and

Marlowe actually wondered if he was going to ask for his money back.

'He says he left a guard?'

'Yeah, *Chunk*. He's sleeping now.'

'She said *Chunk*'s sleeping.'

Cody frowned.

'Who the hell's *Chunk*?'

Trix had obviously heard this, as she immediately started speaking.

'Big guy, dreadlocks, ratty beard.'

'And you called him *Chunk* because he's big?' Marlowe asked. 'That's a bit "fat shaming", isn't it? Why not call him "Dreads" or something cool?'

There was a long pause.

'Piss off, Marlowe,' Trix growled, and the line clicked silent.

'Yeah, she's pissed,' Marlowe crouched, gun aimed at Cody. 'Things aren't going well, are they? And in about, oh, five minutes, your dad is going to have a really terrible speech. We'll be staying here until then, okay? You and me, boys together.'

There was a sound from the other end of the corridor, however, and Marlowe glanced over to see Vanessa run around the corner, her gun in hand, pausing as she saw Marlowe and Cody, the two unconscious guards beside them.

'Brad said you were in trouble,' she explained, slowing to a walk. 'Looks like he was wrong.'

'Hey,' Cody pleaded, looking over at the new arrival. 'I don't know who you are, but I'll give you ten grand right now, in cash, if you shoot this bastard in the head.'

Vanessa looked at Cody, as if realising for the first time he was in the room.

'Do you know who he is?' she asked, pointing at Marlowe. 'He's Tom Marlowe. Ex-MI5.'

Marlowe shook his head.

'I don't think it's time for show-and-tell,' he said, rising – but Vanessa's suddenly dark smile paused him, as she raised her own gun directly at his face.

'The going rate's a hundred grand, and I take bank transfers,' she explained to Cody as she fired her gun.

25

CUT THE FEED

NATHAN DONZIGER STOOD IN THE SHADOWS AT THE SIDE OF the stage, hidden from the gala guests by the heavy black curtains, and glared at his assistant.

'What do you mean, *they sent their apologies?*' he snarled.

The assistant, a young man with horn-rimmed glasses and a trendy blond haircut gulped visibly. He'd not wanted to be the one to pass on the news, but the other cowards had disappeared the moment they heard. Now it was just him.

'That's all I was told,' he said, deciding to pass the buck. 'Saira took the call. Blame her.'

'She'd better have told that bitch to suck up whatever reservations she had, and get on down here!' Donziger exclaimed in anger. 'She's only seven floors above us, for Christ's sake!'

'No, sorry sir, but Senator Kyle checked out this morning,' the assistant used his fingers to push his glasses up his nose. 'As did Senators Tyler and Jones.'

'Bastards!' Donziger screamed in anger, loud enough to be heard by the nearer attendees. 'I'll have them destroyed!'

'Senator Kyle sent you a message,' the assistant passed over a tablet with an email on it.

On it, Donziger could see an image, a photo of an A4 file, placed on a hotel desk. He didn't need to know what was in the file, the photo of the cover alone was the proof needed to explain why Senator Kyle had left.

The message, however, confirmed it.

> Thank you for this lovely gift towards my next re-election campaign, Nathan. I'll be seeing you real soon.

The tablet didn't survive the impact against the backstage wall.

'Find me my son.'

It was a simple phrase, and coldly given, could have been taken either as an order, or a request.

'I'm going on stage in a moment, and I'd like him there.'

The assistant nodded, running as fast as he could from Nathan Donziger, who stood now, watching the party, seething.

Now he understood why there were fewer guests than expected here.

Now he understood why there was a march heading straight for the hotel.

That goddamned spook, that was why.

Straightening his tie, Nathan Donziger took a deep breath.

'Fuck them,' he said as he walked out onto the stage.

It was time to change the narrative again.

MARLOWE DIVED FORWARDS AS THE GUN WAS FIRED.

He'd hoped that Vanessa was as bad a killer as her late partner had been, and luckily for him, he seemed to be correct in that assumption. Her hand shook as she fired, trembling as the anger, adrenaline, and fear at what was happening all hit at once. It was a common feeling, and one Marlowe remembered from his earlier days. There was a chance the simple act of firing the gun would shake her out of this, though, and he needed to solve this problem as quickly as he could. Vanessa fired again, and Marlowe heard the sonic crack of the bullet whip past his ear – she was getting better. But at the same time, she wasn't firing consistently; it was as if she was having to build up the strength and the courage to pull the trigger.

'Why?' he shouted, hoping to shake her out of the mindset she was in. 'The money?'

'You killed Grayson!'

Vanessa was too close to fire now, and instead swung at Marlowe in impotent rage, the gun missing him as he ducked to avoid it. He went to move closer, but Vanessa had gathered her wits again, and the gun swung back to aim directly at him.

'He was trying to kill me!' Marlowe said, slowly rising, hands in the air, trying to find a way, *any* kind of way, to delay the inevitable. 'I won't lie to you, I would do the same again, Vanessa. Not just to your partner, but to anyone who tries to take my life.'

'Does that include me?' Vanessa stared through tears now as she glared at Marlowe. 'Does that include this?'

'Yes,' Marlowe admitted sadly. 'Let's be honest here. You've got the gun, I'm at your mercy. And I would do what it takes, not to end up another dead body.'

He shook his head.

'However, looking at you right now, I really don't think you were the killer in the partnership,' he said. 'You talked of missions you went on, but I feel Grayson was the killer, while you were the backup. You've been used as much as he has, though. I understand you're angry. But tell me, who told you where I was? Who sent you to my hotel—'

Vanessa shut her eyes, and Marlowe knew from the strain on her face she was about to fire again, stopping his words as he realised they weren't working anymore. But then her head erupted into a red mist, as the right-hand side of it simply evaporated, the sound of another gun echoing around the corridor.

Marlowe spun to see Brad standing there, gun in his hand.

'She got away from me,' Brad said simply, staring down at the body on the floor. 'I didn't realise she wasn't an asset until I heard you in the earbud. What the hell were you doing, bringing someone as unstable as that here?'

Marlowe looked down at Vanessa, her one remaining, lifeless eye staring up at the ceiling.

'I needed to know who put her into play,' he said sadly. 'Looks like I'll never know now.'

'Well, sorry for spoiling your day, but it looks to me like you owe me again,' Brad smiled. 'How many times have I saved your life now?'

'Okay, I'll add it to the list,' Marlowe sighed, and then looked back to Cody Donziger—

Who'd escaped.

'Shit,' he said. 'We need to stop him,' he said. 'He'll try to halt his dad's speech.'

'He'll have a fun job trying to do that,' Brad smiled. 'Nathan's already started.'

———

LIBERTY JONES HADN'T LEFT TIMES SQUARE. SHE'D STAYED with half of the protestors as they stood in the middle of it, placards and signs raised in anger. Painted slogans like "Cancel Cody", "It Could Have Been Your Son" and "Human Need Before Corporate Greed" were visible around the square, as were painted Standing Rock Eagle banners, mainly at Dermot's suggestion. It had taken little for the protestors to come out, either. Many had been following the Jericho Falls case with interest, and the thought of big money silencing people with death and destruction was too much to bear. In fact, several of the placards read "No Silence With Violence", with the Donziger Industries logo drawn underneath.

The other half of the protestors had headed towards the hotel, and Liberty had been getting regular updates, especially on how the NYC police had been trying their best to derail the march, but she wasn't there to be the figurehead that night.

She was there to make sure Roxanne Vasquez was.

All she hoped was that Marlowe had been correct, and something world shattering was about to happen, because the cold, the rain and the lateness of the day were starting to take its toll on the protestors.

'If you have a magic bullet, now's the time to use it,' she muttered, before raising her bullhorn and shouting out to the crowd, '*what do we want?*'

As the crowd replied with the expected "justice!" response, Liberty looked back up at the surrounding screens.

'Come on,' she whispered to herself. 'Now.'

NATHAN DONZIGER WALKED OUT ONTO THE STAGE TO A smaller than expected smattering of applause, as the guests of the gala turned to face him.

This was supposed to be my day, he thought to himself. *I paid off Jericho Falls. I got rid of the lawyer. Sure, Cody was outed, but he always was a creepy little prick. It'll do him good. Build character.*

He looked to the side of the stage.

Where was he, anyway? Cody had promised he'd be there beside his father, but to be brutally frank, it was probably better he wasn't.

There was a mic on a stand in the middle of the stage, and Donziger walked over to it, waving to the audience as the band, hired for the night played some rousing tune. He didn't recognise it, and assumed it was an arrangement of some modern, trendy chart-topper. All he'd cared about was that it wasn't "hail to the chief," as the last thing he wanted was rumours of a Presidential run against McKay in two years.

He'd get less done if he was President, after all.

'Thank you, thank you,' he said, realising for the first time that some of the applause had been piped through speakers. *The pricks weren't even applauding him. He'd be taking more heads than expected later.* 'And good evening, to you and the people watching at home.'

This was aimed at Donziger shareholders, watching this on a private feed, the entire speech being broadcast out to them as a way of calming them down. Originally, he was going to keep this quiet, a simple ball with money going to some inane yet popular charity, while in the background quietly forcing his puppet politicians to kill the court case. However, with that finished and Brett's bitch of a daughter removed, he had decided to celebrate a little.

Of course, that was before his file on Cody had been leaked to the press.

Enough of that. Concentrate on the masses.

Behind him, the screen was showing a series of stock videos; farms, cheerful people eating at community picnics, families in New York, a real "best of" playlist for the heart of America, to remind people that Donziger might be *money people,* but they were money people that used money to *help* people.

After all, as the adage said, *buy the lie, sell the truth.*

'My name is Nathan Donziger, and I am the CEO of Donziger Industries,' he said, smiling at a second wave of applause, while wondering how much of this was piped, too. 'And this weekend, we celebrate a win against a great injustice, while mourning the loss of those caught up in last week's domestic terrorism attack.'

———

Watching the screen in the Imperial Suite, Roxanne turned to Trix.

'Is it done?' she asked.

'I've hacked the feed, and Marlowe's activist friends have given me access to the screens in Times Square for the next ten minutes, so I'm good to go,' Trix replied, still typing as she spoke.

'Good. Then, if you would be so kind to do so, please turn this bastard off,' Roxanne pleaded. 'I think he's said enough.'

With a nod, Trix scrolled up with the trackpad, and left-clicked on a button marked "launch virus."

'Here we go,' she grinned. 'Buckle up.'

LIBERTY WAS ABOUT TO TEXT MARLOWE AGAIN AND ASK WHAT was going on, when the screens flickered around her. All across Times Square, the advertising billboards were closing down, turning off, one after another. Even the screens showing feeds of networks were turning off, until apart from the lights from streetlights and shops, the square was plunged into darkness.

And then, at once, every screen lit up with the same image.

'Hello, I'm Roxanne Vasquez,' the giant figure of Roxanne Vasquez spoke, her voice echoing around the protestors as they started cheering. 'This is a recording, made on the off chance that people connected to Donziger Industries have either killed or abducted me by now.'

Liberty's eyes widened, as did the people around her as the woman on the screens continued.

'Assassins sent by Nathan Donziger killed people I worked with, while trying to gain the information I had on the company for themselves, information given to me by my late father, Brett Hendricks, who was once Nathan Donziger's co-founder and partner. It's information that, if it had been allowed to be shown in next week's case, would not only have proven Donziger Industries to be corrupt and criminal, but would also have shown the treasonous acts that both Nathan and his son Cody have performed over the years.'

The crowd was silent, listening to every word.

On the screen, Roxanne smiled.

'And over the next ten minutes,' she said, 'I'm going to tell you every secret.'

Liberty couldn't help herself. All of her professionalism was out of the window now, as, with the thousands of protestors around her, she cheered wildly.

As Nathan Donziger stared at the screen behind him on the stage, the image of Roxanne Vasquez continued.

'I have also sent the proof of these claims to every media outlet in the world, as well as every law enforcement agency head office. Someone, somewhere, will make sure my father's fight to take down this corrupt empire will succeed.'

The gala audience wasn't applauding anymore. In fact, they were scrolling through the feeds on their phones, or staring in horror at Nathan as he looked helplessly around, unable to stop what was happening behind him. He could see the men at the sound desk literally trying to tear the wires out, but this was hard lined, directly into the system. Nobody had hacked the network and—

Cody.

As the noise in the ballroom grew, as each statement claimed by the woman on the screen was met with outrage from the people present, Nathan Donziger ran from the stage.

He'd relied on his son to fix this. And instead, he'd let this happen.

He hadn't appeared at his father's side, either.

Nathan Donziger didn't know why, or even how this passed, but he knew without any doubt that Cody Donziger had done this deliberately. To kill his father's credibility, perhaps, in order to lessen his own damage? Perhaps. Maybe even start a hostile takeover, removing his father before he did the same back? Cody wasn't stupid. He would have known, with his file out there, that his father had been keeping close tabs on his extracurricular activities.

However, he found Cody outside the back doors of the ballroom, in a foetal position against a wall, shaking with either nerves, or an overdose of the cocaine he loved so much.

'What the hell did you do?' Donziger snapped at his son, who looked up at him, his eyes red and raw.

'I thought I was in control,' he said. 'They used me. I thought I'd got the files, but they just needed me to bring them here. The spy—'

'Marlowe?' Donziger grabbed Cody by the lapels, dragging him close. '*Are you telling me he's here?*'

Cody nodded, dumbly.

'Christ, you're the dumbest fuck I know,' Donziger snarled, hurling his son away. 'Fix this. Now.'

As Nathan Donziger stormed off, Cody wiped his eyes, rising and nodding to himself. He might not have much left, and everything might be taken from the family tonight, but the one thing he knew was where this was coming from. And, as he entered the elevator behind him with the last of the three armed guards from earlier, still bleeding from his broken nose, he nodded at him to press the button.

'The Imperial Suite,' he said. 'We need to end them before they end us.'

26

SUITE SHOP

THERE WAS NOBODY IN THE SUITE WHEN CODY ARRIVED.

In fact, the only living person left in there was a gagged and bound, dreadlocked guard, squirming in fear as Cody stared dispassionately down at him, before turning away.

'Give me your gun,' he said, taking it from the broken-nosed guard, turning back into the suite, and emptying the magazine into the laptop on the desk. He didn't know if this would stop the footage, and he guessed it wouldn't, but it made him feel a little better.

In fact, he was so focused on the firing at the laptop; it was only when he emptied his clip and turned to demand another one that he realised the guard he'd brought with him was now on the ground once more.

In fact, he faced Marlowe and another man, older, with a buzz cut. A man he'd seen before, the man who'd killed the woman assassin, before she could sort out his problems once and for all. But he knew the buzz-cut man was a killer – and that could help him right now.

'I'll give you two hundred grand to kill him,' he said to the man, backing away from Marlowe, pointing at him as if the simple spoken offer wasn't enough.

'Tempting,' the buzz cut man said, looking at Marlowe. 'But I'll be honest, Cody. I think your bank accounts have all been frozen by now. There's a lot of high-up folk, Government folk, all looking into you and your pops now. Lots of files being set fire to, up on Capitol Hill.'

'And he'd know,' Marlowe smiled. 'This is Brad Haynes, CIA. He'll probably be the one tasked with sticking a bag on your head and shooting you through it.'

Cody whimpered now, and Marlowe wondered in the back of his head whether this was fear, desperation or a coke come-down. It could have been all three, if he was honest.

'Don't kill me,' Cody said, his voice quavering and weak now. 'I'll testify against my father. I'll do whatever you want.'

Marlowe looked at Brad.

'Could be worth it,' he said.

'I think they'll be happy with that,' Brad replied with a nod.

Marlowe looked back at Cody.

'Are you wired?' he asked.

Cody, confused, shook his head.

'I—'

'Ah, you see, I don't really trust you,' Marlowe smiled, and it was a dark, evil one now. 'Strip to your boxers. Prove it.'

He waved his gun, his finger tightening on the trigger, and Cody quickly pulled off his tuxedo, whimpering as he did so.

'Not quite the man you were on the phone,' Marlowe growled. 'It's quite sad, really.'

Now down to his underwear, Cody stood nervously in the middle of the room, obviously not wired for sound as he wiped his nose, likely to remove any cocaine residue.

'Where's your dad?' Marlowe asked.

'I don't know,' Cody replied. 'He told me to fix this and then left.'

'Left where?'

Cody stood, his face blank.

'Christ,' Marlowe looked at Brad. 'He's getting out of here. Helipad?'

'There isn't space,' Brad replied. 'He's probably heading to the service tunnels. That way he can leave without going through the front entrance.'

Marlowe looked back at Brad.

'Can you deal with this?' he asked.

'Why?' Brad frowned. 'Let Nathan run. He'll get his dues.'

Marlowe pointed at the tied guard on the floor.

'That's what I'm worried about. He doesn't have his gun, and Roxanne isn't here,' he said. 'I'm not hunting Nathan Donziger, I'm saving his bloody life.'

NATHAN DONZIGER ALWAYS HAD AN ESCAPE PLAN, NO MATTER where he was.

New York had its secrets, and one of them was that although built in Midtown Manhattan, the Lotte New York Palace Hotel was actually built on land owned by the Archdiocese of New York, land associated with St Patrick's Cathedral, situated just across the street. The Villard Houses, the original brownstones built, now part of the hotel were designed only a few years after the Cathedral had been built, and Henry Villard, then the president of the Northern Pacific Railway, had created a walkway between the two locations, mainly used now for pipes and cables. Even Presidents used the side entrance on Fiftieth Street to enter and leave the premises in recent years.

But Nathan Donziger wasn't a President. They came and went while he was here to stay.

And so, it was Nathan, with a single bodyguard, walking swiftly towards what was now the Archbishop's House, who stopped when the gunshot echoed down the underground corridor.

Slowly, and with his hands raised, Donziger turned back the way he'd come, seeing a figure walking towards him, gun aimed directly at him.

'Miss Vasquez,' he said calmly. 'I wondered if we'd see each other.'

'Drop the gun,' Roxanne nodded at the bodyguard, who immediately complied. 'Now get on the floor, face to the ground.'

The bodyguard didn't even look questioningly at Donziger before doing this, and Roxanne couldn't help but feel a small wave of triumph pass through her as she saw the expression of disgust on Nathan Donziger's face at this.

'If you're going to kill me, do it quickly,' he said, refusing to back down. 'I'm busy, and I've got things to do.'

'The only thing you have to do is pay for your crimes,' Roxanne replied. 'But while it's just us, you can answer some questions first. Did you kill my father?'

'Brett?' Donziger actually chuckled at the question. 'I didn't even know he was still alive. I didn't even consider him after we had him removed, and the locks changed.'

'You lie,' Roxanne raised the gun, shaking, now aiming at his face. 'Admit the truth.'

Donziger stared at Roxanne dispassionately, his thin lips motionless.

'I said—'

'He can't tell you what you want to hear,' a fresh voice spoke, and Marlowe came into view from the hotel end of the corridor. 'Because he didn't kill your father.'

'That's a lie,' Roxanne shook her head. 'He—'

'He did a lot of shitty things, but the fire was an accident, a pure coincidence,' Marlowe continued. 'I looked into his file while I was in the salt mines. There's nothing about the death, apart from a newspaper clipping about the fire.'

'But that's proof!' Roxanne spun back to face Donziger. 'How would he have known dad was in the fire?'

'Because someone in the Government told him,' Marlowe continued closer. 'Governor Williams was in charge of the district the building was in. Brad told the CIA about how Brett, under his new identity of Daniel Sutton had died there, and he told Donziger, mainly because they had an extensive file on Williams, and could force him to tell them anything. He thought the information would give him some credit with them. He was wrong.'

'And how do you know—' Roxanne paused. 'Let me guess. It's in *his* file.'

Marlowe nodded.

'The video is out there,' he breathed. 'Everything your father put together, everything you wanted to reveal in the court case, it's released to the world. The media are already picking it up, and more and more people are joining the protest above us. You've started a revolution.'

'I didn't want a revolution!' Roxanne shouted in anger. 'I want my father back!'

'Can I speak?' Donziger waggled a hand to gain their attention. 'From what I remember of Brett's words about you and your mother, you were a pretty shitty daughter to him—'

He flinched, ducking as the gun fired, the bullet shooting high and to the side. Realising it was a warning and nothing more, he chuckled.

'If the shoe fits.'

Marlowe grabbed Roxanne's hand, pulling it up, angling the gun away from Donziger.

'Make him pay,' he said. 'He wants you to shoot him. He knows he's about to lose everything, and about to have every dirty secret brought back out. Already, a dozen people in Washington will all be looking to remove him slowly and painfully. If he dies here, it's a quick, pretty painless death—'

'Not if I shoot him in the balls.'

'Sure, yes, that's true, but he'll still be a martyr to people around the world.'

Marlowe looked across the corridor at Donziger.

'Your son is with the FBI right now,' he said coldly. 'Working out what kind of deal he gets for selling you out. Your board is probably doing the same thing. Your only options are to take what they throw at you, or race them to the plea-deal finish line. And believe me, it's already crowded there.'

'I underestimated you,' Donziger nodded at this. 'I won't do that again.'

'Actually, you didn't,' Marlowe replied truthfully. 'You caught me on the back foot and I'm happy to admit it. It's not been the easiest of times for me, and I took my eye off the ball.'

He looked down at Roxanne, letting go of her wrist as he did so.

'Luckily for me, I was hanging around with cleverer people,' he said. 'People who showed me alternatives, and who gave me the inspiration on how to take you down.'

'I'm not going back,' Donziger snapped. 'I won't give you —' this was aimed at Roxanne now '—the satisfaction of seeing me behind bars.'

'And what's your alternative?' Roxanne asked, amused. 'Because Marlowe's right, you have no other—'

She didn't finish as Nathan Donziger dropped to the floor of the corridor, grabbing the gun his guard had dropped, and raising it up, firing in one quick motion. But the bullet flew wide, because as he did this, two more gunshots fired, and his chest exploded into two blossoms of red, his eyes rolling back as he fell to the ground, the gun clattering from his hands.

Roxanne held her gun, shaking now, still aimed at Donziger as Marlowe gently took it from her.

'Self-defence,' he said. 'You didn't have a choice.'

'I'll second that,' the guard, still prone on the floor, said, his voice muffled as he spoke into the concrete beneath him.

There was a commotion from behind them, and Marlowe turned to see Trix standing at the other end of the tunnel.

'Marlowe, you need to go!' she shouted. 'If they find you, there's a shit ton of questions to answer!'

Marlowe nodded. He'd hoped to finish this a lot quieter, but things had got wildly out of hand.

'Go,' Roxanne said, looking up at him. 'I've got this.'

Marlowe nodded, turning and running back towards Trix, currently holding open the door.

'Everything's gone to shit,' she said as they hurried up the stairs and out into the main lobby, Marlowe already wiping down and tossing the gun into a waste bin as they joined the rest of the crowd exiting the hotel. 'They're checking IDs and everything. I'm not sure how we get out of here.'

'I know,' Marlowe nodded at a crowd of FBI agents in

windbreakers, standing at the side of the glass doors, watching the crowd. 'We get arrested.'

He walked over to the agent in charge and held his hands out.

'I believe you're here to take us into custody?' he asked.

Sasha Bordeaux smiled coldly.

'You said you'd bring me Brad Haynes,' she replied.

'I said I'd do that after this was done,' Marlowe waved around the lobby. 'Does this look done?'

'Cody Donziger?'

'Up in his room, in his pants,' Marlowe smiled.

'Actually, he means the Imperial Suite, and in his underwear,' Trix corrected, looking at Marlowe as she did so. 'They call trousers "pants" here. I didn't want them to be confused.'

'Last I saw, Brad Haynes was with him, if that helps at all,' Marlowe added, and Sasha nodded to two of her agents, who peeled off into the approaching chaos, already en route to the suite.

'Nathan?'

'In the tunnels under the hotel,' Marlowe replied carefully, looking around. 'Roxanne Vasquez is with him.'

'You left them together?' Sasha was surprised at this.

'It's okay, he's not going anywhere,' Marlowe shrugged. 'You, um, might need a body bag when you go pick him up, though, although he might still be alive. I didn't really consider checking after we shot him.'

If Sasha was pissed off at this state of affairs, she did an outstanding job of hiding it as she stared coldly at Marlowe.

'We debrief on Monday,' she said. 'I'll send you the details. And I want Brad Haynes, in our custody, by this time tomorrow.'

'Understood,' Marlowe nodded. 'Can my assistant get out of here too?'

'From what we hear, Trixibelle Preston is anything but your assistant,' Sasha smiled at Trix now, giving the strong impression of a shark staring at her upcoming dinner. 'We'd like to talk to you soon, too. I'm guessing the video footage was all you?'

'Dunno what you're talking about,' Trix gave her most innocent look. 'Was there a video? I hope someone filmed it. I'd love to see what happened.'

'Get them out of here,' Sasha looked at one of her agents. 'Get them to the edge of the crowd and let them disappear. Don't worry, wherever they run and hide, I'll know where they are.'

'See you at *Dun Dealgan* tomorrow,' Marlowe smiled.

'What the hell is one of those when they're at home?'

Marlowe shrugged.

'You're the spy, you work it out,' he said. 'See you at lunchtime? Maybe two? Beers on me.'

'Once I have Haynes, we'll see.'

This said, she turned from Marlowe and stormed off into the lobby, most likely to find out whether or not Nathan was truly dead, as Marlowe and Trix were escorted out of the building and into the crowded streets outside.

'She won't find Brad there,' Trix commented as, now away from the lone CIA agent, they moved through the crowd quickly, gaining as much distance as they could.

'No?' Marlowe hadn't expected Brad to stay around either, but couldn't help but stop as he turned to look at Trix. 'Cody?'

'Oh, he's there,' Trix grinned. 'Has a tranq dart sticking in his right arse cheek, too. Brad must have nicked your CIA toy when you weren't looking.'

Marlowe grinned in response, and the smile widened as he recognised another face in the crowd.

'You came through,' Liberty Jones sounded surprised as she shook Marlowe's hand. 'The news sites are already having a field day. Havenford's already been seized by the Feds, and God knows what they're going to find down there.'

'Hopefully enough to screw over a lot of rich pricks,' Trix replied.

Liberty nodded.

'Roxanne Vasquez?'

'Alive, and I think ready to start a new phase of her career,' Marlowe looked back to the hotel, almost as if he expected her to emerge through the doors. 'Our job is done.'

'Your job was utterly stellar,' Liberty said, following Marlowe's gaze. 'I have to say, when Dermot told me about you, I didn't think you'd come through—'

She stopped as she turned back to Marlowe, but he was no longer there. In fact, as she spun around in a circle, she couldn't see the British spy and his companion anywhere in the crowd.

It was as if they never existed.

'Goddamned spooks,' she muttered as she rejoined the partying. 'Goddamned spooks.'

EPILOGUE

Marlowe and Trix had headed south after they escaped the crowds, only stopping at the midtown hotel Brad had arranged for them, what seemed like a year earlier, to gather their items and leave. Marlowe knew the cleaning teams would be here soon – and by that, he meant security service cleaning teams rather than hotel staff, and he didn't want to hang around.

Once they left the hotel, they headed down to Greenwich Village, grabbing two rooms off a hotel chain website booking, using one of Marlowe's newer identities, recently created by Trix, and with no connection to the CIA, MI5, or any other spooky bugger with an agenda.

Once into their two single rooms, with a connecting door between them – mainly for ease but also *just in case* they weren't as clever as they believed they were – they ordered in pizza from *Uber Eats.* Munching on slices while drinking bottles of light beer, they watched the news channel with a growing enjoyment until the early hours of Sunday. Trix had gone to sleep, claiming *jet lag had finally got to her* around one in the morning, and Marlowe, still filled with adrenaline from the night's events and claiming he needed to get some fresh air, disappeared for an hour or two.

On Sunday, Marlowe had started planning his next steps.

When Trix awoke late in the morning, he was already up and showered, and as she stared blearily at him, he'd finally explained what happened during his conversation with his father the previous day, and in return Trix had shown him some CCTV footage she'd picked up while controlling the Donziger laptop, footage that had downloaded onto a USB drive, now uploaded onto the tablet, footage which revealed Vanessa had been working for herself the whole time. Marlowe had expected this, however, and watched the footage dispassionately, only saying anything once it was over, and that was to suggest calling up breakfast, as he was sick of going to diners or bagel shops for it.

The deal had been to guard Roxanne until Monday, and as such the return flights had been booked by Brad for the end of the following day, but Marlowe and Trix both knew they wouldn't be able to take these tickets anyway, as by the time the flights took off, every intelligence agency on the planet would be hunting for them. Instead, Trix bought a new ticket from La Guardia for that night, complaining she hadn't been able to see Phantom of the Opera, while Marlowe said he intended to hang around a day or two more, just to see how things panned out.

Trix had then argued with this, saying that she should stay with him if that was the case, but Marlowe had lightly fended this off, claiming that although she was still suspended, there was more chance of her getting back into

Box, and therefore *she*, more than *they*, should return as soon as. Also, Marlowe suggested that, as she was in London first, she could check into the death of Grayson Long, and see whether it connected Marlowe as a "person of interest" in the case. Because, until he wasn't, he knew returning to the UK was a no-no.

He also gave her the keys to his Jaguar, telling her to place it somewhere safe, and passed a bullion coin to her, asking her to fix the bumper up while she was there. Trix had gone to ask about the coins, but then stopped as the door went, and breakfast arrived.

Marlowe knew he could stay for a good few weeks off the grid, if left to his own devices – he had half a dozen fake credit cards under four unique identities, and a dozen bullion coins in his duffle bag. Trix had reluctantly agreed to this, and by noon of the Sunday after the night before, she gave Marlowe a hug, told him not to get killed anytime soon, and with her bag over her shoulder, and her carry-on cabin bag in her hand left the hotel without a backward glance, on her way back to the UK, promising to check into Taylor Coleman as soon as she returned.

Marlowe was amused to note she'd sorted a first-class ticket home this time. *That was someone who would never go back to economy.* He also wondered what she'd stolen while here, as she hadn't had a cabin bag when she arrived.

Still, finally alone, Marlowe had relaxed, sending a message to Brad to meet him in Bryant Park as soon as possible.

They needed to talk.

'I don't appreciate being told where to meet,' Brad said as he arrived at the park, hugging his arms tight against the cold as he sat on the chair opposite Marlowe, currently sipping a flat white as he relaxed against the folding metal chair. They were to the left of the park as you looked down on it, on the western side, beside some trees and a small coffee shack that looked out across the grass towards the New York Public Museum. Marlowe had thought it amusing to meet there – but not *too close* to there.

Brad looked around.

'Trix not coming?'

Marlowe looked at his watch, counting quietly to himself.

'Currently she's in the first-class lounge, drinking as much champagne as she can get before heading back to London.'

'You changed the flights?'

'She made her own plans.'

'That's probably wise,' Brad nodded. 'The CIA might have worked out who you are through the IDs I used.'

Marlowe nodded.

'Yeah, about the CIA,' he said.

At this, Brad almost fell out of his chair as he jumped up, spinning around, staring across the park at the other tourists embracing the cold February weather, expecting any of them to charge him before he could run for the exit.

'Have you set me up?' he breathed as he looked back down at his coffee companion.

Marlowe, however, hadn't moved.

'Sit down, Brad,' Marlowe sipped his drink. 'You're drawing attention to yourself.'

Reluctantly, Brad sat back down on the chair.

'You could at least have bought me a drink,' he muttered.

Marlowe indicated the coffee stand with a nod of his head.

'It's just there,' he said, watching the American. 'Feel free to get one yourself, although you probably won't want to stay long.'

'There you go again with your cryptic bloody comments,' Brad growled. 'I'm getting pretty damned sick of them.'

'And I'm getting sick of being played with and lied to by you.' Marlowe placed his drink down, turning to fully face Brad.

'I don't know what—'

'Vanessa. You killed her, and you saved my life.'

Brad shifted in his seat.

'Damn right I did.'

'How did you lose her?'

Brad frowned, his eyebrows furrowing as he tried to work out where Marlowe was going with this.

'I didn't realise I was her goddamned babysitter,' he replied.

'Fair point,' Marlowe nodded. 'A lot was going on. And she'd decided to kill me. She would have lost you the moment you gave her a chance.'

He reached into his pocket, placing his phone, as yet still turned off, onto the table.

'Tell me again how you lost her.'

'I saved your life!' Brad was losing his temper now, but Marlowe kept his gaze steady as he watched the older man.

'You did,' he said. 'And now, even if I *wanted* to betray you to the CIA, I'd have that debt over my head, wouldn't I? Convenient, that.'

Brad said nothing to this, wisely waiting to see where Marlowe was going with it.

'I wouldn't have sold you out,' Marlowe added. 'I thought you would have known that. No matter how I was feeling; whether I was angry at the way you kept secrets from us, whatever ... I would never have given you to the CIA. That's your problem to deal with, and I'd expect you to do that in your own time.'

'I know that,' Brad forced a smile. 'I trust you. We went through battle together. I'd—'

He stopped as Marlowe picked up the phone, opening up the video player app on it.

'Trix found footage of you,' he said, scrolling along a CCTV scene on the phone. The camera was positioned high, from the angle of the shot, and at the end of an empty corridor. 'Taken moments before you lost Vanessa.'

Turning it so Brad could also watch, Marlowe pressed play. On the screen, Brad appeared, Vanessa beside him. He was still holding a glass in his hand, and the chances were this was shortly after they'd met in the bar.

They spoke for a long moment, and then Vanessa walked off, Brad watching after her.

Then he pulled his gun out and, after giving it a few seconds more, followed.

'So, we spoke, so what?' Brad snapped. 'I thought she was an asset of yours. I was being polite. But you can see there, I was still suspicious of her.'

'I suspected her too,' Marlowe placed the phone down now as he leant closer, lowering his voice. 'In fact, I was so suspicious that when I sorted her out in a nice new dress for the party, I bugged it.'

He let the sentence hang in the air for a long moment.

'And guess what? When listening back late last night, I got the audio of the conversation we just watched, nice and clear. It even matches up with the video, beat for bloody beat.'

Brad stared at Marlowe, his face paling.

'I wasn't going to let her kill you,' he admitted. 'I just aimed her in your direction, ready to step in—'

'Just in time to save my life?' Marlowe shook his head. 'What if she'd killed me, Brad?'

Brad looked away.

'I had to do something,' he muttered. 'I'd dropped the ball, not trusting you earlier, not telling you the full truth. I thought you'd take the deal with the CIA, that you'd set me up. I had to turn you back to my side of the table and I knew this would put you in my debt.'

Marlowe watched Brad emotionlessly as his mind raced, making sense of this.

There was no recording, and the dress hadn't been bugged.

Marlowe hadn't even considered it when he arranged the clothes.

But Brad didn't know that.

And luckily for Marlowe, Brad's conscience seemed to need a confessional right now.

'They want me to bring you to them by the end of the day,' Marlowe said coldly once Brad had finished. 'Give me one reason why I shouldn't.'

Brad shook his head.

'I don't have one,' he said. 'What will you do?'

'Give you a six-hour head start,' Marlowe replied. 'I know you're packed and ready to go. I also know you probably have someone in the agency who'll go to bat for you while you lie low. So, get out of here and call them up ASAP.'

He smiled.

'And drop me a line when you're okay, yeah? You're a prick, but you're a good man.'

Brad rose, holding out a hand.

'It's been an experience, Brit,' he said, shaking Marlowe's hand briefly, before turning and leaving the piazza, walking off towards the street.

Marlowe watched him go.

He really did like the man, but there had been too many secrets held this time. He'd offered him a lifeline just then, but the chances were, if he was called again, he might turn the CIA agent down next time.

Ah, who are you kidding, he smiled. *You'd be bored if you did that.*

Chuckling, Marlowe rose from the table, picked his phone up, and walked off in the other direction. It was almost two, and he had two more dates on his checklist for the day.

———————

'YOU DID WHAT?'

Sasha Bordeaux didn't even seem surprised as Marlowe stood in front of her. She was sitting in a booth at the *Dun Dealgan*, a pint of beer, untouched, in front of her. To be honest, Marlowe actually wondered if she'd got the pint purely to fit into the bar, and actually anticipated her taking a sip.

'I missed him,' Marlowe repeated slowly. 'It's my fault completely. I thought he trusted me, but he must have suspected something was wrong, and you wanted to ship him to somewhere bloody awful in the middle of nowhere.'

'And why might he have thought that?'

Marlowe sighed, tiring of the lies.

'If I'm honest, it's likely because I told him something was wrong, and you wanted to ship him to somewhere bloody awful in the middle of nowhere,' he suggested.

Sasha didn't react to this; instead, she nodded, sighed to herself and leant back into the leather of the booth seat.

'You knew this was a condition of coming to work for us,' she said. 'Brad Haynes was your key to the executive washroom.'

'Yeah, about that,' Marlowe nodded. 'Looks like I didn't want to work for the CIA after all. Who knew?'

Sasha gathered her things together.

'I suppose I can't be too angry with you,' she said irritably. 'You got us some juicy files. Although we can't find anything on some certain Senators, in the files you passed us.'

Marlowe sat opposite her now.

'That's because I gave them to the Senators,' he replied. 'Wow, I really am shite at this spying thing, aren't I?'

Sasha watched Marlowe for a long, uncomfortable moment, before rising from the seat and walking off without a word.

'If I said I'm sorry, would it help?' Marlowe called after her, but if she heard him, she didn't react to it, walking out of the bar's main entrance, and possibly out of Marlowe's life forever.

Marlowe sighed, walking over to the bar now.

'Dermot in?' he asked.

The barmaid, a middle-aged woman with the look of a bruiser, shook her head with a wry smile.

'Hung over,' she said. 'Had quite a night.'

'Well, tell him Marlowe said hi, and bye, and that I'll catch him and his better half next time I'm in the area,' Marlowe replied. 'I'm off today.'

'Anywhere nice?'

Marlowe frowned.

'I haven't yet decided,' he smiled, placing a ten-dollar bill down for Sasha's drink, nodding thanks, and walking out of the bar.

The question was a valid one. He honestly didn't know where he was going to go now. He knew there was still unfinished news with his father. Also, though Trisha Hawkins was gone, Francine Pearce was still around, and thanks to Brad Hayne's desperation to have Marlowe owe him a favour, Marlowe would never know who sent Vanessa to his hotel – although the chances were it was likely to be any of the three people he'd just considered. And, more importantly, although Trisha was running from Cody, there was a chance she might reconsider now he was no longer the threat he once was – although, there was still the chance he'd be throwing her under a bus for a better deal, so perhaps she would stay under a rock.

Or start to push for her own deal first.

Either way, it was something Marlowe now had the time to properly consider.

But he knew he had one more stop to make first.

Roxanne Vasquez had been arrested for the murder of Nathan Donziger, but this hadn't lasted long, once the full story of what had happened the previous night came out, mainly given as evidence by Cody in an attempt to plea bargain himself out of a life term in a maximum security prison. As such, they had placed her into a US Marshal safe house while people a lot higher up the food chain worked out what to do with her, since she'd effectively whistle blown against one of the biggest corporate blackmailers in recent history.

Trix, with only a touchscreen tablet and an airport lounge Wi-Fi, had worked out the location, sending it to Marlowe by text, and so it was mid-afternoon when he arrived in a small Brooklyn suburb, looking to say goodbye.

Luckily for Marlowe, she was allowed guests, as long as the person running the operation allowed this. And as far as the guards on the door to the safe house were concerned, US Marshal Dexter Garner was a straight-up dude, whose ID was still showing up as active, and Marlowe nodded thanks as he walked in – after a lengthy pat-down, and a very detailed examination of his leather backpack – to see her.

Roxanne was sitting on a sofa in the living room, wearing a hoodie and jogging bottoms, when he arrived, walking through the door and being welcomed with a sad, resigned smile.

'Apparently, this is my life now,' she said. 'They reckon I'll end up in witness relocation, but I'm one of the most recognisable faces on the planet now, so that could be a problem in the short term.'

'Do you *want* to go into witness protection?' Marlowe asked.

At this, Roxanne shrugged.

'It'll probably keep me alive longer, but I won't be able to practise law, and I'll never be able to speak to any of my friends again. So, no, not really.'

She puffed her cheeks out, releasing a stressed-out breath.

'I reckon they'll just do what other whistle blowers do,

and provide me with some security during the trial. And then after that, I'm on my own.'

'What trial?' Marlowe frowned. 'I thought Cody was plea bargaining and Nathan was dead?'

'Nah, the old bastard's still alive, and currently under twenty-four-hour guard in some secret hospital,' Roxanne rose from the sofa and walked over to the window, watching out of it at the Brooklyn street outside. 'We got him twice in the chest, but missed anything we were probably aiming for.'

'You were aiming for something?'

Roxanne laughed.

'Yeah, his head,' she replied. 'Anyway, he's awake and in custody, and now he's claiming it was all his son's work, that poor old Donziger Senior was just a patsy. And he still has a few Senators on his side – the ones who didn't get their files back from you, anyway.'

She watched Marlowe now, looking for any reaction as she continued.

'I heard the Marshals talking this morning. Apparently there was a fire at Havenford,' she said. 'Who knew that a salt mine could burn so well?'

'Nathan?'

'He claims it wasn't him, and I believe him,' Roxanne looked back at Marlowe as she replied. 'Apparently, there was an intruder last night. Used CIA tech to freeze the cameras, knocked out a couple of feds who were down in the salt mine before setting fire to a chunk of stuff. Luckily, it seems to be files that weren't important, but they used the distraction to get the hell out. The FBI now hates the CIA, again, while the CIA is blaming the NSA. It's a genuine confusion.'

She smiled, her mouth pursing a little at the side.

'Where were *you* last night?'

'I was with Trix,' Marlowe shrugged. 'Same room block, but separate rooms.'

'So, no witnesses.'

Marlowe didn't reply to this, instead pulling a file out of his backpack.

'Here,' he said, passing it over. 'It's the file Nathan had on Brett Hendricks. It shows your father was a good man – corrupted, sure, but a man who, in the end, did the right thing.'

'Thank you,' Roxanne said as she read through the first pages. However, the expression turned to one of suspicion as she looked back at him. 'How the hell did you get this? You didn't pick it up last time—'

She stopped.

'It *was* you.'

Marlowe shrugged.

'Let's just say I'm *super*b at what I do,' he replied, as if this answered everything. And, with a last nod, he walked back to the door.

'Will I see you again?' Roxanne asked.

'I'm like a bad penny,' Marlowe smiled. 'I always turn up.'

'When do you return to London?'

Marlowe paused at this.

'You know, I was thinking about hanging around for a while,' he flashed a smile. 'I'm starting to like the place.'

And, with this said, Marlowe left Roxanne alone once more. He knew she was going to have a very busy few months now.

But he also knew, in the back of his mind, that this wasn't the last time he'd see Roxanne Vasquez.

IN THE DRIVING SEAT OF HIS HIRED CAR, MARLOWE LEANT HIS head against the back of the seat and considered his next options. He could return to London, but currently there wasn't much for him there, and until Trix could see what the situation was with Grayson Long, he could be walking straight back into a murder charge. The hit seemed to be removed though, so that was good, and with time to kill, he could stay in the US – but he'd managed to pretty much kill any chance of anyone legitimately wanting to hire him. However, there was always the possibility that one of the many Washington politicians he'd gained files on during his late night jaunt the previous night would find a use for him.

Marlowe looked over his shoulder at the back seat of the car; it had two rucksacks worth of files resting on the leather, the illegal gains he'd made the previous night after his return to Havenford. There was some very interesting reading in there, and this was good, as he needed something to pass the time while deciding what to do next.

His phone rang, which was surprising, as it was a phone that only a handful of people knew the number to. Pulling it out, he frowned at the blank caller ID and answered.

'Yes?' he asked, listening for a moment. 'Ah. I'm glad you found it useful, Senator Kyle.'

He started the engine as he continued to listen to the voice on the other end.

'No, I've never been to San Francisco, but I hear it's lovely,' he said. 'And you're right, currently I am at a bit of a loose end. Send me the details, and I'll check them over as I drive there.'

Disconnecting the call, Marlowe tossed the phone on to the passenger seat. Senator Kyle had a job for him; a small, off the books security issue she needed sorted, in a couple of weeks, and on the other side of the country.

'Just enough time for a road trip,' he muttered to himself as he placed the car into drive, and headed towards the nearest freeway.

It was going to be a *very* interesting vacation.

ACKNOWLEDGEMENTS

When you write a series of books, you find that there are a ton of people out there who help you, and so I wanted to do a little acknowledgement to some of them. There are people I need to thank, and they know who they are. The people who patiently gave advice when I started this, the designers who gave advice on cover design and on book formatting, all the way to my friends and family, and their encouragement.

Editing wise, I owe a ton of thanks to my brother Chris Lee, as well as Jacqueline Beard MBE, who has copyedited all my books since the very beginning, and recent addition Sian Phillips, all of which have made my books way better than they have every right to be.

Also, I couldn't have done this without my growing army of ARC and beta readers, who not only show me where I falter, but also raise awareness of me in the social media world, ensuring that other people learn of my books. and Eben M. Atwater, who helped me fix my rookie weapon mistakes.

But mainly, I tip my hat and thank you. *The reader.* Who took a chance on an unknown author in a pile of Kindle books, and thought you'd give them a go. I write these books for you. And with luck, I'll keep on writing them for a very long time.

Jack Gatland / Tony Lee,
London, December 2022

ABOUT THE AUTHOR

Jack Gatland is the pen name of *#1 New York Times Bestselling Author* Tony Lee, who has been writing in all media for thirty-five years, including comics, graphic novels, middle grade books, audio drama, TV and film for *DC Comics, Marvel, BBC, ITV, Random House, Penguin USA, Hachette* and a ton of other publishers and broadcasters.

These have included licenses such as *Doctor Who, Spider Man, X-Men, Star Trek, Battlestar Galactica, MacGyver,* BBC's *Doctors, Wallace and Gromit* and *Shrek*, as well as work created with musicians such as *Ozzy Osbourne, Joe Satriani, Beartooth* and *Megadeth.*

As Tony, he's toured the world talking to reluctant readers with his 'Change The Channel' school tours, and lectures on screenwriting and comic scripting for *Raindance* in London.

As Jack, he's written several book series now - a police procedural featuring *DI Declan Walsh and the officers of the Temple Inn Crime Unit*, a spinoff featuring "cop for criminals" *Ellie Reckless and her team,* an action adventure series featuring conman-turned-treasure hunter *Damian Lucas*, and a standalone novel set in a New York boardroom.

An introvert West Londoner by heart, he lives with his wife Tracy and dog Fosco, just outside London.

Locations In The Book

The locations and items I use in my books are real, if altered slightly for dramatic intent. Here's some more information about a few of them...

Thames House is the home of MI5, as the building often seen in *James Bond* movies in Vauxhall is the home of MI6. It's a standard looking building, but it you've seen *Spooks* (or *MI5: Spooks* in the US), they use Freemasons Hall off Covent Garden to portray the outside of it.

The Tick Tock Diner is real, and is beneath the New Yorker Hotel. It claims to be the largest diner in New York, and is always busy.

The Stephen A. Schwarzman Building, otherwise known as the main branch of the New York Public Library is real, and was created after the consolidation of the Astor and Lenox Libraries into the New York Public Library in 1895. At the time, it was occupied by the obsolete Croton Reservoir, and before that was part of a "potters field", a graveyard that also utilised the neighbouring (but not yet named) Bryant Park, from the 1820s to the 1840s.

One often forgotten piece of information is that the land the library and park are now built on was the very ground

George Washington's troops crossed, while retreating from the Battle of Long Island in 1776. The road upon which Washington's troops retreated traversed the park site diagonally.

It's best known in film as the library haunted in *Ghostbusters*, but has also been shown in films including *Breakfast At Tiffany's*, *42nd Street* and *The Day After Tomorrow*.

Havenford Salt Mine doesn't exist, but the practice of using salt mines to store archived items is real - in fact, as mentioned in the book, *Winford Salt Mine,* deep under the Cheshire countryside, now run by a company named *DeepStore* had Whitehall paperwork placed during WW2, and now, companies and council departments all over the country use the specially built archive spaces, over a hundred metres underground, to house their most precious papers.

Still a working salt mine, the conditions offer ideal temperatures and very low humidity, the salt pillars creating a naturally occurring dry atmosphere and an ambient temperature of fourteen to fifteen degrees Celsius, great for long-term storage of archival materials, important documents and even priceless artefacts, all held safely below. The YouTuber Tom Scott was one of the few people ever allowed to film down there, and his video is truly eye opening.

Finally, the Lotte New York Palace Hotel is real, originally developed between 1977 and 1980 by Harry Helmsley. The hotel consists of a portion of the Villard Houses, built in the 1880s by McKim, Mead & White, which are New York City designated landmarks and listed on the National Register of

Historic Places. It also includes a 51-storey skyscraper, designed by Emery Roth & Sons and completed in 1980.

The Villard Houses were originally erected as six separate residences in a "U"-shaped plan, with three wings surrounding a central courtyard on Madison Avenue. The houses were commissioned by Henry Villard, president of the Northern Pacific Railway, shortly before he fell into bankruptcy. Ownership of the residences changed many times through the mid-20th century, and by the late 1940s, the Roman Catholic Archdiocese of New York had acquired all of the houses, except the northernmost residence at 457 Madison Avenue, which it acquired from the publishers Random House in 1971, after a very generous donation of $2.25 million allowed them to do so.

The tunnel was an artistic creation, but there have been rumours of such a tunnel for years - it just hasn't been found yet!

If you're interested in seeing what the *real* locations look like, I often post 'behind the scenes' location images on my Instagram feed and in my Facebook Readers Group. This will continue through all the books, and I suggest you follow them.

In fact, feel free to follow me on all my social media by clicking on the links below. Over time these can be places where we can engage, discuss Declan, Ellie, Tom and others, and put the world to rights.

www.jackgatland.com

www.hoodemanmedia.com

Visit my Reader's Group Page
(Mainly for fans to discuss my books):
https://www.facebook.com/groups/jackgatland

Subscribe to my Readers List:
www.subscribepage.com/jackgatland

www.facebook.com/jackgatlandbooks
www.twitter.com/jackgatlandbook
ww.instagram.com/jackgatland

Want more books by Jack Gatland? Turn the page...

Tom Marlowe will return in his next thriller

COVERT ACTION

Order Now at Amazon:

Mybook.to/covertaction

Released May 2023

Gain up-to-the-moment information on the release by signing up to the Jack Gatland VIP Reader's Club!

Join at www.subscribepage.com/jackgatland

But if you want to read something different by Jack Gatland... read on...

T-MINUS TWENTY

DEVIN MACINTOSH WAS IN THE MOOD FOR A CELEBRATION.

The champagne was on ice; the lights turned down low, the room-service oysters now at room temperature and, if he was a little honest, not up to the par he'd expected from the hotel.

The Madison Hotel was as "five star" as you could get, and to rent a suite, even for a Sunday night, was more than most of the staff of the hotel earned in a month.

Devin called it "pin money".

To be brutally frank, though, Devin wouldn't spend so much on such a frivolity; he wasn't one for bells and whistles. Sure, he enjoyed a steak dinner like the next guy, but he was just as happy chomping down on a Burger King bacon double cheese with onion rings - as long as he didn't have to sit in the bloody restaurant, that was.

The places stank of poverty.

And Devin Macintosh hated poverty.

This wasn't some kind of irrational hatred; this was because one time, many years earlier, Devin had been one of those poor, penniless bastards, scraping a living in any way he could, regardless of the legality of the situation. In fact, it was why, many years later, Wrentham Industries poached him from their closest rival with a rather impressive benefits package, including his own box at Madison Square Garden, and the use of a couple of executive suites at the Madison Hotel.

As he'd said, Devin wouldn't spend on such a frivolity. He expected someone else to cover the cost for him.

Lying on the bed, the satin sheets crumpled, Devin ran a hand through his hair. For a man in his late forties, he looked food for his age, at least a good five or ten years younger. This was partly because of his exercise regime, and also because of the hair plugs he'd gotten around five years earlier, when he'd seen his family's genetic disposition for balding had knocked upon his own door.

His wife had called it a vanity exercise and a waste of money, saying he didn't need to do such a thing, that he was "still attractive without hair." But he'd called her a hypocrite, pointing out she'd happily let him pay for her new breasts, and the conversation drew to a close.

Still, they both got what they wanted.

But, for all his complaints about costs, Devin had his fancies. His underwear, currently the only thing he was wearing right now, was worth more than the average suit of his corporate team, and his watch, currently on the sideboard next to his expensive, top-of-the-range phone cost six figures.

But neither of them were as beautiful as the woman laying breathless on the bed next to him. In her late thirties, her own expensive and incredibly flimsy lace underwear had been half removed already, occurring during their first play fight, her incredible breasts free from restraint and quite frankly, in Devin's opinion, spectacular, no matter how much money they cost.

Rising, Devin leaned across those spectacular breasts, grabbing one of the two champagne flutes on the side table. Downing it, he toasted her.

'Happy anniversary,' he said, and was about to speak again, to say something more, maybe even about love, or something equally sappy when the woman grinned, leant closer, and bit him hard on the arm.

'Ow! You bitch!' he hissed, snapping back as she laughed at his response. 'Dammit Gina! Don't leave marks! I exercise with the board tomorrow morning! How will I explain teeth marks to Miles or the others when we're on the treadmill?'

'Tell him you have a very healthy sex life, while your CEO's cock is covered in cobwebs?' Gina lounged now against the bed, her hands gripping the silk sheets, inviting him to retaliate against her.

To retaliate *on* her.

'You should punish me,' she said, in an apologetic "little girl" voice. 'Punish me, daddy.'

Devin smiled in response, tossing the now-empty champagne flute across the room as he rose on his knees, towering over her as they—

The phone on the sideboard *pinged*.

'Leave it,' Gina ordered.

'It could be important,' Devin's attention was now split between the gorgeous, half-naked woman in front of him, and the glowing screen of his phone, just that little too far away to see what the message was.

'*I'm* important,' Gina snarled, and gone was the apologetic little girl. 'If it's life-threatening, they'll send you an email. Or they'll call your PA and she can call you.'

'It's Sunday. She's not at work.'

'She's your PA. She's *always* at work, even when she's home.'

The phone *pinged* a second time. Not a reminder for the message, but a new, second message.

'I swear to god, Devin,' Gina hissed. 'You touch that goddamned phone and I'll punish you.'

'Be serious,' Devin replied, the fun now drained from the situation, rolling across the bed and grabbing the phone. Gina tried to stop him halfway, but he slipped past her, grabbing the phone and holding it high, out of her reach as he looked up at the messages displayed on the screen.

9-1-1 BOARDROOM

9-1-1 BOARDROOM

'Crap,' Devin slumped down, showing Gina the messages. 'I've been called in.'

Gina snatched the phone from him, staring down at the last message, as if hoping that by doing this, she'd somehow change the text on the screen.

'It's all in capitals,' she said, furrowing her brow. 'It's never in capitals when they send this.'

'I know.'

'This probably doesn't mean anything good,' Gina looked up at Devin now. 'Are you in trouble?'

'Why the hell would you think I'm the one in trouble?' Devin now hissed, straightening, as he faced Gina. 'There's ten of us on the board. Well, something like that. I've never counted. But why can't one of them be the one in trouble?'

'Because you're a sneaky, backstabbing shit, and you've always been half a step ahead of everyone else and a firing squad?' Gina suggested. 'Tell them you're sick. Tell them it's a Sunday night and God said you could have the day off.'

'Not with that code,' Devin shook his head, already walking over to his trousers and pulling them on. 'You don't get that unless someone's shit the bed on a massive scale.'

'So, let the person who shit the bed clean it up,' Gina replied.

'*I'm* the one who usually cleans it up!' Devin exploded. 'It's what they pay me an extortionate amount of money to do! This isn't a debate or a negotiation, Gina! I've got to go in!'

He stared at the ceiling, considering the other members of the board.

'Bloody Victoria will go, and she's at her kid's recital tonight.'

'Yeah, but she hates her kids,' Gina pouted. 'You can't go! It's our anniversary!'

Devin, currently pulling on his dress shirt, paused, nodding.

'It's not fair, and I get it,' he said, now sitting on the bed placing a hand on Gina's arm. 'And it's really not how I wanted to spend the night with you. But I have to do this. It's why I get the perks I get. It's why I get...'

He waved a hand around the suite.

'... this.'

Gina said nothing, but her confrontational body language was softening as she glared at Devin.

'This is shit,' she said.

'I totally agree,' Devin leant in, kissing Gina lightly on the lips. 'It'll only take an hour or so. Wait here, crack open another bottle. Go wild on room service. Try to beat the amount we spent here two years back.'

Gina frowned at this as Devin rose, tucking his shirt into his trouser band.

'Do you actually pay for the room service?' she asked suspiciously. 'Out of your own pocket?'

'Fuck no!' Devin laughed, now texting his driver to get off his ass and meet him out front. 'Do you think I'd suggest it if you were spending *my* money?'

Gina folded her arms now, still angry at what was happening.

'I'm not happy about this, Devin,' she said as he pulled on his socks. 'There might be... consequences... when you come back.'

Devin slipped his shoes on and, grabbing his jacket and tie, he blew Gina a dramatic kiss.

'Promises, promises,' he mocked.

'I'm serious!' Gina shouted at Devin as he walked to the door of the hotel suite. But by then he'd already gone, the memories of the beautiful, topless woman in the lacy underwear now replaced with concern about what was so bad, that someone had to send the Defconn tweet.

He knew it wouldn't be good.

THE DRIVER WAS WAITING FOR HIM OUTSIDE THE HOTEL AS HE stormed out, still doing up his stupidly expensive tie as he nodded at him.

'Got your message,' the driver said, without any hint of sarcasm toward the tone of the message, as he opened the door. He waited for Devin to enter before closing the door behind him, walking around to the driver's side, and taking off his own cap as he entered.

Now looking over his shoulder, the driver smiled.

'Home or work, sir?' he asked.

'Why the fuck would I be going home?' Devin snapped, looking at his watch as he did so. The time read 7:02. 'Take me to the office. And knock that stupid fucking smile off your face.'

He'd had the driver, a young, irritatingly handsome Albanian for at least three months now, and as he berated him, Devin realised he'd never once asked what his goddamned name was. He had a very brief moment of concern, a wonder whether he should ask the driver now, but this was wiped away quickly by the simple fact he didn't really care.

Now admonished, the driver turned back to the road, and Devin pressed a button to his side, relaxing as the privacy window rose between them.

Devin hated having to make polite conversation with the drivers. He hated to make any conversation, to be honest. Again, the issues of his past, of having to converse with lower classes rose its head, and Devin reached across the limo seat for the small drinks cabinet, held within a side compartment, pulling out and then pouring himself a whisky, downing it in one hit, and wiping his mouth with his hand before pouring out another glass.

Looking out the window, watching Manhattan pass by, he sighed.

'Fuck.'

Pulling out his phone, he stared at the repeated message one more time.

9-1-1 BOARDROOM

What the hell had happened? Was it a takeover? Maybe Miko Tanasha, that backstabbing bitch, was finally making her play. Either way, he'd lied to Gina; this would not take an hour. Just getting the contrary bastards to sit at the table was going to take half of that.

Sighing audibly, Devin dialled a number on his phone, holding it to his ear and waiting for it to connect, watching the privacy screen intently, as if expecting it to drop at any moment.

After a couple of seconds, the call was answered.

'Hey, it's me,' Devin smiled as he spoke into the phone. He didn't feel like smiling, but he'd been told once by Jason Barnett, director of sales, that if you smiled when you spoke down a phone, you sounded friendlier. Personally, Devin thought it was bullshit, and he thought Jason was nothing more than a mercy hire, but he was happy to try it at that point. 'I've been called into a board meeting.'

There was a pause as Devin listened to the voice on the other end of the line.

'It's the message,' he said. 'The bad one, and you know what that means. I could be there all night.'

Another pause, another conversation from the other end of the phone.

'I know, but there's nothing I can do,' Devin rubbed at the bridge of his nose as he replied, trying to keep his voice calm, to not shout. 'It's gonna be a late one, so kiss the boys for me and I'll see you when I get home.'

He looked back at the privacy wall; it was up, but the glass was opaque, and he could see the driver's eyes through the rear-view mirror, watching him, maybe even judging him for the conversation he was having right now with his wife, at home, with his children, unaware of any anniversary tonight.

'I love you too,' he said, looking out of the window, unable to allow the driver to see his eyes as he lied, disconnecting the moment he said this, holding the phone in his lap.

He'd fire the driver tomorrow, he decided, as he poured himself another whisky, settling back into his seat. The nosey bastard was too interested in what his betters were doing. Or, rather, *who* they were doing.

And that simply wasn't the way they did things around here.

You had to *gain* the power first, before you started black-mailing.

THE OFFICE WAS DARK, AND HE LIKED IT THAT WAY. HE COULD have put the lights on and seen better what he was doing in the office, but he didn't need to. The light from the chrome and glass building opposite was enough for him, bleeding through the windows, casting shadows across the room, hitting the rifle on the floor.

He crouched now; the window was floor-to-ceiling glass, tempered and strong, but not strong enough to resist the glass cutter he placed against it, making a rough circle before using a suction cup to bring the now detached piece of glass back into the office.

The last thing he wanted was for it to fall the other way, crashing to the pavement a dozen floors below him.

Someone might call the police, and that would not do.

They weren't in his plan until later.

Now with a hole in the window around a foot off the ground, he climbed down onto the carpet tiles of the office and, laying prone, he took the rifle, placed the muzzle through the opening, only an inch or so out into the night air, but enough to provide a clear shot. The rough circle was large enough to aim his sight through, too, focusing on the lit up boardroom on the other side of the street, as he unclicked the arms of his stand and readied the rifle, aiming it at the window.

This done, he started on the second part of his plan, pulling a roll of duct tape out of his duffle, and preparing a space beside the sniper rifle.

The night hadn't even started yet, and he was already excited about what was about to happen.

For tonight, *justice* came to Wrentham Industries.

T-MINUS FIFTEEN

THE LIMO PULLED TO A STOP OUTSIDE THE MAIN ENTRANCE TO Wrentham Industries at seven-fifteen pm; for the journey, through midtown and in the middle of theatre traffic to only take that long was actually good, but Devin wasn't going to let the driver know this, instead stepping out of the car the moment the door was open and slamming the now empty whisky tumbler into the driver's hand.

'You should have been faster,' he hissed.

'I couldn't have been any faster,' the driver replied with a surly 'sir,' added after a second's delay. 'The only way we could have been quicker was if I jumped every red light—'

'Next time, jump the red lights,' Devin snapped back, emphasising each syllable with a tap of his index finger on the driver's chest. 'Your delay of even a minute could have cost the firm billions.'

'I'll try to remember that for next time, sir,' the driver replied, stone-faced. Devin almost laughed. He was starting to like the driver. He could even see a future for the man - if he wasn't firing him first thing Monday morning, anyway.

'Do you want me to wait for you?' the driver asked, still staring dead ahead, not even trying to catch Devin's eye.

'No, you're done for the night,' Devin yawned. 'I'll get an Uber back to the hotel when we're done. It'll be faster than you can do it.'

'Very good, sir,' the driver replied and, irritated by this, Devin waved his hand dismissively.

'Just piss off, yeah?' he said, turning away from the car and already starting towards the door. 'You're making the building look lower class.'

As the driver, silently fuming, strutted back to the driver's seat, Devin smiled. He didn't have to be such a dick to the guy, but if you didn't use the power, what good was having it? That great power and great responsibility bullshit was the stuff of superhero comics, and those arrogant, spandex-wearing fags weren't real.

Another car pulled up at the side before he reached the door, and Devin turned to face it as the driver, almost identical in looks, size and uniform as his soon-to-be-fired one, walked around hurriedly and opened the door. Devin wondered whether there was a particular company that only hired chauffeurs that looked like that, but then stopped with a grimace as he realised who was getting out of the car, and therefore would share an elevator with him.

Victoria Harvey was a grade-A, diamond-carat bitch. In her late thirties, but constantly claiming she was five years younger, she was fit as hell - Devin had to give that to her - and currently wore an expensive mink jacket, with an extortionately expensive handbag under the arm.

She seemed to have a better relationship with her driver than Devin did, too, as shown by the slight but visible finger trace along the driver's arm as she told him to wait for her.

They're probably screwing, Devin thought to himself as he faked a smile for the cheap seats. *And if not already, they will be later.*

Walking up to Devin, Victoria didn't even acknowledge the fact he'd held the door open for her, waltzing through and into the lobby as if she expected him to do such a selfless act.

Devin *hated* Victoria.

As they fell into step, walking across the lobby and nodding at the security guard behind the counter in that way people do when they really don't expect to be stopped, Victoria looked over at Devin.

'You smell of fucking,' she said. 'Can't be your wife, it's not her birthday.'

'Always a pleasure,' Devin ignored the jibe as he motioned for the guard at the elevator to call for the carriage.

'Do you know what the hell this is about?' Victoria continued. 'Bloody cloak and dagger bullshit always gives me ulcers.'

Devin raised an eyebrow at this.

'Wait, you didn't call it?' he asked. 'I assumed this was as dramatically drama queen as you can get, so it had to be you or the Asian.'

Victoria sniffed as they entered the executive elevator, the guard leaning in to press the button for them, because *God forbid* they should have to lower themselves to such an act.

'I was at my daughter's recital,' she muttered irritably. 'Had to leave three songs in. Are they called songs? I don't know. All I know is someone had better have died for this, because I'm missing important moments in her life.'

'They usually do die when we get calls like this,' Devin puffed out his cheeks as he watched the number slowly climb upwards. 'I've only had the 9-1-1 once since I arrived. And that was when Ryan whatshisname jumped out the window.'

'God, I forgot about that, the stupid bastard,' Victoria tutted. 'Still, you should be careful, Macintosh. You almost sound like you give a shit.'

'Just stating a fact,' Devin flashed an incredibly insecure smile. 'How was the recital?'

'Fucking abysmal,' Victoria moaned. 'You'd think with the amount of money I was paying, she could play a vaguely recognisable tune. If I hadn't been there when she was born, I'd wonder if she was actually mine.'

'So, with you here, is she with her father right now?'

'Why the hell would I do that?' Victoria stared at Devin with the expression of someone staring at the most stupid man in the room. Which, in her mind, she probably was. 'He's not been around for months. Living in Barbados, I think. No, she's with the Au pair. Hopefully, they'll both be asleep by the time I arrive home.'

Reaching into the inside pocket of her mink coat, Victoria pulled out a small, silver pill box. Opening it up, she took out one of the pink pills from within between a finger and thumb, popping it into her mouth.

'Sharing your sweets?' Devin smiled.

'Acid reflux,' Victoria replied as she closed the box up. 'Been suffering for a little while now. Probably the stress of being near you, and the other pricks I'm going to have to suffer tonight.'

'As long as it doesn't turn into a really painful ulcer,' Devin said with mock sincerity. 'That would be terrible.'

The doors opened onto the twenty-third floor, and with a wave of his hand, Devin offered Victoria the option of leaving the car first.

'Fuck no,' she said, motioning for him to take the lead. 'If the shit's hitting the fan, I'm not the first one walking in. You're junior to me. You can be the meat shield.'

Laughing, Devin walked out into an empty, open plan corridor, the workers on this floor long gone. Only a single cleaner still worked at this hour, a man in his thirties, brown hair under a red baseball cap, headphones on over the top, his face half-hidden as he cleaned the marble floor beside the doors.

Victoria wasn't watching the cleaner as closely as Devin was, however, and bumped into him, her silver box falling to the floor, clattering over to the man as he quickly picked it up, and, rubbing his sleeve on the wet side, where it had fallen on the mopped floor, he passed the box back over to her.

Victoria didn't thank the man, instead snatching the box back and, this time, adding it into the inside pocket it'd originally come from.

'Piss off and do that later,' Devin snapped at him, backing away a little as he walked past the man, resisting the urge to pull out some antibacterial hand gel.

The man grumbled, and then walked into the elevator before it closed, pulling his mop and bucket behind him.

Watching him, Victoria was amused by this.

'Worried you might catch "poor" if you stood too close?' she mocked as they continued down the narrow corridor that led to the boardroom. 'Prick.'

'I wasn't the one who had him wiping his dirty arm all over my property,' Devin muttered.

Victoria went to reply to this, maybe even recover her box from the pocket and wipe it down herself for good measure, but stopped as a sudden thought came to mind.

'What if they're already making alliances?' she hissed, trying to look through the glass walls of the boardroom as they approached. The angle wasn't good for spying, but she could see Miles Fenton in the doorway. The CEO of the company was fat, balding, red faced from years of neglect, and was currently checking his watch. 'We should team up. Strength in numbers.'

'Yeah, right up til you stab me in the balls, Brutus,' Devin shook his head. 'I'll take my chances alone, thanks. Besides, I think it's Miko.'

'You do?' Victoria almost clawed at his arm, to pull him back to ask more, but Devin had already walked into the boardroom, and it forced her to follow suit.

The boardroom itself was swish and futuristic. One side, facing into the office, was opaque glass, blocking the view into the office space, giving secrecy - and the main reason Victoria hadn't been able to count the deals happening inside. The other side of the boardroom was a wall of full length glass windows, looking out into Manhattan. It would have been an incredible view, if it wasn't for the fact that fifty yards away another building, a half-lit floor matching the level of this room, stood, a black monolith in the night, and blocking any postcard panorama.

Devin hated the location here; it meant his office, up on the top floor, could only see half of Manhattan. And, annoyingly, nobody else wanted to help him get the other buildings destroyed, even when he'd drunkenly mentioned he knew men with demolition experience, and was happy to "Fight Club" the whole damn city to get an unobstructed view.

The room itself was nothing more than a boardroom table, with twelve seats at it. In the middle of the table was a conference call phone, a remote next to it, and this remote controlled the massive flat-screen television on the wall at the end, mainly used for presentations and suchlike, or when one of the board couldn't be bothered to attend and "Zoomed" in from their homes, or even, on one occasion when he was so hung over, from his office two floors up - as Devin simply couldn't muster the strength to walk to the elevator.

Apart from that, the room was quite sparse. Against the opposite wall was a mahogany side cabinet, where the bottles of water were placed, and the bottles of scotch were hidden in the deep filled drawers. Devin paused as he realised each drawer now had a small brass number on it - probably some other bullshit HR idea for productivity, decided by Miles while fucked on Ketamine.

Devin was sure Miles took that. Or something similar. After all, it wasn't as if Miles didn't know someone who could get it for him in this very room. Because nobody could be as mind-numbingly boring as Miles Fenton and *not* be on horse tranquillisers.

On top of the cabinet were a coffee machine and a microwave, and Devin made his way straight towards it. He had a feeling this was going to be a long one, and he needed caffeine.

'You're late,' Miles chided both of the new arrivals.

'Piss off, Miles,' Victoria snapped, also ignoring him as she walked past. 'You're only here on time because you've got nothing else to do.'

Miles looked abashed at the insult, but said nothing as Victoria turned her attention to the rest of the room.

'And that goes for you brown nosers too,' she said, pulling off her mink jacket and slumping it onto the back of a chair, its back to the window, effectively claiming the space before anyone else could.

There were six other people in the boardroom, either sitting already at the desk or standing, talking in hushed whispers to each other, probably considering the same short-term alliances that Victoria had, or texting angrily on their phones, annoyed to be called out.

First, there was Jason Barnett. In his late thirties, and in fact only a year older than Victoria, he was Wrentham Industries' fast talking sales director - immaculately dressed in a sharp suit and a trendy tie, his hair on point, with a style screaming loudly he was desperately trying to stay in his twenties, and looking almost as if he'd been waiting for the call, or hadn't actually gone home yet. Which, even though it was a Sunday, was probably the case. He seemed to live in the office.

Next to him was Tamira May. She had just turned forty, as she'd had a really shitty party recently, where she spent the whole night getting more and more shitfaced while telling everyone she was fine, and life *began* at forty, all that self-help bullshit people told themselves when hitting a milestone year, before collapsing after doing some MDMA and telling everyone her life was over. As far as Victoria was concerned, though, it wasn't her age that was stopping her from getting laid; it was the fact she was a mixture of angry Mom and stern accounting governess in her outward appearance; harsh and cold, wearing simple clothing that belayed her status and position in the company.

If Victoria was honest, Tamira was probably the one person here she was intimidated by, and not because she looked like an extra from the *Addams Family*.

Now with a coffee in hand, Devin also looked over the

group, his eye instantly drawn towards a stunningly attractive Asian woman by the wall. Miko Tanasha was one of the older members of the board, only a year or two younger than Devin, but she still looked in her twenties, the bitch. A Japanese woman with steel in her eyes, she wore a simple yet expensive suit, and was watching everyone surreptitiously while pretending to examine her phone.

Devin wanted more than anything to take her there and then, on the table, but even if she wanted to - and he knew she definitely didn't - he already had Gina.

Oh, yeah. And his wife.

Beside Miko, however, was the complete opposite. Hayley Moran, plump, bubbly and with a fondness for pastels puffed nervously on a Vape, pulling her cardigan close around her as she stared out of the window, looking out across the city - or at least as much as she could see, with a thousand-yard stare, her mind far away.

Devin tapped the top of his mouth with his tongue as he watched her, considering what he was seeing, and deciding it was a nervous, guilty woman.

Was HR Hayley the reason they were all here?

There was a loud, bellowing laugh from the other side of the boardroom table, and Devin looked across to see Eddie Purcell, an early fifties gangster of a man, in particular a man built like a brick shithouse and who looked like trouble no matter how expensive his suit was. His gold jewellery and cygnet rings rattled as he shook with laughter at something Miles said, but the moment the decrepit CEO turned around, Eddie's face became one of bitter anger, a stare that was literally burning through the back of Miles Fenton's skull.

The Wrentham Industries board was here. All that was missing was Corey Gregson, but he was always late.

There was, however, someone new in the room. Someone Devin didn't know. A young, scared looking woman with long, mousey-blonde hair, and no older than her mid-twenties, sitting at the table with the look of a woman who really didn't know why the hell she was there.

'Hello,' he said, walking over and sitting down. 'Who are you?'

'She's Donna,' Hayley replied for her, sitting down across the table, away from Devin as she called across it. 'She's from the secretarial bay. To note the minutes.'

Devin nodded at this, and the others, seeing people now sitting, made their own way over.

'Well, sit there and shut up,' he hissed at Donna, while keeping his smile plastered on. 'Two ears, one mouth, yeah?'

'And if anything we say off the record turns up online?' Miles added, sitting at the head of the table, 'I'll personally end you.'

'She's just doing her job. No need for you both to be dicks about it,' Hayley snapped irritably as Donna reddened, as if horrified to find herself the subject of attention.

'Yeah, she's stuck here with you,' Jason joined in now. 'Give her a break.'

He finished this by giving a friendly wink at Donna, sitting back and looking at Miles, a smug expression on his face.

Devin forced the smile off his own face. The two of them were as bad as each other.

The young bull and the wounded old bastard.

Shame neither of them would end up on top. Not while he was around.

'If I wanted your opinion, Jason, I'd look for it in the gutter,' Miles muttered, and was about to continue when

Jason rose angrily to his feet, the chair clattering to the floor behind him.

'Now listen here, you dusty old prick—'

'Guys!'

The word wasn't shouted, but it was spoken with such force that everyone stopped, even Jason, turning to look at Eddie, sitting beside the television.

'Can we just sort out why we're here and get on with it?' he asked, almost patronisingly. 'I dunno about you, but I got better things to do tonight. And I hate wearing a tie on a Sunday.'

'You didn't have to wear a suit...' Jason began, but stopped. Of course Eddie had to wear a suit.

They were on the Wrentham Industries board.

There was a consensus of nods, before Victoria, frowning, spoke.

'Where's Gregson?'

'No show, so far,' Eddie shrugged.

'Probably pissed up in a bar. Again.' It was Tamira who added that, and as the two of them discussed the uselessness of Corey Gregson, Jason took this opportunity to look over at Victoria across the table.

'How was Lucy's recital?'

'Fuck off, Jason. Like you give a shit.'

Reddening, Jason backed off.

'Right then,' Miles eventually spoke. 'Let's get this board-room meeting started while we wait for Gregson.'

———

HE WATCHED THEM THROUGH HIS NIGHT VISION SNIPER SCOPE, stroking the barrel of his rifle as he watched them sit at the table, still arguing. They were probably wondering where Corey Gregson was, unaware that he was sadly unable to join them tonight.

Or ever, even.

They had no idea he was watching them.

They had no idea what he was about to do to them.

He smiled, pulling the bolt back, clicking the bullet into the rifle's chamber and smiling wider as the *ka-chuk* echoed around the empty office room.

It sounded good. *Righteous.*

Soon, there would be blood. Soon, there would be death.

Soon, there would be *justice.*

And soon it would be time to start both the clock - and the game.

———

EIGHT PEOPLE. EIGHT SECRETS.
ONE SNIPER.

THE
B⊕ARD
ROOM

HOW FAR WOULD YOU GO TO GAIN JUSTICE?

NEW YORK TIMES #1 BESTSELLER TONY LEE WRITING AS
JACK GATLAND

A NEW STANDALONE THRILLER WITH
A TWIST - FROM THE CREATOR OF THE
BESTSELLING 'DI DECLAN WALSH' SERIES

AVAILABLE ON AMAZON / KINDLE UNLIMITED

LETTER FROM THE DEAD

"BY THE TIME YOU READ THIS, I WILL BE DEAD..."

A TWENTY YEAR OLD MURDER...
A PRIME MINISTER LEADERSHIP BATTLE...
A PARANOID, HOMELESS EX-MINISTER...
AN EVANGELICAL PREACHER WITH A SECRET...

DI DECLAN WALSH HAS HAD BETTER FIRST DAYS...

AVAILABLE ON AMAZON / KINDLEUNLIMITED

THE THEFT OF A **PRICELESS** PAINTING...
A GANGSTER WITH A **CRIPPLING DEBT**...
A **BODY COUNT** RISING BY THE HOUR...

AND ELLIE RECKLESS IS CAUGHT IN THE MIDDLE.

JACK GATLAND

PAINT
— THE —
DEAD

A 'COP FOR CRIMINALS' ELLIE RECKLESS NOVEL

A NEW PROCEDURAL CRIME SERIES WITH
A TWIST - FROM THE CREATOR OF THE
BESTSELLING 'DI DECLAN WALSH' SERIES

AVAILABLE ON AMAZON / KINDLE UNLIMITED

JACK GATLAND

THE
LIONHEART
CURSE

HUNT THE GREATEST TREASURES
PAY THE GREATEST PRICE

BOOK 1 IN A NEW SERIES OF ADVENTURES
IN THE STYLE OF 'THE DA VINCI CODE'
FROM THE CREATOR OF DECLAN WALSH

AVAILABLE ON AMAZON / KINDLEUNLIMITED

Printed in Great Britain
by Amazon